KEEPING SECRETS

BY

DONAL KERRIGAN

PROLOGUE

THE FISHING ROD

Turning the Philbin building business into a thriving concern had given Brian O'Malley both a sense of purpose and a confidence in his own ability, but he knew that his sense of well-being was down to his wife. It was her love that had enabled him to face down the nightmares that had plagued him since he left Ireland.

He had great plans for the future, but that was for tomorrow. Today, as they walked along the banks of the River Leven the sun was shining. He held his wife's hand as they stopped to watch a fisherman casting his line into the river and before they moved on Brian told her it was time he tried his hand at fishing. It was a chance remark, but Margaret O'Malley remembered it.

There was great excitement in the O'Malley household. Brian O'Malley had announced he was going to try out his birthday present at the weekend. His wife decided that the whole family should take a picnic lunch and explore up the river. Once they'd finished lunch they would leave Brian to fish and later, after she had taken the children home, she would return to help him carry back his catch.

"You seem to be very confident that I'll catch something Margaret."

Her face broke into that wonderful warm smile that almost felt like an embrace. "We wouldn't have wasted money on a rod if I didn't think that Brian," and he'd smiled back and pulled her to him and held her tightly, until eventually she had to push him away.

Katherine O'Malley lay in her bed that Saturday morning. She was remembering the story her mother had read to her and her sister Grace the night before. Kate could always picture in her own mind what her mother described. She always made stories come alive and she and Grace would often talk about them long after their mother had blown out their lamp when she put them to bed. Then Kate began thinking of what treats her mother would have prepared for their picnic lunch when she thought she heard a commotion and voices coming from downstairs. She thought she could hear the voice of Father Joseph from St. Augusta's, but that couldn't be. He never came up to their house.

She snuggled down under her bedclothes, but very shortly afterwards Annie their housekeeper came into the bedroom. She looked as if she had been crying.

"Kate, get dressed and come downstairs. Father Joseph and your father are waiting. Help your sister."

"What's happened Annie? Where's my mother?" Annie didn't reply. "Come downstairs as quick as you can. Hurry." With that Annie left the room.

Katherine and Grace walked down the stairs holding hands. The house was so silent. Something was wrong. Katherine found herself shivering. She held Grace's hand even tighter. There was nobody at the bottom of the stairs. The two sisters entered the living room side by side. Father Joseph stood up, and then slowly their father did the same. They looked at each other as if waiting for the other to speak first. Then Father Joseph spoke.

"Children… I have some bad news for you." Kate looked at her father, but he remained silent. He seemed unable to meet her gaze. She turned and stared at the priest.

Although Father Joseph had faced these occasions many times before, something in the young girl's look almost unnerved him.

"I'm sorry to have to tell you… that your mother died peacefully in her sleep. I'm sure she is now in Heaven with our Lord Jesus."

Kate looked back across at her father, but Brian O'Malley just continued to stare into the distance.

"I think we should say a prayer for your mother," the priest said. Then they knelt down and after a moment their father did too, and the priest led them in saying the rosary.

Annie Dillon told Katherine and Grace the next day that their mother had died of a heart attack. Katherine refused to let anyone see her cry, not even Grace, but when she was on her own she cried so hard that the back of her throat ached and she let out a moan every time she realised that never again would she feel the warmth of her mother's hugs.

The day after the funeral was when Katherine accepted the finality of her mother's death. Their father moved out of the room he had shared with their mother into a smaller room. Dustsheets were placed over all the furniture, the mirror was taken down off the bedroom wall, and the door was locked. Annie Dillon was instructed to place the fishing rod in the storeroom.

Brian O'Malley would never again fish the River Leven.

Patrick Philbin was too ill to travel back from Glasgow for his daughter's funeral, but his wife did. Now the funeral was over, she was anxious to get back to Glasgow. However, she realised arrangements had to be made in respect of the two children. It was obvious that Brian O'Malley could barely cope with his wife's death, and he had a business to run. Two young children would be too much for him on his own. Katherine O'Malley was only twelve and Grace eleven, too young to be on their own.

Mrs. Philbin had always liked her son-in-law since their chance meeting on the ferry over from Ireland. He had saved the family business and, when her husband had finally become too ill to work, had bought her husband out of the business at a very generous price. She told Brian O'Malley that she would take Grace and Katherine with her when she returned to Glasgow.

"Will you tell the children, or shall I?" Mrs. Philbin pushed for an answer because Brian O'Malley looked as if he was unsure what she was talking about.

"I'll talk to them."

"I think you should tell them to-day, Brian. I have to leave the day after to-morrow."

"I'll tell them this evening." Brian O'Malley had promised Kate he would read to them that evening, something his wife had always done in the past.

When their father told his children they were going to Glasgow to stay with their aunt, Grace O'Malley started to cry. "I don't want to go, father."

"I'm afraid you'll have to, Grace. You're too young to stay here. There's no-one to look after you. Your grandmother and her sister-in-law are very fond of you both"

His elder daughter looked at him, dry eyed. "I can look after, Grace, father."

"You're only twelve, Kate."

"That's old enough, father. Annie Dillon will help me." Brian O'Malley shook his head.

"We're not leaving you father." He looked at his eldest daughter. Whilst Grace had barely stopped crying since her mother died, after the first morning Katherine had shed no tears. There was no mistaking the look of determination on his elder daughter's face. "I mean it."

The following morning when his mother-in-law asked Brian O'Malley how the children had taken the news he didn't answer straight away.

"Not very well, I'm afraid." Even as he spoke, he was still undecided. Did he need to lose his children as well as his wife? He thought of his daughter's refusal to leave…the expression on her face.

"You have been most kind, but I'm going to try and keep the children with me."

"Do you really think that will work?"

"I do." Brian met his mother-in-law's gaze. "Katherine's very grown up for her age …it may be possible with Annie Dillon's help. I'm going to try."

Mrs. Philbin looked very hard at her son-in-law.

"Katherine will do anything to protect Grace. They're very close. They'll help each other."

That night their father came to the young girls' room. He told them both they were staying. Then he said goodnight. As the door closed, Grace got out of bed and went over to her sister and hugged her tightly.

"Thank you, Kate."

"Don't worry Grace. I'll always look after you." That night it was Katherine who read to them and who blew out their oil lamp. She lay there in the dark thinking of their mother. Had God taken her because he loved her more than Katherine had, or was she being punished for some sin that she didn't even realise she had committed?

PART 1

KATHERINE'S SECRET

CHAPTER 1

KATHERINE'S FIRST LOVE

Michael Costello was the most good-looking man Katherine O'Malley had ever met, but she was fighting hard to conceal the fact that she thought so.

Michael and Katherine stood together at the summit of Kinnell Hill, getting their breath back after their steep climb. The brightness of the spring sunshine made the colours of the countryside stand out. They looked out along the River Leven towards the hills in the distance. The fields down below them were moving in the wind.

"Isn't that just a brilliant sight?" said Michael pointing towards the waters glinting in the distance, and Kate nodded without looking at him. She had seen this view many times before, but Michael was right. It was a scene that never failed to please.

It was still early May and the sun wasn't warm enough to take the chill off the wind that was blowing. If her mother had been there, Katherine could imagine her pulling up the collar of her coat and telling Katherine there was nothing better than the "bracing" air that brought colour to your cheeks.

Thinking Michael was still looking at the view she glanced across at him, but to her embarrassment he was watching her. As he caught her gaze he smiled and she felt herself reddening and it was not the wind that was the cause. She turned away and then the wind gusted again blowing her hair across her face, helping to hide her look.

Despite that embarrassment as they walked on, she felt an unmistakable nervous thrill and a different breathlessness to that she had experienced on the climb.

When Michael Costello learnt that Brian O'Malley's two daughters went to church every Sunday, he had started to pay more attention to his religious failings. Soon he was a regular face among the congregation at St. Augusta's. The first Sunday he had loitered outside the church until Brian O'Malley and his two daughters arrived so he could be introduced. After that Michael had done his best to make sure that the sisters noticed his presence.

They were both attractive young women. Katherine, the elder of the two, was the more serious of the two and perhaps for that reason appeared slightly plainer than her younger sister. He preferred to look at Grace. She smiled more. She was attractive and flirtatious in a way that her elder sister was not. Grace had been the first that he had managed to speak to at any length and exercise his charm on, but now she had started to avoid him so this Sunday afternoon he had decided he would chance his luck.

He called at the O'Malley's big house unannounced. He was surprised when Brian O'Malley answered the front door himself.

"Michael, this is a pleasant surprise. Come in, my boy. Come in." And so Michael had been shown into Brian O'Malley's living room. There were bookcases all round the room. On the mantelpiece was a square black marble clock and above it a painting of a ship majestically under full sail.

Upstairs Katherine was reading to her sister. "That sounds like Michael Costello."

"Here? Here, in the house?" For some reason that Katherine could not fathom, her sister Grace seemed disconcerted by the thought that Michael Costello might have come visiting them.

"Yes, shall we go downstairs and meet him?" Asked Katherine.

"No... I don't want to see him."

Katherine looked at her sister, surprised at her reaction. "Why not? I thought you liked him." She had noticed that on Sundays after church Grace often hung back to catch a few words with Michael. She'd seen them laughing together.

"I think I've got a headache." Grace put her hand to her brow for a moment. Then when Grace saw the look on Katherine's face she added, "You go downstairs and meet him... if you must."

Downstairs Brian O'Malley motioned to Michael Costello to sit down.

"What brings you here Michael. I can't believe there are problems at the Tannyard on a Sunday afternoon."

"No. No. Not at all. It was just…" For a moment Michael Costello's nerve almost failed him but he took a breath and ploughed on "…It's such a sunny day Mr. O'Malley that I was wondering if Katherine and Grace might like to accompany me on my walk up Kinnell Hill."

"What a grand idea, Michael…"

At that moment Kate O'Malley entered the living room. She put the bible she had in her hand down on the table by the door. "You met my daughter Kate the other day, Michael."

"Indeed, how are you, Miss Katherine?"

"Very well, thank you Mr. Costello." She replied primly. Her father and Michael Costello might be on first name terms, but she and Michael were not. "Michael was just enquiring whether you and Grace might like to walk up the Kinnell."

"I don't think that will be possible father. Grace's is feeling unwell. I have just been reading to her. She says she has a headache"

"I hope it's nothing serious." said Michael Costello.

"I don't think so Mr. Costello. I think she might have a bit of a chill, but it would certainly be better if she rested." She turned to her father. "I'm afraid a walk is quite out of the question." Katherine was pleased to see the disappointment that showed briefly on Michael Costello's face.

"Why don't you and Michael go on your own?"

Katherine was caught by surprise by her father's question, and she paused before she replied. "I don't think that would be proper, do you father?" The proprieties of his suggestion had not occurred to Brian O'Malley, but he wasn't going to admit it, particularly to Katherine. His daughter had become far too proper for his liking. It would be good for her to get out of the house. She was in danger of becoming a recluse.

"Nonsense, what harm can a short walk do?"

What harm could it do? Her father might be right that it might not damage her reputation in Levenside generally, but if the nuns at the convent got to hear of it, they would have apoplexy. She would never hear the last of it.

"Father, I'm not dressed to go out."

"Well run upstairs and change. I've got some business to talk to Michael about." Katherine stood there. "Go on. It shouldn't take more than ten minutes."

It took the best part of half an hour for Katherine to dress into her walking clothes. She made sure of that. Half of her had wanted her father to refuse to let her to go out unescorted with his handsome young foreman, but the other half had longed for him to grant Michael Costello his request. She knew she could have continued to have declined the invitation herself, pretended that she had to stay and look after her Grace, but she hadn't. She looked out of her window. It was windy outside, so she decided against wearing a hat.

When Katherine came back downstairs again, her father was pleased he had insisted she go on the walk with Michael. Katherine spent far too much time moping about in the house, always reading that wretched bible of hers. Maybe it was his fault. He had buried himself in his business since wife had died.

"Take good care of her, Michael. It's blowing a bit out there today." Then Brian O'Malley realised he should put a time limit on the excursion he had permitted. "It shouldn't take you more than an hour and a half to get to the top of the hill and back."

Katherine often went for solitary walks up Kinnell Hill and she knew most of the paths, but Michael chose a path she barely knew and as they walked through the woodland she found herself enjoying his company. The pine cones and needles from the tall Scots pines gave off their familiar scent and she smiled as they both spotted the little squirrels bounding up the pathway ahead of them. As they talked, she found she had slipped into using Michael's Christian name without a conscious decision to do so.

Now Michael and Katherine were standing together holding hands at the top of the hill that looked down on the River Leven. Michael had originally offered his hand to Kate to help her up the final climb at the very top of the hill, but when they reached the summit he had not let go of her hand. As she pushed her hair out of her face with her free hand she saw out of the corner of her eye that Michael was smiling at her.

Then Michael tugged gently on her hand and as she turned to look at him again, he pulled her towards him and she felt her heart racing as he brushed her lips with his. She pushed him away looking shocked and he stood back and laughed, "You look lovely Kate." Then she heard him say, "Let's sit down out of the wind."

She hesitated then she followed his suggestion. She knew that if he tried to kiss her again she wouldn't resist him; and he did kiss her again. This time it was not just on the lips, but so she could taste him. It was a slightly salty taste and she felt his tongue in her mouth. She knew she should be shocked. What she had allowed him to do was terribly wrong. It was like tasting a forbidden fruit. If anybody found out, her behaviour would never be forgiven, but somehow that had made all the sensations even more enjoyable. Eventually she forced herself to pull away from Michael but still she lay on the ground next to him. Then she felt his hands start to move over her body and she pushed him away and stood up, and as the wind caught her hair again she turned back. "Michael, this is wrong. You know it is."

"You're such a good-looking girl Kate. You're difficult for any man to resist." She looked at Michael as he lay on the ground.

"I'm sure that you say that to all the girls you bring up here."

"I've never brought another girl for a walk up this hill Kate." He pushed himself up off the ground and brushed himself down. "Honest to God." She looked at him, at those smiling eyes. Maybe he was telling the truth. She could hear the thickness in his voice. Maybe he did want her every bit as much she did him, but she knew that was not enough. What they were doing was sinful.

"It's time we were getting back." She turned and started to walk down the hill ahead of Michael Costello. He couldn't see her face, but he was sure that she wasn't as displeased about what had occurred as she was trying to make out. She continued striding ahead, fighting to reconcile her conflicting thoughts. Why she did not feel more guilty, why was foremost amongst her thoughts the pleasure she was feeling?

When Michael Costello delivered her to the door of her house he searched for her hand and lifted it very quickly to his lips and then let it fall.

13

"May I see you again, Kate?" She had been thinking what she would say should Michael ask this question. All the way down the hill, she had vacillated over her response. First, she had definitely decided she would tell Michael that a further meeting was impossible. Then she had decided to tell Michael that he would have to ask her father. Then at the last minute a further thought had come to her, and she avoided looking at Michael as she responded, "I shall be visiting the library at 5.30 to-morrow evening. I go there every Monday. Maybe we might meet then."

She turned and went into her house without looking back. Why on earth had she agreed to see Michael Costello and suggest it should happen as if it were a casual meeting? The answer was she couldn't help herself, even though she knew what was likely to happen next time if she were to be alone with Michael Costello for too long.

Brian O'Malley glanced up at the clock on the mantelpiece as he heard his daughter return. He had never doubted that Michael Costello was a man he could trust.

"How was your walk, Katherine?"

"Quite pleasant father, but I don't think I'll be seeing Mr. Costello again."

"Really?"

"Really."

Brain O'Malley looked at his daughter, trying to interpret her expression but she turned away as he did so.

"Yes, unless it's at church."

CHAPTER 2

THE BETRAYAL

On the Monday Katherine arrived at the library before 5 o'clock. She wondered if Michael Costello would take up her suggestion of a casual meeting. If he did, lingering outside the library would make it look as if she was too eager to see him again, so she went inside and sat down to try and read, but by a quarter past five she couldn't contain herself and she made her way outside.

Her heart leapt, approaching down the hill was Michael Costello. He raised his hat and when he expressed his surprise at meeting her again, she smiled. She didn't hesitate when he suggested that they go for a short walk along the River Leven. As soon as they were out of sight of any prying eyes they held hands and when he asked if he might kiss her she did not demur. She savoured the delicious sensation. She knew she wanted more, and so before they parted she agreed to meet Michael the following Sunday for another walk on Kinnell Hill.

They met at an old stone seat they both knew. Katherine told nobody where she was going, not even her sister Grace, and she came empty handed, but Michael brought his worn haversack with him, and packed inside was a small picnic and a rug for them to sit on. He laid the rug over the grass and they sat on it as he cut an apple into small pieces and they fed each other a slice at a time and then he opened a bottle of beer he had brought and she tried a sip, although she had never drunk any alcohol before. It was bitter and she did not like the taste. It caught in her throat and made her cough and some of the beer ran down her chin.

Michael laughed, but in a friendly way. Then he wiped her face with the napkin and lent forward and kissed her briefly on the lips.

When they finished the food Michael finished the bottle of beer and put the empty bottle back in his haversack and then he lifted up the rug and shook it. They lay down together in the sun. They kissed again and she could still taste the slight sourness of the beer he had drunk. She felt his hands moving across her clothing. The sensation of his hands touching her so intimately was irresistible. She felt herself quiver with anticipation. Brazenly she had dressed so as to make the exploration of her body easier for those straying hands.

She did not resist as he loosened her clothing. She couldn't. She closed her eyes as she felt him expose one of her breasts and cup it in his hand. He bent and kissed her nipple. "Please, Oh God." The whispered words came unbidden to her mouth. There was a warmth between her legs. Her whole body seemed to tremble as she felt his hand move down towards those parts of her body that she knew she should not let him touch.

For a moment she pushed down her hand defensively, trying to stop him. "Michael, do you love me."

"Of course I do Kate. How could I not love someone as lovely as you?" She took away her protective hand. "Please be gentle." Then she closed her eyes and the sensations became irresistible. She tried to tell herself that it was all right to behave this way because Michael loved her, he had told her so.

Their lovemaking had continued intermittently over nearly six weeks. Each time Kate told herself that time would be the last but she couldn't help herself. Michael only had to touch her and she wanted him. She wanted his hands wandering over her body, his kisses where she would never have believed kisses could be placed. Once or twice she wondered how Michael came to know how to excite her body in the way he was capable of, but she didn't dwell on those thoughts. He loved her and that was all that mattered. She gave her body shamelessly, but she knew that matters could not continue as they were. If Michael loved her, as he said he did, then there was no problem. He would marry her. She would have to make it clear that this could not continue unless he did.

It was a Monday when she finally decided she must speak to him directly on the subject. They had agreed meet outside the library as usual, but Michael was not there at the appointed time and when he came hurrying up he told Kate he could only stay for a few minutes as he had to get back to the Tannyard. He had some urgent work to finish for her father. Briefly they walked down towards the Leven, but Michael was not his usual lively self. He seemed distracted and more distant than usual and Kate decided it would be better to leave the subject until the week-end when they would have more time. Indeed, there was no opportunity anyway for Michael didn't even walk her back as far as the library before he kissed her perfunctorily on the cheek and made off towards the Tannyard. She called after him to say she would be on Kinnell Hill on Sunday as usual and he seemed to hesitate, but he didn't turn round.

She wondered what was amiss at the Tannyard. She hoped that Michael and her father had not fallen out. That would be a disaster.

She ought to have been angry, but how could she be angry with Michael Costello. "Michael where have you been? I've been here more than half an hour."

In truth she hadn't really minded the wait for Michael. She had been in their special hideaway on Kinnell Hill, the place that only the two of them knew, where they shared each other, where they made their own little heaven. All the time she had waited she had been thinking of what Michael would do to her. She had even run her fingertips over her body pretending that it was Michael doing so. Now she just wanted to feel the warmth of his body against her own as he hugged her with his strong sinewy arms. She knew it would only take moments for her body to respond to his touch, but Michael didn't touch her. She stretched her arms out towards him, but he didn't come to her.

"Kate there's something I've go to tell you."

She dropped her arms to her side. "Michael what is it?" She didn't know why she asked him to go on. His expression said it all.

"We've got to end all this."

"But why Michael? You love me. You told me so. I know it's wrong to do this before we're married, but we can get married. There's no reason not to."

"There is Kate. I can't marry you."

"Why can't we get married?" She searched his face looking for an answer. "My father likes you. He won't object."

"It's not that Kate." She saw the wretched look on Michael Costello's face and then she knew with a dreadful certainty what he was going to say next.

"There's somebody else. There's somebody else I'm going to marry."

"Who? Who is it?" She repeated. "Tell me."

He looked at her silently without speaking.

"Go on, tell me who it is."

"It's Grace."

"Grace? My sister Grace?" She heard a voice ask. It didn't sound like her voice but she knew it was hers. There was a long silence then she managed to get her own voice back. "You bastard! I wasn't enough for you. You had to go rutting with my sister too."

"I'm sorry, Kate." Now Michael made to touch her, but Kate pulled back repulsed by the gesture.

"Don't you ever try to touch me again. Don't ever speak to me again." Kate pushed her way past him and out of the hideaway and walked blindly down the hill. Tears streaming down her face.

She heard Michael Costello calling after her.

"Kate! Kate! Wait! Let me explain."

Explain. What was there to explain? She had been betrayed by her lover and her very own sister.

God, how could she have been such a fool?

CHAPTER 3

THE CONFESSION

The Church of Our Lady of St. Augusta's had been built on a small rise halfway up the hill overlooking Levenside.

Less than forty years before, when it had been first built, it had stood out like a beacon, in splendid isolation above the whole town. Then, gradually over the years, it had become surrounded and then submerged as the buildings from the town below had remorselessly crept up the hill from the original settlement beside the River Leven. Now houses stretched well above the church to the very top of the hill as more and more newcomers sought space to live and work.

Katherine O'Malley knelt at the back of the church, almost hidden from sight in the gloom. In front of her, the twin gas brackets outside the confessional box spluttered and wheezed, and in the far darkness a solitary nun decorated the statue of the Virgin Mary. Katherine O'Malley tried to summon up the courage to make her confession as she had done so many times before to old Father Macdonald, but she couldn't bring herself to do it, not this time. This time the confession would be so different from all of those she had made before. Never before had she had to confess to something that the Church would never forgive her for.

She kept reliving in her mind the events of the previous week. That last meeting with Michael Costello when he had told her that he no longer loved her, and now she knew that they would never be together again because he had asked Grace, her sister, to marry him.

How could she have been such a fool? How could she have believed all his sweet talk, all his lies? She had tried to tell her father, but Brian O'Malley had not wanted to believe her. Michael Costello could do no wrong in her father's eyes.

"Father you can't allow Michael Costello to marry Grace."

"Good Heavens, Kate. Why an earth not? He's a good man. I couldn't want for a better son-in-law. He's the best man I have in the Tannyard. I hope he'll take over the business one day."

"It's not the business I'm talking about father. It's his women."

"What women?"

"He has other women, father. Everybody knows. He'll cheat on Grace, even when he's married to her. He's got another woman even now, even though he's asked Grace to marry him." Brian O'Malley looked at his oldest daughter for a moment before he replied.

"I don't believe it…who is this woman, Katherine?"

She had stood there in silence.

"Well?"

Of course, there was no response she could give.

"I've never seen Michael with another woman. He may have had other girl friends in the past before he came to Levenside, but if he had a woman now, believe me, I would know."

How could she tell her father he was wrong? How could she tell him that she was that other woman?

"It's not that your jealous of Grace's good fortune is it Katherine? It's not that you want Michael for yourself?"

"No, of course not, father." Her denial couldn't have been stronger if it had been true.

What else could she have said? How could she admit to her own father that she was a slut, a fornicator? How could she tell her father that she let Michael Costello do to her, on their long walks together on Kinnell Hill? She could not confess to their trysts.

Her father did not believe that Michael Costello had another woman, and if she said any more her father would think that she was not just jealous, but spiteful enough to pretend that Michael Costello had seduced her just to prevent her sister Grace from marrying him.

She had never known such utter despair. Her father wouldn't believe that Michael had taken advantage of her, or even that she had given herself to the man; and if her father was to ask that bastard, Michael

Costello, just to make sure his eldest daughter was lying, she knew with absolute certainty that he would deny everything. Michael Costello had lied to her, and he would lie to her father. He was obsessed with Grace.

She would never forgive her bitch of a sister. She must have known, or at least guessed, how far things had gone between Katherine and Michael.

"I'm just warning you father. Michael Costello is a bad lot, believe me…"

Brian O'Malley had shaken his head.

"You'll find out in time," she said.

"Nonsense Kate. Unless you can give me some proof of what you are saying I want to hear no more about this." Brian O'Malley looked at his daughter. She dropped her eyes to the ground. He could understand her being in love with Michael Costello. Michael had a way with him there was no doubt, and he was a handsome, good looking young man, but Michael was promised to Grace. Katherine would have to learn to live with that instead of making these wild jealous accusations against him. He had buried himself in his business for too long and let Katherine make all the decisions for Grace. Now was the time for him to help Grace assert her independence.

"If you do anything to ruin Grace's happiness Katherine I will take it very badly. Now let's pretend we never said anything about this."

Katherine had stood there distraught. There was nothing more she could say.

She didn't dare tell Father Macdonald what she had done. Father Macdonald had been brought back by the church to live out his final working years in Levenside after a lifetime of work abroad. She could see the priest's face in her mind, his white whispery hair, and his weather-beaten face. He had always been kind and understanding, but the enormity of her behaviour would be too much for him. She could not he tell him she had lusted after a man so much that she had allowed him to seduce her out of wedlock. Kindly though Father Macdonald was, first and foremost he was a priest.

Then she knew she had to tell someone. She could not bear her secret on her own. She stood up and walked forward towards the confessional box.

CHAPTER 4

FATHER MacDONALD'S SOLUTION

A month after Michael Costello's final meeting with Katherine on Kinnell Hill he married Katherine's sister Grace, in the Church of Our Lady of St. Augusta's.

Brian O'Malley spared no expense. He was genuinely pleased to welcome Michael Costello into his family. He had proved to be an admirable foreman, although he was young, he was well liked by the men, and a hard worker. He was Mungo's son, the man Brian had shared his first lodgings with when he had arrived to Levenside, and Mungo and his wife came all the way from Perth for the wedding; as did Mrs. Philbin and her sister-in-law, who now lived together in Glasgow, in the house they had moved to after Patrick Philbin's last and most serious heart attack five years previously.

Brian O'Malley was determined to make Grace's wedding a happy occasion. He knew that since his wife's death he had left his children too much to their own devices and not given Katherine credit for the way she had tried to fill her mother's shoes. So now, he made a deliberate attempt to come out of his shell. He organised a marquee on the back lawn at Melville House and he provided so much to drink and eat that there were supplies left over for weeks afterwards.

He thought the wedding was a success.

The one blot on the occasion was the behaviour of his daughter, Katherine.

She had been barely civil to the guests that tried to speak to her and she had refused to speak to Grace or Michael, or to Michael's parents, who had travelled all the way from Perth for the occasion. He was very disappointed with her behaviour.

The wedding was purgatory for Kate: not because she had to watch the man she had once loved marry her sister, but because by that time she had recognised that she was pregnant, that she was going to have Michael Costello's child. Nothing was showing, and she decided that before it did she would kill herself, unless she could kill her unborn child first.

She hid herself away in her room. Her ignorance of pregnancy and childbirth was profound. The only time she left Melville House, was to visit Levenside public library. She would even have ceased those visits except that she felt she might be able to increase her knowledge by reading, but she was little the wiser after two weeks as to what she could do. She wondered if she wore a really tight corset she might be able to crush the dreadful seed developing within her. She tried it for two weeks. It caused her excruciating agony but it had little obvious effect on the being inside her. She tried drinking as much alcohol as she could lay her hands on after she had read of a woman losing her child after drinking gin. Each time she tried it, however, she vomited up the alcohol, and she gave up trying after two days.

She was still with child.

She learnt that it was possible to have some sort of medical operation. The Church considered it tantamount to murder and the criminal law provided for those involved to receive sentences of great severity, but none of that mattered to Katherine if she could just kill this insidious thing inside her. Even though Father MacDonald had told her after she had confessed her affair with Michael Costello that there was still time to redeem herself, she knew now that was not true. That was no longer possible.

All this time she had no close confidant she could talk to. Grace had been her one intimate friend but now Katherine would rather die than talk to her, and of course, now that Grace was married, her sister no longer lived at Melville House.

It would not be possible to arrange (what was it called?) "an abortion" in Levenside. Somehow, she would have to travel to Glasgow, perhaps she could make discreet enquiries at the Infirmary, but even as she thought of it she started to despair. She had no money, and her father would never give her permission to go all the way to Glasgow on her own. How much would such a thing cost? Katherine stayed in her room and read her bible. It was part of her penance. Then she spent hours contemplating whether there was any solution to her problem. Alone in her room her solitude only added to her hopelessness and misery.

It was Katherine's behaviour after the wedding rather than her rudeness at it, that made Brian O'Malley decide he had to take some action. She spent all her time brooding in her room and reading her bible. She never came down to eat with Brian when he returned home in time for dinner. Katherine even refused to go to church with him so as to avoid meeting her sister. Instead, she went to a different service. Then she stopped going to church at all.

He spoke to Annie Dillon, his housekeeper. "Annie, I'm worried about Katherine she's not looking well."

"I was going to say something to you myself, Mr. O'Malley. She's not eating and she's looking so poorly."

Brian O'Malley shook his head. He had to stop Katherine moping in her room. "I think I'll speak to Father MacDonald and ask him if he might spare some time to talk to her."

The following Monday Father MacDonald called at Melville House.

"I've told Miss Katherine you're here Father, but she says she's feeling unwell and she hopes you'll forgive her if she doesn't come down to see you."

"Well in that case I'll just have go up and see her."

Annie Dillon didn't know quite what to say, so she said nothing. She followed the priest to the bottom of the stairs and watched him put his hand on the balustrade.

"Are you sure you can manage the stairs, Father."

"Of course, Annie, but thank you for asking." Annie Dillon watched the priest as he slowly climbed the stairs.

Father MacDonald paused half way up and called over his shoulder without turning. "I'm right in thinking Miss Katherine still has the same room?"

"Indeed, Father." The priest continued his unhurried ascent.

Katherine answered the priest's second knock on her bedroom door. He tried not to register his surprise. He could see she had lost weight but it was her drawn features that concerned him most, the haunted look on her parchment white face.

"I'm sorry, Father, not to come downstairs. I didn't mean you to put yourself out like that. Annie should have stopped you."

"Nonsense. I was just going for a walk anyhow. It's pleasant outside. I think it would do you good to come along with me."

"I think I need to rest, Father."

"No, fresh air is what you need, my child. Put on some walking shoes. I haven't walked along the Leven for some time. To-day's just the day for it. I'll wait for you downstairs." Before Katherine could protest again the priest had turned away and started back down the stairs.

They walked along the river in silence. Father MacDonald knew the child needed someone to talk to, but he would let her do so in her own time. Her heart had been well and truly broken. He waited, only glancing at her infrequently, as they strolled along in the sunshine.

Eventually Katherine spoke. "Father, I'm with child."

This was one of those moments when Father MacDonald wondered whether he was up to his calling. Sometimes he found God presented him with problems that he did not feel capable of dealing with. How could the union of two people so often cause more grief than happiness it was supposed to? It was one of those mysteries God made him struggle to grasp.

He tried to imagine the feelings of the young girl beside him. He doubted he would ever understand how much pain she was suffering.

Katherine had passed a harsher judgment on herself than he ever would. He must try and help. Condemnation would make matters far worse for the girl.

He liked Katherine. Her mother had died before he had succeeded Father Joseph as the O'Malley's parish priest and Katherine had, by all accounts, been the one who had done the most to help her sister Grace and her father Brian O'Malley to overcome their loss. Yet when she had looked for love herself, she had found it with someone who had let her down badly. Now, she was paying for it, and paying for it many times over.

"Katherine, have you ever thought of leaving Levenside?"

"Leaving Levenside?" The priests question took Katherine totally by surprise.

Father MacDonald knew that most of his colleagues, even if they agreed that practical help should be offered to a young girl in Katherine O'Malley's situation, would think that he should censure Katherine again for her behaviour, but what good would that do?

The young girl could not be more mortified by her behaviour than she already was. He was in no doubt that the poor girl walking beside him was a remorseful soul. Her pinched, ashen face was testimony to that. What was needed was to give her some hope, however tenuous, that there was a way out of her pit of despair.

He needed to get her to look to the future. The girl was close to the edge. It wouldn't take much to push her into the abyss. When she had first confessed to him of her fornication he had prayed that a situation such as this would not be the result, but he had lived long enough to know it might, that his prayers weren't always answered.

"Yes."

"I can't leave. What would my father do?"

Father MacDonald felt like shaking his head but he did not. The question was asked in all seriousness. "Your father is not helpless Katherine. Annie Dillon is a good housekeeper…"

"…but he will have none of his family."

"Katherine, he will manage." The priest paused on the riverbank and looked across the water to the other side.

"Have you thought what will happen when it becomes known that you are going to have a child, Katherine?" The question was met with silence. The priest watched as the swallows swooped across the water.

Katherine needed to know what faced her. It was going to be hard for her to deal with.

"I have no doubt Katherine that your father will forgive you, in time, but it will be difficult for him. People will talk behind his back, and behind your back. It will be hard to live with. People will speculate. It will be a difficult time for you…your family…and the child."

"Do you really think it would be better if… I went away. Where would I go?"

Father MacDonald didn't answer Katherine's questions directly. "Have you considered what you are going to do about the child?"

For one horrified moment Katherine thought the priest knew what she had been planning, but he continued. "How are you going look after it?"

Katherine stood in silence. She had no idea. She had not thought that she would allow her child to live, or if she did, that she would be alive to have to deal with its needs.

"Adoption isn't such a terrible thing you know, Katherine."

Adoption.

Katherine had not even thought that her child might be adopted.

It was Michael Costello's bastard. She wanted nothing more do with Michael Costello, and nothing more to do with his child. She had no problem giving away the child. Maybe it could be allowed to live.

Father MacDonald took Katherine's silence as acceptance that adoption of her child might provide a solution to her problem.

"So… if I could arrange things, would you consent to your child being adopted?" Father MacDonald turned away from the river to look Katherine in the face as she replied.

"Yes, Father." Her expression had changed.

"You realise that once the child is adopted you will never see it again. You will never know who has agreed to adopt the child. The child will, for all intents and purposes, no longer be yours." He searched the young girl's face to see if she understood the finality of such an act.

"I understand, Father." He saw relief, not regret in her face.

"Let us walk back now, Katherine, and I will tell you what I think you must do."

Chapter 5

Sister Euphemia

The arrangements that he needed to make for the birth of Katherine's child did not worry Father MacDonald as much as how he should approach matters with Brian O'Malley.

Katherine pleaded with Father MacDonald to find a way to avoid her father being made aware of her situation.

"We must tell your father, Katherine." A distraught Katherine shook her head. "I will do it if you want me to, Katherine."

She put her head in her hands for a moment before she replied.

"Please, Father… there must be some way…He's just started to get over my mother's death…"

Father MacDonald reached out and touched Katherine.

She looked at the priest. "Is there no other way, Father?" It was not just the words. Her eyes beseeched him too.

Father MacDonald's heart went out to the poor lost soul in a way he had not expected. He had tried to deal with the situation in the impersonal way expected of him, but now he found his calling failing him. The silent plea her look conveyed was more effective than any words she could have spoken. Her grief re-awakened memories of pleas of his own that were ignored when he was a child.

"I will think on it, Katherine…"

"Thank you, Father."

"…but I would ask that you think on it too."

Katherine said nothing.

It was not just her father that she wished to remain unaware of the fact that she was with child, but she did not tell the priest that. There were two other people that must never know.

Father MacDonald wrestled with his conscience for more than a week before he made a decision.

Then he brought forward the six-monthly visit he was supposed to make to discuss parish affairs with the Diocesan Bishop in Glasgow, and made arrangements to see the Sisters of Charity, an Order of nuns who were situated on the outskirts of Glasgow, whilst he was there.

"The girl's family are willing to have her back to live with them, once the child has been born and adopted, Sister Euphemia."

"That is very generous of them, Father. We are a charity, of course, and we have to consider the needs of many. We always hope any family that we help will be generous in their support for what we do. The order is also responsible for a large orphanage as you probably know." There was something Sister Euphemia's tone that conveyed to Father MacDonald that in the nun's view it was really a waste of time showing any generosity to a girl who had fallen by the wayside, rather it was more important that their families gave their support to the Sisters of Charity and their other good works.

"Indeed." Father MacDonald found it hard to like the nun.

"Normally where we take in girls who cannot pay for the cost of their confinement with us, the girls remain here with us for three years. Of course, they help us out during that time, but it is mainly to ensure that these girls don't resile from their agreement to give up their children. It ensures that they have no chance to contact or find out where their children have gone."

"I see," said Father MacDonald, but the priest wasn't sure he did see. He wondered how those who remained in the nunnery for three years would manage when they returned to the outside world particularly if they had lost contact with their families.

"Of course, in this girl's case…Katherine's the name?"

"Yes, Sister."

"…In Katherine's case, where the family… remains supportive… should a suitable contribution be forthcoming, then, all we would require is Katherine's father's agreement to her child being adopted and that he will ensure that she makes no contact with the child once it is adopted. Of course, Katherine will have no idea who the adoptive parents are so that even if she wants to contact them that would simply be impossible. But in cases such as hers we rely on the family to ensure that happens. Katherine will be free to return to her family as soon as the child is born."

Katherine had given Father MacDonald her trust and he was determined not to fail the child.

"I wish all arrangements to be made through me, Sister Euphemia."

There was a pause before Sister Euphemia replied. "Of course, Father...Will Katherine's family be able to pay the cost of this girl's confinement?"

Father MacDonald said nothing for a moment. He had no money and Brian O'Malley still knew nothing of Katherine's condition, but the nun was overstepping the mark to question him. He stared at her until she dropped her gaze.

"Suitable financial arrangements will be made, sister."

Even then, Sister Euphemia seemed about to say something more, until she looked up and still saw Father MacDonald staring at her, eventually she nodded.

"I have in mind a suitable couple to adopt Katherine's child."

"Indeed?"

"Yes, a good Catholic family. They have a farm, so the child will have lots of fresh food to eat. And the child won't be lonely. They have four children, three of their own and one adopted."

"I would like to meet them."

The nun looked at him sharply. "That is not normal practice, Father."

Father MacDonald met the nun's gaze. There was something about her attitude that he did not like.

"I can assure you, Father, the family is perfectly respectable." When the priest did not respond the nun added, "The wife is related to one of my cousins."

The revelation that the family in question was related to Sister Euphemia simply added to the priest's unease.

"Nevertheless, I would like to meet the family," repeated Father MacDonald.

There was silence. The priest waited.

"I will try and see what can be done."

"Thank you, Sister Euphemia"

It was the Mother Superior who carried out the financial bargaining. She suggested what might be considered a "suitable" contribution for Katherine's family to make. Father MacDonald considered the word that she should have used was "substantial" rather than "suitable".

Father MacDonald wondered where the money was going to come from. Brian O'Malley? He could see no other way, but how could he ask Brian O'Malley? He had promised to keep Katherine's secret. As he listened to the noise of the train as it swayed along the track, the questions kept coming, but the answers did not.

Father MacDonald's next call at Melville House was after a pastoral visit to an elderly woman living in the Tannergate.

The visit had left Father MacDonald depressed. The old woman had swollen joints that caused her a lot of pain. She lived with her grown up children. Unfortunately in these hard times, the family only looked on their mother as a burden, an extra mouth to feed. There was no love there. The only person that seemed to have any time for the old lady was one of the neighbours, a widow called Maureen O'Connor, a good soul, who made a point of regularly looking in on the old lady.

"Will you have a little whisky?" Brian O'Malley asked.

Father MacDonald nodded. A large whisky was exactly what was called for. He wasn't looking forward to this discussion with Brian O'Malley. The complaints of the old lady's family during his recent visit had been depressing. He accepted the offered glass from Katherine's father gratefully.

As the priest took a seat, Brian O'Malley mentioned he was still worried about his daughter.

"The child is unhappy, O'Malley."

"I know Father, but she'll have to get over things." The priest took a sip of his drink. He chose his words carefully.

"I think a rest away from Levenside may be what Katherine needs…" Brian had been about to put his own glass to his lips, but he held it in his hand for a moment waiting for Father MacDonald to go on "…here there is a constant reminder of …her unhappiness."

Brian O'Malley was silent for a long time. "You don't think there's anything seriously wrong with her then?"

"I didn't say that O'Malley. Melancholy can be difficult for some people to shake off."

Now was the time to tell Brian O'Malley the truth. Father MacDonald took a gulp of whisky.

"Physically, I don't think there is anything seriously wrong with Katherine." He looked down at his glass avoiding Brian O'Malley's look, hoping God would forgive him for the lie he was about to tell. "By co-incidence I visited a sanatorium when I was in Glasgow. They help people who find it difficult to get over a bereavement, particularly where their distress starts to affect their health. If Katherine doesn't improve in the next few weeks I would suggest that we send her there so they can talk to her and she can have a decent break from Levenside.

Only then did Father MacDonald look up from his drink and glance at Brian O'Malley. "…I think they might be able to help Katherine." Brian O'Malley searched the priest's face and for a moment Father MacDonald wondered if Brian knew that he was lying, but Brian's look appeared to be one of relief. Any suggestion that there might be a solution to Katherine's problems was what he wanted to hear.

Father MacDonald finished the last of his whisky in one final gulp.

"Can I tempt you to a second glass, Father?" Brian made his offer of another drink out of politeness.

"Just a little more." Brian poured the priest another measure. Brian couldn't recall Father MacDonald accepting a second glass before. The priest looked as if he was feeling his age.

Eventually the priest got up to leave, "I think we should give it a few more weeks and see how matters progress. In the meantime, I will pray for the child."

As the front door closed behind him, Father MacDonald couldn't help feeling more than prayer was required to deal with Katherine's problems.

On his visit to Glasgow, after visiting the Sisters of Charity, Father Mac-Donald had taken the opportunity of renewing his acquaintance with a fellow priest, Father Bruce Tulloch. They had both qualified from the Blackrock Seminary at the same time, but since then their paths had not crossed, largely because Father MacDonald had worked for so long abroad. Recently, they had corresponded as Father Tulloch was now working in the Archdiocesan office, helping to keep the Bishop abreast of what was going on in the various parishes for which he was responsible.

The two priests had High Tea together.

"Thank you for your help with my accounts, figures have always caused me a headache," said Father MacDonald.

"You shouldn't worry you don't give us nearly as many problems as some of the other parishes, Father Andrew," Father Tulloch smiled indulgently.

Father Andrew MacDonald took a deep breath.

"I was wondering if there was something else you could help me with."

Father Tulloch simply raised his eyebrows inquisitively, and as quickly as he could Father MacDonald set out Katherine's story, only leaving out the fact that her father was unaware of his daughter's fall from grace.

There was none of the censure Father MacDonald was half expecting from his colleague.

"A sad tale, but unfortunately one that arises from time to time." They sat in silence for a while, and from his friend's expression Father MacDonald could see that his old friend appreciated at least in part some of the grief and suffering that Katherine must be going through. "I think I might have couple who would make very good adoptive parents. They are a generous couple who run a shop in my home village. Unfortunately, they have not been blessed with any children of their own. It's been a sad disappointment to them. I'm sure they would be good parents. They've been very kind to my mother." Father Tulloch was a practical man, rather than a talker. It was one of the reasons that Father MacDonald liked him.

"Let me write you a letter of introduction to them." Father Tulloch considered for a moment.

"If you go to see them Father, don't mention anything about an adoption, not until you're sure. I don't want their hopes to be raised and then dashed." He gave Father MacDonald an earnest look.

"Of course."

When Sister Euphemia eventually wrote to Father MacDonald with a date for him to visit the family she had in mind to adopt Katherine's child, Father MacDonald took out Father Tulloch's letter to Mr. and Mrs. McBride. As well as responding to Sister Euphemia he wrote to the McBrides.

CHAPTER 6

FATHER MACDONALD PAYS A VISIT

The farmer's name was McLeish. He brought his horse and cart to Stoneyburn station to pick up Father MacDonald. He told Father MacDonald that he and his wife had already adopted a child called Michael as a favour to Sister Euphemia, but they were happy with the boy and that's why they would be pleased to have another son.

Father MacDonald wondered how the farmer could be so certain that Katherine's child would be a boy, but he decided to wait until later to ask the McLeish's intentions if the child were to be a girl.

The rest of the conversation on the way to the farm was monosyllabic, although Mr. McLeish volunteered that the priest need have no worries about how he would bring up the child. "I'm a farmer, but I'm also a God-fearing man, Father."

The priest learnt little else on the journey, despite the fact that it was the best part of two miles to the McLeish farm.

"I'll let my wife introduce you to the bairns," the farmer said when they reached their destination. "You'll excuse me Father, I need to see to the milking."

"I'll make us a pot of tea, Father, and then you can ask me everything you want to know." Mrs. McLeish showed the priest into the kitchen.

The four boys sat at the table. They were all dressed similarly, although the clothes of the two younger boys, particularly the youngest, were more worn. presumably that was because garments were passed down as the older children grew out of them.

The youngest one called Michael watched Father MacDonald as he drank his tea, never taking their eyes off the cake as the priest ate. He was the adopted son. He was too short for the seat he was sitting on. His legs didn't touch the ground and he sat uncomfortably on the edge of the chair with his legs dangling. Although his clothes were clean, the child looked like he could do with a good wash. He had dirt ingrained into his thin pallid neck.

Father MacDonald pushed his plate towards the child.

"Would you like some of my cake." The little boy's hand started to move towards the cake but then he glanced towards his mother." Imperceptibly there was a shake of the head and the little boy withdrew his hand as quickly as it had moved towards the plate.

"The children will have High Tea once you have gone Father."

Father MacDonald nodded. "Thank you for the cake Mrs. McLeish. Do all the boys help on the farm?"

"Yes, but the youngest is only seven. He's still a bit small for any real work, but he collects the eggs and helps me around the house. Don't you, Michael?"

The boy didn't react. He was still staring at Father MacDonald's plate. "Michael?" The boy wrenched his attention back to his mother and nodded.

"Do you like living on a farm?" Michael was still looking at his mother and then he nodded again. "What do like most about it?" The boy looked at him in silence.

"You like collecting the eggs, don't you?" said Mrs. McLeish. He's very good a finding where the hens lay their eggs." The boy nodded. Father MacDonald realised he would get nothing out of the child while he sat at the table with his mother.

"Perhaps you could show me round, Mrs. McLeish?"

"Of course, Father. Michael, you stay with me, you others run along and help your father."

Mrs. McLeish showed him round the farmhouse. She told him the two eldest shared a room and the two youngest another. There were no beds, just straw mattresses, two in each room, but all the indoor living spaces looked clean and tidy. She showed him round the farm too, all the time holding Michael firmly by the hand. Each time he asked the child a question, Mrs. McLeish answered. When it was time for the priest to leave, she took the young boy with her to fetch her husband so that the priest wondered why she appeared frightened of leaving the child alone with him.

The priest was in plenty of time for his train. He had half an hour to wait at least, so after Mr. McLeish's cart was out of sight, he wandered into the small town. He originally thought of walking down to the church that was at the far end of the town, but he changed his mind.

The bell rang as he entered the shop.

"I wondered if you might have a newspaper?"

"I'm afraid they're all sold for to-day, Father. They go quickly once they come off the train in the morning." Father MacDonald nodded.

"Anything else I can get you, Father?" The priest shook his head. The wizened old man behind the counter seemed anxious to talk, probably because business was slow. "You're not from round here, Father?"

"I've been visiting the McLeishs. Do you know them?"

Of course the man knew all the locals. "Oh yes. They've a farm a couple of miles out. They've a cousin in the Church. They come in every month for the market. They sell their eggs and produce on one of the stalls. Mrs. McLeish comes in here every time with the three boys…buys them a bag of boiled sweets. She spoils them, if you ask me."

"Three boys?"

"Yes, they bring in all three of them. Quite a handful."

"I thought the McLeishs had four children."

The man shook his head. "Not as far as I know. Father."

"How old is the youngest?"

The man shrugged, "Ten, I think."

"When is the market?"

"The last Wednesday of every month. You need to get here early though, Father, if you want the best produce."

Father MacDonald's next visit to the farm outside Stoneyburn was the following market day, when the McLeish's were selling their produce on their stall. That was when he found seven-year-old Andrew McLeish alone in the barn, which was bolted from the outside. The child had welts on the back of his legs, he told Father MacDonald his father had beaten him with his belt for misbehaving during the priest's previous visit to the farm.

CHAPTER 7

KATHERINE RETURNS FROM GLASGOW

Father MacDonald brought Katherine home from the convent where her child was born. At first Katherine appeared to Brian O'Malley to be much better for her visit to the "sanitorium" that Father MacDonald had organised. It had been expensive, but it seemed like money well spent. Katherine ate her meals with him again, and though she had never been talkative they resumed some kind of discourse. There was one thing that Katherine would not talk about though, that was her time in Glasgow, but that didn't worry Brian O'Malley. He was pleased to have Katherine back and over her depression.

He prayed it would last.

Then another crisis occurred, one that was a greater trauma for Brian O'Malley than Katherine's unhappiness. Grace and Michael Costello announced they were leaving Levenside. They were going to South Africa. The decision threw Brian into a spiral of despair.

Brian simply couldn't understand why. There was still no reconciliation between Katherine and Grace and Michael Costello, but after Katherine's return there appeared to be some kind of unhappy truce between the three of them. Surely it couldn't be the rift between his daughters that was the cause? Whatever it was, both Michael and Grace were adamant that they were going.

He couldn't see the logic to it. South Africa was no place to start married life. Why travel hundreds, no thousands, of miles away when

Michael had a good job and a decent home to live in? Why give up that, for the hardships of a foreign country? The chances of becoming rich as a gold prospector were close to nil. It was a gamble no sensible man would take. He made all these points as he argued long into the night with Michael Costello.

"You left Ireland to better yourself Brian. That's all I am doing."

Brian threw his hands in the air in exasperation. "You have a good job and you're earning reasonable money, aren't you? I had no job. We couldn't pay the rent. Our farm was going to be taken from us."

"You built up your own business. I want to make my own way like you, Brian."

Brian could only shake his head. He'd always thought his son-in-law had more sense. The more they argued the more stubborn Michael Costello became. For a fleeting moment Brian thought of telling his son-in-law the real reason why he'd left Ireland, but that was something he had decided long ago he would never reveal to another living sole. It was a secret that would die with him.

He tried persuading Grace.

She told him the decision had been made. Michael had never intended to make his life in Levenside. He had stopped there to pay off his father's debt to Brian O'Malley. He had been on his way to Glasgow and then onto America to make his fortune, but now he was convinced the way to riches was prospecting in South Africa.

"Well at least stay here until he's established himself out there Grace. Wait until he's found a place for you to stay."

She shook her head. "He's my husband, father. Where he goes, I go."

Then Grace told Katherine. It was the first time they had spoken at any length since Katherine's return from Glasgow. Katherine barely reacted.

"You'll do what you want to do. You always have." But there was no venom in Katherine's words. In her mind she had lost her sister a long time ago, now her mind was filled with the thoughts of a different loss.

"I will write to you Kate."

"As you wish."

Katherine couldn't believe how painful giving birth to a child could be, but the physical pain was as nothing compared with the emotional suffering she had gone through since. Now her feeling of loss was stronger than ever. She longed to know what had become of her child.

She had not been allowed to see her baby, let alone hold her offspring. She didn't even know whether she had a son or a daughter.

"Can't I just see my child once?"

"You have no child. You never had a child, Katherine." The nun who had delivered her child had said. How cruel the words had been, but then the nun had never had a child of her own and never would.

Katherine had made an appeal to the Mother Superior as soon as she was able but her plea had been rejected. "If you were to see the child it would only make it more difficult for you to give it up." Katherine was certain in her case that seeing her child would have had the opposite effect on her. She was sure it would have reminded her that the child was Michael Costello's and then she would have wanted nothing to do with it, but that was not something Katherine could say to the Mother Superior.

Now Katherine had changed her views, she longed to find her child. She felt she had lost a part of herself. The more she thought about it, the more in her mind the feeling of bereavement grew, and the less she could resign herself to it. The feeling was like a physical pain and it was unremitting. It never left her, but Brian O'Malley didn't notice. He was in a fever of activity helping Grace and Michael prepare for their departure.

Katherine, on her part, was barely affected by the preparations for their going, for she had taken to her room again. When Grace came to say her final goodbye she had to do so through Katherine's closed bedroom door. Katherine wouldn't open her door so she could say her farewell.

Brian O'Malley went with Michael and Grace as far as Glasgow and saw them off there.

After Michael and Grace had left Levenside, Brian O'Malley threw himself back into his business. He was without a foreman, but he didn't need one. He wanted to work to forget the loss of his son-in-law and his favourite daughter, and so he didn't notice the gradual change in Katherine.

The only person that noticed was Father MacDonald.

Grace sent Brian O'Malley a letter from Southampton from where she and Michael embarked for South Africa, but it was several weeks later that he received her first letter from South Africa. It was posted in Durban, before they set out for a place called Johannesburg. By this time the priest's weekly glass of whisky had become a fixture and Brian O'Malley was always home on a Thursday evening to welcome his friend, Father MacDonald.

After he received Grace's second letter Brian O'Malley purchased an atlas and he and Father MacDonald looked for both places mentioned in Grace's correspondence as they drank their whisky. Then the priest told Brian of some of his experiences in the Far East. Brian had always felt leaving Ireland had been a bold adventure but compared to what his son-in-law and the old man sharing his malt whisky had done, it was nothing. They sat in silence for a while.

"How's your other daughter?"

"Katherine?" Brian O'Malley considered the question for a moment. "Much the same."

The answer didn't satisfy Father MacDonald. "I haven't seen her at St. Augusta's recently," said the priest.

"She's gone a bit quiet again, I think she misses Grace and Michael."

"Do you think I might call and talk to her if she doesn't come to church this Sunday."

"That would be kind of you, Father, I would appreciate that." Brian O'Malley felt a moment of guilt. He had been so wrapped up in Grace and Michael leaving he realised he had neglected Katherine. Despite her antagonism, particularly to Michael, she must miss Grace as much as he did.

Father MacDonald and Katherine walked along the River Leven taking the same path as they had when she had announced she was going to have a child. She mentioned that to the priest.

"I often wonder what has become of my child. Father."

"That is only natural Katherine."

"Do you think I'll ever get to see the child?"

"Katherine, you know that it isn't possible."

"Just to see the child from a distance, Father." The appeal in her look was heart-breaking.

The priest stopped walking. "Katherine you have to stop thinking about your child. It is best that you do, for both your sakes. You're just torturing yourself."

"I can't forget, Father."

"You have to try, Katherine. Now, have you heard from your sister Grace?"

Katherine told the priest that she had received a letter from Grace posted near somewhere called Johannesburg. Where they were staying was very hot and that there were lots of flies.

"I can imagine," said Father MacDonald. Brian O'Malley might not realise how deep the fissure was that had caused his daughter and son-in-law to take flight, but it was all too clear to the priest. Father MacDonald felt sadness over what had happened to the O'Malley family, perhaps it was that which caused his indiscretion.

As they walked on he turned to Katherine, "Don't worry Katherine. I will see your son comes to no harm."

Katherine was looking out across the Leven when she heard the words, so the priest did not see her expression change.

She had a son. Not only that, but Father MacDonald must know where her son was. How else could he give her that assurance?

Katherine made sure she had regained her composure before she turned to the priest.

"Thank you for talking to me, Father. You have been so kind to me. I can never thank you enough for all the support you have given me."

Even as she expressed her thanks Katherine's mind was elsewhere. She turned once more to look across the river. She was thinking of the future, and a plan was starting to form in her mind.

CHAPTER 8

TUGELA HEIGHTS

The night of Tuesday 23rd January 1900 was dark and rainy. Unpleasant weather, but Michael Costello wasn't one for complaining. They had crossed the Tugela River four days before and since then they had just camped and waited for something to happen. Occasionally the Boers fired at anybody stupid enough to expose themselves too close to their positions, but now at last, the decision to advance had been made. The objective was to take the hill in front of them, Spion Kop, just north of the Tugela River. Spion Kop was the height that commanded the way through to the besieged town of Ladysmith.

What worried Michael was that there was only one way up Spion Kop from the Tugela River side of the peak. That was up a barely discernible track that led up the southern spur of the mountain. To Michael, the path looked like one meant for trained climbers.

Like the other men recruited in Durban Michael had signed up for a year. The recruiting sergeant had told Michael the war wouldn't last anything like as long as that. Michael hadn't argued - what was the point? After he had finished prospecting Michael had worked as a builder for the Boers. The sergeant didn't know what he was talking about. He didn't know the country and he certainly didn't know the Boers.

For months Michael and the rest of the local recruits had moved around from one skirmish to another, and always it seemed one reverse followed another, until finally they had heard that Ladysmith had become surrounded and 10,000 men besieged. Then General Buller had been sent out with troops from England and now the General was determined to relieve the town.

As Michael and the rest of the Imperial Light Infantry marched towards the Tugela River, and the Rangeworthy Hills beyond, they passed wagon after wagon of supplies. They could see all the "essential" equipment being brought to the front. Cases of wine for the officers, a tin bath for them to bathe in, and even a piano for entertainment. The wagons and the hundreds of oxen pulling them stretched for miles. It had taken four days for the all the troops to cross the Tugela River over the pontoon bridges. If General Buller thought he was going to surprise the Boers, he certainly had a strange way of going about it. His officers had yet to understand the Boer concept of travelling fast and light.

By the time they'd reached the Tugela River, Michael had found himself the senior NCO in his company. His promotion had been rapid. He'd only been a corporal for just over a month when at the start of the march north his sergeant had fallen sick and been declared unfit for duty.

The word went round again from Captain Vertue. No talking, no smoking and if they came across the enemy, they were to use their bayonets. There was to be no firing. The intention was to surprise the Boers. As much chance as catching the Pope asleep at Communion, Michael thought. He saw the Colonel moving off in front, carrying a rifle like the rest. Soon the lead group disappeared into the inky blackness and Michael saw Captain Vertue leading the next contingent forward. Michael's men were next and he got them to close up behind him.

Michael's wife, Grace and their child Meta, were in Durban. They had a good friend there, a young widow, running a boarding house and she had offered Grace and their daughter Meta room and board, provided Grace cooked and helped her run the place. For now, Michael felt satisfied his family was in no danger, but once his year was up, even if the war wasn't over, he was determined that he and Grace would be on their way back to Scotland. His father-in-law, Brian O'Malley, had written several times asking them to return home. The future for them here in South Africa now looked bleak, particularly as they had Meta.

Maybe Katherine had got over what had happened. Brian O'Malley's last letter said Grace's sister had got over her breakdown. He could only hope so. Katherine had taken it very badly when he had told her he was going to marry Grace. He was allowed to give no explanation. He had not been able to tell her that his only physical encounter with her sister had left her pregnant and so he had no alternative but to marry Grace. He had never been able to tell Kate how much he wished he had not been so foolish, that she was the one he had really loved.

Then just after their marriage Grace had lost her baby. They told nobody about losing the baby, but that, and the unbearable atmosphere whenever Kate was present, had made him decide they had to get away and make a fresh start. That they should take their chances in South Africa.

It had been hard, but they had made a new beginning and some of the guilt he felt for the way he had wronged Katherine had faded.

It had been pure luck that he had ever ended up in Levenside working for Brian O'Malley. His father had asked him to visit Brian O'Malley when Michael was on his way from Perth to find work in Glasgow. His father had given him some money for Brian O'Malley. Some longstanding debt that had to be paid, his father had said.

He would not sign up again in South Africa. He would leave this fight to the regular army. The Colonel had said that now General Buller was here in South Africa, Ladysmith would be relieved and then the Boer's would capitulate, but Michael wasn't so sure.

The Boers were fighting for their homes, and they were masters of the guerrilla tactics. They went to war with nothing more than a horse, a Mauser rifle, and the clothes they stood up in. This war was going to drag on for a lot longer than most people thought and a warring country was not where he and Grace wanted to bring up their daughter. There would be too much bitterness, too much strife. Meta deserved better.

Much to Michael's relief the rain stopped almost as soon as they moved forward. Strict silence had been ordered but, as they stumbled forward in the darkness amongst the rocks and boulders, every so often you could hear a strangled oath as someone tripped and fell on the hard rocks. To reach the southern spur of the mountain it was clear that they were having to make a considerable detour. They struggled amongst the boulders and rocks and moved in and out of various hollows of the watercourses and dongas but eventually they reached the start of the steep narrow path that led up the mountain.

Michael began the climb upwards leading his men in single file. He couldn't afford to let his concentration waver. The path was steep, rough and extremely difficult to pick out in the darkness. Whoever was leading the way must have local knowledge because the path was too indistinct to be followed in the darkness by anyone who didn't know it. Michael just prayed that they didn't lose contact with the company in front, or that any of them lost their footing. He sensed more than once that one side of the path dropped away vertically. One slip and God knows how far you would fall, probably fifty to a hundred feet.

They climbed for more than an hour, stopping from to time as the lead group checked to make sure that they had not lost the track to the top.

Then Michael walked straight into the man in front of him. "What the…

"Shut up," The man hissed. "There's a problem up ahead." Michael bent close to the man. "What is it?"

"Dunno. Anyhow, we've been told to wait here." They waited. The minutes passed and Michael could hear nothing and then Captain Vertue came scrambling back along the path. He peered at the man ahead of Michael and then at Michael.

"Who's in charge of your company?"

"I am, sir."

"Is there anybody in your company that knows anything about dogs?"

"Sir?"

"Do you or any of your men know about dogs?" The Captain repeated quietly. "There's a dog on the path."

"What's a dog…"

The Captain interrupted, "Look, there's dog on the path and they can't catch it. It keeps running away and coming back down the path. If it starts barking the Boers are going to know for sure we're on hill."

"Jesus." Whispered the man next to Michael. The Captain ignored his blasphemy.

"We can't shoot it and we can't get close enough to cut its throat, so I want to know if there's anyone who knows anything about dogs in your company."

Michael thought quickly. "There's Jock Simmons. He might be able to help. He's good with animals. Had lots of animals on the farm he worked on back in Scotland."

"Anybody else?"

"I can't think of anyone, sir."

"Pass the word for him to come up the line."

It didn't take long for Jock Simmons to squeeze past the five or six men ahead of him in the line and then the Captain explained the situation in whispered tones.

"Do you think you can catch the dog?"

"Aye, I might be able to…" then Jock paused before he said very quietly but very firmly, "I'd not be wanting to catch the dog just to kill it Captain."

In his exasperation the Captain almost forgot to whisper his response. "We don't have any choice. The dog's a real danger to us all."

"Well Captain, if I can get hold of the dog without him barking, will you not trust me to make sure he keeps quiet after that?"

Michael could just make out the two men looking at each other in the darkness. Captain Vertue needed Jock Simmons to catch the dog, but letting it live would just prolong the danger. Yet Michael knew how stubborn Jock could be. It was obvious to him that Simmons wasn't going to agree to kill the dog. He wondered what Captain Vertue was going to do.

He turned to Michael, "It's Costello isn't it?"

Michael nodded in the darkness, he was surprised that Captain Vertue recognised him.

"You go forward with Simmons. If he catches the dog and it looks like it'll stay quiet and it's a spot where you can stay put, wait there for your men to catch up; but if that dog so much as growls while you're with it, cut its throat. Do you understand me?"

"Yes sir."

The Captain's face was very close to Michael. Michael sensed that the Captain wanted to say something more. What? Cut the damned dog's throat whether Jock Simmons wants you to or not?

"Right. Follow me." Captain Vertue squeezed back up the line with Michael Costello and Jock Simmons following him until they reached the spot where the line ended.

"Alright, you two go forward now." They had only felt their way forward about thirty or forty paces when Michael saw a white object through the darkness; just visible, but out of reach, the dog sat on its haunches.

Jock Simmons motioned Michael that they should go back and they retraced the distance they had advanced to where the Captain was waiting at the head of the column.

"Well?"

"I need some rope and can you and tell the rest of the men to fall back a bit, sir. The dog won't come close to me if thinks there are lots of others about."

The Captain passed the word for some rope and it materialised very quickly.

"Here's the rope. I'll stay here with the men, but you'll have to take Costello back with you." The Captain looked at Michael. "You know what to do, Costello." He turned away and told the man next to him to try and fall back. Jock Simmons started to inch slowly back towards the dog and Michael Costello followed him.

"Don't look at the dog," whispered Simmons, "Just look at me." Michael caught sight of the white dog again and turned his attention towards Jock. He heard him say something in a very low voice to the dog and watched Jock hold out his hand, palm down with his fingers slightly bent. For a moment the dog did nothing. Simmons looked away from the dog and waited. Michael wasn't quite sure when the dog moved towards them, but Jock Simmons had hardly moved for ten minutes. Then out of the corner of his eye Michael saw the dog was up on all fours moving slowly towards Simmons' outstretched hand. Jock Simmons let the dog sniff his hand for a while and then he rubbed the dog on the side of the neck and then it came right up to Jock.

Jock turned to Michael, his arm resting lightly on the dog, "It'll be alright now you can tell the Captain." As he said those words without looking at the dog, Jock Simmons slipped the rope round the dog's neck as a makeshift lead.

Michael Costello felt his way back to Captain Vertue. He whispered his news.

"Simmons has got the dog, sir. I think you can leave him here with it." Captain Vertue hesitated for just a moment. Then he said, "All right, but you stay here with Simmons, just in case there's a problem with the dog. I'll take your company up with the others. I think there's room for the men to get past here. Then you bring up the rear. Remember what I said. Any noise from the dog and you use your bayonet. Understood?" Michael nodded back in the darkness.

Michael Costello, Jock Simmons and the dog were the last to reach the summit of Spion Kop that night. The Boers had only left a handful of men guarding the path near the top of the hill. Nobody knew why, maybe the Boers had too few men or they just didn't think the British would try to take the heights in total darkness. A bayonet charge and a few shots and they were driven off with little trouble.

When Michael and Jock reached the peak they found Captain Vertue hadn't forgotten them.

"Your company's in the middle of the line, over there Costello. The engineers should be digging them in, but the ground's pretty solid so make sure they do a good job. The Boers will be up here in the morning. They won't like losing the hill."

Michael found that the engineers had provided very little protection for his men. Entrenching tools were pretty well useless when faced with hard rock. Michael got his men to move as many large rocks and boulders as they could find to act as additional cover to the minimal trench the engineers had provided. By the time the men had finished they were all exhausted.

The morning was misty. It wasn't until about eight o'clock that the cloud broke and the visibility started to improve as the sun came out. Then a fusillade of shots rang out from the Boer lines. One of Michael's men was among the first to be hit, a bullet full in the face as he peered over the top of their makeshift protective wall, and for the first time Michael realised how dreadfully exposed the British line was. They were going to be in for a difficult day. It took a little longer for it to become obvious to him just how bad it was going to be.

In the darkness the night before someone had made a major error. The ground that the British occupied was not the highest point of Spion Kop. There were at least three higher points on the hill and in the misty conditions the Boers had quickly seized these points that the British had failed to occupy. To make matters worse the British line was not in fact a straight line, but more like a crescent and each end of the crescent was particularly exposed to the Boers on the high ground. Michael quietly thanked the luck that had made Captain Virtue allocate Michael's company a position in the middle part of the line.

After the initial fusillade of shots, worse followed. The Boers had brought up artillery and they started a bombardment with the field guns they had concealed on the adjoining hills.

"Keep you heads down," he shouted down the line of his men, but nobody had any intention of moving. The large rocks and boulders Michael had got his men to move in front of their positions helped, but they only provided concealment of your entire body if you lay sideways. Michael's men barely had enough cover from the Boers on the high ground, many of the rest of the British troops on Spion Kop were sitting ducks. As the day started to warm up so did the Boer sharpshooters.

Patiently the Boers started picking off anybody that moved. A shot rang out and rock splinters flew past only inches from Michael. It took less that an hour for it to become obvious just how hopeless the situation on Spion Kop was. The Colonel over to Michael Costello's right, tried to lead the two companies of men closest to the Boers in a charge towards one of the sections of higher ground to clear the Boer position, but before he had gone ten yards a bullet hit him full in the chest and as he fell a second one tore away the side of his face. His uniform had made him an easy target for the Boers.

Most of the men retreated once the Colonel fell. None of those that carried on, got further than twenty yards. It was clearly suicide to be in open ground, and it wasn't much better behind the few rocks that protected Michael and his men.

Jan de Moeuve was a member of the Primloo commando. When his Commandant had called for volunteers to regain Spion Kop he had volunteered. Now he concentrated his attention on the group of men off to his left at the centre of the British line. They were slightly better protected than most of the others. They had tried to build a stone protective wall. Maybe the others had taken the view they didn't need protection because they were high enough above their attackers, Jan thought. He smiled. When daylight had come they must have had a rude awakening and now it was too late for them to do anything about it.

He decided to leave the easier targets to the others. The men he was watching would be more difficult to dislodge. Difficult but not impossible if you were patient, and Jan was a patient man.

The men had realised that looking over the parapet of stones was too dangerous. That's what the first man he had shot had done. Now if they wanted to take a look, the man on the end would look round the end of the stones but only for a second and even then he didn't do so very often, but if he was patient… He decided to let off two or three shots against the stone parapet to see if that had any effect on the men pinned down behind it.

The point he chose was where Jock Simmons was lying. The dog had slept under Jock Simmons jacket and it had continued to lie beside Jock despite the noise of the battle, but the closeness of the shots on the parapet clearly terrified it and Michael saw Jock was fighting to restrain it.

"Let it go Jock. The Boers won't bother shooting a dog."

Jock looked at him and then finally he let the dog go, but just then there was a lull in the firing and instead of running away the dog just stood there out in the open. It didn't want to leave Jock.

The appearance of a dog was not what Jan de Moeve had expected. For a moment he ignored it, but when it didn't move he realised it must belong to one of the soldiers.

Carefully he took aim, squeezed the trigger and the shot rang out. The dog went down. Incensed Jock Simmons lifted himself above the protective stones and took aim at the Boer position from where the last shot had come, but before he could fire his rifle Jan de Moeve's second shot rang out flinging Jock backwards so that he fell dead beside the dog. Jan nodded. Patience that was what it took, patience.

Michael cursed. Captain Vertue had been right they should have killed the dog. He should have ignored Jock's protests and slit the dog's throat. It was too late now. Jock Simmons was dead and so was the dog.

"Stay down," he hissed, but he didn't need to tell the others that.

Jan de Moeuve waited to see if the other men would react to his killing the dog and its owner, but they didn't. He was impressed. Clearly these soldiers were disciplined, or their officer was. Never mind, thought Jan, time is on my side, especially in this sun. A few hours in this heat and they'll start to get desperate.

Getting rid of these soldiers would be a challenge. Jan de Moeuve liked a challenge.

Michael lay there wondering if they could survive on the amount of water they had. It was going to be a long, long day. "I don't want to see any of you drinking from your canteen until I pass the word."

They were going to have wait until darkness fell before they could do anything. Another charge like the Colonel's would be suicide, surely everybody would realise that.

The next charge was led by Captain Vertue at the other end of the line. His attempt was intended to dislodge the Boers from one of the other high points they held. He got further than the Colonel, but not much further. Once again the Boers picked out the distinctive insignia on the uniform of the officer leading the charge. Jan was one of the two sharpshooters whose shots hit Captain Vertue. That Captain Vertue got so far was probably because Jan did not turn his attention away from the group of men in the middle of the British line until he realised they had no intention of leaving the protection of their stone wall to join in the charge. Then he, like the other Boer sharpshooters picked off the charging men. First the officer who led the charge, then his men, often two or three different Mausers felled one man. Off to the right of Captain Vertue, Michael watched in anguished silence as he saw so many men he had got to know over the last few months run blindly to their deaths. It was only 10.30 in the morning and both their Colonel and Captain Vertue lay dead.

As the sun rose the heat started to become unbearable and Michael struggled to coax his men to lie still. Every attempt they made to discard part of their uniforms he stopped. Bare flesh would turn to raw flesh in less than an hour and the men listened. They listened as he made them ration their water and Michael began to feel with luck they might survive. His men drank sparingly and although the sun was merciless, they hugged their bodies to the stones. By mid-afternoon the stones exposed to the sun had become so hot that you could have boiled a kettle on them - if you had one.

The carnage was worst at either end of the crescent that formed the British line. Men were continuously being caught in the crossfire from the Boer lines and the bombardment from the Boer artillery. It was impossible not to hear the cries of pain or close your eyes to dismembered bodies thrown in the air by the artillery shells.

The fire from the Boer lines slackened and Michael's attention was drawn to the far end of the line where Captain Vertue had died. Michael saw the white flag appear at the same moment as Colonel Thorneycroft, now the most senior officer, did. Michael didn't understand what the flag signified until the firing ceased completely. Then he saw some Boers coming forward to disarm the men in front of them. Moments later Colonel Thorneycroft, who was now the Colonel in command, rushed forward waiving a pistol in the air shouting at the approaching Boers. "Get back! Get back before I open fire. There's going to be no bloody surrender here." The Boers hesitated. Thorneycroft was big man, broad shouldered and six foot two inches tall. As he ran forward he shot his pistol in the air. The Boers hesitated and then started to move back. As the Colonel reached the British soldiers the men who had thrown down their rifles picked them up and ran back. Most got back before the Boers started firing again. The moment had passed, but the position was even more precarious than Michael had thought.

Michael and his men held on all through the afternoon. They heard that reinforcements were being sent up and that some dismantled naval artillery was being manhandled up the heights, but as the sun started to cool at last, all Michael and his men were thinking about was water. The only news Michael longed for, was of fresh supplies, most of all the word he wanted to hear was "water". Gradually darkness began to fall. Maybe they would push forward under cover of darkness but only if they had fresh water.

"Who's the officer in charge here?"

"We don't have an officer, sir. Captain Vertue was killed this morning."

"Are you the senior NCO, sergeant?"

"Yes sir."

Michael was surprised to find the officer that had dashed forward, bending as he ran was none other than Colonel Thorneycroft.

"Well sergeant we're pulling back down the hill when it's dark. Your company and the one to your left will form the rear guard. We need to hold the centre here until the last. Hopefully the Boers won't realise we've gone until it's too late. I'll send Lieutenant Lawson forward. He'll be in command." The Colonel looked at him. "Do you understand?"

"Yes sir."

"Good man." Colonel Thorneycroft turned to move off, but then the Colonel paused for a moment. "What's your name?"

"Sergeant Costello, sir. Sergeant Michael Costello." Colonel Thorneycroft nodded in the gathering darkness, "You and your men did well to-day sergeant." Then he was off running again towards the top of the cliff top pathway. He had almost reached when a shot rang out. It missed the Colonel by inches, ricocheting off the rock face by his feet. Then before the Boers could fire again he was out of sight.

Jan de Moeuve couldn't believe it. They were pulling out. The British were all but beaten and the Boer Commando were going give up the hill to them. Jan felt like weeping. Two of the Primloo Commando who had volunteered to come up Spion Kop with him were already on their way down the hill. The British had launched some kind of diversionary attack over to the east of Spion Kop and Schalk Burger had panicked and withdrawn his men. He pounded his fist against the rock in frustration. General Botha had asked them to retake the hill. He was damned if he would just crawl away.

It was getting dark and because of the news of the proposed withdrawal Jan missed the officer running forward to the British front line. By the time his attention was back on the British line the figure was departing at speed in a crouched run. He fired his Mauser but it was a snatched shot and he missed. He cursed. The next moment the figure had disappeared over the lip of the hill.

He was doubly certain now he wasn't going to leave. Something was happening over there. He lay there and waited. Darkness fell. He could no longer see the British line. Then he thought he saw a movement way in the distance not where the front line had been but at the lip of the hill where the path led down the hill. He fired into the darkness. He thought he heard something after the shot but he couldn't be sure.

Lieutenant Richard Lawson was very young. By right, as the officer in charge, he should be the last to leave the hill. As the other company slipped back in the darkness to the head of the path down the hill, Michael spoke to him.

"Perhaps you would lead the company down the hill, sir."

"No sergeant. I'll bring up the rear."

Michael Costello felt protective of the young man. He was sure this was Lieutenant Lawson's first action.

"Well sir. I think we might get the men faster down the hill with you leading and me chasing the stragglers from behind...there's one other thing sir."

"Yes sergeant?"

"Well sir...I was the last man up the hill. I'd rather like to be the last man down." He tried to give Lieutenant Lawson a wry grin, but his mouth was so dry he couldn't. He wasn't sure that the Lieutenant could see his expression in the darkness anyhow, but he was sure how the young man would interpret his request. Michael was asking to be given the honour of being the last man to leave the field of battle. Regular soldiers took these things with great seriousness.

The young man thought for a moment. "Very well sergeant. You bring up the rear." Then he held out his hand and Michael Costello shook it.

Michael was almost at the top of the pathway when the blow to his back lifted him off his feet. The sound of the shot reached him a fraction later as he felt himself dropping to the ground. He struck his head on the hard rock as he fell to the ground. He couldn't see anything. He couldn't move. One final thought flared into his mind. He was never going to see Katherine again.

Then there was nothing, only that darkness.

Days after Spion Kop Brian O'Malley read about the battle in the Times newspaper. The report from the Times War Correspondent was clear. The British army through incompetent leadership had managed to snatch defeat out of the jaws of victory. It was weeks, however, before he learnt that his son-in-law Michael Costello was among those that had died in South Africa. The news came in a letter from his daughter Grace telling him she was coming back to Scotland with her daughter Meta.

Chapter 9

Grace's Homecoming

Originally Katherine had no intention of accompanying her father to meet her sister Grace on her return from South Africa, but she changed her mind. Something told her that it would be easier if, after all these years, her first meeting with her sister was not in Levenside but on some neutral ground.

Grace and her daughter returned by the *Southern Star* to Southampton. Grace sent a telegram, once she landed, with details of the train she would take to Glasgow. It was there, at the Central Station that Brian and Katherine met Grace.

The two of them searched for Grace among the faces streaming towards them down the platform, but for some time they did not see her. It was only when Katherine saw a thin figure half way down the platform that she thought she recognised someone similar to Grace. Even then, had a young girl not been clutching the young woman's arm, Katherine would have dismissed the woman as her sister. It wasn't until the young woman put down the two small suitcases she was carrying and bent down to the young girl and started pointing toward Katherine and her father, that Katherine was sure that the woman was indeed Grace.

Her sister had lost weight. Kate could see that even from a distance, and she was also clearly wary of her first encounter with Katherine, for she walked towards them with a measured step, but once her sister had pointed them out to the young girl, the girl waived and ran forward. She stopped uncertainly in front of Brian O'Malley, not quite sure of how she should greet her grandfather.

"Do you know who I am?" asked Brian O'Malley.

She nodded. "You're my grandfather." The girl held out her hand and Brian O'Malley shook it with great solemnity.

"I'm pleased to meet you Meta."

Then Brian O'Malley bent down on one knee so that his face was level with Meta and smiled. Meta, hesitated for a moment and then threw her arms round her grandfather's neck, burying her head in his shoulder, and Brian O'Malley reciprocated by giving his granddaughter a tight hug.

Katherine felt a pang of jealously as she looked at the two of them but she had no time to dwell on what she saw before she heard her sister's voice. She turned to see Grace standing in front of her.

"It's been a long time Kate."

"Yes." She couldn't bring herself to say any more, so she just looked at her sister. Grace had always been the more attractive of the two of them, but now her face had a tired and careworn look.

"You're looking well, Kate. How is Levenside?" Grace was the one to fill the silence between them, and Katherine forced herself to reply.

"Much the same." She shrugged. "Nothing much happens in Levenside." Katherine realised her response was terse, but she couldn't help it. She was being battered by conflicting emotions. She had missed her sister, but she still couldn't forgive her.

"How was South Africa?" She would make an effort for the child's sake at least.

"It was summer when we left Durban."

For the first time Katherine noticed that Grace and Meta were not dressed for the cold, as she and her father were. She turned to Brian O'Malley.

"Father, Grace and Meta will catch their death if we stand about here."

"Yes, come along all of you," and Brian O'Malley picked up the suitcases and Meta attached one of her hands to her grandfather's. Brian O'Malley ignored Grace's protests that she could carry her own luggage.

Brian O'Malley had booked for all of them to stay overnight at the new Central Hotel. It was late afternoon, too late to set off for Levenside.

They would catch the train in the morning and now he led them down the platform to the grand new hotel at the front of the station.

As they entered the hotel lobby Katherine surprised Brian O'Malley and Grace by saying, "Let's have an early dinner and then Meta can eat with us. I'm sure the hotel won't object - not if we tell them this is a special occasion."

Katherine led the way forward to the front desk and she missed the relieved glance that passed between Grace and her father.

Brian O'Malley saw his younger daughter and Meta up to their room, and Katherine made her way to her own room, wondering about Grace's life in South Africa. It must have been hard. She shook her head. Two small suitcases, …all of Grace's former life with Michael Costello was contained in just two small suitcases.

Once Grace was in her room, Meta ran over to the window to look at the view and Brian O'Malley took the opportunity to voice his condolences.

"I can't tell you how sorry I was to learn of Michael's death." He said in a quiet voice.

"Thank you, father. I think I'm over it now. It was hard at the time being so far away."

"It must have been difficult."

"It was…I got a very nice letter from the officer who was with Michael when he was killed. I'll show it to you when we get home if you like."

"I would very much like to read it." He paused, and now he smiled, "I can't tell you how pleased I am that you decided to come back home."

"Thank you." Grace looked at her father. There were so much that she wanted to know and there was one particular cloud overhanging her return. "How is Kate?"

Brian O'Malley looked at her uncertainly for a moment. "Katherine has some news for you, but I better let her tell that to you herself."

"What is it, father?"

Brian O'Malley shook his head. "I must be going. I'll confirm with Kate that we can eat as soon as the restaurant opens at 6.30." Then he called across a goodbye to Meta and left.

Grace wandered over to the window and rested her hand on Meta's shoulder. "I wonder what news Katherine could have for me?" Grace said it aloud, but there was no one to hear her, nobody but Meta.

Grace had told Meta she would have to be on her best behaviour if she was going to dine with all the grown ups in the restaurant and she sat quietly as she had been instructed whilst the others talked. Although in truth it was mainly her mother and her grandfather who did the talking.

"How are my grandmother and her sister? Does Glasgow agree with them?" asked Grace.

"They seem to have taken to life in Glasgow like ducks to water. Your grandmother used a fair bit of your grandfather's money to buy an annuity. She got a very reasonable rate from the Western Bank of Scotland."

For once Katherine chipped in. "They seem have tea parties all the time. No doubt you'll get an invitation." Then she added, "They might even take you to the new music hall that's opened in Sauchiehall Street."

After the discussion about the matriarchs of the family, there was a lull in the conversation so Meta thought it would be alright if she said something. "Grandfather says you have some news for my mother, Aunt Katherine." For a moment there was silence. Katherine looked across at her father. Her father's discomfort amused rather than annoyed her, but she showed no reaction. "And did your grandfather say what the news was?" Katherine asked Meta.

"No, he said you would want to tell mother yourself."

"I'm sorry Katherine I didn't mean to be indiscrete."

"It doesn't matter, father. It is no secret and we need to talk about arrangements now that Grace has returned." Grace noted the emphasis on the word "arrangements", but she said nothing. She waited for Katherine to continue.

"Grace I'm engaged to be married."

Grace's face broke out into a smile. "What wonderful news Katherine." Katherine face didn't display the same enthusiasm as her sister, in fact as she looked across at Grace she wondered why Grace should be so happy to hear her news.

"Do I know the lucky man? Who is he?"

"Seamus Thomson, he owns a number of shops in Levenside."

To Brian O'Malley, Seamus had simply started life as a 'butcher' pure and simple, now that Seamus owned several shops it seemed important to Katherine that everybody saw Seamus as a business owner. Why Seamus' status was so important to her, Brian O'Malley couldn't quite understand. Maybe it was because Katherine had not married for love.

"Oh yes, I remember him. He was the butcher in the High Street. Mama always used to buy her black pudding there."

"He owns three shops."

"It sounds like he's doing rather nicely. He sounds like a great catch, Katherine." It was only then that she saw Katherine's hostile look.

Brian O'Malley intervened. "Perhaps Katherine you would like to tell Grace about the arrangements that you mentioned."

For a moment Katherine continued to favour Grace with the same look, but then she said, "The main reason, Grace, that I wanted to tell you about Seamus is that I will be moving out of Melville House very shortly. Father has very kindly bought Seamus and I a house on the Howes Road as a wedding present."

Katherine paused, and Grace wondered if she was waiting for Grace to comment on her father's generosity, or possibly show some resentment. However, Grace didn't feel any resentment at her father's wedding gift. Clearly her father's business had continued to prosper in the years she had been away and if he could afford it, no one deserved to be rewarded more than Katherine. It was Katherine who had held the family together after her mother died. It was Katherine who had looked after their father after she and Michael had left for South Africa.

"That's very kind father. I am pleased."

Katherine heard what her sister said, but she wondered if she was being disingenuous. Her distrust of Grace still ran deep.

"It will mean that you and Meta will have much more room in Melville House when you move back. Indeed, once I have gone, Meta will have a choice of rooms."

Grace smiled, "That will be grand for her."

However much Katherine dressed up the arrangements Grace understood what remained unsaid.

Katherine had made sure that the two of them would never live together again under the same roof.

61

CHAPTER 10

THE FINAL PARTING

It wasn't until Grace was settled back in Levenside that Brian O'Malley became aware how seriously ill she was. As her raking cough became more frequent he insisted that Grace should see a doctor.

That was when he first came across Dr. Cunningham. Brian O'Malley had heard good reports of the young man from Father MacDonald who had met him visiting some of his poorer parishioners and, although the young doctor was not long qualified, Brian asked him to examine his daughter.

Doctor Cunningham diagnosed Grace as having tuberculosis.

Brian O'Malley immediately arranged for Grace be seen by a consultant at the Glasgow Infirmary. The consultant confirmed the diagnosis of young Dr. Cunningham. He also confirmed that doctor's prognosis. There was little or nothing that could be done for Grace.

The Mrs. Philbins insisted that Grace stay with them. It was much more sensible for them to look after her. They were within easy reach of the Infirmary if further treatment proved possible.

Grace refused their offer. She insisted that she be allowed to return to Levenside. Fresh air was the best treatment she could have, according to Dr. Cunningham, and she would get that in Levenside, better than in Glasgow. Grace said she would see no other doctor.

It was only two or three weeks after her return that Grace took to her bed. She was not to leave it, until she died. She wrote to her sister Katherine asking if she would return to Melville House to look after her.

"I do not think it will be for any long time," she wrote. There was no disguising the fact that the disease was rampant.

Katherine refused Grace's request. She did not believe Grace was dying. However, Grace asked both Dr. Cunningham and Father Mac-Donald to speak to Katherine. In their different ways they made it clear to Katherine that Grace was terminally ill, and so Katherine decided she would visit Grace on her sick bed.

As she opened the door to Grace's bedroom her sister was in the middle of a violent coughing fit. Just as it subsided Grace had her first serious haemorrhage. Katherine watched in horror as the bright red frothy blood issued from Grace's mouth, soaking her handkerchief and staining the bedclothes.

That evening Katherine moved back to Melville House. She barely left her sister's side until the night that Grace died. Dr. Cunningham warned her that Grace's consumptive illness was highly contagious and that it was best if she and Meta kept their distance from Grace. Katherine accepted the advice in respect of her niece, but not as regards herself. She slept in Grace's room and she read to her as she had when Grace was a child.

The swiftness of the Grace's decline took everybody by surprise. That final day Katherine thought Grace looked better that she had for some days. Her natural beauty seemed to have returned. The worried drawn features had disappeared.

They had left the windows of her room open for most of the day, and as usual Katherine had read to Grace, but that evening Grace had asked that Katherine read from Dickens, rather from the bible. When she finished Katherine saw that Grace looked almost serene.

"Will you sit here with me on my bed for a moment? Just hold my hand." Katherine looked at her sister sharply. In the lamplight, Grace's eyes looked much brighter than she remembered. They were almost shining.

Katherine sat on the bed as she had been bade and waited.

"Will you fetch Father MacDonald?" Katherine started to rise from the bed on which he had been sitting, but Grace still held her hand. "One more thing before you go." Katherine waited for her sister to speak.

"Will you forgive me?"

Katherine looked away. She fought to control her emotions. Now was the time to bury those wounds however deep they might be. It only seemed a matter of a few moments before she turned back to look at Grace but, whatever words she had decided to use, she never uttered them, for Grace no longer grasped her sister's hand, and although Grace's eyes still stared at Katherine, the light had gone from them.

At Grace's funeral Katherine found herself too numb to respond even to Father MacDonald's expressions of sympathy. As she had sat with Grace on her sick bed she had decided that with Michael Costello dead, given time, that it would be possible for Grace and her to rediscover at least some of the closeness that they had enjoyed as children, but cruelly they had not been granted that time.

Two weeks after Grace's funeral Father MacDonald came once again to visit Brian O'Malley at Melville House and share a whisky.

"I understand that in her will, Grace entrusted the care of Meta to Katherine."

"Yes, Father. Katherine seems unlikely to have children of her own so I think in time it may be a good thing, although she seemed quite upset about it at first." Brian paused. "We've agreed that for the time being Meta will live with me and Katherine will visit every day."

Father MacDonald sat silently for a while. Now was the time to confess to Brian O'Malley the terrible secret that he thought about every day, but he found himself shaking his head. He could not break his promise, he could not betray Katherine's secret.

"You may be right."

He looked down at the book of poetry he had brought with him. "Have you read any of the Richard D'Alton Williams' poetry?"

"I'm afraid I haven't had the chance, Father."

The priest nodded. "Brian take this. Once Grace's departure is less raw in your memory, if you get the time, read 'The Dying Girl'. Williams wrote it before he left Ireland."

"Thank you, I will."

Father MacDonald finished his whisky. "There's no point wondering if there is something more you could have done Brian. There's no escape once you catch that disease. Grace never had a chance. It's a disease that kills more of us than any other."

As the priest stood up to go, Brian picked up the book from the side table and found a place for it in his bookcase.

He heard the priest say, "The ironic thing about William's poem is that I think he probably thought by going to America that he had escaped the terrible disease he wrote that poem about, but in the end it that was that disease that killed him too."

Although Doctor Cunningham certified Grace's cause of death as tuberculosis, in Brian O'Malley's mind it was the death of her husband that had killed Grace. It seemed to him that although she had told him that she had got over Michael's death that was far from the case. Grace did not have the will to fight her illness.

When Brian O'Malley went through his daughter's few belongings he found two letters. The first was in an envelope addressed in Grace's handwriting to her sister "to be given to Katherine in the event of my death".

Brian O'Malley hesitated over what to do with that letter. In the end he decided not to give it to Katherine straight away. Whatever the contents he feared it would fuel the antagonism that he hoped would now die with Grace. He locked it in the safe he had installed in his study.

The other letter he put in his desk drawer. It was the one that Michael Costello's commanding officer had written to Grace following her husband's death in South Africa. After he read the letter he stared at the signature and name at the foot of the letter, **Lieutenant the Honourable Richard Lawson.**

The name next to the signature registered straight away. The letter had been signed by the grandson of the man Brian Costello held responsible for the death of his father and his sister Tara.

CHAPTER 11 - THE MCBRIDES

Throughout his life, Matthew McBride swam in the North Sea every day from the first day of May until the end of October – except on Sunday. Too many fishermen died because they couldn't swim, and Matthew's father had been determined that Matthew wouldn't be one of them. So, as soon as Matthew was old enough, his father had taken Matthew down to the sands and into sea with him.

By the age of ten Matthew had become one of the best swimmers in Eyemouth. At the age of thirteen Matthew signed on for his first trip on his uncle's boat. There was never any doubt that Matthew would be a fisherman, like his father, but his mother wouldn't let him sign on with his father. Fishing was a dangerous livelihood, and she didn't want to lose her husband and her son at the same time. That was when Matthew's plans, and his father's plans, fell apart.

Matthew McBride suffered from chronic sea sickness.

He persevered, everybody agreed that, but Matthew was next to useless for long stretches on each voyage he took. In the end, his uncle spoke to Matthew's father. He was blunt about it. It was unreasonable to make Matthew suffer anymore. It was agreed that Matthew would need to find a shore job.

That was how Matthew McBride came to run the general store in the little fishing village of Eyemouth, and that's how he came to marry Christine.

Christine's father had also been a fisherman, but he drowned when she was still a teenager, one of the one hundred and twenty-nine fishermen from Eyemouth to perish in the Great Storm on Black Friday.

She remembered how calm that Friday morning was. She always went down to the harbour with her father to watch the boats go out, and she did that day, although her father told her that it was unlikely that any fishing boats would be putting out to sea. The barometer was giving one of the lowest readings he had ever seen.

She listened as her father and some of the other fishermen argued against going out to fish. As usual, the men had all met up at the pierhead weather glass. There was a lengthy discussion, but in the end most of the men wanted to take the risk. The sun was shining, the sea looked flat and calm, and they all needed the money from the next catch.

Christine's father swallowed his misgivings and took his boat and crew out too. In Eyemouth it was understood if one boat sailed, the rest of the fleet did so too. So, at 8 o'clock the boats set off. Christine watched them sail out in tight formation, fanning out as they passed the Hurkur rocks at the harbour entrance. The russet sails of her father's boat standing out among the white canvas sails on the other boats.

Forty-five boats went out, but only twenty-two boats came back, and her father's was not one of them, neither was Matthew McBride's uncle.

Four hours after the little fleet set sail, the wind dropped, the skies darkened and the hurricane struck. The boats were hit by massive waves. The fishermen cut their lines and tried desperately to run for home - less than half made port.

By nightfall there were ninety-three new widows in Eyemouth. Christine's mother was one of them, and Christine found herself the eldest of five siblings without a father.

Matthew McBride's father was the skipper of the last boat to return. He brought his battered boat in two days after the Great Storm. Instead of running for port he had decided to sail into the storm, and his boat survived. He didn't make port until the Sunday morning, two days after the Great Storm.

Although Christine's mother received five shillings a week from the Disaster Fund, money was short. There were few jobs for women in Eyemouth that paid any money.

Christine was a practical girl. She realised quite quickly that the only way to escape a life of poverty was to marry. By the time she was sixteen there were already several young men that were interested in her. There was no doubt she was a 'good looking lass'. The only problem was

Christine was determined that after Black Friday she would not marry a man that went to sea. In Eyemouth, that didn't leave many eligible young men, particularly as he had to be from a Catholic family like herself. In the end she decided it only left Matthew McBride.

It was surprisingly good choice. He was quiet man, but he proved to be kind and generous. She grew very fond of him, and then one day she realised to her surprise, that she was in love with him.

Just a small cloud hovered over their world. They would have liked to have children, but gradually, as Christine and Matthew McBride reached middle age, they became reconciled to the fact that they were not to be blessed, despite their prayers. They told themselves they were lucky because at least they had each other.

Then they received a letter from Father MacDonald, a friend of Father Bruce Tulloch who had been born in Eyemouth. Another man who had not gone to sea.

Katherine felt sure that her father held her responsible for the deaths of Michael Costello and Grace, although he never said anything about it to her. For a time after Grace's death, the two of them said little to each other about anything, and once again a barrier grew between them.

Brian O'Malley would eat the evening meal that Annie Dillon his housekeeper would prepare for him and then he would shut himself away either to check over the ledgers he kept there or to read in the room he had converted into a study after Grace's death, but Katherine no longer lived at Melville House and she told herself she did not care what her father thought about her. Her son was all that occupied her thoughts.

It was about twelve months after Grace's final illness that Katherine became aware that every spring Father MacDonald took a short holiday. She had no proof it had anything to do with her son, but she was curious.

Katherine knew better than to ask the priest directly where he went, but she determined to find out. He still invited Katherine for occasional walks and when he mentioned his travels she asked the priest if he hadn't missed his family being abroad for so long.

"No child, the Church has always been my family."

Katherine was not so easily put off. "But you did have a family, didn't you, Father. You weren't an only child?"

"Yes, but most of my family died even before I was sent abroad."

Father MacDonald knew he'd always been an afterthought on the part of his parents. He was by far the youngest of the family. That was why he was in the Church. There was nowhere else for him to go. Everybody had thought his mother beyond childbearing age, including his mother, when Andrew MacDonald had made his presence felt; and as with many other not very well to do middle class families, there had been no land or money left for the youngest of the brood. The Church was the only answer and Father MacDonald had done his best to adapt to the path imposed upon him.

Katherine also sought information from her father who she still had lunch with after church on a Sunday, after all the two men often had a drink together.

"Don't you think it's sad that Father MacDonald has no family."

Brian O'Malley looked at his daughter considering what she had said. He was surprised that his daughter had initiated what was a new topic of conversation but Father MacDonald, as a man, interested Brian.

"Why should I be sad about that, Kate? Father MacDonald is not unhappy. I can't remember him complaining, not once." Brian O'Malley paused. "Well there was one time, but that was when he thought I'd given him too short a measure of whisky."

Katherine humoured her father by smiling, but his response didn't, even for a moment, deflect her from her pursuit of information.

"Does Father MacDonald not have any close friends?

"He has lots of friends, Katherine. I count him as my friend as well as my priest."

"Apart from you father?"

"He doesn't talk about other people much. He sometimes mentions Father Tulloch who works in the Bishop's office in Glasgow. They went to the same seminary."

"Have you ever met him?"

"Who? Father Tulloch? No." Brian O'Malley didn't bother to consider why Katherine was so interested in Father MacDonald's family background. He was pleased that she was making the effort to talk, so often Sunday lunch was punctuated by long silences. "I think Father MacDonald was quite fond of Father Tulloch's mother. The two of them went to see her shortly before she died."

"Where was that, father?"

"I'm not sure I remember." Katherine willed her father to remember the place name.

"It was that fishing village that had that terrible disaster." He shook his head. "The name's gone."

Katherine said nothing. She filed away the information.

Then, when during one of her walks with Father MacDonald he told her that he would have liked to live by the sea if he had not become a man of the cloth, Katherine was almost certain she knew the secret of her son's whereabouts. Although she'd been quite young at the time she remembered the Great Disaster. Even in Levenside there had been a collection for the families, so many fishermen had died.

She set about planning a visit to Eyemouth.

Money was not a problem. She did all her father's housekeeping purchases and he was always generous, but there were difficulties. Eyemouth was a long way from Levenside. Even if she could travel there in a day, Meta was a problem. She couldn't take the child with her, and she couldn't leave her on her own in Levenside.

She was right about the distance. Eyemouth turned out to be virtually on the English border. To get there she would have to travel to Edinburgh and then take the train to Berwick, but a return journey could be done in a day if she planned it carefully.

The week after Father MacDonald returned from his next annual break Katherine O'Malley arranged to stay for a week with the two Mrs Philbins in Glasgow. Once she was there, she asked if they would be willing to mind Meta for the day whilst she took a break to visit Edinburgh. The two old ladies jumped at Katherine's suggestion. It gave them a day to spoil their only grandchild.

When Katherine O'Malley got to Edinburgh, she changed at Waverley station straight onto the train to Berwick.

Katherine became more and more nervous as the train trundled along. She had no idea what she was going to do when she got to Eyemouth. She knew that her son was now eleven years old, but she had no idea of his name or what he looked like. She hoped Eyemouth was a small place…not too small though.

She looked out of the train window at the strangeness of the North Sea, it was so cold and uninviting. The grim greyness of the water was almost indistinguishable from the dull cloud overhanging the sea, and on another occasion it would have dampened her spirits, but not that day. She was certain she was going to see her son for the first time. Nothing was going to stop her. Her initial feeling of nervousness started to fall away to be replaced by a feeling of exhilaration.

She had to avoid being noticed. She discarded the idea of visiting the school. A casual question while making a minor purchase might not be too obvious. There must be a shop where she could make enquiries.

When she climbed down onto the platform at Eyemouth she still hadn't got a clear plan as to what she would do. She stood there uncertainly.

"Can I help you ma'am?" The member of the station staff who took her ticket had noticed her indecision.

"Not really. I'm staying a few days in Berwick. An old friend of mine, a priest, was born here. I thought it would be interesting, as I'm so close, to see where he came from."

The man nodded his head. "That'll be Father Tulloch he hasn't been here since his mother died. His friend Father MacDonald was here not so long ago. He stays with his friends, the McBrides. They run the general store and rent out rooms."

The ticket collector had volunteered nearly all the information she wanted without her asking any questions. She relaxed.

Just for a moment she thought of asking if the McBrides had any children, but she thought better of it. She had learnt patience over the years.

"I think you've got a problem though ma'am." The statement broke into her thoughts. Had she relaxed too early?

"There's not a train back to Berwick until late this afternoon. I doubt it'll take you more than half an hour to see the whole of Eyemouth."

"Maybe there's somewhere I can get some lunch while I wait?"

The station staff member looked doubtful. "The McBrides only do breakfast and High Tea for those staying with them."

Katherine was not put off. "Where do I find their establishment?"

"If you turn left out of the station, and then straight over at the crossroads, the road runs down to Eyemouth. As the hill drops away you'll see the general store and the McBrides' house, next to the foot-bridge over the river."

"Tell me are the McBrides a family business?"

The man nodded. "Matthew McBride started the business. There's just him and his wife. They've got a young son, John. He's a bit young to be helping in the business, but he's a great swimmer, like his father."

John, she approved of the name. She might well have chosen it herself.

Her informant was right, there wasn't much to see in Eyemouth. The name described the situation of the village exactly. The fishing village had grown up round the mouth of the River Eye. A stone harbour had been built to one side where the river met the sea, and it was the home for a number of fishing boats of various sizes. On the harbour side were the buildings where the fish were stored and sold once they were landed. Katherine could tell that from the overpowering smell. Most of the houses were on the left bank of the river, but on the far side of the river, that could be reached by a bridge, were two or three rows of artisan dwellings.

She had not gone into the general store, on her way down the hill but she decided she would have to now. The one or two people she had seen, had looked at her inquisitively as she'd passed. She couldn't sit by the harbour wall for hours without becoming the subject of speculation.

She set off back up the hill, walking past the houses that ran up to the station and towards the general store.

Then she saw him, and her heart started racing. She had to force herself to keep walking. Down the hill came a young boy with a towel rolled up under his arm. She knew straight away he was her child. There was nothing distinctive about his features that immediately reminded her of Michael Costello or herself, but he was her son. She just knew.

As he reached her, he touched his flat cap and said, "Good day, ma'am."

She felt an overwhelming urge to take hold of him and hug him tightly and tell him how many years she had been searching for him, but she did not. Instead, she returned his greeting, "Good day, young man," and the two of them walked past each other, so close that she was able to see the colour of his eyes.

She walked past the McBrides store without looking back, until she came to the crossroads. One road led to Berwick, the other to Coldingham. Which way to go? She couldn't think.

She turned towards Berwick.

She had on her walking shoes and she strode along, paying no attention to the cold blustery wind. She didn't notice anything about her surroundings. Her heart was singing.

She'd found her son. Her son was called John, and he had clear blue eyes.

CHAPTER 12

JOHN McBRIDE
COMES TO LEVENSIDE

After her visit all Katherine could do was to hope that no one in Eyemouth would mention the visit of a strange woman to Father MacDonald on his next stay. There was no reason that they should, she had never mentioned the priest by name, and she hadn't spent that much time in the fishing village. She had even gone for a long walk rather than waiting for her train in Eyemouth station.

As time passed, she was proved right. All the same, Katherine couldn't go back to Eyemouth. The fishing village was too small. She would never get away with another visit. Even more than before, she longed for information of her son, but however hard she tried, she could not think of way of obtaining it without betraying her new knowledge. Ten years was a long time, but that was how long she had to wait before she saw John McBride again.

When she did. It was in Levenside of all places.

Christine McBride was adamant that her son would not go to sea. Matthew McBride said they should wait and see what the boy wanted to do, and, in the end, it was indeed their son John who made the decision. It was one that surprised both his parents. He told them he intended to go into the priesthood. He said he wanted to follow in Father MacDonald's footsteps.

Father MacDonald only had dispensation to be away from his parish for two nights and he was not permitted to be away on a Sunday, so his time with the McBrides always fell during the working week. John McBride and the priest would walk over to Coldingham Sands and John would swim, often with a couple of brothers who were his close friends, and Father Macdonald would watch and enjoy the sea air, and John and his friends would listen impressed as the priest told tales of the Far East and his missionary work.

John McBride was quiet and studious like his adoptive father. He did well at school, and eventually with Father MacDonald's help he secured a place at the priest's old seminary.

Father MacDonald was surprised when he received notification that a pastoral assistant was going to join him. Father Tulloch had suggested he should consider it and he had willingly agreed. He had told Father Tulloch he would always been willing to help those considering entering the church, but that had been over a year ago and he had forgotten about it. He had been happy at the original suggestion, Levenside was a busy parish and he had to admit that he found it difficult to provide for all its demands. The right young man would be a real help.

However, now he had learnt that the novitiate coming from his old seminary was John McBride, he was not so sanguine about the proposal, indeed as he read the letter informing of the appointment, he was deeply troubled.

In normal circumstances he would have given him pleasure to encounter John McBride again. He would have liked nothing better than to aid John's progress in his chosen vocation, but the fact that John McBride's real mother lived in Levenside was a complication that could not be overlooked.

He had made sure that Brian O'Malley's daughter, Katherine Thomson, had had no contact with the son she had given up for adoption. John McBride had grown up as far away as possible, and there was no reason, after all this time, why Katherine should realise that John McBride was her son, but if they were to come into contact and she did realise…

Father MacDonald didn't want to imagine the consequences.

It was better not to take any chances, so he wrote to Father Tulloch in the Archdiocesan office, asking if he could visit him to discuss the matter, but his friend was no longer there. He had been seconded at short notice to Rome. He would not be returning for at least six months.

Brian O'Malley had not seen Father MacDonald for over three weeks and he wondered why. True it was an informal arrangement, and there were occasions when demands upon the priest prevented his visit to see Brian at Melville House, but Brian O'Malley felt it was something both men looked forward to, and he couldn't remember the priest missing his glass of whisky for three consecutive weeks.

As he was leaving church the following Sunday and Father Mac-Donald was saying farewell to his congregation Brian mentioned to the priest his recent absence.

"Will you be coming round this Thursday, Father? I miss our discussions."

"I do, too, Brian. I've been rather busy. I have this new novitiate."

"He'd be welcome too, Father. Bring along with you."

The priest appeared to hesitate. "If I can, I'll be there, Brian." As Brian O'Malley walked away he puzzled over the priest's reaction. Could it be that Father MacDonald was worried about this young novitiate seeing the old man imbibing whisky? No, not Father MacDonald, but the priest had seemed reluctant to accept the invitation. That Thursday Father MacDonald reappeared at Melville House and he brought John McBride with him. The priest had dithered about accepting the invitation but he asked himself how much harm could it do? Katherine Thomson no longer lived at Melville House so they were unlikely to meet her and Brian O'Malley had no idea of the existence any grandchild, other than Meta.

It was Brian O'Malley that troubled the priest most. Was he once more betraying his good friend?

Meta Costello was the person that opened the door to Father Mac-Donald and John McBride. Maybe it was the absence of those three weeks, the old priest was not sure, but he couldn't help noticing what a striking young woman Brian O'Malley's granddaughter had become.

Father MacDonald was not the only one who noticed how attractive the girl who opened the door was. John McBride would normally have been only too interested to listen to Father MacDonald and Brian O'Malley talking about the matters that interested them. Brian O'Malley was very well informed about politics and had a particular interest in Irish affairs, but as he watched the two older men sipping their drinks John McBride's thoughts were elsewhere.

He couldn't forget those lovely blue eyes.

As Meta walked back towards Melville House, she felt uneasy. She had never felt troubled by her friendship with John McBride until the moment he had told her that he would be returning to the seminary the following week.

John had been very busy. He had been assiduous in his support of Father MacDonald, but he had managed to snatch a little time to be with Meta Costello, and they had spent it walking over the braes that surrounded Levenside, marvelling at the views of the Lomond Hills and the River Leven. Aunt Katherine had repeatedly told her that young women were not supposed go walking unaccompanied with young men, but John McBride was studying to be a priest so what harm there could be in their walks together?

Neither she, nor John, saw any reason to mention their meetings to anyone else. They enjoyed being together. They made each other laugh. They looked forward to their walks on Kinnell Hill and along the River Leven.

It was only natural to arrange one final meeting to say goodbye.

They decided to try and forget that their time together was coming to an end, and they nearly succeeded. On the final evening before John's return to the seminary, they decided to go for a final walk-up Kinnell Hill.

Once they had climbed away from the town John began to push the pace along so that by the time they reached the open ground at the brow of the hill Meta found it a struggle to keep up. She paused for a moment to catch her breath. She looked at the view of the river winding away in the distance below them in the fading light. Then she realised that John hadn't stopped so she ran after him. Just as she tugged at his arm to slow him down, she caught her foot. She clung onto him as she fell and that pulled him down with her.

A moment later the two of them were rolling over and over on the coarse grassy hillside, laughing just like a couple of little children. They came to a stop almost side by side.

For a while, they both lay there among the grass looking at the sky as dusk fell.

"Red sky at night, shepherds delight…" Meta heard herself reciting the children's verse that her grandfather had taught her. As she finished

John lent across to her. She turned towards him and found herself looking up into his eyes. She closed her eyes as he lent down towards her. He brushed his lips across her closed eyelids and then she felt his mouth on hers. She didn't resist as he pulled her body close and tightly encircled her with his arms. She felt his body hard against her own.

A moment later he pushed her away.

She heard a strange voice say, "I'm sorry Meta … I didn't mean to…." She looked at him. She tried to smile, but her confused thoughts must have registered in her expression.

"It's getting late…" John seemed to stumble over the words. "We'd better get back." She reached out. For a moment their hands touched, but John pulled his hand away almost instinctively, as if he had held it too close to a flame.

They walked back to Howes Road slowly, and gradually a barrier of silence grew between them. Neither of them looking at each other.

Finally at the door to her grandfather's house in the Howes Road she turned towards John.

It was John who spoke first. "I have to leave first thing in the morning." He paused, keeping his eyes downcast. "I think it's best if we say goodbye now." He looked at her briefly.

She searched his face for some recognition of the feelings that she knew had existed back on the hill, but John dropped his gaze. Without another word he turned and walked away. She watched him walk along the road. She waited for him to turn and wave, but he did not turn back, and she watched him until finally, in the fading light, he turned the bend and was out of sight.

It wasn't until a week later that she heard from him again. The letter was waiting for her on the sideboard in the hall when she returned home from teaching at the convent. For some reason she did not open it straight away. She took it up to her room before she read it. "Dearest Meta…." She read it slowly, savouring its contents. She could feel its warmth and tenderness. It was only as she started to read the final page that the significance of what she was reading came to her …." I long to lie beside you again, to hold you **naked in my arms** …."

The words stood out as if they were burnt onto the page. She walked over to the mirror. She looked at the reflection in front of her.

Dear God, what had she done?

78

CHAPTER 13

THE QUARREL

As Meta walked back from St. Augusta's she barely noticed the threatening clouds gathering in the sky above her. Even when she entered her grandfather's house in the Howes Road, she was still lost in thought.

She took off her coat and she was about to make her way to her room when she saw her grandfather standing in the living room with his back to the fire, with his hands clasped behind his back. His presence and the fire made the room both warm and welcoming, a complete contrast to the miserable day outside. It made Meta hesitate in the doorway.

"Grandfather…" Then she changed her mind. "If you don't mind, I think I'll go up to my room… I'm feeling rather tired."

"Of course, Meta."

Brian O'Malley's watched his granddaughter retreat from the room. As Meta started up the stairs she put her hand on the balustrade as if to support herself. He frowned and momentarily a look of concern showed on his face. There was a lot of illness down in the Tannergate. He wondered if he should follow just to check on her. He stood undecided. Meta hadn't looked unwell.

When she reached the top of the staircase Meta didn't notice that the door to her room was partly open. So once inside the room, she was startled by a darkly clad figure standing in front of her. The woman swung round, her eyes blazing, her face like a storm cloud.

"You whore!" Her aunt's vitriol burst upon Meta.

"How could you … " Her aunt seemed to choke as she tried to get the words out. Then she hissed at Meta, "My God! He's to be a priest."

To Meta's horror she saw that John's letter, was in her aunt's hand. Meta stood in a daze as her aunt advanced towards her.

The blow across her face made Meta stagger backwards, but the pain didn't register. The shock of being struck froze her senses.

"You slut! Your mother was the same…. throwing herself at men, but you'll not seduce John McBride. I'll see you in hell first." There were flecks of spittle at the sides of her aunt's mouth and she spat out the words at Meta like venom.

Meta stood fighting back her confusion. What had she done wrong? She had only shared a fleeting kiss with John McBride. It was he who had written of his feelings for her. It wasn't her fault.

Her aunt raised her hand and struck Meta again. Meta stood motionless. Her arms were limp by her sides. She closed her eyes and waited for the next blow… but the next blow did not fall.

"That's enough!" Meta opened her eyes and saw her Aunt Katherine's right arm was held in a vice like grip. Just behind her aunt stood her grandfather. Neither her aunt, nor Meta had heard him enter the room. Meta watched as her aunt turned to face Brian O'Malley. Her aunt's face was still contorted with hatred.

"You're just as bad! You let Grace throw herself at that nobody Michael Costello." A sneer crossed her aunt's face. "He was common as dirt. Even when she decided to run away with him you wouldn't stop her. No wonder Meta's turned out the way she …"

A sound like a rifle shot stopped Brian O'Malley's daughter in mid-sentence. Meta saw a red weal appear on her aunt's cheek, her aunt's shoulders sagged, the letter dropped from her hand. Then Meta heard her aunt, pleading with her grandfather, "Father you can't let her ruin John McBride's life. He's going to be a priest."

Brian O'Malley's voice was ice cold, "Wait for me downstairs." Very slowly, Aunt Katherine walked out of the room and down the stairs.

Meta felt her grandfather put a comforting arm round her shoulder. He led her slowly across to her bed. She moved unthinkingly in the direction she was led. Quietly, he said, "Have that lie down. We'll have a talk in a while."

Without saying a word, Meta lay down on the bed and shut her eyes. "People talk a lot of foolishness in the heat of the moment." Meta didn't respond to her grandfather's words. She kept her eyes closed. She just wanted to be left alone. Her grandfather's spoke again. "I'll leave you be, Meta." His voice sounded far away. After a while she heard the slight click of the catch as her grandfather closed her bedroom door as he left the room.

As she lay there, she didn't feel any pain from the blows her aunt had struck. Her thoughts blanked out the physical pain. She knew she had to forget John McBride, forget about her feelings for him, forget everything he had written.

She felt tears welling in her eyes and she turned and buried her head in her pillow as she had when she was a little girl.

Brian O'Malley descended the stairs slowly. After all these years, after all that had happened, the jealousy was still there. He shook his head. Michael Costello hadn't seemed so "common" when Katherine had her eye on him. Katherine had only turned against him when it became obvious that Michael preferred her sister Grace, Meta's mother. It was so difficult to forgive someone who broke your heart. Love so easily turned to bitterness, and then the bitterness to poison.

When Brian O'Malley entered the living room, Katherine was sitting hunched in one of the leather armchairs. It would not be long before that gnawing bitterness would get the better of her again.

"Kate, I think you should go home. I'll talk to Meta." He paused, "Promise that you'll never speak to Meta again about this unless you've talked to me first."

For a long time there was no reply. Slowly Kate got up from her seat, and he saw the hardness in her expression as she spoke, "You've always sided against me, haven't you father?" Then without another word, and before Brian O'Malley had a chance to reply, Katherine turned and walked out. She slammed the door shut behind her.

It resonated with her anger and bitterness.

Brian sat down in the armchair. He looked around his living room, hoping to gain some comfort from the familiar surroundings, but there was nothing there to lessen the pain of his daughter's remarks. If only there was someone he could unburden his feelings to, but there was no one he could share his thoughts with. This was not something he could share with Father MacDonald. Without realising it, he gave a loud sigh. Once there had been Maureen O'Connor and then his wife Margaret, but now there was no one, just Katherine and she was unable to escape the bitterness that welled up inside her.

As she walked down the road Katherine realised how weak all her passion and emotion had made her. Suddenly she felt vomit rise to her throat. She stopped, feeling a cold sweat on her brow, and waited for the nausea to pass.

It wasn't just Meta's behaviour towards a priest, that was bad enough but John was her son, the son she could never admit to.

Unbelievably her father thought that she, Katherine, the daughter of the family who had no child, should be thankful for being given the chance to bring up her sister's child…and now, more than ever, that child's behaviour meant she could never forget the pain and loss she felt. Not just of her child but of the love of her life.

Even though he was in his grave far away in South African veldt Michael Costello had left behind his child as a constant reminder of all that she had lost.

She leant against the stone wall as she started to retch, but there was only bile in her stomach. There was nothing else to bring up.

It had never occurred to Meta that her aunt would go through her personal letters. Letters were sacrosanct. She blushed as she realised what her aunt must have read.

She got up from her bed and retrieved the letter that was still lying on the floor. She read it again, but her aunt's behaviour had robbed it of all the warmth that it had held before. It was no longer a love letter. Now it was just an appalling confession. She put it back down on the table and walked over to the long mirror in her bedroom.

She looked at her reflection and tried to smooth down the flounces on her dress that had become crushed as she lay on the bed. She went to her wardrobe and selected another dress. She slipped out of her clothes. Was it so sinful to want John McBride as she did? She caught sight of her naked body in the mirror. She pulled her dress in front of her to hide her nakedness. Had she behaved like a slut? She remembered when she'd first realised how strong her feelings for John McBride were. For a moment she moved her hand down across her naked body, she felt a quiver of pleasure.

There had seemed to be no good reason why they should not become good friends. Even Aunt Katherine had been quite taken with the young novitiate the one time she had been at Melville House when he called.

Meta remembered John McBride kissing her on the back of her hand after he had walked her back to her grandfather's house, not something a priest would do. How she had started to blush and how she had fought to persuade herself that he was just being gallant. How later she had hoped that he found her attractive.

Only now did she realise how much she loved listening to John tell her stories. She remembered how she had sat in front of their grandfather's living room fire while John McBride told her his version of her favourite story. She had almost been able to see the demoralised Robert the Bruce shivering as he hid from the English in the damp cave to which he had fled. The emotion she had felt had not just been because he brought the story alive.

She remembered the last time they had walked up Kinnell Hill together. How she had accidentally pulled him down as she fell on the hillside, how they had lain together, his body against hers and how she'd felt when he briefly kissed her lips. The longing as he crushed his body against hers, only for him to suddenly pull away.

She stopped herself. There was no future in such thoughts.

She buttoned up her dress and brushed back her hair. She sighed and walked across the room and sat down at the table. Usually when she wrote letters the words tumbled off her pen, but not this time. This time it was different. Why of all the people in the world was she the one to fall in love with a man who wanted to be a priest? Why?

When she finished, she sat for a long while. She had told John that for some time she had been thinking of leaving Levenside. Would he believe it? It would be so much easier if he did. She wanted to hurt him as little as possible. She was just folding the letter into the envelope when Brian O'Malley entered. She stood up.

"Grandfather, I'm going away. I've written to John McBride. I've explained I'm leaving Levenside."

Brian O'Malley tried not to show how upset he was by Meta's announcement. He stared intently at his granddaughter, trying to judge if she really meant what she said.

"There's no reason for you to go, Meta. Your aunt didn't know what she was saying. She was just overwrought. I'm sure there's nothing for you and John McBride to be ashamed of. I'm sure it's just a misunderstanding."

'Just a misunderstanding'. Meta thought of the kiss that she and John McBride had shared on Kinnell Hill. She dropped her gaze. "I'm afraid my mind is made up grandfather."

Brian O'Malley desperately wanted to dissuade his granddaughter but the words wouldn't come. How could he explain to Meta the feud that had blighted her parents' lives?

He turned away and looked out of the bedroom window at the two apple trees at the end of the garden, but they provided him with no inspiration. He didn't want his granddaughter's life to be scarred by a family feud that should have been buried long ago, but it still lived on – in Katherine's mind at least.

Meta looked tenderly at the figure staring out of the window.

"I've got to leave grandfather. While I'm here John…" Meta's voice tailed off. She was going to say, "will be tempted", but she stopped as she found herself blushing as she recalled the words that John had written in his letter.

"I'm going to London. I should be able to get a teaching job there and…."

"You don't need to go as far as that Meta. I'm sure that we could arrange a post for you in Glasgow… or Edinburgh." She shook her head.

"No grandfather that wouldn't work. I've got to get right away."

Brian O'Malley said no more. He looked helplessly at his granddaughter one final time, then he turned and walked out of the room.

CHAPTER 14

META LEAVES FOR LONDON

Meta finally left Levenside for London at the end of July. King George V had summoned a conference in the capital under the Chairmanship of the Speaker of the House of Commons as the political situation in Ireland was deteriorating by the day. There was even talk of a civil war across the Irish Channel. Each day Brian O'Malley avidly read the reports in the two-day old copies of the Times he had delivered to Melville House, but to his granddaughter Meta the political situation meant little. Her only thoughts were about the man she was in love with, John McBride. The man she had to learn to forget.

It was so easy to say, it was so much more difficult to do.

The arrangements for Meta to leave Levenside took longer than she expected and each day she hoped for just one final word from John McBride but there was only silence, nothing else, not even an acknowledgment of her last letter. Indeed, she had no way of knowing if he had even received it.

The day before her departure Meta felt she should go round to her aunt's house. Her aunt's behaviour and her angry words weren't easy to forget but Meta hoped that telling her aunt that she was going away might help to heal the rift.

Her aunt refused to speak to her. In the end it was her Uncle Seamus she said goodbye to and who wished her well.

That evening she also said farewell to her grandfather. He had told her that he would make arrangements for her to be taken to the station but she insisted that she would do it herself. Catching the first train leaving the next morning for Glasgow meant getting up at first light, but she wanted to make the journey to London in one day.

She had left her luggage downstairs and she tried to creep quietly down the stairs from her room so as not to wake her grandfather, only to find Brian O'Malley was standing patiently in the hallway waiting to accompany her to the railway station.

Once the porter had installed Meta and her luggage in the first-class compartment that her grandfather had insisted on paying for, Meta lowered the window and lent out to say a final goodbye. She just managed to reach out far enough to give her grandfather a kiss on the cheek.

"Thank you, grandfather. Thank you for everything."

Then she heard him say, "Meta, I know you were annoyed that I asked Alex Field to meet you at King's Cross but London is a very different place to Levenside. It's useful to have at least one friendly face in a strange place. You can rely on him."

The whistle blew and as the train pulled slowly away, she settled down in her seat. Until the last few weeks her grandfather had been something of a remote figure. She loved him dearly but there were lots of things she did not know about him. She had never realised until the previous evening that he had any business interests outside Levenside or that he had dealings with this lawyer, Alex Field, in London. According to her grandfather Alex Field was the youngest of three partners in Ashby, Crisp and Field, and by far the most able.

Later that morning, Alex Field stood at the window of his office in New Square, Lincoln's Inn and looked at the flowers in the centre of the square. The Inn's gardeners kept the centre of the square in impeccable order. The rose beds surrounding the grass lawn looked particularly attractive, the red and white flowers standing out against the green leaves in the sunlight. He regretted having to work on a day like this, but that was the price of success and later that afternoon he would have to take time off to meet Brian O'Malley's granddaughter at King's Cross. He sat down at his desk and for a moment rested his elbows on his desk and placed his fingertips together in a steeple in front of him. He smiled.

His business dealings with Brian O'Malley now spread over the best part of 15 years. It had started with a small property transaction in

London but now O'Malley had some quite substantial commercial investments, including a number of quite lucrative investments in American railway and steel company shares. O'Malley's older brother was an executive in one of the major steel companies in the United States. Prior to his latest letter Brian O'Malley had written to ask Alex Field to sell his large holding in Brazilian government bonds. Alex Field have been quite surprised at the instructions for the price of the bonds was rising, and they were being actively promoted by a number of investment houses. Then, last week the news that the Brazilian government was in financial difficulties and that there was rioting in São Paulo had filtered through to the London markets. This week you couldn't give away Brazilian bonds and yet six weeks before Brian O'Malley has got out at the top of the market. Brian O'Malley, in an out of the way place like Levenside appeared to have more information than Lloyd's of London.

Alex Field smiled as he thought how the timing of this disposal had cemented the reputation he already had with his firm's brokers at Lloyds. The previous year when O'Malley had advised Field to sell any Mexican bonds that he or any of his clients held. O'Malley had never offered advice in such a fashion before, but Alex had to admit that if any of his clients had held such investments he would have advised them to follow O'Malley's advice. What Alex Field had done was to pass the advice on to his broker over lunch at the Garrick Club. A week after that lunch, the Mexican government had suspended all interest payments. Since then, Alex had frequently had to refuse invitations to lunch from his broker who seemed to want to discuss numerous investment opportunities with him, Alex's sale of Brian O'Malley's Brazilian stock and his advice on the Mexican bonds meant that Alex was now considered to have either government or international connections. Since the Marconi scandal the year before everyone was obsessed with government leaks. He was obviously considered a man with access to all sorts of confidential information but in fact Alex Field's most influential connection was Brian O'Malley. Brian O'Malley who lived far away in Scotland but was now one of Ashby, Crisp and Field's major clients.

It intrigued Field as to why Brian O'Malley had selected him as his legal adviser. They'd never even met. Alex Field had never been across the border to Scotland and he had no Irish connection. He was also fairly certain that Brian O'Malley had never been to London.

The only Irishman Field knew was the lawyer, Serjeant Sullivan, one of the last of the Irish Serjeants - but he also doubted if Brian O'Malley and Serjeant Sullivan had met each other either.

He thought back. It was nearly twenty years since Sullivan had started to try and build up his English legal practice. Field had used Sullivan before the Serjeant had become fully established in England. It had been a breach of promise case. The girl had come to see Alex Field in Lincoln's Inn.

Field specialised in commercial work and had done so for a number of years. His initial reaction had been to refuse the case. The girl had been twenty two or twenty three years old, well spoken, and quite striking. She had insisted on seeing him. Alex Field hadn't immediately recognised the girl, although he realised from the name that the girl was the daughter of the former partner of his firm who had died in his early fifties and to whom Alex Field had originally been articled.

"Miss Mansfield I would like to help, but breach of promise isn't an area of law I deal with. I realise this is your father's old firm but you would do far better to use a firm that specialises in matrimonial matters." He paused and looked at the girl. She had shaken her head.

"I would be happy to recommend a firm here in Lincoln's Inn."

"No, Mr. Field I want you to deal with my case."

"I'm not sure that is the best course of action."

"Mr. Field I want you to act for me. I would consider it a favour. My father advised me that if I ever needed a lawyer that you were the lawyer I should use."

Alex stared at Caroline Mansfield. He was flattered, but that didn't alter his judgment. Miss Mansfield would do better to find herself someone with experience in handling matrimonial matters. However, he felt a certain obligation to the girl. He did not wish to disappoint her. There was a vulnerability about her. For a moment Alex Field was undecided.

"I think you should take my advice."

"I will Mr Field…in all matters, other than who is to act on my behalf. My father left me very little except his advice…" There was a pause. "However, I loved and respected him."

Up until that moment Alex Field had not considered what Caroline Mansfield's financial circumstances might be, she had simply asked to see him on a personal matter. He recalled her father had had to retire quite early through ill health, well before the firm had become as successful as it now was. Such money as he had had probably all gone to Caroline Mansfield's brother in any event.

Alex Field's resolve collapsed. He found himself saying, "Very well Miss Mansfield I will take your case. I hope I can ensure the court is persuaded of the correctness of your case as effectively as you have persuaded me that I should act for you."

As she thanked him and left his office he sat there trying to persuade himself he had done the right thing. After all, a case for breach of promise of marriage was really no different from the breach of any other contract. He shook his head. It was not a convincing argument. If the case came to court he resolved to make sure Caroline Mansfield would have the best counsel he could find to argue her case.

The Defendant was adamant. There would be no settlement. The case would be contested. As soon as he realised this, Field consulted the other members of his firm. One of his colleagues, who did more litigation work than Alex, had recently seen the Irish lawyer, Serjeant Sullivan, appear in a highly contentious libel case in the High Court. "Field I've never come across an advocate with a more detailed grasp of their brief."

Alex Field decided to instruct the Irishman.

The case had been so one sided that Serjeant Sullivan barely needed to exercise his obvious talent and despite the Defendant's initial intransigence Alex Field once again expected the other side to seek a settlement before the judgment went against them, but they did not, and the inevitable happened.

After the case he congratulated Sullivan on his conduct of the case.

"To be honest with you Field, there was nothing to it. That young man was too honest for his own good. I'm still not absolutely sure if he did promise to marry our client, but he's certainly still in love with her. He'd marry her to-morrow if he could."

"Why won't he? She'd still marry him."

"Ah yes Field, but there remains one insurmountable problem."

"…That is?"

Sullivan said nothing but simply looked across the court to the elderly man who had just risen from his seat at the back of the court. Then

Sullivan shook hands with Alex Field and walked away, leaving his clerk to pack up his law reports and unopened papers. Alex Field glanced once more across the court watching the man who stood at the back of the court, his back ramrod straight. Then Colonel Sir Frederick Lawson Bt. turned on his heal and marched out through the court doors, without saying a word to his grandson or even glancing at Miss Mansfield. The coldness of the defendant's grandfather was apparent even from a distance.

As the defendant Richard Lawson shook hands with his barrister and made to follow, Alex saw the young man steal a quick glance at Caroline Mansfield as she stood with her mother in the well of the court. Personal tragedy was written in that look. Serjeant Sullivan was right. Captain Richard Lawson was clearly still in love with a woman he would now never marry.

Alex Field had been surprised that the case had been reported in the newspapers; even the Times carried a report. "Baronet's heir loses breach of promise suit." It had been something of a cause célèbre at the time. The Baronet as well as being a distinguished soldier was a wealthy Irish landowner. His grandson, the defendant, had also seen distinguished service in the Boer War and was said to have a bright future in the army, but following the case he had resigned his commission and disappeared. No one knew quite where.

Alex Field had been approached to take several more cases of a similar nature. He declined them all.

Alex had been somewhat intrigued by his instructions from Brian O'Malley. The direct financial provision O'Malley proposed to make for his granddaughter was quite parsimonious considering his obvious wealth. Brian O'Malley could easily have bought a house in London for his granddaughter to live in. In fact, O'Malley owned a number of investment properties in London so he did not even need to acquire one. Quite recently he had bought out the mortgage of a substantial property in Park Lane.

Instead, Alex have been charged with finding cheap but respectable rooms for Meta to live in. He could not help but be puzzled. For a moment he had wondered if Brian O'Malley and his granddaughter were estranged. However, the final sentence indicated otherwise.

"I would be grateful if, as a personal friend, you would also take an interest in my granddaughter's welfare whilst she is living in London."

Alex was rather touched by the request. He sat behind his large oak writing desk thinking over the contents of Brian O'Malley's letter. He was looking forward to meeting his client's granddaughter.

Meta Costello travelled down to London via Glasgow and then Edinburgh. The Edinburgh to London train was late. Alex Field had been waiting for almost half an hour when early that evening the steam engine with its LNER livery pulled into the platform at King's Cross. The train let out an unpleasantly loud hiss of steam as it came to a slow stop. Field had bought a platform ticket in order to meet Meta Costello as soon as she got off the train and he searched diligently for her face as the passengers thronged out of the train and along the platform. Brian O'Malley had sent him a description of his granddaughter, but the train was packed and there was a throng of people milling about on the platform.

He was just starting to feel a slight sense of panic when he saw the dark red coat that O'Malley had written to say his daughter would be wearing. The young woman wearing it also wore a burgundy coloured hat with a black velvet brim. She stood out in the crowd. Alex had little hesitation in going forward to introduce himself.

He raised his hat. "Miss Costello?" The young woman smiled. She had a pleasant face, but the most striking feature was her eyes.

"You must be Mr. Field." He nodded.

They shook hands. The noise and bustle made further conversation difficult. Alex tried to raise his voice above the hubbub.

"I've made arrangements for some rooms as your grandfather instructed. If you'll just come with me." He beckoned to the porter with Meta's cases to follow them.

Alex made a point of using a hansom cab if he could, simply because he was more accustomed to them, but to-day he was unlucky. They had to make do with a roomier but more spartan motor cab, but if he had been trying to impress Meta he couldn't have made a better choice because being in a motorised hackney carriage was a new experience for her. In Levenside motor cars were still a novelty.

"Where are we going?"

"I've arranged some rooms with a very respectable landlady not far from here, in the Gray's Inn Road. How is your grandfather?"

"Very well, thank you."

After a few more questions, the conversation petered out. Meta was quite happy just to sit back and absorb her new surroundings. She was so interested in all the new sensations around her that she gave no thought to talking to her escort.

As the short journey progressed Alex Field continued to observe his young escort. She was a pleasant, attractive young girl. She had those striking blue eyes, but she had so little to say. He was a little disappointed. There didn't seem much to this young woman.

In later life Alex Field was to admit that his initial assessment of Meta Costello was one of the very few misjudgements he made in life.

However, Meta was unaware of his assessment. She was far too excited. She was going to make a new life for herself here in London.

She would forget John McBride.

END OF PART ONE

Part 2

Brian O'Malley's Secret

CHAPTER 1

LEAVING IRELAND

Many of Brian O'Malley's memories of life in Ireland had gradually faded with time, but the final early morning walk he and his father had made to see their landlord's agent remained clear in his mind even forty year later.

He saw himself pulling on his trousers and a clean shirt. There was a mist outside so that when he glanced out the window he could see little of the field outside. He and his father had started towards the big house where Hobson lived as Brian's sister Tara stood at the door. She gave a gentle wave but she let her hand drop to her side as she realised both Brian and her father's only thoughts were on what lay ahead of them. They would not be looking back.

The black iron gates were open in front of them but both men stopped almost as one. His father rested a hand on Brian's shoulder, and then they began the long walk up the driveway. The crunch of their feet on the gravel made it seem as if the drive went on forever. Then they became aware of the grey unyielding stone of the house staring out at them through the swirling mist. The building was even bigger and more intimidating than Brian remembered it as a child. Beside him his father hesitated again, and Brian knew his father felt the same sick apprehension as he did.

They made their way round to the back of the house. His father knocked at the dark green door. An anxious young girl answered, and his father asked if they could speak to Hobson. As the child turned away to tell Hobson of their request, Brian saw a bruise on the side of her face.

Then they were standing in front of Hobson, the land agent for Colonel Sir Frederick Lawson. Hobson sat behind his big table with his back to the window. He steepled his fingers and simply stared at the two of them. For the first time in his life Brian became aware of how unsettling a silence could be.

As Brian, and then his father, dropped their gaze Hodgson still said nothing. He just let them stand there, holding their caps in their hands, with their heads bowed.

"And what can I do for you gentlemen?"

Brian remembered the sneer in Hobson's voice and how he had emphasised the last word, leaving them in no doubt that Hobson considered them anything but gentlemen. Brian saw his father hesitate and Brian decided to speak, "Mr. Hobson we need more time to pay the rent."

There was another long pause.

"Do you indeed?" The tone of Hobson's voice and the way he looked at Brian made Brian realise that Hobson considered his intrusion into the interview, an impertinence. Hobson continued to stare at him until Brian lowered his eyes again and looked at the ground and when he did so he missed the look of satisfaction that briefly flitted across Hobson's face.

Brian O'Malley realised how dry his mouth had become. Although he had spoken on their behalf, it was his father to whom Hobson eventually turned and addressed his next response. "More time … well maybe I can come to some arrangement with you O'Malley."

For a moment what Hobson said didn't register, but when it did, Brian and his father didn't dare to look at each other.

"Yes…" Hobson paused as if thinking about what he was about to suggest, "maybe if you were to work Three Fields Farm and bring in the harvest for me there as well as your own I could give you another quarter to pay your rent. Of course, if there is no decent harvest then I'll have to think again…"

He paused, "What do you think about my proposal?"

Brian and his father were too dumbfounded to think, let alone answer.

Then Hobson addressed Brian's father again, adding a further proposal as if it was an afterthought, "… and I'll tell you what I'll do O'Malley, to make sure there's a little bit of money coming into the house I'll give that young lass of yours a job up here at the big house. That'll bring in a shilling or two." This time Brian looked at his father in disbelief.

As Hobson gave them a deathly smile, which showed his rotten teeth, Brian's father managed to find his power of speech and Brian heard him mumble, "I don't know how to thank you Mr. Hobson."

"I'm not as unreasonable as people make me out to be." Once more Hobson's teeth showed as he gave the semblance of a smile, but as he turned and looked at Brian it disappeared. His beady protruding eyes met Brian's with a cold stare and as they looked at each other something told Brian that they should not have sought the favour that they had, but it was too late.

At least, they had been granted some more time.

The Three Fields Farm was but one of many owned by the O'Malley's landlord, Colonel Sir Frederick Lawson, who had recently retired from the army. He owed his large estate in Ireland, along with his Baronetcy, to James 1. The lands in question had been gifted to the Lawson family in exchange for a large financial consideration when James 1 had been desperate for money. Colonel Lawson, did not consider the transaction to have been good value for money. He had no interest in Ireland. Indeed, he had not visited Ireland in fifteen years. What he hated most all about Ireland was the weather. A good day in Ireland, according to Sir Frederick, was when it rained for less than two hours.

Sir Frederick lived in a large house overlooking Hyde Park in London. As the summer of 1870 came to an end, he had other things than Ireland on his mind. At long last his son had agreed to marry, but of much more interest to Sir Frederick was a new distraction.

Returning early from his club he had found his valet in a rather compromising position with one of the young housemaids. That his valet should have sex with one of the housemaids did not offend Sir Frederick's sense of decency but that he should do so in his very own bedroom offended him greatly. Sir Frederick dismissed his valet, who had served him loyally for the best part of twenty years and refused to give him any kind of reference. He did do not the same for the housemaid.

Instead, Sir Frederick gave the young woman some personal instruction as to how he expected her to behave in the future and she responded in such an exciting and delightful way that he even gave her a modest promotion within his household.

Having left his regiment, earlier than he anticipated, Sir Frederick had only one intention, and that was to enjoy himself. The fields and pastures of Ireland were of no interest to him. He barely recalled the name of the agent responsible for running his estate and he was totally oblivious to the existence of Brian O'Malley, his family or any of his other tenants.

The first day they started work on Three Fields Farm, which lay at the far end of Sir Frederick's estate, Brian's father fell ill. There had never been a previous occasion when his father had even admitted to being unwell, but after repeatedly vomiting during the night he could barely stand when the next morning came so Brian worked on his own that day. Luckily Hobson was nowhere to be seen and Brian was able to leave the fields early. Even so, by the time he reached home darkness had fallen.

His father always insisted that they leave a lamp burning in the kitchen until the last member of the family reached home. The light from the house guided Brian for the last part of his journey and as he crossed the field next to their house he could see lights shining through both front windows. That was unusual and perhaps that should have been a warning to Brian, but he was too exhausted and hungry for any concerns to register. He just wanted to make sure his father was all right and then collapse onto his straw mattress. Maybe there might be a bight to eat if Tara might had been allowed some scraps of food from the big house.

As he walked past the little outhouse where once they kept their hens he noticed the door was slightly ajar. He retraced his steps and pushed the outhouse door fully open. As he entered, he stumbled over something lying on floor. His hand touched something warm and wet.

The side of his father's head was matted with blood and as Brian brought his hand away he could see it was covered with blood. He stood transfixed until a scream penetrated his thoughts. He stumbled outside and started to run towards the house. As he reached the window to the back room, he stopped. The only table in the room lay on its side, the bowl and the jug that normally rested there lay smashed upon the floor. There were two men inside the room and on the bed was his sister Tara.

One man was holding her arms over her head, pinning them down on the mattress so that she was helpless. Her skirt and underclothing had been torn off and lay on the floor. The other man was Hobson. He stood there his trousers undone, his penis hideously erect, and as he moved towards Tara. She struggled violently, throwing her head from side to side.

As Hobson bent over her, Tara managed to lift her head and spit in his face.

"You little bitch!" Hobson slapped Tara viciously across the face with the back of his hand.

Brian watched in disbelief as the two men forced Tara's kicking and struggling body face down on the mattress so that her cries were smothered by the bed clothing and he saw Hobson start to force her legs apart with his knee.

Rage seared through him like heat exploding from a furnace. Brian flung the front door open, and raced across the main room ignoring the disorder that met him and burst into the back room.

"Bastard!" He screamed as he threw himself at Hobson. He forced Hobson down onto the floor. Then with a knee in Hobson's back, he seized Hobson's head in his hands and twisted it was all his might. Brian felt rather than heard the crack as Hobson's neck broke.

Then Brian dropped the limp body and stood up to face the other man. Brian had seen the animal look in the man's eyes as he had watched Hobson, waiting his own turn to violate Tara.

Like Hobson, the other assailant had been stunned by Brian bursting into the room, but as Brian rose to his feet the man let go of Tara and lunged for the shot gun lying on the floor. He raised it before Brian could get to him. All Brian could do was throw himself at the man's midriff as he fired the weapon. The explosion was deafening in the confined space, but Brian felt no pain.

In his panic the man had fired too wildly and missed. The recoil from the weapon and the weight of Brian's charge carried the attacker backwards. The man fell to the ground winded, with Brian on top of him. As the man struggled to break free of the weight pinning him down, Brian rolled aside and grabbed the empty gun by its barrel and as Hobson's accomplice started to get to his feet Brian brought the stock crashing down on the man's skull, cracking it. The man slumped to the floor. Brian O'Malley stared in shock at the dead man lying on the floor.

It took him seconds to hear Tara calling his name. He turned his gaze away from the body lying on the floor and saw that Tara was no longer on the bed. She was lying on her back on the floor. He made to lift her back onto the bed but she held his arm to stop him. He could see the pain in her eyes. It cut through him. She asked him to let her rest and give her a moment to recover.

He told her that as soon as she felt able, she must tidy herself up and put on some warm clothes. They had to leave.

Tara gave him a weak smile and tried to nod, but she winced as she did so. Brian squeezed the hand resting on his arm, stood up and made his way into the front room. The place was wrecked.

He started to look for some food for them to take with them and made a pile of everything he could find on the kitchen table. Then he decided he must do something about his father. He went outside and carried his father's body back into the house. He laid it gently on the floor in the far corner of the main room. Then he went over to the dresser, the only piece of furniture that was still upright, and lifted out the red tablecloth they had never used since his mother died. It had been a wedding gift, and despite everything his father could not bring himself to part with it.

Brian took one final look at his father's body and then he covered it with the red cloth. He didn't want Tara to see her father's disfigured face.

He realised now why Hobson had been so accommodating when they had gone up to the big house. The offer of a job in the kitchens for Tara had not been generosity on Hobson's part.

He must have thought he would find Tara all alone in the house knowing they would be up in the fields – and he would have, if his father not been too ill to come with Brian that morning. What had Hobson intended to do? Maybe up at the big house Tara had resisted his advances. Perhaps he'd always planned to get her on her own when there were no witnesses who would report his behaviour.

Brian thanked God he had come back early that evening. Then he tried to clear his head. They had to run, the further the better. There was no alternative. Maybe they should even try to get a ferry to Clydeside.

He ran back up the stairs. Tara was no longer lying on the floor. It looked like she had tried to stand up and had then fallen over onto her side and for the first time he saw the red blood showing through the back of her torn clothes.

He leant over to take a closer look. Tara was no longer breathing. The gun shot that had been meant for him had hit Tara as she ran for the doorway.

He cradled her head in his arms, rocking Tara back and forth, as if he could breathe life into what was now a lifeless body. As the numbness of the shock wore off, he let out a long, pitiful moan. His throat ached so much he could not even swallow. In the end, the sheer exhaustion caused by his grief made him accept reality. Tara was gone.

He carried her into the other room. He lifted the cloth that covered his father and laid Tara's body beside him and then he lowered the red shroud over the two of them. He stood back and bowed his head.

He had no time to do anything more. Despite what Hobson had done, Sir Frederick Lawson would seek retribution for his agent's death.

He pulled the battered wooden door of the small farmhouse closed behind him and started to walk away, then he turned and looked at it for one last time. He had an urge to set the house ablaze, turn it into a funeral pyre, but that would be madness. He needed to disappear quickly and without attracting any attention, but for a moment he couldn't move. He stood there momentarily rooted to the spot as he felt his previous life shrivelling up like a burning piece of paper. Whether he burnt the building or not made no difference, all that he was left with now were the ashes of his past life.

He turned away again, and this time he did not look back. What had occurred that day had to remain a secret. A secret he could tell no one.

CHAPTER 2

THE WESTERN BANK OF SCOTLAND

Friday 16th September 1870 was the day that Brian O'Malley arrived in Glasgow from Ireland. It was also the day that the Chairman of the Western Bank of Scotland realised that the bank he had fought so hard to create was in real danger of collapse.

Sir Robert McPherson's meeting with his fellow partners that afternoon had not been pleasant. Two or three of the other partners had only been interested in one thing, apportioning blame, when what needed to be done was sorting out the crisis the bank faced. The only man who had really grasped the gravity of the problem and had tried to address it was young Henry Wrightson.

Although the whole board had agreed to the opening of a London office to aid the bank's expansion, Sir Robert had acknowledged that it had been his decision to put Tinsley in charge, and now it was clear that George Tinsley had been the wrong choice. Originally it had looked like Tinsley had made a number of bad lending decisions, but following some enterprising detective work, much of it by Wrightson, it appeared that Tinsley had siphoned off a substantial amount of money from the bank that it was unlikely to ever recover. A number of transactions Wrightson had investigated were in reality loans to Tinsley, the borrowers being men of straw.

The Chairman sat behind his large wooden desk. The coal fire was lit in his first-floor office. The porter knocked on the door and came in to bank the fire with more coal. Autumn was coming. There was nothing more Sir Robert could do, but he couldn't bring himself to go home.

Banking was all about confidence. Once depositors lost confidence in a bank, it was doomed. He had been prudent over the years and the Western Bank had substantial reserves and in the end the Board had agreed to the support arrangements he had personally negotiated with two Edinburgh banks, should additional funds be required.

The most important thing for the moment was to keep the reasons for George Tinsley's departure from being made public. If Tinsley's behaviour became known there might be a run on the bank.

He couldn't believe he had been so wrong about Tinsley. The problem it transpired was George Tinsley's wife, rather than the man himself. According to Henry Wrightson, she had been caught up in the social whirl of London Society and Tinsley had been forced to live well beyond his means to fund her extravagant life-style.

He got up, put away his papers in the drawer of his partner's desk and slowly pushed it closed. It was getting late. Lady Caroline, would want to know how the meeting had gone.

He turned off the gaslights in his office one by one and then walked through into the main banking hall. The dimly lit hall with its high vaulted ceilings had a forbidding look about it. The head porter was still there. He came across as Sir Robert walked down the hallway taking one final look at the bank, his bank.

"Shall I find a cab for you, sir?"

"No, thank you, James. I feel like walking this evening."

"Very good sir." The head porter did his best not to show what a bad idea he thought that was.

"Will I let you out the side entrance, sir?"

Sir Robert McPherson looked at the head porter for a moment and then he nodded. "Thank you." Was the man being unusually solicitous? Did he know what was going on? He must know something was afoot.

"Goodnight, sir." The Chairman stood for a moment, but he did not turn round so he didn't see the concerned look on the Head Porter's face as the heavy door swung shut behind him. The yellow gas lamps threw a sombre, dull light on the roadway. Slowly he began to make his way home. It was a lengthy walk to Kelvingrove Park but it would help clear his head. Lady Caroline would be waiting. At that thought, he smiled.

As he turned into Sauchiehall Street he saw that Godenzi's Restaurant had still to come alive. It would be different once the music halls came out. He had walked almost half a mile when he realised that he was being followed. He started to turn round, but as he did so he found himself seized on either side. Two burly men took hold of him and half lifted him, half pushed him, down the side street to his left.

For a moment Sir Robert McPherson was too surprised to utter any protest. Indeed, he had been bundled into a side street before he even started to struggle, but by then it was too late, as a shout for help left his lips a sickening blow to the back of his head knocked him to the ground and a second rendered him unconscious.

Brian O'Malley had spent most of his first day in Glasgow wandering through the city looking for lodgings. The stench of the dreadful closes in which so many people were crammed still lingered in his nostrils. The buildings were so squalid. Despite the washing festooned between the floors of the grey sandstone tenement buildings the only rooms in which he was offered a space to sleep had been fetid and filthy.

Back in Ireland they'd had an outside privy behind the farm. Here there was no sanitation. The night soil was carried out through the squalid dwellings with the rest of the rubbish when it became unbearable.

He'd had several offers of a space in the dreadful tenements in Bridgegate and off Saltmarket from families desperate for help to pay their rent, but he'd turned them down. He could not bring himself to stay there, amongst the disgusting smells, hemmed in with so many people.

Now he had found himself a doorway away from the worst slum areas and he decided to sleep where he was and renew his search in the morning, although he was not sure how safe he would be.

As he was settling down in the doorway, he heard a disturbance at the end of the street. He was almost invisible in the dark and badly lit side street. Brian thought he was witnessing a robbery but this was clearly turning into something else. Three men had thrown to the ground the senseless man they had dragged off the main street but they weren't making any attempt to take anything. They just went on relentlessly beating and kicking the man.

Brian assessed the odds.

Three to one, and they were all big men. The man on the ground would be taking no part in the fight even if he recovered consciousness. One of the robbers had a vicious looking cudgel and another had a wooden stave.

If Brian stayed where he was, the doorway would cloak his presence. His clothes were too dark and drab to stand out in the gloom. He would be safe, but it was likely the man on the ground would never get up again.

Still, he hesitated. He had the advantage of surprise, but that was not enough. Most likely he would end up senseless on the ground.

He moved rapidly into a run.

One of the men had just started to turn as Brian crashed into him. Brian sent the man flying so that he cannoned into the stocky man opposite him with such force that the impact floored both attackers.

The third man, the biggest of the assailants, gave an angry shout, without waiting for his accomplices to regain their feet, he rushed at Brian with his stave raised. At the last moment, Brian flung himself to the ground swinging his outstretched legs so that he took the man's legs from under him.

As the man hit the cobbled stones his wooden stave was knocked from his hand. Brian grabbed it before the man could recover and swung it with all his might at the back of the man's head. The contact almost knocked the stave out of Brian's hands, but the man went limp.

Brian turned to face the other two attackers. The odds were much more even now. Brian was now armed and only one of the others was. However, if they rushed him together…

Possibly, the unarmed man was still winded, but for whatever reason, he made the mistake of holding back, waiting for his companion to make the first move, and when the armed man came for Brian, he was ready for him.

Again, this man ran at Brian, but this time Brian stood his ground. He didn't try to trip the man. He just swayed to his right. The impetus of the attacker's lunge and the man's weight carried him past Brian as he side-stepped the man. As the attacker's side and back became exposed, Brian swung his stave, putting all the force that he could into the blow. Brian heard the sound of bone breaking. The man dropped his makeshift wooden cudgel and slumped to his knees, clasping the side of his chest with one of his hands.

The third attacker hesitated. Brian moved forward slowly, one pace at a time. The man glanced at his fellow attacker groaning, lying on the ground and holding his ribs. He glanced back towards Brian who saw the fear in the man's eyes. This man started to back away. Brian raised his stake, but the man had seen enough. He turned and fled.

Brian stood and watched him go, then he bent down to examine the man in the black frock coat lying on the ground. For a moment he thought the man was dead. Brian bent towards the man's face. The man was still breathing… still alive. Brian stood back up and looked at the figure on the ground. The man's clothing indicated he was a man of substance. Certainly worth robbing, so why had the men not grabbed whatever money he had and run?

Brian heard a noise behind him. Stupidly he had turned his back on the other two assailants. He whirled round as quickly as he could, but there was no immediate threat. The noise he had heard was man with the damaged ribs struggling to get up off his knees. The other man still lay unconscious on the ground. Brian bent down and picked up the wooden stave and readied himself, but the man only wanted to escape. As soon as he had got himself more or less upright, he turned and staggered off back up the street.

Once he was certain that man was no longer a threat, Brian checked the other assailant again to make sure he was still unconscious and then knelt down again by the injured man lying on the ground. The last thing Brian wanted was to get involved in something that would interest the police, but he couldn't just abandon the man. He doubted the attackers who had fled would be back. They had no stomach for a real fight, but the injured man needed help.

He hesitated to go through the man's clothing. If anyone came upon them, they might well take Brian as one of the thieves, but there was no alternative. If he could just get the injured man home, then Brian could disappear.

There was more money on the man that he could hope to earn in a year, but he found nothing to identify him. He couldn't leave the man there.

He threw the injured man's arm round his shoulder and carried his dead weight the length of the side street and back to the main street. The few passers-by there were avoided Brian as he approached them. No Good Samaritan came forward. From a distance all they could see was a drunken businessman, befriended by a shabby down and out.

Then he realised the man in the frock coat was trying to speak …"Bank…Western Bank…"

Maybe that was the man's workplace. With no other option, he decided he would try and take the man there. He tried to hail a passing cab, but the cabbie ignored him. In desperation Brian stepped right in front of the next one, grabbing at the horse's bridle and pulling it to a stop. The cabby swore, leant forward and struck Brian a blow with his whip. Despite the pain Brian held onto the horse.

The cabby raised his whip to strike Brian a second time, but Brian let go of the horse and jumped forward grabbing the whip out of the cabby's hand. Holding the horse again, Brian demanded that the cab driver step down.

"Put him in the cab." The cabby stood there. Brian raised the whip. "Now!" Grudgingly the surly cabby moved. Brian watched as he loaded the injured man into his cab. "Gently now."

Once the injured man was properly in the cab Brian motioned to the cabby to step back out to resume his own seat. "Do you know where the Western Bank is?"

"Of course, but I'm nae moving 'til you pay the fare."

"You'll get your money when we get there."

"If you've got nae money, you'll nae get there. There'll be nae body at the Bank to pay me at this hour."

The two glowered at each other. Then the cabby nodded his head in the direction of the man lying on the seat in his cab.

"It looks to me if 'yon' needs to get to the bank sooner rather than later. I'm sure he's more than enough to pay me."

There was no alternative. Brian took some of the coins Sir Robert had in his waistcoat pocket. As he opened the palm of his hand to look at the coins the cabbie leant down and grabbed the only gold coin.

"That'll do."

"That's a half sovereign."

"Do you want me take you and your drunken friend or not." Brian hesitated.

"This man's not drunk, can't you see he's hurt." The cabbie was as good as robbing the injured man.

The cabbie shrugged. "Looks to me like he fell over after he'd had a few too many."

There was no point in arguing. The injured man needed attention. "Get a move on."

"If you say so." The cabbie put the coin to his mouth and bit it, and then remounted his cab.

Brian put the remaining coins back in injured man's inside pocket as the cabbie flicked the reins and the horse moved forward. Brian sat back and wondered what he would do when they got to the bank.

He hoped there might be a night watchman, but as the cabby pulled up in front of the bank Brian could see no sign of life, all the doors of the solid looking building were firmly closed.

"What now?" said the cabby.

"Wait here." Brian got down from the cab and walked up to the bank door and hammered on it. There was no response. He waited and then hammered a second time. Nothing. As he turned round, he saw that the cabby was dragging the injured man out of his cab. He started running back towards the cab.

"Stop! What are you doing?"

"Here take him." The cabby thrust the inert body into Brian's arms and as Brian struggled to hold the injured man the cabby jumped back up onto his cab and as soon as he was on board cracked his whip.

"Wait …" Holding the dead weight of the injured man Brian could do nothing. Brian turned and dragged the limp body to the wall of the bank and tried to lay the man on the ground, but the inert body was difficult to handle and before he could prop the body against the wall the cabbie was on his way.

"Stop! This man needs help," but his shouts only had the effect of making the cabby take his whip to his horse again. Brian started to give chase but the cab was too far away for him to stop it. Brian walked back to the bank. He bent down. The man's breathing was very shallow.

Brian started to stand up again but before he could rise fully he was seized from behind. He tried to struggle but two men had him pinned by his arms so he was unable to break free. They turned him round and bundled him through the now open bank door.

"There's an injured man outside."

"I know that," said the man dressed in a frock coat, standing just inside the door.

Brian had been wrong to assume the bank was unoccupied. One of the changes that Sir Robert Macpherson had introduced when he became Chairman of the Western Bank was that one of the partners of the bank should be present on its premises at all times. The partners' flat and the servants' quarters were occupied and the head porter who lived on the bank premises was also inside the bank.

The noise of Brian's hammering had brought the junior partner to the window of the flat in the premises adjoining the bank. He had been just in time to see the limp body of the bank's Chairman and senior partner being thrown to the ground by what he took to be a footpad.

CHAPTER 3

IMPRISONED

"Lock that thug in the Safe Room. Get Sir Robert up to my rooms … gently now" The orders from Henry Wrightson, the most junior partner of the Western Bank of Scotland, were obeyed without question. Moments later Brian heard the heavy vault door swung shut behind him.

As Sir Robert McPherson was being carried upstairs to the partners' flat Henry Wrightson ordered his servant to summon Sir Robert's wife to the bank as soon as possible and make sure she brought a doctor with her.

Lady Caroline McPherson and Doctor Hillyard arrived at the bank in less than half an hour. The junior partner of the Western Bank had not met Dr. Hillyard before but he knew he was not just Sir Robert's doctor, he was one of Glasgow's most distinguished physicians. Lady Caroline he had met before. She had impressed him as someone who knew more about banking than many of his male colleagues. Henry Wrightson showed the two arrivals into the bedroom where Sir Robert lay and withdrew.

"I'll be in the sitting room if you need me. Please let me know how Sir Robert is once you have examined him."

As soon as the door closed behind Henry Wrightson, Dr Hillyard turned towards his patient to examine him. He knew better than to suggest to Lady Caroline that she wait outside the room.

It was twenty minutes before Lady Caroline emerged from the room alone. She showed herself into the partners' sitting room. Her face did not betray her deep concern. Her husband had briefly recovered consciousness after her arrival, but he had been in such pain that Dr. Hillyard had given him laudanum. Rest the doctor said was essential. Sir Robert was suffering from severe concussion and other injuries consistent with a sustained and brutal assault.

As soon as Lady Caroline entered, Henry Wrightson spoke. "How is Sir Robert?"

The Chairman's wife chose her words carefully. "Dr. Hillyard says it is too early to tell if Sir Robert has any serious injuries, but my husband has regained consciousness." She paused. She knew her husband had at least two or three broken ribs, there was also the possibility of a fractured skull and damage to his internal organs, but she decided not to disclose those facts to the junior partner of the Bank.

"I'm sorry. We were just too late to help Sir Robert."

"Tell me what happened," Lady Caroline asked.

"I'm afraid a thug tried to rob Sir Robert as soon as he left the bank. I heard him hammering on the bank doors trying to get help. When I got to window he was being thrown to the ground. The head porter and my servant managed to seize his attacker."

"Where is the man?"

"I had him locked in the safe room."

"Have you called the police?"

Mr. Wrightson hesitated, "Not as yet, I decided to wait until after the doctor had seen him before I took any further action."

Lady Caroline looked thoughtfully at the youngest partner of the Western Bank and then she nodded. "I think it might be advisable to wait a bit longer. In view of this afternoon's Board Meeting the bank needs to be careful about …any adverse publicity."

The junior partner avoided showing his surprise. Lady Caroline obviously knew of the confidential subject matter of their last Board Meeting. Sir Robert clearly put considerable trust in his wife.

Lady Caroline's next question startled Henry Wrightson again although once more he avoided showing it. "Do you think this attack could be in any way related to what occurred at to-day's meeting?" Henry Wrightson was sufficiently astute to realise that making public the Chairman's serious injuries could be extremely damaging in the current circumstances but until Lady McPherson posed her question he had not considered that Sir Robert's assault was anything apart from an isolated incident.

"Tell me did my husband's attacker have a weapon?"

"Weapon?"

"Yes. A cudgel or an iron bar?"

"I didn't see one. I'll get my servant to have a look outside. The man we apprehended may have dropped it during the attack."

"Yes, do that. You say it was your servant and the head porter who caught the attacker?" Mr. Wrightson nodded.

"I'd like a word with them if I may."

"Of course."

Lady Caroline interviewed the head porter first. She expressed her gratitude for the assistance he had given her husband and then she asked him to recount what had occurred. His version of events proved similar to those of the bank's junior partner until near the end of the interview.

"All this happened very shortly after you let my husband out of the bank?"

"No, Lady Caroline. I showed Sir Robert out of the bank at least half an hour before the commotion occurred."

"Are you sure?'

"Yes, my lady. After the Board Meeting he stayed for a short while in his office then I let him out by the side door. The main door had already been secured for the evening."

Strange thought Lady Caroline. What could have brought her husband back to the bank?

The servant told the same story about the attack but could not say when Sir Robert left the bank. What he did say was that he had carried out a thorough search and had found nothing that could have been used as weapon in the vicinity of the bank.

Lady Caroline went back to her husband's room. She took out her husband's clothing and went through the contents. If Sir Robert's attackers had been after his money, then they had missed most of it. Her husband's gold pocket watch was also still in his fob pocket.

She sought out the bank's junior partner again.

"Mr. Wrightson I think we should interview the man you're holding in the Safe Room. I am not at all sure that he is responsible for my husband's injuries."

"I'm sorry Lady Caroline. I don't think that would be wise. The man's dangerous." Lady Caroline just looked at Henry Wrightson.

"I saw him manhandling Sir Robert with my own eyes Lady Caroline."

"How do you account for the fact that none of my husband's money is missing?"

"The man was still bending over your husband when he was seized. Maybe he had no time to take anything."

Lady Caroline thought for a moment. "I think it is important that we know exactly what is behind this attack. This man has to be questioned."

"I cannot allow it Lady Caroline. It is too dangerous. I am responsible for the bank and Sir Robert would never forgive me if something happened to you."

"If you are responsible for the bank then you will realise that we need to know as soon as possible the reason behind my husband's attack." They stared at each other.

"Very well. Please wait here a moment." Henry Wrightson left the room. He returned five minutes later carrying a shotgun.

"Mr. Wrightson is that really necessary?"

"If I cannot dissuade you from speaking to this man I intend to do everything possible to ensure your safety." Lady Caroline said no more. If this young man was as earnest in carrying out his banking duties as he was in protecting her, the bank was in safe hands.

Brian was no longer sitting at the table, instead he was lying on the stone floor trying to sleep. As the door to the safe room opened, he stood up quickly. He saw the man who had ordered him to be locked in the room was now armed with a shotgun. Surely matters couldn't get any worse. He backed away as the man entered the room. The Head Porter lit the gas lamps on the wall by the door.

"Sit down over there." The man with the shotgun motioned to Brian to sit at the table. As he sat down a well-dressed woman entered the room.

"If you move an inch from that chair, I will shoot you. Do you understand?" Brian nodded.

"Do you understand?" Brian's nod had not been enough.

"Yes."

"Good. This is Lady McPherson. She has some questions to ask you. You would do well to tell her the truth."

Brian didn't make the mistake of nodding this time.

"What's your name young man?" Lady Caroline McPherson's tone was not friendly, but it was not hostile like the man with the gun. Lady Caroline must have been very attractive in her youth, and she remained striking now she had reached middle age.

"Brian O'Malley, ma'am."

"Well Mr. O'Malley, how did you come to be with my husband outside the bank this evening."

Brian told his story. When he told her that he had taken on three men, two of whom were armed, Lady Caroline wondered if he was exaggerating, but as she listened she judged not. The state of her husband and the nature of the injuries described by Dr. Hillyard seemed to confirm his story. Mr. O'Malley was either a brave young man, or a foolhardy one.

"Where did this happen?" The description of the main street where he had managed to stop the cab sounded like Sauchiehall Street. It was on her husband's route home.

"How did you pay for the cab?"

"I didn't, ma'am. Your husband did."

"My husband was unconscious."

"I know. I had to take the money from his pocket. The cabby wanted a lot more money than I had to bring us to the bank."

"How much did he ask for?"

"He took half a guinea."

"Half a guinea!" Mr. Wrightson's voice was full of disbelief.

"Half a guinea for a cab from Sauchiehall Street to the bank?" Lady Caroline's voice echoed Mr. Wrightson's disbelief.

"I didn't know what else to do ma'am. Your husband needed attention badly. Nobody else would even stop. The cabby said he wouldn't shift for less." Brian kept his eyes on Lady Caroline rather than the man with the shotgun. She had to believe him, so he said again. "Your husband needed help."

"What did you do when you got here?"

"I hammered on the door ma'am but there was no reply. I thought there was nobody inside." Brian explained how the cabby was decided to make off as soon as possible and how he had been unable to stop him because he was holding her unconscious husband.

"I put your husband down on the ground as soon as I could and ran after the cabby but he'd gone too far. He was too fast for me. Then I came back to see how your husband was and two men came out of the bank and grabbed me from behind."

"Where are you from?" Lady Caroline saw his hesitation. "Ireland?"

Instinctively Brian didn't want to reveal anything about himself but he could see from Lady Caroline's reaction to his hesitation that he had no alternative. The franker he was the more she was likely to believe him and the less anybody was likely to investigate his background.

"Yes," said Brian.

"What did you do there?"

"I helped my father on the farm,"

"And when did you arrive?"

"This morning, ma'am."

"This morning? You've had quite an eventful day Mr. O'Malley." Brian looked at the shotgun pointing at him.

"Indeed ma'am."

"And what are your intentions?"

"Intentions, ma'am?"

"Yes, young man. What are you intending to do with yourself?"

"Well, as soon as I've found somewhere to stay ma'am I'm going to look for a job here in Glasgow, maybe down in the docks. If I can't get a job there I was thinking of going onto Levenside. I've some friends from Ireland who are going there."

"Just one more thing Mr. O'Malley. Will you stand up." Brian looked over at the shotgun still pointing at him and hesitated.

"Do as Lady Caroline asks," said Mr. Wrightson. Brian stood up.

"Please empty your pockets." Brian did as he was told. All he had in his pocket was his knotted handkerchief. He placed it on the table. Lady Caroline asked him to open the handkerchief. She counted the coins it contained. They amounted to less than half a guinea.

"Thank you, Mr O'Malley. I would like to thank you for everything you did to-day to help my husband. Both he and I are in your debt." Brian felt himself relax. Lady Caroline seemed to have accepted his story was true.

Brian watched as she rose from the table and left the room followed by the man with the shotgun. The door closed behind them. Then a moment later he heard the door being locked again.

Despite what the lady had said, he was still a prisoner.

CHAPTER 4

LEAVING GLASGOW

Mr. Wrightson rejoined Lady Caroline Macpherson in the sitting room of the partners' flat. "Mr. Wrightson was that shotgun really necessary?"

"I thought so Lady Caroline," replied the banker.

"And tell me Mr. Wrightson, would you really have shot Mr. O'Malley if you thought it necessary?"

"I think it unlikely Lady Caroline."

"Indeed. Why do you say that?"

"Well, I've never used a shotgun. The gun belongs to your husband."

"I see."

There was a pause.

"There was another reason…"

"…And that was?"

"The gun wasn't loaded." He shrugged. "I couldn't find any ammunition."

Lady Caroline stared at the youngest partner of the Western Bank. If Mr. Wrightson gave up banking he might have a future playing poker.

"I don't think Mr. O'Malley assaulted my husband…"

"…I gathered that Lady Caroline."

"I don't think we should keep him locked up in the safe room. However, I think we need to prevail upon him to remain here until tomorrow. Hopefully my husband will be somewhat more recovered by then. I think in the meantime you need to make some immediate enquiries into the whereabouts of George Tinsley."

"You think Tinsley could be behind this assault?"

"Let me just say I don't think Mr. O'Malley was part of it and there doesn't appear to have been any attempt to rob my husband. So, where does that leave us?"

Mr. Wrightson thought for a moment. "Do you wish me to summon the constabulary?"

"No. I think we should leave them out things until to-morrow. My husband isn't up to talking to them yet. Let's see how your inquiries go."

Once Mr. Wrightson had left the room Lady Caroline dropped her guard for a moment. The concern showed in her expression for the first time. There was little more she could do for her husband. The main problem to be resolved was Tinsley.

She'd never liked him, or his wife, and she had told her husband so, but he had been impressed with Tinsley's grasp of financial matters. Well, there was a lot more to banking that being good at figures. You needed to be able to assess people's characters and it hadn't taken her long to realise Tinsley was no good. He'd been too smarmy and ingratiating from the start. Mr Wrightson was a different kettle of fish. He didn't pretend to be something he wasn't.

She decided to go and sit quietly by her husband's bed. Any further discussion with Mr. Wrightson could wait until after the bank's junior partner had more information about George Tinsley.

When Mr. Wrightson opened the door to the safe room for the second time Brian O'Malley saw he no longer carried a shotgun.

"Come with me Mr. O'Malley." Brian quickly looked around as soon as he was through the doorway but here was no obvious escape route. He had no alternative but to follow Mr. Wrightson through the bank's main hall and up a flight of stairs to the partners' private living quarters. He found himself in the impressive sitting room.

"Mr. O'Malley the man who you saw being assaulted is Sir Robert Macpherson, Chairman of this Bank. We need to investigate what happened to him in more detail."

"I've told you all I can," Brian tried to convey his truthfulness in his response.

"Quite so, Mr. O'Malley, but the police will want to hear your story

118

too. It's too late for me to summon the constabulary this evening and anyhow Sir Robert is not fully recovered. I'm afraid I'm going to have to ask you to spend the night here at the bank." Mr. Wrightson's words made it clear that Brian was not being given the option of leaving. Mr. Wrightson reached over to the wall behind him and pulled a rope. Brian heard a bell ring and a moment later the servant appeared in the doorway.

"Please show Mr. O'Malley to the spare bedroom on the second floor."

As Brian followed in the wake of Mr. Wrightson's servant it was obvious that an escape was still not going to be easy but escape he must. He could not wait and allow himself to be questioned by the police.

Brian had never had more than a straw mattress to sleep on. He sat on the bed and looked about him. This was the most luxurious room he had ever been in.

He didn't see the manservant close the door behind him, but he did hear the key turn in the lock. He walked over to the window, drew back the heavy curtains and looked down at the street below. It was a long way down, but it was an outside window. He could see the sombrely lit street below.

The manservant stood outside listening for a moment. He couldn't understand why a farm boy had been given a bedroom in the partner's quarters, possibly because it had a decent lock, but so did the safe room. He shook his head.

CHAPTER 5

LADY MACPHERSON

Lady McPherson stayed overnight at the bank because her husband was too badly injured to be moved. She was about to start breakfast in the partners' dining room when Mr. Wrightson's servant approached Mr. Wrightson.

"When I unlocked the top floor bedroom the man had gone, sir."

"How did he get out?" Lady Caroline intervened without being asked.

"He climbed out the window ma'am... I mean my lady." The servant was clearly worried that he might be held responsible for Brian O'Malley's escape and having to answer to the Chairman's wife deepened his concern.

It appeared that instead of sleeping on the high-quality linen he had been provided with, Brian O'Malley had knotted his sheets together and let himself down from his second floor window.

Mr. Wrightson asked Lady Caroline whether O'Malley's escape made her question her view of Brian O'Malley innocence. She shook her head. "The fact that Mr. O'Malley doesn't want to be locked up doesn't make him a thief." She paused, "It's a pity we don't know more about his intentions I would have liked the opportunity of rewarding Mr. O'Malley for helping my husband."

Mr. Wrightson raised his eyebrows but said nothing.

"However, I think it makes it easier for us to decide how to deal with matters Mr. Wrightson."

"Why do you say that Lady McPherson?"

"I think we can proceed without involving the Constabulary for the moment."

"Indeed?"

"Yes. My husband is not well enough to be bothered by police officers. So, with O'Malley gone there is little information we can give the police about the assault."

"Even so I think the police should be notified of such a serious assault. Those responsible need to be caught and punished."

"Quite so…and in normal circumstances I would have no hesitation in encouraging you to follow that course of action." She paused, "However, I don't think we want the police to become…interested in any other matters. If they become aware that attack on my husband was not simply an attempt at robbery their investigation could follow an embarrassing line of enquiry. The bank's circumstances are, as you are most certainly aware, at a somewhat delicate stage as present."

Mr. Wrightson hesitated. He had not contacted any of the other partners. The fact that it was the week-end gave him some sort of an excuse, but if anything went wrong and he had kept his colleagues in the dark they would have no hesitation in hanging him out to dry.

However, Lady Macpherson might be right that it would be better to keep the assault and her husband's injuries secret for the moment. Lady McPherson had proved correct in most of her assessments up until now. She was an impressive lady, not only the Chairman's wife but also the source of much of the Chairman's original wealth. Nevertheless, any decision Henry Wrightson took now would be seen as his decision and his decision alone.

"What do you suggest I do then if I don't notify the Constabulary?"

"What I suggest, is that you call on Mr. Tinsley. I have been impressed by your abilities Mr. Wrightson. I think you will be able to ascertain fairly easily if Tinsley has had any involvement in my husband's assault."

"And if he has Lady McPherson? What do you suggest I do then?"

"You will persuade him that it is in his best interests to leave Glasgow. No… let us say Scotland, as soon as possible, and not return."

"Let him go?"

"Yes."

"And how do you suggest I persuade him to leave Lady McPherson?"

"That is a matter for you Mr. Wrightson but may I suggest you do not use a shotgun this time." Wrightson looked at the Chairman's wife. He thought he detected the hint of a smile.

If she was right that Tinsley was involved in what had happened then the further he was away from the bank and Glasgow the better for the bank at the current time. However, Henry Wrightson wasn't as convinced as Lady McPherson that he could engineer that outcome. Flippant discussions over breakfast were one thing, he wouldn't be able to take matters so lightly when he met Tinsley face to face.

"If Mr. Tinsley arranged for the assault on your husband should I not consider Mr. Tinsley … dangerous?"

"Once you make it clear to Mr. Tinsley that you and the Bank are aware of his involvement in my husband's assault and that it is your intention to inform the police I do not think that Mr. Tinsley will consider resorting to violence." She paused and then added, "Anyhow I have no doubt that you would be a match for a wimp like Tinsley."

Wrightson returned Lady Caroline's look. He was not sure he appreciated her confidence in him.

"I thought we had decided not to involve the Constabulary?"

"Quite so. Quite so, Mr. Wrightson, but Mr. Tinsley doesn't know that does he?"

When Henry Wrightson arrived at the Tinsley residence it was George Tinsley himself who came to the door. Henry smelt whisky on the man's breath, and that worried Henry because he had no idea how the alcohol would affect George Tinsley's reactions.

"Well Henry this is an unexpected pleasure. Come in." Tinsley gave no appearance of being surprised to see Henry Wrightson as he showed him through to his study. The house appeared deserted. An empty glass on George Tinsley's desk confirmed that he had indeed been drinking. George Tinsley didn't offer Henry a drink.

What can I do for you?"

"The partners of the bank have instructed me to have the constabulary arrest you for your involvement in an assault on Sir Robert Macpherson yesterday evening."

George Tinsley had turned away from Henry Wrightson. He paused momentarily, then picked up the empty glass from his desk and walked over to the sideboard and poured himself another drink from the half empty decanter.

"I had nothing to do with it."

"But you know he was assaulted?"

"Yes."

"Then if you weren't involved, how do you know he was assaulted?" Tinsley didn't answer for a moment.

"Word gets out."

"I don't think so George. Apart from those responsible for the assault, there are less than half a dozen people who know about it, and I'm certain none of those would have told anyone, certainly not you."

George Tinsley shook his head. Then he repeated his first answer but this time his words sounded a slurred. "I had nothing to do with it."

If you're going to bluff, don't stop with half measures Henry Wrightson told himself.

"I'm afraid we have a witness, George."

"Who?"

"I'm not going to give you his name George, but one your thugs was so badly beaten that his ribs were broken. He told us enough for us to be able to prove you were involved."

"What! You'd take the word of a foot pad, a common criminal against the word of a partner in your own bank?"

"In this instance…Yes, yes I would." The two men stared at each other until Tinsley lowered his gaze.

"How does this 'evidence' implicate me Henry? You don't have any evidence you can use in court."

"Well, I'm happy that we have… and more importantly, so are the other partners." Henry Wrightson met George Tinsley's gaze with a look that conveyed his absolute confidence that he was speaking the truth. George Tinsley turned away again and gulped down the rest of his drink.

"Look George, I was instructed to go straight to the police, but I've come here first."

"Why?"

"To give you a chance."

"A chance for what?"

"To get away before I come back with the police."

"Did the other partners tell you to do that?"

"No, it was entirely my own idea."

The other directors still don't even know about the assault Henry thought, only you do. He watched George Tinsley, as Tinsley appeared to consider his situation for a moment.

"Well?" said Henry Wrightson. George Tinsley shook his head, but it wasn't a rejection of Henry's proposal.

"You're a good sort Wrightson." Henry Wrightson ignored the compliment, but he felt a sense of relief at Tinsley's remark. It appeared that Tinsley was no longer pretending he was innocent of Sir Robert's assault. He waited to see if George Tinsley would accept the proposal that he should flee to escape the consequences.

"How long do I have?"

"How long do you need?"

"Until to-morrow."

"I can't do that George." The more time Tinsley had, the more likely he was to change his mind and brazen things out. His continued presence in Glasgow was a danger to the Bank.

"You can have until two o'clock this afternoon. I can't give you longer than that."

"I can't make arrangements in four hours!"

Henry looked at George Tinsley very coldly and said, "Well that's all the time you've got." Then Henry Wrightson turned and made his way to the study door, only when he reached it did he look back.

"Don't worry, I'll show myself out."

As Henry closed the door behind him he heard a glass shatter against the door. He could hear Tinsley shouting at him through the closed door.

"Bastard! You're all a bunch of bastards. None of you thought I was good enough for your bloody bank."

When Henry Wrightson arrived back at the bank he sought out Lady Caroline.

"Well, how did it go Mr Wrightson?" asked Lady Caroline.

"Much as you expected," said Henry Wrightson. "I left my servant outside the house. He'll let me know as soon as…" He paused and then rephrased the sentence. "…He'll let me know if Mr. Tinsley leaves."

"He'll leave. All we have to do is wait."

"I think the time is approaching Lady Caroline when I need to inform the other partners of the assault on Sir Robert."

"Let's just wait a little longer and see if Mr. Tinsley does do a runner. I have every confidence that he will, but I'd like to be sure."

Henry Wrightson wondered why Lady Caroline appeared willing, indeed eager to see the man, who deserved to be tried by a jury for arranging the attempted murder of her husband, escape justice. Then he realised that it was not what she wanted, it was what her husband wanted. The Western Bank of Scotland was more important to Sir Robert Macpherson than any revenge or punishment, and his wife knew it.

Shortly before three o'clock Henry Wrightson's servant returned to the bank with the news that Mr. George Tinsley had left in a cab shortly after two, taking with him two large suitcases. Mr. Wrightson told Lady Caroline.

"I didn't think you'd have any trouble with George Tinsley Mr. Wrightson."

"So it has proved Lady Caroline. I can't say I was as optimistic of this result as you."

"You should have been Mr. Wrightson. I have every confidence in you."

"Lady Caroline every time you say that to me you want me to do something."

"You're very perspicacious." Lady Caroline looked at Mr. Wrightson for a moment.

"I would like you to find out where that young man, Mr. O'Malley has gone."

Henry Wrightson shrugged his shoulders. "He could be anywhere."

"He was thinking of working in the docks."

"Lady Caroline there are hundreds of people working in the docks."

"Well, what do you suggest?"

"I don't know… but in view of what has happened to him since he came to Glasgow, I think O'Malley's more likely to try and get away from Glasgow than stay here and we have no idea where he's likely to end up."

"Levenside." Said Lady Caroline.

"Levenside? Why Levenside?" Asked Mr. Wrightson.

"He said he had some friends there."

"Who could he know in Levenside? He's never been outside Ireland before."

"O'Malley said he had friends who came over on the same boat and told him that's where they were going." Lady Caroline paused for a moment. "Doesn't the Western Bank have a branch in Levenside?"

"Yes, but how does that help?"

"You could ask the manager to make inquiries, keep his eyes open for Mr. O'Malley." Henry Wrightson shook his head.

"Lady Caroline, O'Malley's not a man who is likely to be opening a bank account."

"What do you suggest then?"

Mr. Wrightson thought for a moment. "Well, we know the day O'Malley's boat arrived from Ireland. There will be a list of the luggage it shipped."

"And if that is the case?" Asked Lady Caroline. Henry Wrightson was pleased to see the puzzled look on Lady Caroline's face.

"If O'Malley's friends had too much luggage to carry, they'll have arranged for it to be send on. If I can trace their luggage, I should be able trace them. Then the bank might be able to help us."

"Will you make enquiries for me?"

"I will, but I doubt I'll come up with anything."

Ten days later the shipping company Mr. Wrightson approached informed him that one of their passengers, a Mr. Patrick Philbin who had arrived on same boat as Brian O'Malley, had arranged for two trunks to be forwarded to Levenside.

Henry Wrightson went to visit the Chairman at his home where he was recuperating. Lady Caroline was pleased to see him. "You handled Mr. Tinsley's departure very well."

"I did nothing more that suggest he leave, and as I recall it Lady Caroline, that was your idea."

"I meant that I was impressed by the way you've handled the reason for his disappearance. Everybody seems to accept that his sudden departure was due to his marriage breaking down. There seems no suggestion that it relates to problems at the bank."

"Thank you."

"Do you have any information on Mr. O'Malley? I would really like to thank him properly. My husband has told me the young man was not one of the men who attacked him. It does seem that O'Malley must have intervened to stop the assault."

Henry Wrightson told her of the information he had obtained. "I'll write to the manager of the Western Bank in Levenside and ask him to keep an eye open for Mr. O'Malley and this man Patrick Philbin," said Lady Caroline.

Mr. Wrightson shook his head, "I wouldn't hold up too much hope that he'll come back with anything."

CHAPTER 6

THE PHILBIN BUILDING BUSINESS

Angus Wylie was a big man, perfectly able to do physical work, but to make a lot of money he realised it was better to organise others to do the hard work.

He started by providing labour to unload the boats coming up the river from Glasgow to Levenside, but by the time Brian O'Malley arrived in Levenside, much of his business was building work. This included building cheap, shoddy housing for the ever-increasing number of Irish immigrants coming to Levenside. He didn't like the new Catholic immigrants, but he was happy to make money out of them. They were desperate for work, so he didn't need to pay them a great deal and most of what he did pay them he was able to take back in rent.

Part of Wylie's success came from cultivating a relationship with Alan Ready, the Town Clerk. When eventually Levenside recognised that it had grown enough to spread its wings and build new civic buildings, few were surprised that much of the work went to Angus Wylie.

He was the first builder in Levenside to employ a young Irish immigrant called Daniel Philbin. Daniel was useful to Wylie because he had his own gang of men, but it didn't take long before the two fell out. Danny started to push up the rates he charged Wylie because other firms were offering to pay him more than Wylie. Angus Wylie reacted with fury at such disloyalty. The exchanges between the two men were worse than acrimonious, and one of Wylie's men, Jamie Alexander, became involved in a bruising fight with Mungo Costello, one of Danny Philbin's workers.

Danny set up his own business in the old Tannyard next to the Tannergate, doing both building work and providing seasonal labour for some of the landowners farming the areas around Levenside. Wylie continued his business from his quayside yard. He tried to kill of Danny Philbin's business by undercutting his prices for farm work, but that proved a mistake. That work was already badly paid. Instead, he should have cut his rates for the lucrative building work that he had always seen as his own.

Daniel Philbin bought one of the large houses up on the hill above Levenside. Not nearly as big as Angus Wylie's own, but a significant dwelling. It was that purchase which made Wylie realise the Philbin business was doing better than he had realised.

"It wasn't the fall that killed him. They say it was Danny Philbin's heart. He had some kind of turn and then just toppled over." It was Jamie Alexander who told his employer of Daniel Philbin's death. Daniel Philbin's heart attack took most people by surprise, including Wylie, but it had happened just as he realised what a serious competitor Daniel Philbin had become. As Wylie listened, he realised he might have an unexpected opportunity to finish off his rival's business.

"When's the funeral?" asked Wylie. Wylie's foreman paused and looked at his employer, not sure if he had heard correctly.

"You're never going to the funeral, Mr. Wylie?"

Wylie didn't hide his irritation. "Did I say I was?" He had no more intention of attending a Catholic Requiem Mass than his foreman did.

"Who is taking over the business?"

"I dinnae ken, Mr. Wylie."

"Well find out." Alexander scratched his head but said nothing. Wylie was in one of his foul moods. There were few of Danny Philbin's men Jamie still talked to, but some of Philbin's new lads drank in Nevin's Bar, maybe he could get the information Angus Wylie wanted.

Jamie Alexander and Angus Wylie met down by the docks the following morning. "I understand that Mungo Costello and a few of Daniel Philbin's men spoke to his widow …"

"…And what did she say?" Angus Wylie seemed even more impatient than usual, and he didn't seem inclined to take Jamie into his confidence, but then when did Wylie ever do that?

"The widow has asked Mungo Costello take over as foreman. The men think she's trying to keep the business ticking over until she can sell it. There's a couple of new jobs Danny was working on."

"What do you know about Mungo Costello?"

Jamie Alexander shrugged. His employer obviously didn't know he'd had a fist fight with the man. "Not much. He's over fond of his drink in my view. He spends a lot of time in Nevin's Bar."

"Keen on the drink, is he?"

Angus Wylie turned away. Their conversation was over. Jamie Alexander watched as his employer walked back down towards the quayside. As Wylie approached the yard, Jamie Alexander saw a tall, heavyset man was waiting for Wylie. Apart from his height the man was distinctive because of his crooked face. He had a badly set broken nose.

Two days after the Daniel Philbin's funeral Angus Wylie decided that a visit to Daniel Philbin's widow to express his condolences was called for. It was Wylie's first visit to Daniel Philbin's house on the hill. When the door opened, Mrs. Philbin's unhappiness was obvious. There were tell-tale dark circles under her eyes. Although she hadn't got over the shock of her husband's death, she tried to pull herself together as Angus Wylie introduced himself.

"It's kind of you to call Mr. Wylie. Won't you come in for a moment?"

"I don't want to trespass at a time like this."

"Don't worry, come in."

Mrs. Philbin showed Angus Wylie into her living room. He looked around. He still considered Daniel Philbin as nothing more than an Irish hod carrier, so he was surprised by what he saw.

There was a rich mahogany table at one side of the room with matching dining chairs, the armchairs were made of leather, and the covering on the settee on which he was offered a seat was leather too.

It was obvious to Angus Wylie it wasn't just in business that Daniel Philbin had ideas above his station.

"Did you know my husband well Mr. Wylie," Angus Wylie's turned his attention back to Mrs. Philbin. For once Angus Wylie felt there was no harm in relying on a semblance of the truth.

"Not well. I suppose we were more in the way of business associates. He helped out with a couple of building contracts when I needed more men."

He had wondered how much of a grasp of her husband's business Mrs. Philbin had. Not much, it appeared. A moment later she confirmed it.

"I'm afraid Danny didn't discuss too much of his business with me Mr. Wylie." He saw Mrs. Philbin's eyes glisten again.

"Your husband's death was very sudden and unexpected and I dare say he hadn't thought of making provision for the business after he'd gone."

He could probably pick up Danny Philbin's firm for next to nothing. He went over the sums in his head again, whilst he watched Mrs. Philbin try to regain her composure. "Now may not be the best time for me to say what I had in mind, Mrs. Philbin, but I don't know when would be a better time."

"What is it that you wish to say Mr. Wylie?"

"I had in mind to mention to you the possibility of purchasing your husband's business whilst it's still a going concern."

"Well, it's kind of you to think of doing that …both for my sake and for the sake of Daniel's men, but it's not something I need to consider at the moment."

Angus Wylie fought to prevent his look of sympathetic concern changing into a frown. He had been wondering if he should reduce the offer he had in mind.

"Just before he died the one thing my husband discussed with me was the future of his business. I think he was finding it difficult to manage on his own. He asked his younger brother to join him here from Ireland. Patrick and his family were going to come over next summer but since Daniel died, I've written and asked if they could come over as soon as possible."

'Damn'. Angus Wylie just stopped himself from saying the word out loud.

Mrs. Philbin continued, "You see Daniel and I have no children."

Angus Wylie mulled over this new information for a moment. It was not what he had wanted to hear. If Danny Philbin's widow had written appraising her brother-in-law of the current situation, he would have to act quicker than he had anticipated.

"Quite so, quite so." They sat in silence for a moment. Wylie let the silence grow before he spoke again.

"When do you expect your brother-in-law to let you have a response?"

"Oh. I've really no idea… I've only just sent the letter and it will be week or two before I can expect any reply. I think it'll be two or three months before he's able to arrange his affairs so that he can leave Ireland."

Wylie kept his expression impassive.

"I see, and what is going to happen to the business in the meantime?"

"Daniel set up a trust of the money he had in the bank to take effect on his death. I am the sole beneficiary. The manager from the Western Bank doesn't think there will be any problem in my using the money in the trust account to pay the men for a while, if that's what I want."

"I see…" Angus Wylie liked less and less of what he was hearing. "Who is going to act as your foreman?"

"Mungo Costello has offered to do the job for the time being. Daniel used to work on each of the contracts he took on. He always used to say he was his own foreman."

That's the reason why the stupid bugger had his heart attack. Daniel Philbin had taken too much on his own shoulders, but Wylie didn't say that. Instead, he forced himself to smile, "Well, I pleased that you seem to have matters sorted out for the time being."

Mrs. Philbin nodded. "Hopefully the present arrangements won't be for too long." Angus Wylie stood up, keeping his thoughts to himself.

"Well, if there's anything I can do to help don't hesitate to get in touch… and if circumstances change and you do decide to sell the business…" He left the rest of his proposal unsaid.

"That's very kind of you Mr. Wylie and thank you for calling. It was very considerate of you."

As Angus Wylie walked down the hill a dog trotted hopefully towards him. Wylie aimed a vicious kick at its head and the dog skeltered away.

The week after Angus Wylie's visit, Mungo Costello had a bad fall. He'd been drinking. He been very upset by Danny Philbin's death. They had left Ireland together. It was Jamie Alexander who told Angus Wylie the news. Wylie didn't seem surprised.

Mrs. Philbin had given Costello his pay early, as it was his first week as foreman. Costello had suffered concussive injuries, a broken arm and possibly a fractured skull in his fall. The accident had happened near Nevin's Bar, but nobody had seen Mungo fall. He remembered little of what had happened.

"It looks like he'll be off work for some weeks. The Philbins don't seem to have much luck, do they?"

Wylie had just nodded.

CHAPTER 7

ANGUS WYLIE'S HELPING HAND

Angus Wylie took off his hat as Daniel Philbin's widow opened the door and held it to his chest as he spoke. Worry, rather that grief showed in her expression on this occasion.

"Mrs. Philbin, I've just heard the terrible news about Mungo Costello. I thought I'd call round to see if there was anything I could do."

"Please, come in, Mr. Wylie." She showed him into her attractive living room and invited him to sit down on one of the leather chairs. "I'm afraid Mungo Costello is quite poorly Mr. Wylie. I arranged for the doctor to see him, and he says it may be several weeks before he's back at work."

"That must be a blow."

"Yes, it is." Mrs. Philbin moved her hands, which had been resting on the arms of her chair and clasped them together in her lap.

"Is there anything I can do?

"That's very kind Mr. Wylie, but I don't see how."

"Something did occur to me Mrs. Philbin. As I was walking over here, I started to think how you would need to replace Mungo Costello for a while …you need someone with experience and … well it occurred to me that there was an experienced man, Jamie Alexander, who might be talked into keeping an eye on things for you. He worked for me until recently and I think he worked with Danny in the past so I know he would be able to help you supervise what's going on quite easily. He's been trying to set up on his own, but business has been slow, and I think

I could convince him to help you out for a month or two." Wylie waited to see Mrs Philbin's reaction.

Mrs. Philbin bit at her lip. The name Jamie Alexander sounded vaguely familiar.

"Jamie would provide the experience I think you need to keep your business going."

Mrs. Philbin thought for a moment. She desperately wanted to try and keep things going until Danny's brother, Patrick, could get over from Ireland.

Perhaps she should speak to Mr. Scott the bank manager again before she made any decision. What would Danny say? Probably there's no point in speaking to Mr. Scott - building work isn't something he would know about. She had to learn to stand on her own two feet.

"Are you sure, Mr. Wylie? You must have a lot of work on yourself at the moment, you might need him back to help you."

"Well, I'm sure I can manage for a couple of months. Like your husband, I act as my own foreman more often than not."

These days Angus Wylie rarely ventured out of his office. He certainly didn't demean himself with any menial labouring work. He looked straight at Mrs. Philbin, "I'm still interested in your business Mrs. Philbin. It's in my interest to keep it as a going concern."

"Thank you, Mr. Wylie, that would solve a real headache for me."

"Good. That's settled. I'll ask Jamie to come over to meet you first thing in the morning and then we can all go over to the Tannyard together and you and he can talk to the men." He paused and then added as if it was something he had just thought of, "I might be able to put some farm work your way as well. I'm not keen to take on any extra work just now."

As she closed the door, Mrs. Philbin couldn't throw off a nagging uncertainty. What harm could it do to accept Angus Wylie's offer? His wish to buy Danny's business seemed genuine. Surely it was, as he said, in his best interests as well as hers to keep it going for the next couple of months. This offer of help would buy her more time.

Mrs. Philbin looked at her husband's employees. She was standing on a wooden box so her men could see her better. Most of the men she barely knew and she was ill at ease. Jamie Alexander had turned up on time and although he told her Mr Wylie was delayed, she decided to introduce him straight away.

She lifted her head. "You will all have heard by now of Mungo's accident. Despite that I am determined to keep Danny's business going." She heard a few supportive noises. "I think I've found an experienced man to help me manage things until Mungo is fit and well again."

She turned towards Jamie Alexander who stood as tall as her although she was standing on the wooden box. "I'd like to introduce Jamie Alexander." When Jamie's name was mentioned, it didn't receive the reception Mrs. Philbin hoped. There was a lot of muttering and a number of the men looked quite sullen, but none of them said anything. Nothing at least that carried to her.

Jamie didn't say much. Just that he looked forward to working with all of them and he was sure that they would all want to carry on as before and help Danny's widow.

"Has anybody got anything they wish to say?" She waited for a moment, searching the faces in front of her, particularly the men at the back of the group but nobody caught her eye. One or two appeared to give Jamie Alexander a hostile look.

"Well, if nobody has anything to say…" No one spoke. "I'd like thank you again for giving me your support. Good luck to you all." She stepped down and then she motioned to Jamie to walk over to the Danny's office with her.

"I don't think the men have got over Mungo's accident coming so quickly after Danny's death." They stopped outside the office Danny had used. "If you need to talk to me at any time you can find me over at the house." She held out her hand.

Outside the Tannyard gates she paused. Then she saw Angus Wylie striding up the hill. He raised his hat.

Angus Wylie apologised for his unfortunate absence, "I'm so sorry to be late. How did it go?

"I'm not sure Mr. Wylie."

"This arrangement is for the best Mrs. Philbin. Take my word for it. Jamie's got a lot of experience and hopefully Mungo will soon be on the mend."

"Let's hope so. It's kind of you to help me out."

"Not at all. I'm sorry I wasn't here when you introduced Jamie."

Mrs. Philbin didn't say anything. Neither Jamie nor Angus Wylie had given a reason for the latter's absence.

"Well unless there's something else I can do, if you'll excuse me, I must get back." As Alex Wylie walked down the hill Mrs. Philbin watched him uncertainly. It was only a temporary arrangement she'd agreed upon, she told herself.

After work two of her husband's men called at Mrs. Philbin's house.

"What can I do for you?"

"We wanted to speak to you…" The spokesman paused, "…about the new arrangements at the Tannyard."

"Yes?"

"Some of the men are going to find it difficult to work with Jamie Alexander…"

"Why?" Neither of them spoke. She waited. "Well?"

"We've worked with him before. He left Danny to go and work with Wylie."

She looked at them. "Yes, Mr Wylie told me. That was one of the reasons I decided to employ him."

The two men looked at each other. Then one of them blurted out. "Danny and Mr. Wylie didn't get on."

"If you thought Mr. Alexander was the wrong choice, why didn't you speak up this morning?"

"We didn't know until we say you talking to Mr. Wylie afterwards that he had anything to do with it…"

She shook her head. What did they expect her to do? She looked at their unhappy faces. She tried to think of something, anything, to say by way of encouragement. "Mr Wylie's been quite helpful since Danny died. I think his death shocked Mr. Wylie like the rest of us. He's already put some farm work our way."

A further glance passed between the two men and then the spokesman said, "Jamie Alexander doesn't like working with the Irish Mrs. Philbin …and I don't think you'll find there's much profit in farm work."

She thought for a moment. Maybe she had the wrong decision

about Jamie but if she changed her decision straight away it would look as if she didn't know what she was doing.

"It's only for the short-term, until Mungo Costello's better or my brother-in-law gets here. Let's see how things go…."

Although Mrs. Philbin was unaware of it, the next day neither of the two men who had spoken to her showed up for work. They weren't the only ones, but Jamie decided not to bother mentioning any of the absences to Mrs. Philbin, although he let Alex Wylie know.

Wylie realised he needed to be careful. "Take on a few more Paddies but try and make sure they're new arrivals." He'd certainly expected to lose some of Philbin's men when they learnt who was to be new foreman of the business, but not many. There was not that much work to be had in Levenside, Glasgow possibly, but not here in Levenside. It was lucky that Mrs. Philbin had no idea about how bad his relationship with her husband had been.

He smiled, now he had more than one option. At the very least he could offload a couple of contracts he was losing money on.

A week later Angus Wylie called on Mrs. Philbin. He checked there were no problems that Jamie Alexander was unaware of and then he moved onto the main purpose of his visit. He had promised to take on a contract with the Council as a favour to the Town Clerk, but the rates meant there was no profit in it, and he could use his men elsewhere.

"It's a little bit of work for the local Council here in Levenside, Mrs. Philbin. My business has as much as it can handle right now, but if your happy with the idea I could put in a bid on behalf of Philbins."

Mrs. Philbin hesitated before she responded, after what the men had told her the other evening, she was more suspicious of Angus Wylie now. Was he genuinely trying to help her keep the business going or was there some catch.

"Do you think that's advisable at the moment Mr. Wylie?"

"I do."

She needed advice from someone, but a contract with the local council must be worth having. "Very well. See what you can do. Thank you again for your help Mr. Wylie."

There was no need for him to bid for the contract, of course. It was already won. Mrs. Philbin vacillated. Should she speak the bank manager? No Danny would expect her to make her own decisions.

On Angus Wylie's next visit, she signed the contract …and a second one for farm maintenance work.

CHAPTER 8

ARRIVING IN LEVENSIDE

The oldest part of Levenside lay next to the waterfront, and most of the newer developments were on the hill behind. That was also where the ghetto called the Tannergate was that provided a home for the Irish Catholics that had fled the famine. Brian had been told on the ferry that if there was anywhere cheap to stay, it would be there. So, he set off up the hill towards the tight rows of shoddy houses that curved round the hillside.

The first thing that Brian became aware of as he approached was the smell. It was a warm day and the gulleys that ran between the rows of houses he was approaching gave off an unpleasant stench. As he walked between the first two rows of houses, a group of dirty barefoot children watched him without interest.

Every time a door was opened to him, the response was the same, a silent shake of the head. Brian started to wonder if all the inhabitants of Levenside had lost the power of speech, then near the end of one of the rows he came to a house with a dark green door. He knocked once again, resigned to receiving another silent refusal.

He couldn't be sure of her exact age of the woman in front of him because the dark patches under her eyes made her look older than she was. Even so, she was a much younger woman than those he had encountered up to now. Brian guessed she must be about thirty. Her skin had the unhealthy look of someone who spent most of her time indoors. She stood at the door, wiping her hands on her apron.

"Do you have a room to rent, by any chance?" said Brian. The woman looked at him. He could see the hesitation.

"Anything would do." He didn't bother trying to keep the desperation out of his voice.

"If I have, how are you going to pay? You don't look to me like you've any money." The woman was certainly blunt. She stared at his unshaven face and his old, dishevelled clothing and almost instinctively Brian moved his hand up to his chin in the hope of covering some of the stubble.

"I've got a job."

"And where would that be?" Maureen looked him straight in the eyes as she fired off the question. She had seen many Irishmen come to Levenside.

"Philbins, …the firm works out of the Tannyard."

"Next you'll be telling me you're a friend of the new owner." The sarcasm in her voice was barely hidden.

He ignored it, and smiled, "Indeed, I travelled over on the ferry with him and his family."

"Indeed."

"Yes." Despite his confident response there was no hint of a change in Maureen Connor's expression. She shook her head, if this man knew Danny Philbin's brother why was he struggling to find a room? Why did he look like a tinker?

Brian sensed that she was about to turn him down. "I came over with Patrick Philbin on the boat, but you needn't worry about whether I have a job or not. I can pay the rent in advance," and he dug into his pocket and pulled out the last of his money. He unwrapped his handkerchief to show two half crowns and a sixpenny piece.

Maureen continued to stare at him hard. The man in front of her didn't lack confidence, but his story that he was a friend of the new owner of the Philbin building business, had to be just that, a story. On the other hand, in his grubby handkerchief he did have two weeks rent in advance for his board and lodging. Times were hard. Her only lodger now was Mungo Costello. He owed two weeks rent and he still wasn't fit enough to go back to work. Her other lodger had decided to leave for Glasgow to try his hand at shipbuilding as soon as Jamie Alexander had taken over at the Tannyard. One lodger was not enough, not just because she would be short of money, but people would start to talk if a young widow only had one man living in her house for too long.

Finally, although she wouldn't admit it even to herself, despite all the dirt and grime, Brian O'Malley was a good-looking man.

"You'll have to share the downstairs back room and the rent is half a crown a week. That includes your evening meal. You can take it or leave it." Maureen made her offer briskly, an air of finality in her voice. He felt like smiling but sensibly he did not. Instead, he quickly nodded his acceptance and before she could change her mind he stepped forward and Maureen held the door ajar.

There was barely room for the two of them to pass in the narrow corridor but he ignored the cramped surroundings. What was more difficult to ignore was the smell of food cooking in the kitchen as he passed. He glanced through the kitchen door he caught sight of a pot on the stove and an iron tub on the floor. He realised he was starving.

After his new landlady had showed him the tiny room he was to share at the back of the house that was barely large enough to hold two straw mattresses, Brian decided to chance his luck. He went back to the kitchen.

"I was wondering… would it be too much trouble to let me have a bath and something to eat?" he asked.

"For what you pay you get one evening meal and that's all." She turned away. "Now, if you don't mind, I've plenty of washing that needs to be done."

"I'll willingly pay." She looked back at him.

"I haven't the time to be pampering the likes of you."

He held out the sixpenny piece, the last of his money. Maureen Connor looked at it for a moment and then shaking her head she took it.

She gave him some bread and some thick broth to eat. It was surprisingly tasty. He couldn't stop himself from wolfing the food down although he tried not to as Maureen was watching him closely. It was a relief, when finally, once she had boiled enough water to fill the bathtub, she left him alone in the kitchen.

He put his clothes on the chair by the door and got into the tin bath facing away from the doorway. It was a wonderful sensation just lying there and letting the warm water lap over him, feeling his tired limbs coming back to life.

He sat in the bath until the water started to cool then he stood up and turned to the chair by the kitchen door on which he had left his clothes. He stared at the chair. His shirt was not there, nor were his trousers.

He didn't hear the door open and it took him a moment to realise Maureen Connor was standing looking at his naked figure. Before he could do anything, she held out a worn pair of clean trousers and a shirt that she had in her arms.

He felt himself blushing to the roots of his hair, but if his landlady recognised how awkward he felt, she didn't show it. Her face showed no hint of embarrassment.

He hesitated for a moment, then he took the proffered clothes, and before he could properly recover his composure and do something about his nakedness or thank her for the clothes, his landlady had turned and quietly closed the kitchen door behind her. As Maureen Connor made her way back up the narrow steps to her room, a hint of a smile crossed her face.

Brian felt annoyed. He pulled on the shirt. He was still not properly dry, and almost tore it. Why should he be embarrassed? It was Maureen who should be embarrassed.

Eventually, his irritation began to fade as he felt the cleanness of the shirt against his skin. He pulled on the clean trousers and then he sat on the chair and eased his boots back on. The one thing he hadn't been able to do was wash away the blisters on his feet.

How had Maureen Connor come back into the kitchen without him hearing her? What had made her do it? Maybe behind that cold facade there was a warmer friendlier side to Maureen Connor, maybe she just felt too vulnerable to show it. He'd pay her for the clothes when he had some more money.

After he had emptied the tin bath in the gulley outside the back door, he decided to thank Maureen properly for the clean clothes so he went up the stairs and knocked on her door. When she came to the door, he smiled.

"It was kind of you to lend me these clothes."

Maureen Connor looked at him,

143

"They're my husband's clothes. He was about your size."

"You're married?"

His landlady shook her head. "I was. He died of pneumonia two years ago."

"I'm sorry."

"Don't be. He was a drunken bastard." Brian wasn't sure if he was more shocked by what she said or the way she said it. Maureen's face was expressionless. He found himself feeling uncomfortable again.

"I was thinking of going for a walk up the hill … to have a look at the town."

She carried on as if he hadn't spoken, "Don't expect me to be doing your laundry free of charge. That's not included in what you pay." He nodded.

She started to close the door. There was nothing more to be said. He turned and made his way downstairs again. He shook his head. Maureen Connor was too much of a contradiction for him.

Half an hour later he set out in search of the Philbins' house. Margaret Philbin had given him the name of the house and told him it was at the lower end of the Howes Road. She'd said it was lovely big house with apple trees in the garden, but he wondered what it was really like. She'd only visited her uncle's house once and that had been ten years ago.

If he had glanced back as he walked away from his lodgings, he would have caught a glimpse of his landlady watching him from her upstairs window as he made his way up the hill, but he didn't. He was no longer thinking of his Maureen Connor and her equivocal behaviour. He was thinking of the girl he had met on the ferry and her family. Tomorrow he would ask Margaret Philbin's father for a job and if that went well, he told himself he would ask if he could call and see his daughter. He smiled to himself.

He began to walk up the cobbled road away from the Tannergate towards the highest part of the town. Despite the climb, there was a lightness about his step. Although it was a warm sunny day he noticed that some of the leaves on the trees were starting to turn brown and the gardens had that variety of colour that showed that autumn was beginning. He heard a bird singing in one of the trees, it sounded carefree and for the first time since he left Ireland he felt himself relaxing.

At last, he came to the house he knew belonged to the Philbins. Melville House. He looked at the large house. The knocker on the imposing front door was of polished brass. For a long time, he stood outside the house looking at the solid stone walls, wishing he could see inside, perhaps catch a glance of Margaret, but there was not a soul to be seen. He walked past the house and looked across the well-kept garden in the hope he could see into at the rear of the house. He could not get a clear view, but Margaret had been right. He could see at least two apple trees.

Eventually he turned away and instinctively he knew he would not be coming back. He wouldn't be calling on Margaret Philbin. This was a different world to his. Margaret Philbin would know nothing of the slum dwellings in the Tannergate where he was now sharing a miserable back room. He thought back to the boat, although the Philbins had shared their food with him on deck as they left Ireland, they had retired to sleep below in their cabin. They had not been deck passengers like him. Margaret wouldn't look at a common labourer, even one who worked in her father's business. He walked sadly on up the hill leaving the town behind him.

When he came to the top of the hill he walked along the top of the Howes Road where there were three or four even larger houses standing in isolation. When he reached the bend in the road where it crested the hill, he turned round. As he looked back down over Levenside he realised why the grand houses had been built where they were. He stood there for quite a time. It was not the town that caused him to stand and stare, it was the view beyond of the Lomond Hills and the River Leven. The beauty was breath-taking. He could see the vast expanses of mauve heather and the roaming hills and the sun flashing and sparkling on the river as the waters rippled and ran away in the distance. The impressive stone houses on the Howes Road stood like guardsmen looking out over Levenside and the marvellous view beyond.

He walked down the hill more slowly than he had climbed it. His only thought was that one day he would own one of those big houses on the Howes Road. Then, and only then, would he be able to approach Margaret Philbin, the girl he had fallen in love with on the boat from Ireland.

CHAPTER 9

BRIAN FINDS WORK

The next morning as he made his way past the kitchen to the front door Brian O'Malley was surprised to see that Maureen was already at work although it was only just starting to get light.

She got up off her knees where she had been using her washboard on the dirty clothes soaking in the old tin bath and came to the kitchen doorway.

"Good morning," he said.

She nodded. "Wait a minute." He paused. Maureen went across to the table and picked up a package. "Here, take this piece, it's your first day, you'll need something to eat later." She thrust the package into his hands and turned away before he could thank her. Outside the front door he stood for a moment then he shook his head and set off for the old Tannyard.

Brian was not the first to arrive. Three men were already lined up outside the gates of the yard where Danny Philbin had set up his business. They all stood in silence and gradually more men joined the line. Eventually Brian turned to the man standing behind him. "Do you think they'll be taking on more men today." Even as he spoke another couple of men joined the queue. The man didn't reply at first, he just hawked and spat on the ground.

"Who knows."

"Why?"

"There's no telling with this new foreman."

"Has the new owner appointed another foreman?"

"What new owner?"

Brian O'Malley looked at the other man trying to gather his thoughts. Patrick Philbin should have arrived in Levenside by now.

"Who's been running the Philbin business since Mr. Philbin died?"

"Good question laddie."

At that moment the gates to the Tannergate swung open.

The man next to him said, "That's the new foreman." Jamie Alexander walked through the gateway and then along the line of men standing outside the Tannyard.

On his way back up the line he stopped in front of Brian O'Malley. "What's your name?"

"Brian O'Malley."

"I haven't seen you before."

"I'm only just over from Ireland. I got into Clydeside the day before yesterday." Jamie Alexander nodded. Brian thought of mentioning he had travelled over with Patrick Philbin, but something told him not to.

"What did you do back home in Ireland. laddie?"

"I worked on my father's farm."

"Your father owned a farm?" Brian O'Malley saw one of the men next to him smirking. "He rented a smallholding." Jamie Alexander was about to say something more but instead he walked back to the front of the queue.

"You three …away into the yard." He pointed to the three men in front of Brian O'Malley. Then he walked past Brian and the man behind him and picked out another three men further down the queue. Brian couldn't see any reason why he and the next man had been missed out, but he waited to see if anything else would be said before he protested.

As Jamie Alexander walked back, he stopped. "So, you're a farm boy are you laddie?" Brian nodded. "Well, you're in luck I've got some farm work that needs doing, so you and your friend here can do that …if you want it."

"Thank you," said Brian. Jamie Alexander smiled. Farm work was the dross here in Levenside. It was the hardest work and it paid the worst too. Then Jamie Alexander turned to the man beside Brian. "What about you?" The man looked at Jamie Alexander without enthusiasm. "Yes."

"Yes what?"

"Yes, thank you Mr Alexander."

"That's better. A wee bit of civility never hurts, does it?"

"No Mr Alexander."

"Come on then." They followed Jamie Alexander into the Tannyard where a couple of horse drawn carts were waiting. "Josh here will give you a lift out to the farm. You can pay for your transport at the end of the week when you get your wages. There's some ditches to dig and some dry-stone walling needs repaired." He looked up at Brian. "I take it you know how to build a dry-stone wall?" Brian nodded.

They climbed up onto the back of the cart and Josh nudged his horse forward. The man next to Brian waited until they were out of the Tannyard before he spoke.

"He always gives the Irish the shite work." He paused briefly as he coughed then he added. "Danny Philbin never made us pay for being ferried about either".

CHAPTER 10

CONFRONTATION

It didn't take long before Josh trusted Brian O'Malley with unloading the cart at the end of the day. Brian was a reliable worker, willing to help his work mates.

As Brian O'Malley jumped down from the cart the Monday after he had started helping Joss, he saw there was a stranger standing in the yard. Brian lifted the picks and shovels off the back of the cart and carried them round into the storeroom. When he came out the man was still standing there, watching him. He didn't recognise the man. He didn't work at the Tannyard. If he had, Brian wouldn't have missed anyone of his stature. He was a large solid individual, taller than Brian by two or three inches. He also had a distinctive broken nose that made his face look crooked.

"I hear you've been asking questions."

Brian paused unloading the cart and turned towards the voice behind him. Joss was sorting out the horses. There was no one else in the yard. Just Brian and this man he'd never seen before.

"What do you mean?"

"Just what I said. You've been asking questions ...about Mr. Wylie."

"What if I have?"

"I wouldn't go on doing that if I was you." The man moved forward almost imperceptibly.

"Why shouldn't I?"

"Mr. Wylie doesn't like it. I don't like it."

"…And who are you?"

"I'm a friend of Mr. Wylie."

The man's hostility was obvious.

"I just wanted to know how Jamie Alexander came to be here, helping Mrs. Philbin out."

The man looked at Brian O'Malley, "And what business is it of yours."

"I was just surprised."

"And why's that?" The man had narrowed his eyes.

Brian shrugged, "I just thought Jamie Alexander would have had enough to do already for Angus Wylie."

The man was so close to Brian now that Brian would have backed away but he found his back was already right up against the side of the cart. Without realising it he had already been backing away from the man.

"What are you suggesting?"

Brian met the man's stare with his own.

"I'm not suggesting anything." The man pushed his face forward so that his forehead was almost touching Brian O'Malley's.

"You better watch yourself laddie if you want to carry on working here. Mrs. Philbin asked Angus Wylie for help after Mungo Costello got so drunk he fell over and nearly killed himself. He suggested Jamie Alexander help her out for a while. Satisfied?"

The man paused and then added, "Don't you go causing any more trouble," and before Brian could respond the man head butted him. The sudden pain was excruciating. Brian staggered sideways catching hold of the cart to stop himself falling. As he did so the man turned and walked away calling over his shoulder, "I'll be watching you laddie."

Before Brian could recover the man had walked through the Tannyard gates and was gone.

CHAPTER 11

MR PAGET

Brian missed Ireland and the little stream that he and his sister Tara used to walk beside, but the River Leven provided a surrogacy of sorts. Occasionally he walked up the hill that rose above the town, to where he had first discovered the magnificent views of the river and beyond, but nearly every Sunday he would walk along the banks of the Leven, stopping now and then to watch the water as it flowed past him, alone with his thoughts. His only family now was his brother in America. He often wondered if he would ever see him again.

For the time being Jamie Alexander ran the Philbin business and Brian had to accept that. It was not sensible to make enemies before he needed to, so Brian tried to make sure he had as little contact with Jamie as possible.

Brian thought of asking after Patrick Philbin at the Philbin house, but he decided his enquiry might get back to Jamie so for the moment he decided to bide his time. The new foreman only allocated him badly paid jobs on the farms outside Levenside, but it was regular work and it was enough to pay Maureen Connor. However, as he wandered along the Leven he thought about his future. An illiterate jobbing labourer would never aspire to a house on the Howes Road or impress the girl he had met on the ferry. He had no education and there was no one in Levenside he could turn to for advice. He started to think he ought try following his brother to America.

Then late one afternoon, he found Levenside public library. He was still wearing his work clothes, so he didn't go inside until the following day. There was a little bald man wearing glasses reading behind a desk as he entered. Brian walked down the rows of books. He had no idea where to start.

Physically, Brian O'Malley and Mr. Paget the librarian were exact opposites. Brian was tall, broad shouldered and fit from hard labouring work. Mr. Paget was only a little over five foot and looked smaller because he hunched his back. He had lost most of his hair and wore round shaped spectacles. Brian made sure he sat out of sight of the librarian.

At the end of Brian O'Malley's second week of visiting the library, Mr. Paget found Brian asleep at one of the tables when he came to close the library.

He shook Brian's shoulder. "Are you alright?"

"No…Yes." Brian was disorientated. He had been in such a deep sleep he had to fight hard to work out where he was. Mr. Paget watched Brian recover his thoughts.

"Are you studying anything in particular young man?"

Now he was awake Brian couldn't hide his embarrassment. "I'm… just trying to find my way around."

"Well, if there's anything I can help you with …"

"No. I'm sorry I just…thank you." Brian made his way to the library door as quickly as he could.

Mr. Paget picked up the book that Brian had been reading. Mr. Paget shook his head and turned and to look after Brian. The library door had already closed behind the young labourer.

Despite Brian O'Malley's embarrassment Mr. Paget was certain that Brian O'Malley would be back; and two days later he was, but Mr. Paget waited until the two of them were entirely alone in the library before he approached Brian.

"Are you teaching yourself to read?" Brian felt his cheeks burning.

"No…I…" before Brian could complete his denial Mr. Paget continued, "…because if you are, I could help you."

Brian stared at Mr. Paget, not sure if he had heard him correctly.

"I'd be happy to help you if you're trying to teach yourself to read."

Brian O'Malley was at a loss. His greatest fear had been that if Mr. Paget learnt that he couldn't read properly that the librarian would ask him to leave the library.

"I … I don't know what to say."

"Yes, would be sufficient," said Mr. Paget and he smiled at Brian, and it finally registered that the little man's offer was genuine.

"That would be more than kind of you."

"Young man I will only be too pleased to help you." And Mr. Paget held out his hand and without hesitation Brian grasped it.

It was a struggle to work in his room, much of it by candlelight, but Brian persevered. At least Mungo Costello, his roommate was out most evenings drinking so Brian wasn't disturbed but with only the window ledge to use it was hard going.

One evening he heard at knock on his door. When he opened it, he was surprised to see Maureen standing there. She looked across at the book propped on the window ledge. "I'm told that you study every evening."

"Yes, is it a problem? Mungo's normally out in the evenings."

"There's no problem." Mungo had told her Brian O'Malley was an idiot, pouring over books he could hardly read, with a candle in his room. Despite Mungo's accident, Danny Philbin's widow was still giving Mungo money for his rent, but he was drinking it away. To Maureen, Mungo was the idiot. If he continued as he was, she would have to put him on the street, but she'd been interested in what he'd told her about her other lodger.

"I just thought I'd say…if you are going to be studying in the evenings you can use the table in the kitchen."

"Are you sure?" Brian couldn't keep the surprise out of his voice.

Maureen looked at him, "Yes… provided you keep out of my way."

"Of course, that's very kind of you." Maureen looked embarrassed Brian wondered if she was thinking he might misinterpret her thoughtfulness.

The use of the kitchen with Maureen's paraffin lamp and the table on which he could write and rest his books was a godsend. Quite often when he came back from the library Maureen would still be busy in the kitchen. She rarely said anything or interrupted him and that suited Brian. He would get straight down to his work after he ate. Sometimes he saw her glancing at him but as soon as she realised that he had noticed, she would look away.

Most evenings it was only those glances that passed between them. Maureen never said anything until she wished him a goodnight and told him to blow out the paraffin lamp when he had finished.

153

A couple of weeks after the new working arrangements started, Brian found his attention wandering. His head dropped and he fell asleep without realising it. He awoke to find Maureen placing a cup of tea down beside him.

"Drink that," she said. Brian saw the lamp needed adjusting but before he could stand up to do it Maureen had done it for him. "There's more tea in the pot. It'll keep you awake."

He took the cup, "This is kind of you."

She looked at him for a moment. "You need to be careful Brian. If you do that again you could easily knock over the lamp." It was the first time Maureen had used his first name.

He wasn't sure if it was his pointing out her kindness towards him or her new familiarity, but as he looked at her he could tell she was feeling awkward.

"I don't know where you think those books will get you," she inspected the pot of tea she was still holding, "…but I'll say one thing for you, you persevere." Then she turned away and went back to the sink and began scrubbing hard at the pots in the sink. He watched her for a moment. She paused to flick some strands of her hair out of her eyes. She had an attractive face. He waited to see if she said anything else, but she paid him no more attention and when she had finished her chores she gave him her usual cursory goodnight and left him alone in the kitchen.

He tried to get back to the exercise Mr. Paget had given him, but he couldn't. Maureen was a real enigma. One moment she tried to be distant and cold towards him the next minute her innate kindness took over and she would lend him some of her husband's clothes or make him tea to help him stay awake. Maureen seemed to want to be more than just his landlady, friends at least, but she seemed embarrassed to show her feelings. He wondered if she was frightened that if she lowered her guard and showed an interest in him, he would turn out like her husband.

Mr. Paget made Brian read out loud to him after the library was closed and he gave Brian exercises to ensure that he wrote every day. To Brian his progress appeared terribly slow, but with Mr. Paget's encouragement he gradually gained in confidence, until one evening when he came in late Mr. Paget smiled at him.

"Mr. O'Malley your handwriting has come on a pace." There was no doubt that Brian O'Malley's juvenile script was now starting to take a form that many adults would be more than pleased with.

Mr. Paget handed him a book. "I think you should keep a journal, Mr. O'Malley. It'll help you with your writing."

"What do I have do Mr. Paget to keep a journal?"

"Each day, or whenever you can, you simply write in it anything important that had happened to you. Do you think you can do that?"

Brian nodded.

"I've written to-day's date in it, to start you off." said Mr. Paget.

That evening Brian made his first diary entry, something he was to do again nearly every evening for the rest of his life. For the first few days he showed the entries to Mr. Paget, but after the librarian told him the journal was a "personal document" Brian started to read it over to himself at the end of the week and try to correct any errors himself.

Sometimes when he finished his journal he would wonder about Margaret Philbin and what had happened to her and her father and he tried to puzzle out what was going on at the Tannyard and why Jamie Alexander was there and not Patrick Philbin.

He tried to ask Mungo Costello about Jamie, but Mungo didn't want to talk about the Philbin business. Once he asked Mungo how he had fallen and injured himself. All Mungo would say to Brian was, "I've never fallen down drunk." After that the subject was closed.

Eventually Brian decided to ask Mr. Paget what he knew about the Philbin building business. Brian learnt for the first time the full extent of the feud between Danny Philbin and Angus Wylie, but what he was told made the current situation even more difficult for him to understand.

CHAPTER 12

MAUREEN AND BRIAN O'MALLEY

Once Mungo Costello's rent was four weeks in arrears, Maureen had had enough. Her face, as Mungo staggered past the kitchen, said it all. Brian had seen the warning signs, but Mungo had not, or maybe he no longer cared.

One evening Maureen packed up all of Mungo's belongings and placed them outside in the street. Then she barred the front door. Brian heard Maureen bolting the door, but he paid no more attention until Maureen came into the kitchen and stood in front of the kitchen table.

"I'm going to bed now. If you let that drunk in tonight, to-morrow night you'll find your things on the street too."

Brian said nothing but once Maureen closed the door he wondered what he should do. Mungo had done his best to help Danny Philbin's widow until his bad fall. He had never interfered with Brian's studies even though he thought they were a waste of time and, on the one occasion Brian had gone to Nevin's Bar, Mungo had done his best to introduce Brian to the regular workers from Philbins drinking there.

Brian opened the door to the corridor and walked to the back room he shared. Mungo didn't have many belongings, but they were all gone. Brian lay down on his own mattress. He couldn't let Mungo back in, but he wanted to help if he could. He went back to the kitchen to try and study again, but it was no good. He couldn't get over feeling guilty that he had been so taken up with his studying that he hadn't tried to help Mungo.

Eventually, he got over his indecision. He went back to his room and took the tin box in which he hid his money from under the loose floorboard. He counted out two weeks' rent and put that back in the box, and then he put the rest of his money in his pocket. Maureen had barred both the front and back doors so, in case she came back down and checked, he packed his books up as if he had gone to bed and let himself out the window of his room at the back of the house and made his way down into Levenside.

Brian knew where to find Mungo. He hoped it was still early enough in the evening to talk some sense into the man.

He stepped past the young children sitting on the steps of Nevin's Bar and pushed his way through crowded interior searching for Mungo amongst the fug and blue smoke. There was good chance that if he tried to help Mungo all he would find was, like Danny Philbin's widow, he was throwing good money after bad, but he had to try.

He was certain that Mungo Costello would never work at Philbin's again, particularly now Jamie Alexander was foreman. He was sure Mungo knew that himself, although he hadn't said it, that was why Mungo hadn't made any attempt to stop drinking since his injuries and why in one relatively sober moment Mungo had talked to him about making a new start in Perth. Brian was sure that the only future for Mungo was somewhere other than Levenside, particularly if he kept bad mouthing Angus Wylie.

First, he had to get Mungo out into the cold air outside and try to sober him up. After that was to find him a roof for the night. Then he had to make sure that in the morning Mungo and his belongings were on their way to Perth.

Joss Freebody and two other Philbin men were standing at the bar. They greeted Brian warmly and invited him to join them.

"Is Mungo here?" With a movement of his head Joss pointed Mungo out. Joss was standing on his own in the far corner of Nevin's with a pot of ale in his hand. Brian explained to Joss what Maureen Connor had done and what he was going to try and convince Mungo to do.

Joss looked at him doubtfully. "Well Brian …even if he's still sober it'll take some convincing to get Mungo to leave Levenside."

"We've got to try. He can't go on like this." Brian looked across at Mungo Costello. Mungo was staring into his pot of ale, apparently oblivious to everybody else in the bar.

"Can any of you let Mungo have a bed for tonight?"

The two men next to Joss looked down at the floor, inspecting the floor as if there were some items of interest to be discovered among the sawdust. Joss was the only one that looked at Brian. "If it's just for tonight, I can probably get away with him sleeping on the floor, but after that…"

"Help me get him outside so I can try and talk to him."

Brian couldn't remember in detail how he convinced Mungo he had to leave Levenside, but the next day Joss confirmed that he had taken Mungo to the railway station before the Tannyard opened and Mungo had left on the first train.

Brian was surprised that Maureen never asked what had happened to Mungo. All she did was ask Brian if he would see if anyone looking for lodgings. Despite her harsh treatment of Mungo, he said he would ask around.

"I'll let you know if I hear anything." He had still not fully shaken off the sleepless night he had spent sorting out Mungo. He decided to go to bed early. He was tired and needed some sleep.

"Shall I blow out the lamp?"

Maureen shook her head. "I need that lamp upstairs. Can you carry it up for me?"

Brian hesitated for a moment, normally he and Maureen just took a candle to their rooms but maybe she had some sewing or darning she wanted to do upstairs.

"Of course," he picked up the oil lamp and followed her up the stairs.

Maureen walked in front of him, so Brian could not see the expression on her face, but her face was impassive when she stood aside to let him in through the door. She followed him in and then lent back against the door closing it behind her.

"Put the lamp over there on the dresser." He did as she bade and turned to leave.

"Come over here." He came towards her like an obedient child. She was certain that Brian had no idea of what she intended as she stepped forward. She took him in her arms and kissed him. For a moment, there was no response, but it was only a moment, then his lips parted before her searching tongue and she tasted him for the first time, and after that she pulled him onto her bed.

They lay there kissing each other. Saying nothing, just whispering each other's name. Maureen was surprised at how gentle Brian's kiss was, not that she could remember her brute of a husband even bothering to kiss her after they were married.

"Do you want me?" Brian didn't answer so she slid her hand downwards. She smiled. She could feel the answer with her fingertips. She started to pull at his clothes, and he helped her. Soon they were both naked.

She heard him groan as she held his hardness in her hands. She guided him between her legs and straight away she felt him thrust himself inside her, but she was ready for him. She had been longing for this to happen for so long. She felt the warmth of him inside her and although she was sure he had never had a woman before, his movements made her cry out with pleasure.

Sleeping together became a regular occurrence. Each night as Brian lay beside her, Maureen tried to convince herself that she was just seeking consolation from her loneliness. Brian was much younger than her; there was no possibility of things lasting. She told herself that the ache she had felt before they shared the same bed was nothing more than the ache of loneliness, but she knew that was not the case.

Brian was not just someone she was using to get over her loneliness. Her feelings went much, much deeper than that. She realised that she had probably fallen in love with Brian the very first day she had seen him. Her husband had been a brute, who had often forced himself on her when he was drunk. It had been a blessed release when he had fallen ill and died of pneumonia. There had been no love there.

Brian was different. From the first, he had been kind and considerate to her, and for all his strength he was a gentle lover. Try as she did, she could not stop her feelings for him getting stronger and stronger, but her happiness was tinged with sadness for she knew one day she would lose him, and he would move on. She just prayed that he would not happen for a long time.

CHAPTER 13

LADY MACPHERSON'S LETTER

One Friday after they had been paid their weekly wages Jamie Alexander called Brian over. Brian's immediate thought was that Jamie had decided to get rid of him, but that turned out not to be the case. It appeared that Jamie had been talking to Joss about Brian.

The fact that Brian was one of the few men that signed his name when he was given his pay had not gone unnoticed. In addition, Jamie had found out from Joss that it was Brian who helped a lot of the men check that they paid the right amount for their transport. Mr. Paget had moved on to teaching Brian some elementary bookkeeping and Brian had been happy to help his fellow workers to sort out what they needed to pay. It enabled him to practice his figures.

"I've been thinking O'Malley. I was wondering if you would like to start doing some building work for me."

"I would." Brian wondered what was coming.

"Well O'Malley…if I make sure that you do some building work for me in town then perhaps you could help me out."

Brian hesitated. He didn't trust Jamie, but Jamie seemed to take Brian's silence as confirmation of his willingness to help.

"It would make things easier if we did more of the bookkeeping up here at the Tannyard. I want to stop using the bookkeeper down at Mr. Wylie's yard. If I arranged for you to work on one of the building contracts here in Levenside you could be back at the Tannyard earlier than if you were doing farm work. You'd have time to help me sort out things here in the office."

161

Brian thought about the proposal. Jamie clearly wasn't offering him any extra money for this bookkeeping, but the building work would mean he was paid better than before, and he'd be able to find out more of what was going on in the Philbin business.

"Well? What do you say, O'Malley?"

"Yes Mr. Alexander I could do that."

"Good. If you help me O'Malley, I'll look after you."

Brian didn't make a direct response to this last remark. All he said was, "Shall I come to the office when I get back to the Tannyard each day?" Jamie nodded.

When he got outside Brian stood for a moment looking about him. He could hardly believe it. He had gone from being Joss's helper on his cart doing odd jobs on local farms to being Jamie Alexander's assistant in the Tannyard office all in the matter of months. Mr. Paget's insistence that he learn the rudiments of all "three R's" was paying off, just as Mr. Paget told him it would. Brian O'Malley was now effectively the bookkeeper for the Philbin business.

Nobody thought it necessary to tell Angus Wylie of the new arrangements. Jamie Alexander simply gave a copy of Brian's records to Angus Wylie's bookkeeper each week and for his part the bookkeeper at Wylie's yard was more than happy to get rid of some of the extra work Angus Wylie had given him.

But Brian noticed something straight away. Jamie expected him to keep two sets of records. What the men were paid each week and what each man paid back out of their earnings for Joss transporting them about to whatever job they were on.

Brian kept a second copy of all the records he gave to Jamie.

Jamie Alexander went with Danny Philbin's widow to the bank every Friday to withdraw the necessary cash to pay the men, but he never took Brian O'Malley along with him, until one week there was a query that Jamie couldn't deal with.

The following week when Jamie Alexander knocked at the door of Melville House, Brian O'Malley was with him. Ironically, although Brian had procrastinated about meeting Mrs. Philbin in case it got back to Jamie Alexander, it was Jamie who introduced them.

It didn't occur to Jamie Alexander even to acknowledge Brian O'Malley's presence, until Mrs. Philbin asked to be introduced to Brian.

She seemed pleased to meet a "new man" working in her husband's business. Once Brian spoke to Mrs. Philbin he realised he needn't have worried about approaching her. Not only was she friendly but she seemed interested that he had only recently arrived from Ireland.

When they arrived at the doors of the bank, the first thing that Brian noticed was the nameplate on the wall. It read, "The Western Bank of Scotland".

"Wait here O'Malley." Brian received Jamie Alexander's instructions with relief. His encounter with the Western Bank in Glasgow was still very vivid in his mind. What if someone in the bank recognised him?

As soon as Jamie and Mrs. Philbin went inside Brian moved away from the front door and stood at the side of the bank where there was an alleyway he could slip down if he needed to.

Jamie and Mrs. Philbin seemed to take forever to conclude their business. Brian's apprehension was growing when at last Jamie Alexander came out.

"Where's Mrs. Philbin?" Jamie was alone and he seemed distracted.

"Oh, the manager Mr. Scott wanted to speak to her." Brian waited for Jamie to elaborate but all he said was, "Let's go".

As they walked back to the Tannyard he kept asking himself why would the manager want to have a discussion with Mrs. Philbin without her foreman? Surely it couldn't be about him?

Brian often thought back to his encounter with the Philbins on the ferry. Despite his established intimacy with Maureen Connor, he couldn't get Margaret Philbin out of his mind. He remembered her striking blue eyes, how her smile had charmed him on the quayside, and how much he had enjoyed her company as they had sat on deck eating her mother's picnic.

Over the weekend Brian decided to go and see Mrs. Philbin. He was determined to find out what had happened to Patrick Philbin's family, and particularly his daughter, Margaret and if his problems with the bank were not over she might be the best source of information.

Donald Scott, the manager of the Levenside Branch of the Western Bank of Scotland had been surprised to receive a letter from the wife of the Chairman of the Bank. To be precise Donald Scott received two letters from Lady McPherson but only one was addressed to him, the other was addressed to a "Brian O'Malley Esq."

Sir Robert McPherson, the Chairman of the Bank had appointed Scott, at the relatively early age of 38, five years previously. The Chairman had been convinced that Levenside was one of those towns near to Glasgow that was likely to expand in the next few years and he had determined that the Western Bank would benefit from an early presence there. Within a couple of years Sir Robert had been proved right. One of the first substantial accounts that the bank had acquired in Levenside was that of Angus Wylie. Somewhat later Daniel Philbin had started to use the bank's services.

Donald Scott had a great deal of respect for his Chairman. He had never met his wife, Lady McPherson but one or two of his colleagues had told him that she was a formidable lady, and that she had also been the initial source of much of his wealth, so he read her letter with interest.

"Dear Mr. Scott,

I am writing to you in the strictest confidence. Although I have not yet made your acquaintance my husband has the highest regard for you and so I know that you will treat the contents of this letter with the utmost discretion.

You may be aware that recently my husband suffered a serious assault from which I am pleased to say he is now fully recovered. Had it not been for the intervention of a young man by the name of Mr. Brian O'Malley my husband would have undoubtedly suffered much more serious injuries than he actually occasioned.

Unfortunately, Mr. O'Malley left Glasgow before my husband or I had an opportunity to thank him for his endeavours on my husband's behalf. It is my belief that Mr. O'Malley is acquainted to a Mr. Patrick Philbin who has business interests in Levenside. Should you become aware of Mr. O'Malley's presence in Levenside, I would be grateful if you would write and keep me informed of his whereabouts. In addition, if you do discover the whereabouts of Mr. O'Malley I would be grateful if you would arrange delivery to him of the letter I have enclosed with this one.

I hope you do not find my requests too much of an imposition and I hope that I will have the pleasure of making your acquaintance on one of your future visits to Glasgow.

Most sincerely,

Lady Isobel McPherson".

Donald Scott pondered the contents of the letter. He knew neither Brian O'Malley nor Patrick Philbin, but he had no doubt that Patrick Philbin was the brother of Daniel Philbin, the recently deceased client of the bank. Daniel Philbin had made a favourable impression on Mr. Scott and despite Philbin's obviously humble origins, the manager of the Western Bank of Scotland had assessed Daniel Philbin as an astute businessman. Donald Scott considered Philbin's untimely death most unfortunate.

During his lifetime, Daniel Philbin had been anxious to safeguard both the future of his business and the future of his wife. Daniel had sought the bank's advice as to what ought to be done to secure her position. Donald Scott in turn had obtained advice for Philbin from one John Dawson, a lawyer who had recently moved to Levenside from Glasgow, and who was well thought of by the Bank.

The result was that now, following Daniel Philbin's death, most of the money in Daniel Philbin's account was held in trust for his wife's benefit. John Dawson refused to be one of the trustees of the "married woman's" account. He never acted for "Papist" clients, so in the end Danny Philbin had suggested that Mr. Scott himself should be a trustee and that the other trustee should be a Mr. Paget, a retired schoolteacher of Danny Philbin's acquaintance. Mr. Scott had had dealings with Mr. Paget over the setting up the new public library in Levenside and he had thought both Daniel Philbin's suggestions eminently sensible.

As a result, dealing with matters following Danny Philbin's death had proved much easier to deal with than might normally have been the case. Mrs. Philbin had told the trustees of her intention to keep her husband's business going until her brother-in-law could travel over from Ireland to take it over and her two trustees had both agreed to make available the money she needed from her trust fund.

Mr. Scott knew that Mrs. Philbin came into the bank with her foreman once a week to arrange the withdrawal of money to pay her employees. Once he had received Lady McPherson's letter Mr. Scott had instructed his staff that on Mrs. Philbin's next visit he would like to speak to her personally.

"Good day Mrs. Philbin. I hope this isn't inconvenient."

"No, no, not at all, Mr. Scott." There was silence for a moment. Mrs. Philbin waited for Mr. Scott to go on. Although Daniel Scott was younger than her, Mrs. Philbin felt intimidated by her bank manager. Had she not been, she might have sought more advice from Mr. Scott over her husband's business.

"Is there some problem with my account?" asked Mrs. Philbin.

"No. It isn't really about your own affairs Mrs. Philbin. I was going to ask if you might be able to assist the bank."

"I'll be glad to help if I can." Mrs. Philbin made her response more out of politeness than any belief that she could be of any assistance. She'd had no dealings with the bank before her husband's death. The only thought that occurred to her was that it was unlikely that Mr. Scott would want to borrow money. She fought back a nervous smile.

"One of the bank's clients has been trying to get in touch with a Mr. Brian O'Malley." Mr. Scott looked at Mrs. Philbin, trying to gauge if the name meant anything to her but there was no change to the expression on her face. "They are under the impression that Mr. O'Malley might be one of your employees, Mrs. Philbin."

"Oh… I'm afraid…" Mrs. Philbin was about to say she didn't really know any of her employees by name, apart from Jamie Alexander and Mungo Costello, when she remembered the rather good-looking young man she had been introduced to on the way to the bank and who she understood helped Jamie Alexander with the bookkeeping. Wasn't his name O'Malley?

Maybe she could be of some assistance.

CHAPTER 14

THE MEETING
WITH MRS. DANIEL PHILBIN

When Brian got to the Philbin house on the Howes Road he stood for a moment irresolute in front of her house. Then nervously he let the brass knocker fall against the door of Melville House.

"Mrs. Philbin we met yesterday. My name is Brian O'Malley. I work in the Tannyard."

Mrs. Philbin smiled. "Yes, I know. You came here with Mr. Alexander." Mrs. Philbin held the door open. "Do come in, Mr. O'Malley."

Brian O'Malley followed Mrs. Philbin into her house. As he looked round he was pleased he'd changed into his best clothes.

"Please sit down, Mr. O'Malley."

Although Maureen Connor had freshly washed Brian's clothes, he brushed the seat of his trousers before he sat down in the leather chair that Mrs. Philbin indicated.

"It is very fortuitous that you called. I wanted to speak with you."

"Indeed?"

"Yes, is there a particular reason for your visit to-day?"

"Yes, ma'am." Brian hesitated. He desperately wanted to know what had happened in the bank, but the most important thing he decided was to find out what had happened to Margaret Philbin and her father.

He took a deep breath, "I travelled over from Ireland on the same ferry as your husband's brother…I was wondering what had happened to him."

"You were on the same boat as Patrick?" Mrs. Philbin looked at him, as if searching for confirmation of what he said in his expression.

"Yes ma'am. He and his wife, and their daughter Margaret."

"How were they when you saw them? How was Patrick?" Brian O'Malley recognised the anxiety in Mrs. Philbin's voice. He was unsure how to answer.

"They seemed pleased to be coming over to join you. Mr. Philbin seemed keen on helping you with the business. They were very kind to me on the boat."

"And my brother-in-law seemed well?"

"Yes."

Mrs. Philbin paused before she spoke again. "Is Patrick the reason you're here in Levenside, Mr. O'Malley?"

Brian hesitated, "Well…yes."

Mrs. Philbin didn't respond immediately.

"You mustn't repeat what I'm going to tell you Mr. O'Malley. Not to anyone. Can I trust you?"

"Of course, Mrs. Philbin."

"My brother-in-law and his family are still in Glasgow, Mr. O'Malley. Patrick was taken ill as he was leaving Glasgow to come here." The worry was now clearly to be seen on Mrs. Philbin's face. "The doctors in Glasgow feel he may have a similar heart problem to my husband's."

Brian tried to digest the news. "I'm sorry to hear that Mrs. Philbin."

"I don't want that information getting back to Mr. Wylie…or anybody else"

"Of course not, Mrs. Philbin."

She wondered if she had said too much already, but for some reason she felt better now that she had confided her secret to Brian O'Malley. She hoped her trust in the young Irishman was not misplaced. However, he knew Patrick, and he seemed genuinely concerned about what had happened to her brother.

"Tell me Mr. O'Malley, how are things at the Tannyard?"

Brian paused, he needed to choose his words carefully. She must know about the workers now having to pay for their transport. She must have agreed it with Jamie or Angus Wylie, but she might not know how much bad feeling this deduction from the men's pay had caused. "I don't really know Mrs. Philbin, but I'm afraid the new arrangement with Joss Freebody hasn't gone down well with the men."

"Joss Freebody?" She thought for a moment. "Isn't he the man with the horse and cart?

"Yes Mrs Philbin, that's the man."

"He used to help Danny move his materials. What's this new arrangement?"

"Well, Mrs. Philbin Joss ferries the men out to the building sites and farms that we have contracts to work on. Your husband used to pay Joss for doing that, but now the men are having to pay Joss. I understood it was something Mr. Wylie suggested to you, to save money. I'm afraid it hasn't gone down well with the men."

Mrs. Philbin looked troubled. "When did this happen Mr. O'Malley?"

"About six weeks ago."

"Mr. Wylie never suggested any new arrangement to me Mr. O'Malley, and if he had, I certainly wouldn't have agreed to it. It's not fair on the men." Mrs. Philbin pulled out a small handkerchief she had tucked up one of her sleeves and made a ball with it and closed her hand round it, squeezing it tight. "I'm not surprised it hasn't gone down well with them, Mr. O'Malley."

The scheme to charge the men for transport must had been thought up by Jamie Alexander. He had lied to the men that it was something agreed by Mrs. Philbin. Jamie was creaming off the extra money for himself from the business. Probably no one else knew about it, not even Angus Wylie. Brian wondered if the pay cut he had imposed "to save the business" was also something else Mrs. Philbin hadn't been told about.

"…and I would like to discuss matters with the Bank."

"I'm sorry Mrs. Philbin, I didn't hear what you said."

"I was saying that I have other matters of concern about my late husband's business. I have arranged a meeting at the bank with the trustees of my account. It would be useful if you were there."

Mrs. Philbin transferred the handkerchief to her left hand, and now she placed the flattened palm of her right hand on the arm of the settee, looking at the back of her hand rather than Brian as she spoke.

"There is another reason for you to be there Mr. O'Malley. Mr. Scott, the manager, tells me that there is an important client of the bank who has been trying to get in touch with you." Brian tried to keep his face impassive. He had been pleased to receive Mrs. Philbin's invitation and been about to accept it until he heard the additional reason for involving him in the meeting. He hesitated.

"I'm sorry, did you say that one of the bank's clients wants to get in touch with me?" Now Mrs. Philbin glanced at him again.

"Yes Mr O'Malley, that is what the manager told me." Mrs. Philbin watched as Brian O'Malley tried to digest her unexpected disclosure. She had been somewhat surprised herself that one of the bank's clients wanted to get in touch with the part time bookkeeper in her husband's business, so she explained, "Mr. Scott is holding a letter for you and he asked if I could arrange for you to collect it. In the circumstances I thought we could combine you doing that, with my meeting."

Brian didn't like what he was hearing. Why would one of the Western Bank's clients write to him? The only people he knew connected with the bank had accused him of a serious assault. If he went with Mrs. Philbin, he was more likely to end up meeting the constabulary than the bank manager.

"Of course, I'll pay you for any lost wages Mr. O'Malley." Mrs. Philbin had mistaken the reason for Brian O'Malley's hesitation about the proposed meeting.

"It's not that Mrs. Philbin it's just…"

"…Mr. O'Malley there are clearly things going on at the Tannyard that I do not know about. I need to get some advice and it would be most helpful if you could come to the meeting I am arranging. I was going to ask Mr. Alexander to be present too, but in view of what you have told me I'm not sure now how much I should be relying on his advice."

Brian realised that Mrs. Philbin had decided to put a lot of trust in him even though she barely knew him. She must be genuinely worried about what was going on. He had no option, if he wanted to help Margaret Philbin, and her family, he'd have to take the risk. He had come to Levenside hoping that the Philbins might help him. From what Mrs. Philbin has said and from what he knew of what was going on in the Tannyard it might be that it was the Philbin family rather than himself that needed assistance.

"I'd only be too glad to help."

He could see that Mrs. Philbin's relief at his response. "One final matter Mr. O'Malley I would be grateful if, even at the meeting with the bank, you did not mention that my brother-in-law's ill health."

"Of course."

CHAPTER 15

A MAN OF BUSINESS

Brian O'Malley had arranged to meet Mrs. Philbin outside the Western Bank of Scotland. Although Brian was unaware of it, the impressive new building had been personally commissioned by Sir Robert McPherson. Sir Robert had wanted something that gave the impression of solidity and permanence, rather than affluence. In that he had succeeded, and the building reminded Brian uncomfortably of the main bank in Glasgow in which he had been incarcerated. Once again, he was looking at a building that would be neither easy to break into or escape from.

He had convinced himself that Mrs. Philbin's meeting was not part of a conspiracy to entrap him. He was sure that if Lady McPherson knew of his presence in Levenside, and still considered him responsible for the assault on her husband, there would have been no lure of a letter, the first he would have known about it would have been a constable at Maureen Connor's door.

However, as he stood there waiting for Mrs. Philbin, his confidence started to wear thin, and his feeling of unease started to grow. He was relieved when at last he saw Mrs. Philbin approaching down the hill.

"Thank you for coming Mr. O'Malley. Shall we go in?"

When Mrs. Philbin and Brian O'Malley were shown into Mr. Scott's office she said, "This is Mr. Brian O'Malley. I know you have business with him later Mr. Scott, but I think it would be useful to have him at our meeting."

"Of course, as you wish Mrs. Philbin. I am pleased to meet you Mr. O'Malley." Mr. Scott held out his hand. He thought he did well to contain his surprise, for at his previous meeting with Mrs. Philbin had barely been able to recall who Brian O'Malley was, and that had led Mr. Scott to believe O'Malley was simply a labourer in her late husband's business. Unfortunately, it was on that basis that he had written to Lady McPherson in Glasgow, to brief her on his success in discovering Brian O'Malley's whereabouts.

The presence of the other person in the room somewhat bemused Brian O'Malley. It was Mr. Paget. He was sitting at Mr. Scott's conference table when they arrived. He stood up as the others entered. After shaking hands with Mrs. Philbin, Mr. Paget shook hands with Brian O'Malley.

"It's good to see you again Mr. O'Malley," said Mr. Paget with obvious warmth. Then he turned to Mr. Scott and said, "I have already had the pleasure of making Mr. O'Malley's acquaintance."

The fact that his other trustee knew Brian O'Malley was not only a surprise to Mr. Scott, it was also one to Mrs. Daniel Philbin. Realising that both were re-assessing their views of Brian O'Malley, Mr. Paget sat down again which prompted Mr. Scott to invite the others to take seats at the oak table and while Mr. Scott helped Mrs. Philbin pull in her chair Mr. Paget spoke again, "I assume Mrs. Philbin that we are here because you have some concerns about how your late husband's business at the Tannyard is being handled on your behalf."

"That is quite correct Mr. Paget," said Mrs. Philbin.

"I know Mr. O'Malley is a man of discretion but perhaps he has raised a few matters of concern with you Mrs. Philbin?"

"He has." Mrs. Philbin now she started to relax. It seemed that she had made a correct decision in placing her trust in the young man sitting beside her.

"Mr. O'Malley has raised a particular problem that I was not aware of, and I am grateful for his doing so." Mrs. Philbin turned to Brian. "Please tell Mr. Paget and Mr. Scott what you told me Mr. O'Malley."

All eyes now turned towards Brian, but he didn't feel self-conscious as he told them of the change in the transport arrangements at Philbins and how the workers now had to pay for it.

"I had no idea this had occurred until Mr. O'Malley told me. I certainly never agreed these new arrangements with Jamie Alexander." said Mrs. Philbin.

"I understand Mr. O'Malley that you carry out much of the bookkeeping for Philbin business these days?" said Mr. Paget.

"Not really, Mr. Paget. I only prepare details of the wage payments for Jamie Alexander to give to the bank and Mrs. Philbin. I only have a limited knowledge of what the business receives."

"Yes, most of the payments would be directly to the bank. No doubt the bank keeps Mrs. Philbin informed," said Mr. Paget looking at Mr. Scott.

"That is correct," Mr. Scott looked uncomfortable. He felt he should be leading the discussion rather than Mr. Paget.

Mr. Paget nodded. "Well, the most important question is probably for Mrs. Philbin to answer. You have no knowledge of this charge made to your employees. You receive none of this money from Jamie Alexander?

"I knew nothing about it until Mr O'Malley told me. I receive no money from Mr. Alexander I simply arrange for him to collect the men's wages here each week."

"Well Madam, if that is the case, I believe that you and your business are being defrauded." Mr. Paget raised his eyebrows in silent interrogation of Mr. Scott, obviously looking for corroboration of his assessment of what was going on at the Tannyard.

For a moment there was silence and then finally Mr. Scott spoke. "I fear that Mr. Paget may be right. Mr. O'Malley can you let me have a copy of the records that you keep each week without Mr. Alexander knowing about it?"

Brian nodded. "That shouldn't be a problem Mr. Scott."

Brian was just beginning to feel a bit more optimistic about the future, when Mrs. Philbin spoke again. "There is another matter that I think I need advice on." Mrs. Philbin produced two documents from the bag resting in her lap. As she placed the papers on the table she explained they were contracts for extra work that Angus Wylie had suggested Philbins should take on including a farm contract that she had agreed should be transferred from his own firm.

Brian's heart sank as he saw Mr. Scott frown and glance at Mr. Paget.

"These are copies of the contracts you agreed with Mr. Wylie, Mrs. Philbin?" asked Mr. Scott, the bank manager.

"They are. Mr. Wylie told me the extra work would help tide my business over."

"I see that you have signed both contracts." Mrs. Philbin nodded. "Did you take any advice before you did so?" asked Mr. Scott. Brian couldn't help feeling sorry for Mrs. Philbin. He watched her shake her head.

"Only from Mr. Wylie, he said it was work that could easily be combined with what my husband's firm was already doing. He said he was interested in purchasing the business, so he wished to ensure it carried on as a going concern."

"I see." Mr. Scott seemed oblivious to Mrs. Philbin's discomfort. "I think it would be sensible if I asked Mr. Dawson, one of the bank's solicitors, to have a look at these..." He looked inquiringly at Mr. Paget who had throughout maintained his usual imperturbable expression. The schoolteacher nodded.

Mr. Scott turned back to Mrs. Philbin. "I think any further advice will have to wait until we hear from Mr. Dawson. Is there anything else Mrs. Philbin...Mr. O'Malley...Mr. Paget?"

No one spoke.

"Good, well I think that concludes matters for the moment. I will arrange another meeting as soon as we have Mr. Dawson's advice and I have had a closer look at your accounts."

The bank manager stood up obviously feeling more in control of what was happening. "Mr. O'Malley would you be kind enough to wait a moment, while I see Mrs. Philbin and Mr. Paget out."

Brian O'Malley waited uneasily in Mr. Scott's office. It seemed ages before Mr. Scott came back, but when he did so there were no constables, no handcuffs - all Mr. Scott had in his hand was a pale white envelope.

"I have been entrusted with a letter for you Mr. O'Malley. I told Mrs. Philbin that it was from a client of the bank, but that is not strictly true. It is from Lady McPherson. She is the wife of the Chairman of the Western Bank, Mr. O'Malley." Mr. Scott looked at Brian O'Malley to see if the significance of the name had registered, but Brian had determined that whatever happened on Mr. Scott's return he would not react or show any surprise, so he remained silent, his face expressionless. Mr. Scott pushed the letter across the table.

"You have …encountered Lady McPherson previously?" Mr. Scott could not help his inquisitiveness getting the better of him. Even he, a senior manager of the bank, had not met her.

Brian hesitated. "Yes Mr. Scott…I have met Lady McPherson."

"Indeed?"

"Yes…I'm afraid I must be going Mr. Scott. Thank you for delivering Lady McPherson's letter." With that Brian stood up, picking up the envelope as he did so, frustrating Mr. Scott's attempt to continue his cross-examination.

As they reached the door of the bank Mr. Scott spoke, "There's just one further thing, Mr. O'Malley." Brian tried to keep the same expression on his face as he turned and faced the banker.

"I'd just like to thank you for your help. Mrs. Philbin needs someone who knows something about business to help her until her brother-in-law gets here." Brian stared at Mr. Scott for a moment.

"I've been only too happy to help the Philbins."

Mr. Scott shook his hand. As he walked away from the bank Brian O'Malley was smiling.

He waited until he got back to Maureen's before he read the letter. The letter was both a letter of apology and a letter of thanks from Lady McPherson. Those responsible for assaulting her husband had been identified. She concluded the letter with an offer to help to Brian O'Malley in any way she could, including assistance in finding employment in Glasgow.

He hadn't felt bitter about what had happened in Glasgow, but it was relief to know that he could at least put that episode behind him. It was thoughtful and generous of Lady McPherson to write. A few days previously he might have taken up her kind offer but there was no way he could leave Levenside now. The Philbins needed his help. Levenside was where his future now lay.

CHAPTER 16

BRIAN LEAVES MAUREEN

The second meeting at the bank ten days later with Mr. Scott, Mrs. Philbin and Mr. Paget was a more sombre occasion than the first. Once more Mrs. Philbin had asked Brian O'Malley to be present and Mr. Paget and Mr. Scott seemed to assume that he would be present.

However, this time Mr. Scott made sure there was no doubt that he was in charge of the meeting. He came straight to the point.

"Mrs. Philbin we have considered the current outgoings of the Philbin business and its future obligations." Mr. Scott paused ensuring he gave added weight to what was to follow. "It is the view of your trustees that you cannot afford to keep your husband's business going in its current state for much longer. You are paying out much more than the business is receiving. If you carry on like this you will end up without enough money to live on. Do you have a definite date yet for when your brother-in-law will be here in Levenside?"

Mrs. Philbin glanced at Brian O'Malley before she shook her head. "No. I'm afraid I don't."

"In that case Mrs. Philbin I think you have no alternative. You will have to sell the business," said Mr. Scott.

Mrs. Philbin looked shocked.

Brian glanced at Mr. Paget, but Mr. Paget's face gave nothing away. "Who are you suggesting Mrs. Philbin should sell the business to Mr. Scott - surely not Angus Wylie?" asked Brian.

Mr. Scott raised his eyebrows, "Why not? …If Mr. Wylie is willing to pay what the business is worth…"

"…What about the money Jamie Alexander has been taking out of the business?"

"My suggestion is that matter should be handed over to the constabulary. I am doubtful if much of that money will be recovered. There is no evidence that Angus Wylie is involved in Jamie Alexander's fraud."

"…What about the contracts that Mr. Wylie got Mrs. Philbin to sign?"

"Mr. Dawson has advised that Mrs. Philbin may be able to set those contracts aside in the long term because Mr. Wylie may have misled her. However, I think in the short term the threat of litigation is likely to be a useful tool to ensure that Mr. Wylie pays a proper price for her husband's business."

Mr. Scott's view that the Philbin business would struggle to survive might be correct, and that selling the business was the most practical solution but handing the business to Angus Wylie would have awful consequences, for all the men who worked at the Tannyard, including Brian. There had to be another way.

"Before Mrs. Philbin decides to sell her husband's business she will need to consider if there are any other options open to her," said Brian.

"Indeed, but I think her options are limited, Mr O'Malley…very limited."

There was little more that could be said. Mrs Philbin left first asking Brian O'Malley to call and see her the following day and then Brian and Mr. Paget left the bank together.

Brian asked the question that he had been wanting to ask Mr. Paget since the first meeting at the bank ten days before. "Mr. Paget I never realised you were Mrs. Philbin's trustee. May I ask how that came about?"

"It's quite simple Mr. O'Malley. Just like you, Danny Philbin couldn't read or write very well when he came to Levenside. We didn't have the library then, so he came down to the school and asked if I knew if there was anybody who could help him. I thought it was brave of him to ask, so I helped him." Mr. Paget smiled. "He set up his own business and when it became successful he wanted to make sure his wife was

provided for, and he set up a trust for her, and asked me to be a trustee."
He paused, and then he added. "I'm afraid I couldn't tell you I was Mrs.
Philbin's trustee without obtaining her permission."

"Do you have a moment to discuss the Philbin business, Mr. Paget?"

"Of course, why don't you come and have tea with me."

The two of them walked to Mr. Paget's small house on the outskirts
of Levenside. It had a view across the road to the River Leven. Brian had
never been to Mr. Paget's home before.

The biggest problem for Danny Philbin's business they both agreed
was the contract with the various farms on the Balloch Estate. It provided
for an hourly rate that made it barely profitable, so it was no wonder
Angus Wylie had tried to get the contracts off his books, but that wasn't
the major problem for the Philbins.

The agreement was for ongoing maintenance work, as well as farm
work, and the owner of the Balloch Estate had only allowed Angus Wylie
to transfer the contract over to Philbins provided all payments for the
maintenance work to be carried out under the contract were deferred.
No money would come into the Mrs. Philbin's account until the following year, after the harvest was complete. Philbins would receive nothing
for the best part of a year in the meantime it would be required to carry
out much of the maintenance work on the Balloch Estate.

Mr. Paget told Brian that Mr. Scott took the view that it was just
too much a risk for Mrs. Philbin to finance that contract. Mr. Scott had
been very firm about that, and Mr. Paget said he agreed.

"How long do you think Mrs. Philbin has to come up with any
proposals Mr Paget?"

"Mr. Scott won't let things drift for very long. I would say she has
two weeks at the most. Then he'll insist we approach Angus Willey on
Mrs. Philbin's behalf to sell the business."

"Why is Mr. Scott so keen on letting Angus Wylie have the business?"

"I don't think he's keen. It's just that he can't see any alternative.
He thinks with Mr. Dawson's help he can ensure Mrs. Philbin can get a
good price from Wylie, certainly enough for her to live comfortably on."

"The bank could lend the business some money to keep it going."

"Mrs. Philbin is not a businesswoman. I'm afraid if Mr. Scott won't
let her risk her own money, he's unlikely to risk the bank's money."

Brian thought for a moment. "Would he loan money to me, do you think?"

Mr. Paget saw the earnest look on Brian's face. "Mr. O'Malley there's no doubt you have a head for business, but you are not what a bank would consider a good risk. You are not what they would describe as a man of substance."

The initial discussion with Mr. Paget cleared Brian's mind. He knew what needed to be done. He had two weeks. During that he find to find them enough money to get the Philbin business through the next twelve months.

Once the Wylie contracts had run their course or been set aside, once the Jamie Alexander situation was sorted out, and once there was a new foreman he had no doubt he could make Philbins back into a profitable business again. He had enough experience now to be able to help Patrick Philbin tender for new work when the time came.

That evening he sat at Maureen Connor's kitchen table and worked out exactly how much of a loan he felt was required, and the following day when he finished work he went back and saw Mr. Paget again. The librarian didn't ask Brian where he thought the proposed loan was coming from all he said was, "When you ask for your loan add an extra 10% on top of that figure."

"Why?"

"Because any serious lender will expect you to ask for a reserve of that nature, in case something unexpected happens, and nothing is certain, you may need it." So, Brian amended his proposal and added another 10% to the total of the loan. Mr. Paget told him to call it a contingency provision.

Mrs. Philbin was the first person Brian O'Malley told of his intention to go to Glasgow. She assumed that Brian intended to see her brother-in-law to check on his health and to discuss the future of the Philbin business and Brian didn't disabuse her, but that was not his immediate purpose in going to Glasgow.

He accepted that Mr. Scott would not entertain an application from him for a loan and so he decided that he would go and see the only other person who might help him. He would go and see Lady Macpherson.

He had nothing to lose. With her connections she would know someone who could help him save the Philbin business. The worst Lady McPherson could do was to say no. In view of her letter, he didn't anticipate facing a shotgun on this occasion.

Correspondence between the bank in Levenside and the bank in Glasgow was swift and Lady McPherson replied to his request to see her by return of post. Mr. Scott's curiosity increased incrementally as he had passed on the correspondence, but he remained none the wiser of the relationship between Lady McPherson and Brian O'Malley for neither Lady McPherson, nor Brian O'Malley chose to enlighten him.

Brian tried to convince himself that he was going to Glasgow because he owed it to the Philbin family to try and save their business, but he knew wasn't doing it just for that. Of course, he wanted to save the Philbin business both for himself and for them, but there was more to it than that. He wanted to see Margaret Philbin again.

He knew Margaret Philbin was the woman he wanted in his life. He couldn't forget her, despite his involvement with Maureen Connor.

Once he had spoken to Mrs. Daniel Philbin and agreed that he would go and see her brother-in-law, it became clear to Brian that he had no other choice but to make a clean break with Maureen. He shrank from telling her. She loved him. More than that, she hoped that one day he would marry her, but he couldn't pretend to Maureen that he would be coming back to her. If he had the chance, he was going to tell Margaret Philbin of his feelings for her, so he had to tell Maureen he was leaving her for good, that he could no longer stay in the Tannergate with her, sharing her bed.

There was no way he could tell that to Maureen without hurting her so he put it off for as long as he could. At first, he simply told her that he would be going to see the bank in Glasgow about a loan for the Philbin business, but the evening before he planned to travel to Glasgow, he knew he had to tell her the truth.

The two new lodgers had gone to bed and he and Maureen were sitting in the kitchen. Just as he steeled himself to tell her, Maureen spoke. "You'll be leaving in the morning?"

"Yes."

"How long will you be gone?"

Brian's courage failed him. "I don't know."

Maureen just looked at him for some time without speaking. Then it came to him. Maureen already knew what he was leaving her. He dropped his gaze. "Maureen…"

"You're not coming back, are you?" Brian forced himself to meet her gaze. He could see the pain in her eyes. "No, … not to the Tannergate."

The look on Brian's face told Maureen everything. There was no point in arguing. The next morning he would be gone, gone for good. She turned her head so that he could not see how badly his words had wounded her and then she got up and left the room.

He sat in the kitchen feeling wretched and wrestling with his guilt. He knew how much Maureen had done for him, but worse he knew how much she still loved him. He sensed rather than heard her come back into the kitchen.

"Will you be coming back for your stuff when you get back from Glasgow." Brian heard the hope in her voice.

"No. I'll take everything I need with me in the morning." He did not meet her anguished look. "It'll be easier for us both that way."

"But you need your clothes washed. Your things aren't ready." Brian looked at her. She knew more than anyone how pitifully few his clothes and possessions were.

"Maureen…"

"Don't say anything more Brian." She sat down beside him and took hold of his hand. They sat in silence for a while. Then Maureen stood up and walked back out of the kitchen. She sat on her front doorstep until she heard Brian go up to bed.

How would she bear it if she saw him when he came back to Levenside? How could she smile and say, "good day" and just pass him by? She sat for some time on the step alone. She stared into the distance in front of her, but she saw nothing.

Brian slept alone in Maureen's bed that night. He heard her moving around in the room during the night when he woke briefly from his troubled sleep, but she did not come to bed.

In the morning he found Maureen had neatly packed all his clothes and belongings in an old cardboard suitcase that had belonged to her husband. It was lying open on the kitchen table. All his washing had been done Maureen had kept the kitchen stove alight all night to dry his clothes.

"I think everything is there. There's a couple of things I still had of my husband's as well."

"Maureen. I…" He looked at her, but she didn't meet his gaze.

She closed the case and pushed it across the table towards him. "You'd better be going."

She still wouldn't meet his gaze, so he picked up the suitcase.

Maureen didn't try to touch Brian or kiss him goodbye. Even a final hug she knew would have been unbearable, but she followed him to the door.

He turned around once he was outside. He stood on the doorstep for a moment.

"Look after yourself," as he spoke Maureen lifted her gaze for just one fleeting moment and once again he saw the pain in her eyes before she looked away. Then he turned and walked away down the hill. As she watched him go, she raised her hand to wave, but then she let it drop, for he did not look back.

She watched him all the way down the hill. At the bottom of the hill he appeared to hesitate, and for just a moment he stopped. Then he walked on.

"Goodbye and safe journey," she spoke out loud but only she heard the words. Brian was too far away to hear anything she said.

As Brian O'Malley listened to the noise of the train clattering along the rails taking him towards his appointment at the Head Office of the Western Bank of Scotland in Glasgow, he wondered what would have happened to him if Maureen Connor hadn't taken him in all those months before. Then he thought about Ireland and all that had happened to him since he had left his homeland and he vowed that he would save the Philbin business. He would make it successful and then…then he would seek revenge for what had been done to his family.

END OF PART TWO

PART 3

LONDON AND LEVENSIDE – WORLDS APART

CHAPTER 1

A MAN OF SUBSTANCE

Brian O'Malley sat with a two day old copy of the London Times unread in his lap and stared unseeingly at the fireplace. Without his granddaughter the big house was a lonely place. No longer could he look forward to a lively greeting from Meta when he returned from work.

Only the ticking of the black marble clock on the mantlepiece incessant like the drip of a tap broke the silence. He wondered if Meta had got over the young priest she had fallen in love with. There had been no mention of John McBride in her letters and he wondered if he had spoken to Meta before he had fulfilled his intention to join up and go to France. The young man was driven by good intentions but he wasn't cut out to be a priest, even less was he cut out to be a soldier. Brian doubted whether John McBride could survive the awfulness of what was going on in France.

It was strange how some of the young man's mannerisms had reminded him of Mungo Costello. Brian O'Malley's thoughts wandered back to his arrival in Levenside forty years before and to his first lodgings with Maureen Connor, where he had shared a room with Mungo. Even then, the squalid houses in the Tannergate had been a breeding ground for disease so when Dr. Cunningham had told him that illness had again broken out in the Tannergate he hadn't been surprised.

He had encountered a drained looking Dr. Cunningham late the previous afternoon. The doctor's expression was not simply the result of exhaustion. The emotion as he spoke was obvious. He had told Brian that John Murphy a young boy of seven, a child the doctor had helped to bring into the world, had died that morning. Brian O'Malley started pacing across the room. There must be something he could do. He owed so much to the town and the people who had taken him in so long ago.

Just after 9.00 o'clock the following morning, he made a telephone call to the head office of the Western Bank of Scotland in Glasgow. This was only the second time he had presumed on his personal relationship with the current Chairman of the Western Bank. After that short call, he walked down into town to keep his appointment with Mr. McCann, the new manager of the bank's branch in Levenside. In Brian's view McCann he didn't have anything like the ability of his predecessor.

Mr. McCann welcomed Brian O'Malley into his office. O'Malley was a good customer. However, the manager couldn't stop himself from gently shaking his head as Brian outlined his request. The loan he was seeking was well beyond Mr. McCann's discretion, but he was certain that even if he referred it to his head office Brian O'Malley's proposal would never be agreed.

Mr. McCann didn't say that to Brian O'Malley's face. O'Malley had a sound building business but he simply wasn't a man of sufficient substance to be considered for a loan of the magnitude he was suggesting. Certainly, not at the rate of interest O'Malley was proposing. Had it been someone like Angus Wylie then the proposal might have been worth discussing in detail.

However, when Mr. McCann suggested that it was unlikely that a loan would be forthcoming Brian O'Malley had sought an assurance that Mr. McCann would refer the matter to his Head Office for a further opinion, and he was so quietly insistent that Mr. McCann eventually promised that he would raise the matter with his Head Office. He quite liked O'Malley. As he showed him out of the bank he couldn't help thinking it was unfortunate that O'Malley didn't understand more about banking and business.

Mr. McCann decided to put through the call to the Manager at the main branch of the Western Bank of Scotland in Glasgow straight away. Best get it out of the way. To his surprise, after he outlined the nature of his call McCann found himself being passed through to the Chairman's office. It took some time for the Chairman to come on the line.

"Is that you McCann?"

"Yes, Sir Henry I…"

"…How much detail have you gone into with Mr. O'Malley over this loan?"

"Well …I thought in view of the amount of the loan and the interest…"

"…What is the purpose of this loan? Is it a personal loan?"

"… Not really, Sir Henry."

"What do you mean by 'not really'."

"Well…he wants to negotiate a preferential loan for the local council on the basis of his personal guarantee. I thought the amount of the loan was so substantial that the bank would…." McCann's response tailed off.

"…that the bank would what?

"Well …that the bank wouldn't consider it."

"I see. That was your view?"

"Well…yes."

"Did O'Malley indicate if he was willing to give any security for this loan?"

"Yes he did. He offered his personal guarantee and a charge over some of his business interests."

"And his business interests are?"

"He said he had some substantial shareholdings with brokers in Glasgow and London. He stated they would be adequate for the bank's needs."

"Well, are they?"

"I'm…not sure. I didn't make a full note of them at our first meeting because… He's got quite a reasonable building and labouring business here in Levenside. It's quite successful, but not big enough to be security for a loan of this size."

"I see. Did you ask him for a list of the shareholdings he was talking about?"

"No. I didn't…"

"Would it surprise you to know that I have a full list of those assets?'

"Well…"

"What is the most recent set of accounts you have seen for his company?

"I …I don't recall. …I don't have them in front of me…clearly I check the figures on his bank accounts with us fairly regularly. There is a reasonable balance for the company's ongoing needs but not the kind of substantial balance that some of our other customers hold."

McCann thought of the cash that Angus Wylie held in his business account. It was almost ten times that in O'Malley's account. He had details of Wylie's accounts at his fingertips. Wylie's business was the one that would lead financial expansion in Levenside. However, that wasn't what the Chairman wanted to know.

"Did you ask Mr. O'Malley if he held other bank accounts apart from his business accounts with you?"

"Well no… he obviously has his own personal account, but that is only a small account."

"What property does Mr. O'Malley own in Levenside?

"Well he owns two houses on the Howes Road, which is one of the best residential roads here in Levenside. He bought them some time ago. He gave a long lease of one to his eldest daughter when she married. We hold the deeds on both the properties, but only for safe keeping. There is no loan outstanding on them. He owns quite a lot of property in the Tannergate but those are mostly just tenement properties that his workers rent."

"And did you ask Mr. O'Malley what property he owns outside Levenside?"

"I wasn't aware that he owned any property outside Levenside."

"So, you didn't ask him?"

"No… No, I didn't ask him." Mr. McCann had not noticed before how stifling his office was. He needed a glass of water. His mouth was very dry.

There was a pause at the other end of the line.

"Well Mr. McCann it may surprise you to know that Mr. O'Malley holds a number of other accounts with the main branch here in Glasgow and has considerable property interests as well, both here in Glasgow… and in London."

"I see."

"I hope you do," said Sir Henry Wrightson. There was silence again at the other end of the line. Mr. McCann swallowed hard, aware of the threat implicit in this last sentence.

Then Sir Henry continued, "The Western Bank of Scotland is a bank Mr. McCann. The purpose of a bank is to lend money so that it can charge interest. That is how the Western Bank of Scotland makes its profits. The Bank particularly likes to lend money to persons it considers as being a good risk. If it can identify such persons it is even willing to give them preferential rates. I have taken the time since Mr. O'Malley has been with this bank to identify Mr. O'Malley as such a person. Local authorities also tend to be bodies the bank likes to lend money to." There was another pause. "Do I need to say any more Mr. McCann?"

"No, Sir Henry."

"Good day."

There was a click at the other end of the line.

As Mr. McCann put the telephone back in its candlestick cradle he shook his head. He decided that he needed more than a glass of water. He walked over to his drinks cabinet and poured himself a large glass of whisky. He wondered how he had managed to misjudge the situation so badly.

Later in the day, on his way to the monthly meeting of the Levenside Burgh Council, Brian O'Malley called into the bank once again as he had arranged. For the first time in their dealings together, McCann produced a bottle of his best whisky and offered him a glass. Brian politely refused the invitation, but nevertheless McCann poured two glasses and drank his own down in a series of nervous gulps. "Are you able to let me have a list of the shareholdings you referred at our previous meeting?"

"Indeed." Brian O'Malley produced a list from the small attaché case he was carrying. "I think those should be sufficient to provide security for the loan of the size we were discussing. However, here is list of my property investments should you require further security."

"These are properties in Glasgow and London?"

"Yes …and now Mr. McCann I'm afraid I have a Burgh Council meeting to attend. Could you be as good as to let me know if the bank is willing to agree in principle to make the loan I am seeking?"

Mr. McCann glanced at the documents in front of him and took a deep breath. "I can confirm that in principle the Western Bank of Scotland is willing to make such a loan."

"At the rate I am requesting?"

"Yes, subject to your lodging sufficient of these securities with the bank, we are willing to make the loan at the preferential rate you have requested." Brian O'Malley immediately stood up, shook hands with Mr. McCann, bade him good day, and set off for the town hall.

After the door closed behind him Mr. McCann stood staring at it for a good thirty seconds. Then he noticed the second untouched drink and after only a moment's hesitation he picked it up and drank it down quickly.

CHAPTER 2

THE COUNCIL MEETING

Since his election as a Bailie, Brian had not missed a single Burgh Council meeting. Most meetings of the Council just rubber-stamped the recommendations of Arthur Finlay, the Town Clerk. Finlay had taken over from the previous Town Clerk ten years previously. He was a dour little man who had a puffy face, and who, whatever the weather, perspired a lot. The sweat betrayed his fondness for drink, but Brian found Finlay was a capable and competent Clerk who rarely put propositions before the Council without carefully considering them.

The meeting would be divided into two. The first half would deal with general Council matters and the second would deal with local Board of Health matters. That second part was the part of the meeting that concerned Brian.

When he neared the town hall Brian saw ahead of him the tall figure of John Dawson, the senior partner of the firm of solicitors that the Western Bank of Scotland in Levenside used. Dawson was also a Bailie. Like Arthur Finlay, he rarely smiled. Dawson was pre-occupied and he was tugging irritably at his wing collar as he mounted the steps to the town hall. He reached the top of the steps and glanced round. He saw Brian but made no attempt to acknowledge him. Dawson was an ardent member of the Presbyterian Church.

Despite John Dawson's coldness towards him, Brian had a great deal of respect for him. Dawson did not handle Brian's legal affairs, but that was only because Brian knew that it would have been futile to ask him.

Dawson's attitude at the Council meeting was going to be important. As would Angus Wylie's, the man Brian O'Malley had been in competition with for most of his working life. Wylie was probably the wealthiest man in Levenside; he certainly owned more of the land and houses around the town than anybody else. There was even a rumour that he had recently purchased 400 acres of the Balloch Estate, which had a frontage of over a mile on the River Leven and Loch Lomond. Brian had a feeling that Wylie had probably started the rumour about the Balloch Estate himself because he knew Brian would love to acquire a part of the Balloch Estate.

Wylie was a big man in every sense of the word, well over six feet, with broad shoulders and a large paunch.

Brian frowned, without the support of Wylie or Dawson, he could only count on four, or possibly five, Council votes. He had to get the support of one of these two, because nearly all the rest would follow their lead. Because of their business rivalry he was sure that Wylie would be implacably opposed to any proposals Brian put forward. Brian's main hope was that Dawson would support the proposals, but that too presented a problem, for Brian's relationship with Dawson was tainted by the religious divide that split so much of Levenside.

However, Dawson had sided with Brian once the previous year when the Council had agreed Arthur Finlay's proposal for the Council to acquire a new fire engine with a petrol engine driven pump. It had been more Finlay's persuasion than Brian's that had convinced Dawson on that occasion and Brian hoped that something similar would happen on this meeting. He was sure that Dawson would at least give any proposals a hearing, and he had taken Dr. Cunningham to see Arthur Finlay prior to the meeting to ensure he was aware of the urgency of the proposals.

The Council Chamber was set out in a semi-circle. There was a hard wooden bench seat for each member, with a small wooden desktop in front of them. It reminded Brian of a schoolroom. Brian's seat was at the left hand end of the semi-circle that faced the Chairman, and at the other end, with only a couple of seats separating them, sat John Dawson and Angus Wylie. Wylie was a great one for posturing. Dawson was the opposite, and when he spoke what he said was very much to the point.

Brian had a clear view of the two men. He studied Wylie carefully; he was still not sure of the best way to deal with his opposition. Wylie couldn't forget Brian had thwarted his attempts to take over the Philbin building firm and he still saw Brian as a common Irish labourer.

The business of the meeting went quickly, too quickly. Within half an hour most of the items on the agenda had been dealt with. Brian took out his half hunter pocket watch and looked at the time. There was no sign of Dr. Cunningham. The doctor had promised he would be there for the start of the meeting. He needed the doctor to be there. He looked down at his watch. It was now half past three.

They had come to the proposal that Brian had been waiting for, the public works item. The renewal of the existing sewer and drainage system in the lower part of Levenside and its extension to deal with the older properties in the Tannergate area of the town. Brian glanced round to the door of the Council chamber.

Still there was no sign of Dr. Cunningham.

The Chairman of the meeting was Seamus Thomson, Brian's son-in-law. He asked Arthur Finlay to outline the details of the proposal. As Finlay stood up he glanced over at Brian. He had also noticed the absence of Dr. Cunningham. Brian could only shrug his shoulders.

The Members listened attentively enough as their Clerk pointed out the importance of the project, but when he mentioned that a substantial capital investment would be required Brian O'Malley immediately saw some of the members start to shift uncomfortably on their hard wooden seats.

"The estimated cost of this project is £10,042 10s. 6d." There was a sharp intake of breath from Angus Wylie and there were mutterings from a number of the others. Such expenditure would involve substantial borrowing; borrowing was something the Council nearly always refused to consider.

Angus Wylie was the first to speak. He was frowning.

"This isn't a renewal project." He was looking at Brian now. "This is a totally new drainage system. The Tannergate's never been part of Levenside's main drainage system. Why should it be now?"

Brian looked anxiously over at Arthur Finlay. Brian was tempted to interject, but he sensed that this was not the time.

"The present arrangements seem perfectly adequate to me," continued Wylie. Brian thought of the stench of the open gulleys in the Tannergate in the height of summer, but still he said nothing. After a long pause, it was Arthur Finlay, the Town Clerk, who replied. Arthur Finlay knew as well as Brian O'Malley not just how unpleasant the Tannergate could be and what a danger to health its open gullies presented.

"You will see from the papers I have circulated that the Medical Officer of Health has recommended these proposals."

Wylie was not to be deflected. "Well let him pay for the proposals." Was the comment he flung back at Finlay, but the Town Clerk persevered, seemingly unperturbed by the seated interruption.

"Chairman, you will see the reasons for Medical Officer's recommendation. Clearly, however, the expenditure on this project cannot be met from the annual rate. If the Council is to contemplate such expenditure it would have to consider taking a loan and repaying the money over twenty-five or thirty years…"

"Aye, and the interest too," interjected Angus Wylie.

"I have not formally approached the Council's bank to negotiate such a loan until such time as I have instructions from the Council…." continued Arthur Finlay, as if he had never been interrupted, and Brian found himself admiring the little man.

"However, the Council has been very sensible over its borrowing in the past and, as such, is creditworthy as far as the bank is concerned. I anticipate that such a loan could be arranged at an annual rate of four per cent." As Finlay announced the figure a few of the members turned and exchanged meaningful looks at each other. Creditworthy or not, they were going to have borrow a lot of money and, even at four per cent, pay a lot of interest over the years.

"It's out of the question," boomed Angus Wylie, and this time several heads nodded in agreement. Brian tried not to let his feelings show. It was now clear to everyone present that Wylie was implacable opposed to the project. No amount of persuasion was going to convince him of its merits, but Brian knew his opposition wasn't the cost of the project. Wylie had more to gain than anyone else at the meeting from the proposals. He owned much of the property that would benefit from the new drainage system. Wylie's opposition was because he thought that Brian was in favour of the scheme.

Brian glanced over at John Dawson. His face remained impassive.

Silence was no longer an option if the scheme was to be saved. It was clear that already a majority of those present were against the drainage scheme because of its cost and he didn't even have Dr. Cunningham there to help him convince the other Bailies that the dire health problems in the Tannergate were caused by the absence of a proper drainage system. He had to intervene now, or it would be too late.

Slowly he rose to his feet. He sensed the other nineteen members of the Council turn to watch him. His interventions in their debates were rare.

He knew that he had to get one point out of the way first before Wylie could use it against him.

"You will all be aware that like Angus Wylie that I own a number of the properties in the Tannergate, but it is not for that reason that I am in favour of these new drainage proposals. I hope you will accept that."

He caught sight of the smirk on Angus Wylie's face.

"You will know that there has been a serious outbreak of fever in the Tannergate and that has already resulted in a fatality. It is likely there will be a number more deaths, mainly young children."

Brian paused and looked up, but apart from Wylie, most of the faces opposite him were expressionless. He felt his best approach was a direct statement of the facts. If he did that without emotion perhaps it would be accepted.

"Dr. Cunningham tells me that the child who died recently was probably suffering from para-typhoid." One or two of the members murmured to each other and Brian could see that now there was concern on their faces. More importantly, he thought he could just detect a change in Dawson's usual impassive expression.

"Dr. Cunningham is still awaiting news from Glasgow of the results of the tests that he has carried out to confirm his diagnosis, but he is confident that he is right." Brian let his voice fall away at the end of the sentence. He had their full attention now.

"We must have proper sanitary arrangements for the properties in the Tannergate. Unless that we do, I can tell you that it is Dr. Cunningham's view that there's a risk of an epidemic, not just this year, but any year we get the kind of hot weather that we have now."

Brian looked round the meeting. There was silence for a moment.

"Where's Cunningham? Why doesn't the good doctor tell us all this himself?" It was another intervention from Wylie, making the point he had feared most. Where was the doctor?

Brian continued as if the answer was obvious. "Dr. Cunningham has more on his hands than he can cope with, Mr. Wylie, I'm sure he would be here if he could, but as he knew he was likely to be needed dealing with the cases in the Tannergate he gave me a letter which he asked me to put before the meeting if he was unable to attend."

Brian was thankful that he had the foresight to insist that Dr. Cunningham write it. He held it out to the Town Clerk and Finlay came forward and took it from him. Finlay passed it to Seamus Thomson who read it and then indicated that it should be passed round the meeting.

Wylie waved the letter past without making any attempt to read it, but John Dawson read its contents closely.

After he had finished, he looked straight across at Brian. It was difficult to detect if there was concern in his expression. What was Dawson thinking?

"I anticipated that some of you might consider the costs of this project prohibitive…" He glanced across at Wylie as the Town Clerk continued, "…so I have made some enquiries about possible loans to finance it. I am pleased to say that my own bank, the Western Bank of Scotland, would be willing to make the necessary loan at 3% interest per annum."

Brian paused, he had their attention now. He didn't tell the meeting that his personal guarantee had been required to secure this favourable interest rate. He just waited for the lower figure to sink in.

"What are you after O'Malley? Are you trying to buy votes - or are you after the contract for the drains yourself?"

Brian heard Wylie's sneering voice. He felt the raw emotion building up inside himself, like water building up behind a dam and he fought to contain it. He knew he mustn't let Wylie provoke him. He wanted to grab Wylie by the lapels, and tell him not to be so bloody stupid, but he caught sight of John Dawson watching him, waiting for his response, and he bit off the reply that was about to spring to his lips.

Wylie was a lost cause. He always had been.

There was only one response he could give, so he said very quietly. "I will not tender for any works if the Council agree to this project." He paused. "I also undertake that I will not personally vote on this proposal." He was looking at Dawson as he made his response so he didn't see the look of surprise on Wylie's face, but what he did see, or at least he thought he saw, was an almost imperceptible nod from John Dawson.

Then he looked across at Wylie and saw that for the moment Wylie was at a loss as to how to reply and so Brian sat down before Wylie could think of anything.

The remaining debate was a short one. Most of the Bailies who spoke were concerned, as Brian had expected, with the cost of the project. His negotiation of the preferential bank loan had given the project at least a chance, but there was still no sign of Dr. Cunningham. He was sure that the doctor would have clinched the argument, but it looked as if the vote would be taken without his presence.

After he had allowed all those who wished to speak to have their say the Chairman was about to put the matter to the vote when Peter McDonough, who Brian got on well with, stood up. Brian thought he might be suggesting an adjournment to give the doctor more time to be present but he was wrong. McDonough proposed that the motion be amended so that the proposed sewage and drainage works should go ahead, but only if the loan from the Western Bank of Scotland at 3% was available. Two or three of the members nodded their support and no one objected to the proposed amendment, although Brian heard Wylie mutter, "What's the point".

The vote was called on the amended proposal.

Brian could barely watch as the hands were raised. Three, four, five hands went up in favour. Then he saw John Dawson raise his hand as well, and then another three hands were raised. Nine votes in favour. Then came the votes against, and as Brian counted those he realised that he had gambled and failed. There were also nine votes against.

He wanted to get away from the meeting as quickly as he could but the weight of his failure was like an invisible hand pushing him down in his seat. If only he hadn't waived his own right to vote. He could have agreed not to tender for the contract and still voted. No, he was sure it had taken both his promises to convince Dawson to vote for the project. He sat for a moment, almost in a trance.

Then he looked around. No one else had moved. What were they waiting for?

They were all looking at the Chairman. Then it dawned on him. It wasn't all over. The Chairman had a casting vote.

What would his son-in-law do? He could see the hesitation written on Seamus' face. Seamus shuffled the papers in front of him and cleared his throat. Seamus avoided looking at Brian. Seamus cleared his throat a second time. They still waited.

"This is a matter which involves major expenditure on the part of Burgh Council…." Seamus paused for a moment and swallowed. Still he avoided looking any of them in the eye. "…I think it would be wrong, therefore, for it to be agreed on a casting vote. I propose to abstain."

Brian looked at his son-in-law. He should have felt disgusted but he did not. Ever since he had married Kate, Seamus had been a disappointment. This was just one more. He wondered if Seamus had discussed the project with Katherine. He didn't seem to have the guts to make any decisions without consulting her these days. Slowly Brian got up and walked out of the chamber. As he passed Angus Wylie the man could not contain himself.

"The Council knows better than to waste money on your stupid gestures O'Malley."

Brian had to work hard to control himself. Wylie couldn't contain his pleasure that he had got one over on the "Irish hod carrier" he hated so much. That was all that mattered to him. Brian could have felled the man with a single blow, but he didn't. He just walked away.

It wasn't he who would suffer because of Wylie's selfish stupidity. It was the people of the Tannergate. As he walked slowly down the town hall steps he was surprised that John Dawson came across to him. When he spoke, it was in a formal way as if they were still in the meeting.

"I regret that the Council did not decide to proceed with the drainage project. I wish more people would think of the good of the community than of their own personal advantage." With that, John Dawson turned and walked away. It was only a couple of sentences, but Brian could never recall the man speaking directly to him before. He watched Dawson's retreating figure. It must have taken a lot for Dawson to say what he had.

It was only a few minutes after he arrived back at Howes Road that Brian heard a knocking at his door. He opened it to find himself facing a worried, breathless Dr. Cunningham.

"How did it go O'Malley?" Brian didn't need to answer the question. Dr. Cunningham could read the result in his expression.

"I'm sorry," said Brian.

"So am I," said Cunningham. "Sean Kelly's bairn is down with it now. That's why I wasn't at the meeting." Brian felt helpless, but there was nothing more that could be done for the moment.

He was saddened by the news about Sean Kelly's son. Sean was his foreman, honest and reliable, a good man. He had worked for Brian for almost ten years. Michael Kelly was his only child.

"Come in and have a drink." He stood back and made way for Cunningham to enter. He put his hand around the man's shoulder. He had never seen the doctor so tired and worn out.

"Don't worry, we'll think of something," but even as he said the words, Brian knew he had no solution to the problem, other than for the two of them to get drunk.

CHAPTER 3

THE GREAT FIRE

Two weeks after the Council Meeting Brian O'Malley was alone in his sitting room. Once again, his thoughts were of his granddaughter. He wondered how she was managing on her own in London.

He started to draw the curtains on the darkness outside. As he did so, he became conscious of a distant glow from the Tannergate. He focused on the light in the distance and saw quite clearly a house was burning in the distance.

"Annie! Annie! The Tannergate's on fire."

His housekeeper must have been on her way from the kitchen, for she ran into the room within seconds of his calling her.

"Tell Arthur Finlay to get that damn fire engine of his up to the Tannergate as fast as he can."

Brian was out the front door before Annie Dillon could open her mouth. As he ran down the hill he felt for the first time how strong the wind was blowing. Flames were now clearly visible in another of the houses and the flames in the first house were licking through the upstairs window towards the roof. They weren't just facing a couple of houses going up in flames; they were facing a major conflagration. If they didn't catch the blaze early enough, it would take the whole of the Tannergate with it. Once the fire really caught hold, there would be little chance that they could stop it spreading. The ghetto in which Brian had once lived was facing disaster.

He found himself overhauling others running in the same direction. Not just the inhabitants of the Tannergate were converging on the fire, but people were coming from further parts of Levenside. He wasn't the only one to realise the enormity of the threat.

He could see from the illumination given off by the flames that Sean Kelly, whose son Michael Dr. Cunningham thought might have the fever, was already there. Sean had gathered some of the other workers from the Tannyard around him and was already trying to organise them.

"What can I do Sean?"

"We've got a real problem Mr. O'Malley. I've organised the lads to get everybody out of the houses down wind of the fire and drag out as much the stuff inside that'll burn, but there's no water."

"Jesus, …what do you mean, no water?" Brian didn't notice his blasphemy. Without water there was no hope. The flames were too fierce to get anywhere close to them without water. They had to have water.

Then Brian realised the problem. The standpipe in the Tannyard had been dry for over a week. It must be the same here in the Tannergate. He could see a third house was now alight. He pointed to the first of the burning houses.

"Whose house is that?"

"Patrick Callaghan's, Mr. O'Malley." Callaghan was one of the regular workers in the Tannyard.

"Is anyone still inside?"

Sean shook his head. "No, he's over there with his wife". He pointed to a couple that were huddled together at one side of the crowd. The woman was heavily pregnant. The couple stared mesmerised by the dancing flames that had engulfed their house. Then Brian O'Malley saw them both flinch as with a crash the roof collapsed. Then with the building now open to the sky there was a roar as the wind caught the flames again and drove them even higher up into the sky and moments later the front wall of the building collapsed inwards. The woman buried her head in her husband's chest and he hugged her tightly.

Some of the men from the Tannyard that Sean had organised were helping the occupants of one of the adjoining properties to drag their pitiful belongings from their property but the fire was becoming too fierce. They were driven back by the heat as the flames started to take hold of that house too. There were now four houses ablaze with the wind fanning the flames like the bellows in an ironworks. Soon the whole row of houses would be burning and Brian felt a sense of dread, for with the strong wind blowing down towards the town there was nothing to stop the blaze engulfing the whole of the Tannergate and spreading to the rest of Levenside.

Brian turned to Sean Kelly, even in the dancing shadows of the half-light Brian could see Sean's face looked drawn and haggard, "How are you Sean?"

"Fine."

"Are you sure?"

The big man nodded.

"Arthur Finlay should be on the way with that fire engine of his, but we can't wait for him."

Sean nodded again in agreement. They both glanced across at the blaze. They watched for a few seconds in frightened fascination as the tongues of fire danced and leapt in the sky. Then Brian spoke.

"Take a dozen men. Get up to the Tannyard and find as many buckets as you can carry. Bring them down here. We've got to get some water on that fire…" Brian's eyes met Sean Kelly's. Sean understood the danger as much as Brian did.

"Break open the gates if you have to but get a move on for God's sake." But Sean was already had his back to Brian. Brian heard him shouting to others as he ran off up the hill to the Tannyard.

Within a matter of minutes, a chain of men was passing buckets of water up the hill. The nearest standpipe that was working was almost halfway down the hill and the blaze had started near the top of the Tannergate. As the men struggled to pass the heavy buckets up the hill Brian got Sean to organise a second line, this time made up of women and children to pass the buckets back down again to be refilled.

There was no absence of willing hands. The inhabitants of the Tannergate were fighting for their homes. However, it didn't take Brian long to realise as he moved up and down the line that despite everybody's commitment there was a problem.

The buckets they were using were not proper fire buckets. They were builders' buckets. Each weighed at least thirty pounds when they were full of water. It was back breaking work to pass those up the hill and soon he started to see men having to stop and put down the bucket passed to them.

He knew he couldn't let any of those in the chain stop and rest for more than a few moments. Water was all they had to fight the fire with, and they needed as much of it as they could get as quickly as they could get it. Brian moved up and down the line, tightening it. He made sure no one had to stretch for the bucket being passed to them. Instead, he made sure that they were all close enough to catch the buckets as they were still being swung toward them so the man next in line was helped by the momentum built up by the man before him. Then he began calling out, "One, two, three - give," and as the men picked up the chant down the line everybody started to swing the buckets rhythmically. Instead of the men trying to move the buckets as fast as they could they started to move the buckets along the line in one steady movement.

Then as new men arrived Brian used them as reserves and when he saw part of the chain faltering he joined in with these fresh men getting them into the rhythm almost without the line pausing.

Brian also put Sean Kelly in charge of the few men he could spare so that Sean could continue with the work of dragging out the contents of buildings that lay in the path of the growing inferno.

Brian knew they couldn't let up. They had to save the Tannergate. In the orange and yellow flickering light he could see the fatigue etched in the faces of everyone around him. As he looked at some of them, he wondered if it was illness as well as fatigue. His own muscles ached with pain. Like those around him he was soaked with sweat.

But it was no use, despite all their efforts Brian could see that the fire was so fierce now, that attacking the flames directly was a losing battle. Even when they shifted the water to dowse buildings further down the line all it did was slow the fire down, but they could not prevent the flames spreading. Nearly a dozen buildings were ablaze.

Brian could see not just exhaustion etched in among the sweat and grime on the faces of the men and women alongside him, now there was also despair. He felt the despair himself, but he refused to show it. As men half his age started to wilt under the heat and the physical effort involved, Brian struggled to keep the line of buckets moving.

"Come on boys. The fire engine will be here anytime now."

"Keep at it lass. You're as good as any of them."

All the time he tried to think of a way to save the situation. His urging managed to keep the line of buckets going but it was no use unless something else was done. Only a miracle or Finlay's new fire engine could save them now. Where was he? If he didn't arrive soon there wouldn't be much need for a fire engine or the Burgh Council because there wouldn't be anything left of Levenside in the morning. The wind was driving the flames down the hill and into the town at an alarming rate. Only a motor driven engine could pump enough water onto the flames.

"It's no good Mr. O'Malley, the wind's too strong. We need more water." Brian had not seen Sean Kelly approaching him. He didn't answer Sean straight away. The two of them stared at the flames.

Then Brian O'Malley thought of something, the idea that they were to talk about in Levenside for many years afterwards.

He tugged at Sean's arm, "Come on," and he started to run up the hill towards the Tannyard. Sean followed without any hesitation. A couple of minutes later they were through the gates of the Tannyard. Brian pointed to the office at the back of the yard. He had no keys but it didn't matter. Within seconds Sean Kelly's massive shoulders had the door splintering on its hinges. One final effort from the two of them and the heavy door gave way entirely.

In the gloom inside it was difficult to see. Sean Kelly waited while Brian searched around in the darkness at the far end of the office. Brian cursed as he stumbled over unseen objects. Then he found what he wanted, wrapped in oilskin paper.

"Sean, I want you to shorten the chain of buckets. When there's a gap of half a dozen houses between the flames and the end of the chain, dowse as much water as you can on the next house and keep throwing water on it. Do you understand?"

"I understand well enough Mr. O'Malley, but we've tried that…. the wind is too strong," replied Kelly.

"Trust me, Sean. This time we're going to make a proper firebreak," and then he showed Sean Kelly what was beneath the oilskin wrapping paper. In the gloom, Sean Kelly looked at Brian O'Malley for just a moment, then he turned on his heal and ran down the hill, shouting to the men he had been working with as he went.

Brian followed, the oilskin packages clasped firmly in his grasp. He knew he had to demolish at least two of the terraced houses. Only if they used dynamite could they make a sufficient firebreak. At least two or three buildings had to be flattened to the ground.

There wasn't much time. Brian knew the weak points of these buildings. After all he and Sean had built a lot like them over the years. If anyone could find their way around them in the dark he and Sean could. He realised how much he'd come to depend on Sean over the last few years. He prayed Sean's son wasn't down with the fever as Dr. Cunningham feared.

By the time he was inside the first of the firebreak houses he realised he didn't need to know his way around in the dark. The glow from the encroaching fire was already starting to light up the interior of the house and a reflection of the orange flames skipped up and down the walls beside him as he worked. He could feel the heat too. The water being thrown onto the roof and walls of the adjoining buildings would gain them a little time, but not much.

It was getting much too warm. He worked as fast as he could. All the dynamite was in place. There were only the fuses to light.

He made one final check and then made his way outside and signalled Sean Kelly to move his men and the end of the chain back to a safe distance.

As he turned, he could see the new Merryweather fire engine in the distance, grinding slowly up the hill, with Arthur Finlay and his fire auxiliaries standing on the running boards. The fire engine was towing a trailer with the extra lengths of hose Finlay had realised they needed.

For the first time he felt there was just a possibility that they could avoid a complete disaster. If they could blow the dynamite now there was still a chance that they could save most of the Tannergate. Finlay had told him that the fire engine could pump over 300 hundred gallons of water a minute on to any fire. He'd better be right.

Sean Kelly ran across to him and confirmed that all the men and women in the chain had been moved back. Brian knew they must hurry. He needed Sean to help him light the fuses. Each of them would take one of the houses. Brian estimated they would have only a couple of minutes to get clear. He gave Sean a nod and they ran back into the houses. They both emerged from the back of the buildings within a few seconds of each other.

That was when matters went wrong - just when it looked like the situation could be saved. Many times in later years Brian was to wonder if there was something he could have done to avoid what happened next, but he could never be sure. Fate is its own master.

Before he motioned Sean Kelly to follow him down the hill Brian turned to look at the fire. To his horror he saw a figure in one of the houses closer to the fire. That very second, the back room burst into flames silhouetting a woman inside.

The outline was familiar and then he realised who it was. The house was the very one that he had stayed in when he first came to Levenside as a young man.

Despite all the offers of help he had made over the years Maureen Connor, the person who had first provided him with a roof over his head when he had arrived in Levenside, had steadfastly refused to move from the Tannergate. Now she was hopelessly trying to drag a chair to the back door and out into the yard. Even as he watched, her clothes caught alight and he could see, rather than hear her scream. Maureen must have been so desperate to save some of her possessions that she had slipped back into her house when everybody else was too pre-occupied to notice.

Without thinking Brian ran back and into the building. He grabbed Maureen, barely noticing that her clothes were already alight. A moment later he found Sean Kelly next to him and together they dragged Maureen as far away from the building as they could and then rolled her over and over on the ground, beating out the flames.

When the dynamite went up, they were still far too close to the houses.

Brian O'Malley should have died that night, but he did not. Sean Kelly was between him and the blast, and it was Sean Kelly and not Brian that took the full force of the explosion. All Brian could remember was Sean smashing against him, and then there was oblivion.

When he regained consciousness, he had no idea where he was. His head hurt. Very gingerly he raised himself on one elbow and what had been a throbbing pain changed immediately into excruciating agony. He thought he would pass out again as a pulsating red film seemed to cover his eyes, but gradually the pain began to ease and the mist to clear. Then he remembered the fire and he looked anxiously across towards the flames. To his relief he saw that the firebreak had worked. Indeed, the explosion had done even more than he had intended. The break in the line of back-to-back houses was more than three houses wide, and in the gap barely a brick of the middle two houses stood higher than waist high.

What was even more heartening was what he could see through the gap. He could just pick out the diminutive figure of Arthur Finlay. He was directing two men who were holding a canvas hose that was spurting a stream of water onto the house beyond the break in the line of houses that had been created.

The human chain had started back with the buckets and, with water being pumped up the hill from the fire engine, it looked like the flames could now be beaten. Brian's demolition skills had not let him down, nor had Sean Kelly.

He wondered what had happened to Sean and Maureen. He tried to turn his head to search for them. About twenty feet away, Maureen was kneeling beside the figure of a man, who could only be Sean. Fighting the throbbing pain in his head Brian forced himself to stand. Half limping and half shuffling, he managed to hobble his way across to them.

He could see that Maureen appeared to have some painful burns to her face and arms but she looked as though she had no other serious injury. Her heavy clothing had protected her from the worst of the flames and then she had been lying flat on the ground, so the blast that had caught Brian and Sean Kelly had for the most part missed her.

Sean Kelly was a different matter. Brian knew instinctively that the man did not have much longer to live. Despite his own pain Brian managed to kneel down beside him. He lent forward towards the man whose head was cradled in Maureen Connor's lap.

For a moment Sean opened his eyes and a glint of recognition showed.

"I'm sorry Mr. O'Malley," was all he said.

"It's alright Sean, you lie still," and then Brian fought in his aching head for something more to say to the man who had struggled so bravely with him through that night and who had once more given him such unstinting support.

He remembered Sean Kelly's son.

"How's your boy doing?" he asked, but if Sean heard him there was no reply, for even as he spoke Sean's eyes closed for the last time.

There was a long pause and all Brian could hear was the crackle of the fire that was starting to die behind him. Maureen Connor looked across at him, the last of the orange glow played on the burnt black dress that she wore. For a moment he wondered if she was remembering what there had once been between them so many years before.

Very quietly she said, "Sean's son died this morning." Brian looked at the man that lay there in her arms. All night he had striven to help fight that terrible fire and Sean hadn't said a word.

Brian watched as Maureen Connor laid Sean Kelly's head to rest on the ground. Brian felt the tears slowly run down his cheeks. Maureen saw them, but she said nothing. There was nothing more to be said.

Brian insisted on attending the funeral of Sean Kelly and his son. He was able to remember little of what occurred. He sat through the event in a chair. It was almost another month before he was able to venture outside his house again and then he needed a stick to walk.

His housekeeper, Annie Dillon, was against him even getting out of bed, let alone going any further, but Brian was adamant. He wanted to see for himself the extent of the damage to the Tannergate. As he walked slowly down the hill in the sunshine leaning on his stick he encountered John Dawson. To his amazement, for the first time in ten year's John Dawson raised his hat to him in the street as he passed by.

As he walked on, he was surprised by a number of other people going out of their way to acknowledge his passing. Further down the hill, the news of his approach to the Tannergate seemed to have gone ahead of him. It was as if someone had telegraphed the news of his presence to the inhabitants, for when he arrived there he found himself surrounded by a crowd of well-wishers. The same thing was repeated over and over again as he walked down the hill; men nodded and doors opened and women came out drying their hands on their aprons and stood on their doorsteps smiling a welcome to him. His own men working in the Tannyard stopped working and the new foreman made no attempt to stop them as they left the Tannyard. Instead he joined them as they all followed Brian on what was rapidly becoming his pilgrimage down to the ruined houses in the Tannergate.

It was only then that Brian O'Malley fully understood how the people of Levenside felt about what he had done for them that night: the night that became known to all in Levenside as the night of the Great Fire.

Two weeks later there was a meeting of the Burgh Council. At the end of the meeting John Dawson proposed a motion that the Council should proceed forthwith to carry out the sewage and drainage works previously proposed for the Tannergate and the lower half of Levenside. There was no debate. The motion was carried by seventeen votes to one.

CHAPTER 4

META AND THE ALMA
ELEMENTARY SCHOOL

Several of Meta's applications for a teaching job in London were rejected, often without her even being interviewed. She had anticipated that it might be difficult to find a post in London, but it was turning out much harder than she had anticipated.

Eventually she was offered an interview at the Alma Elementary School near Mile End in the East End of London. The interview panel was supposed to consist of three persons appointed by the education authority, but one of the members was a clergyman who had been called away to attend a bereaved parishioner. That left the headmaster, Mr. Fairfax, who Meta thought was rather full of himself, and a local councillor who appeared intimidated by the headmaster, to conduct the interview.

"It won't be easy to fill your predecessor's shoes, you know. Mr. Davidson certainly taught his pupils how to behave. Quite a disciplinarian... of course, he was just the type to enlist at the first opportunity. Very patriotic... I like to think that I'd have done the same thing myself if I'd been 20 years younger."

"I'm sure, headmaster."

Mr. Fairfax nodded and for a moment appeared to reflect upon his own, and Mr. Davidson's patriotic fervour. "Mr. Davidson's class is the biggest in the school unless you can keep discipline you won't be able to teach them anything."

"I will certainly do my best, headmaster."

"Of course, of course."

Two things became apparent to Meta. Firstly, that the headmaster thought that the essence of teaching was strict discipline. Secondly, Mr. Fairfax considered teaching was a man's job. She began to wonder why she'd been invited for interview, and she waited in vain for an explanation of exactly what teaching duties her appointment would involve.

She only made a perfunctory attempt to ask questions. Her heart wasn't in it. The interview appeared to be a charade and when eventually Mr. Fairfax stood up and thanked Meta for coming she was relieved.

As soon as she got back to her rooms, she took off her heavy dress and bathed her aching feet. She was annoyed she had wasted her time again. She tried to console herself that Mr Fairfax was not a headmaster she would have wanted to work for.

She had enjoyed teaching back in Scotland. She felt she had a natural aptitude for it. All she wanted was the opportunity to continue with her vocation. She sighed.

Two days later she received a letter from Mr. Fairfax offering her the appointment at Alma Elementary School. She read it twice to make sure it was correct.

On her first day Mr. Fairfax did introduce Meta to the other staff and show her around the school, but when they came to her classroom he did not take her inside but left her at the door so she had to introduce herself to her pupils.

As Meta entered the classroom alone she saw chalked on the blackboard two messages. "Pupils should be seen but not heard," and "Speak when you are spoken to." Her predecessor, Mr. Davidson, had left his pupils his instructions as to their future conduct.

By the end of her first day Meta was exhausted. Getting any reaction from her pupils had been a struggle. On her way home she bought a newspaper for the latest war news. As soon as she got into her sitting room she threw of her shoes and started to read it. It was full of the latest offensive in France. Meta looked down the endless columns of the dead and wounded. It was hard to believe the numbers.

As she carried on reading the description of the current battle in 'The Times' two words stood out, "poison gas". The young men in France were not just being shot and killed, they were being poisoned as well. It was difficult to imagine the suffering the soldiers in France were going through. She closed the paper. She thought of John McBride, the man she was trying to forget, and she thanked God he was safe in Scotland.

Meta had only been at Alma Elementary School for two or three months when Mr. Fairfax, saw Mr. Davidson's name in one of the casualty lists published in the papers. A few days later he received a letter from Mr. Davidson's wife. It appeared Mr. Davidson had been blown up by a mortar shell.

At morning assembly, once Mr. Fairfax had been informed of the details of Mr. Davidson's death, he made the whole school stand in silence as a tribute to the "bravery of the man" and Meta with head bowed couldn't stop herself from wondering if it really required any bravery to be blown up by a mortar shell and whether Mr. Davidson had appeared as fearsome to the Germans as he obviously had to the pupils of Alma Elementary School. Then she felt guilty for such ungenerous thoughts towards a man who had died for his country.

Mr. Fairfax constant lecturing on discipline had led to a growing antagonism between them. Her failure to refer any of her pupils to him for punishment seemed to be a source of frustration to him. He seemed to think examples had to be made of pupils on a regular basis. It had the effect of colouring her feelings not just of him, but also towards anyone she associated with him.

The previous week, Mr. Fairfax had come into the staff room when Meta had been alone there. Once again he had taken the opportunity to give her a lecture about how important it was to be strict with her class. "Discipline is everything in a school like ours, Miss Costello, most of these children have no idea how to behave."

"Has there been a problem with the children in my class Mr.Fairfax?"

"Regrettably yes, Miss Costello."

For a moment she wondered what Mr. Fairfax was talking about, then she remembered seeing Mr. Fairfax hovering outside her classroom the previous day. She had started to read to her class at the end of each day. She sometimes allowed her pupils to choose the stories she read. The children were often so keen for their favourite stories to be chosen they became overexcited and called out the names. She remembered on that occasion she'd had to quieten them down.

"Mr. Fairfax it's in the children's nature to get excited at times. I think we need to help our pupils to develop their abilities. Children often respond to encouragement as much as to discipline."

"I am not in favour of allowing boisterous behaviour in the class-room, Miss Costello. Respect, that is what children must learn. Give these children an inch and they will take a mile. Believe me." He paused and then before Meta could respond he added, "Unquestioning respect for authority that is the only essential our children need to learn. That is why the British Army is so formidable. Discipline. If you can't keep your pupils quiet send them to me. A good birching will soon teach them the proper way to behave."

Then Mr. Fairfax strode out of the staff room. Meta looked at the doorway through which Mr. Fairfax had disappeared. The headmaster seemed as determined to inflict corporal punishment on her pupils as she was determined that it would not happen. She shook her head. They were dealing with children, not soldiers.

Miss Thompson, another member of staff, came into the staff room as Mr. Fairfax left. Miss Thompson put the books she was carrying down on the table and hesitated for a moment.

"May I give you a word of advice Miss Costello?" Miss Thompson had been at the Alma Elementary School longer than even Mr. Fairfax. From what Meta had seen and heard of her, Miss Thompson would have made a much better head teacher than Mr. Fairfax, but she hadn't even been considered when Mr. Fairfax had been appointed. Women had to give up teaching when they married as marriage was a full-time occupa-tion so they were rarely considered for senior posts if they were still of marriageable age.

"Of course, Miss Thompson."

"Take care how you speak to Mr. Fairfax." For a moment Meta thought of saying keeping quiet just allowed Mr. Fairfax to get away with his bullying behaviour. She was determined not to be intimidated, but she realised Miss Thompson was trying to give her a friendly warning. "Do you think I'm too forthright?"

"You would do well to try and be less …argumentative with Mr. Fairfax. It's not good for your career to antagonise the headmaster."

"I'm not trying to do that Miss Thompson. It's just that Mr. Fairfax doesn't seem to realise that the children respond to encouragement as well as discipline."

"I know. I know, but if you feel you must query Mr. Fairfax's views try to be a little less confrontational." Miss Thompson smiled. "I was young once…sometimes it takes a little longer than you would like to change things."

"I'll try and watch what I say," said Meta.

Miss Thompson smiled. "Good. You're an asset here and I'd hate for us to lose you before you've sorted the school out." Then Miss Thompson expression became serious again. "Once Mr. Fairfax takes offence he doesn't forget. He's got a long memory."

Meta nodded. She wondered if Miss Thompson had crossed swords with Mr. Fairfax in the past.

Mr. Fairfax might be an arrogant bully, too full of his own importance, but Miss Thompson was right, he had absolute power over her future as a teacher. If he were to sack her without a reference her teaching career would be as good as over. There was one thing she was certain of though, none of her pupils was going to be birched by Mr. Fairfax.

She could still remember her own childhood experiences back in Scotland of the tawse being wielded with such severity that even the bravest of pupils cringed at the sight of it. Visualising Sister Frances bringing the flailing strips of leather, cracking down on her palm still made her wince.

She had witnessed the agonies of pupils leaving Mr. Fairfax's study. One young boy with glasses could barely walk.

CHAPTER 5

JOHN MCBRIDE
DECIDES HIS FUTURE

Once John McBride had made his decision to leave the Seminary and turn his back on the priesthood there was only one place for him to go, Eyemouth.

His parents told him he could stay with them as long as he wanted. They had been proud of his decision to join the priesthood, but they welcomed him home after his change of heart. Neither of them had been convinced that the Church was his vocation.

John had a lot of time to think. He tried to understand why his country had gone to war. He reluctantly accepted that small countries such as Belgium needed to be protected, but his decision as to his future course of action was decided for him by more personal matters.

He swam in the freezing North Sea as he thought of his future. Many of his school friends were no longer in Eyemouth they had joined up to fight. More and more his thoughts turned to Meta. He wondered how she was faring. He longed to try and get in touch with her, but he had broken her heart once, he did not want to do so again.

It was when he learnt the fate of the two brothers who had been his closest friends during his school days and spoke to their parents about their loss that he decided what he must do. The brothers had often swum with him off Coldingham Sands. Being fishermen, they had both joined the navy, but they had not gone to sea. They had been sent to Western Front as infantry, members of one of the Naval Divisions sent over to the continent by Winston Churchill, the First Lord of the Admiralty. They had died together holding the lines against the Germans near the Belgium front.

When he told his parents of his decision they tried to understand, but the change from being a priest to a soldier was so fundamental they found their son's choice difficult to accept, particularly his mother. She talked to him at length and when it became clear she couldn't change his mind she persuaded him to return to Levenside and talk to his old mentor Father MacDonald before he went to any recruiting office. Already in Eyemouth too many mothers had lost their sons.

The priest listened quietly as the young man unburdened himself. As John explained his uncertainties about the priesthood so much of the young man's troubled thoughts reminded Father MacDonald of his own youth and his own doubts as to whether the Church was truly his vocation.

He made no attempt to persuade John to return to the Seminary but when he realised that John was thinking of joining up and going to France, he tried very hard to dissuade him from that course of action.

"Leaving the Seminary John is a momentous decision, enough for the moment. Take one step at a time."

Their discussions went on for a long time, but the more Father MacDonald spoke about the horrors of the fighting in France, the more determined John McBride became he must face them. In the end the priest gave up, but he decided to take John on his weekly meeting with Brian O'Malley in the vain hope his friend might succeed where he had failed.

When Brian O'Malley opened his door, John was surprised by how much Meta's grandfather had aged. The fire that had occurred must have been every bit as serious an event as Father MacDonald had described.

Brian O'Malley was as welcoming as ever but he grew very concerned when he heard that John McBride proposed to go to France. He liked the young man a great deal. "There are other ways you can contribute to this war than becoming involved in the fighting John."

Because Father MacDonald and Brian O'Malley were both so insistent, John McBride agreed to "think on it" before he made a final decision, and so he stayed another night with the priest. Before he went to bed Father MacDonald emphasised again to him that fighting in

France would mean killing other human beings. "Do you believe that you can kill someone, John?" He studied the young man intently. "When the fighting starts others may depend on you doing just that. You won't have time to think about it." Despite those words John met the old man's gaze.

That night he lay awake wondering. He had convinced himself his conscience would allow him to kill. He could kill if it meant saving the lives of other men. Was that enough? He would never forgive himself if he did not put that question to the test. Hiding at home was no longer possible. He knew that from the moment he had encountered the grief of those parents in Eyemouth who had lost their sons.

The next morning, he told Father MacDonald that his mind was made up. He was going to do what he had to, and with a heavy heart Father MacDonald accepted his decision. There was nothing more he could say.

Before leaving Levenside John decided he ought to say goodbye to Brian O'Malley. He walked over to the Howes Road and Meta's grandfather invited him in. John hesitated. He did not want to listen to any further persuasion, but in the end he went inside.

Meta's grandfather made no further mention of France. He simply asked John whether his decision to give up the priesthood was final.

"Mr. O'Malley, I'm even more certain of that, than about going to France."

Brian O'Malley gave him a searching look. "Was it my granddaughter that changed your mind?'

"I had doubts about my calling before I met Meta, Mr O'Malley. She didn't realise it, but she helped me make the decision I needed to make." They sat in silence for a short time and then Brian O'Malley stood up and walked over to his desk and came back with a piece of paper.

"Meta told me never to give this to you, but I think circumstances are different now." John looked at the paper. Meta's address was written on it. Brian O'Malley put his hand on John's shoulder.

"You should try and see her, or at least write to her before you finally make up your mind about France." Then they had shaken hands, but neither said goodbye, as if they both felt it would bring bad luck.

Once John McBride had gone, Brian O'Malley went back inside. He frowned. Had he had done the right thing? What harm could it do now to give him Meta's address?

The next day John McBride took a train to London. He decided against writing to Meta. He would go and see her, but not until he had gone to one of the recruiting offices in London. He was sure she would not want him to go to France and she was the one person who might persuade him against it.

It never occurred to Brian O'Malley to mention what he had done either to Katherine, or Father MacDonald.

When Meta heard the second knock at the downstairs door she remembered her landlady was away for the weekend. She folded the newspaper carefully and placed it on the table. There was no point in rushing to open the door. If it was for her, it could only be Alex Field. She always found him a struggle to talk to.

For a moment she blinked in the bright sunlight as she looked at the face of the man standing in front of her. Then a voice said rather shyly, "I know I shouldn't have come…" and then it tailed off.

In front of Meta stood the man she had been trying so desperately to forget. She stepped forward and John put down his suitcase. She couldn't stop herself. She hugged him to her with all her strength, burying her head deep into his shoulder. Then she pushed him away holding him out in front of her so she could look at his face.

"Come in. Come in. Don't just stand there." She smiled and pulled him by the hand into the house. She couldn't think of anything else but how delighted she was to see him.

John had barely sat down before she started her questions.

"What are you doing here? How did you find me?"

"Your grandfather gave me your address. He's almost back to his old self again."

"I told him not to…" She started to frown. "What do you mean, "he's almost back to his old self'? Has he been ill?"

"Well …he was quite badly injured in the fire. It took a lot out of him."

John saw the expression on Meta's face changing as he spoke.

"You didn't know?"

Meta shook her head.

She wrote regularly to Brian O'Malley, but her grandfather rarely wrote back and when he did, he mentioned little about himself. There had been over a month when he had not written at all and she had been quite concerned.

"I'm afraid Meta, there was a serious fire in Levenside, but for your grandfather and his foreman, the Tannergate might have been destroyed. He was badly injured in the fire. His foreman died."

"Sean Kelly is dead?" Meta hand had moved involuntarily to cover her mouth. She shook her head in disbelief. "Tell me what happened."

She listened in silence as John described all he had learnt whilst he was in Levenside. How a fire had swept through Levenside fanned by high winds, and how her grandfather had led the desperate fight to save the Tannergate from destruction.

When John finished, for a moment she said nothing, trying to take in what she had been told.

"…is my grandfather alright now?

"He still walks with a bit of a limp, but he's back at work."

"Why did nobody tell me?"

"I suppose your grandfather didn't want to worry you. There's nothing you could do."

"Yes, but Alex Field must have known."

John looked at the expression on her face. "Maybe he wasn't told either."

Meta shook her head, "Wait 'til I see that man."

John didn't envy Alex Field his next meeting with Meta.

"What have you been up to Meta?"

Meta dragged her thoughts back to John. There was so much she wanted to tell him about London. The famous museums she had seen, her visits to the National Gallery.

He was impressed by her enthusiasm. "I wish I had more time. There so much you could show me."

Meta looked at John. Why had he said, 'I wish I had more time'?

However, before she could say anything John spoke again. "…And how is teaching here in London, Meta?"

Meta couldn't help herself. She had longed to tell someone of her frustration and of her battles with Mr. Fairfax. She poured her heart out and John listened without any interruption until she finished.

"It's seems you've got quite a problem on your hands Meta … I think Miss Thompson's advice is very sound though."

"The man's a bully."

"He sounds like one, but if you're going to take him on. Wait until something really important happens. Then you'll find you get support from people like Miss Thompson."

She nodded. It was so good to be able to talk to John.

She saw him glance at the clock on her mantelpiece.

"Meta, I'd better sort out somewhere to stay for the weekend. I've only got until Monday."

Meta didn't stop to think. If he had to get back to Scotland after the weekend there was no way they were going to waste time looking for somewhere for him to stay. "There's no problem. You can stay here. I've got a spare room."

For a moment John looked at Meta in silence.

"No Meta. I'll find somewhere close by."

Meta was having none of it. "You've come all the way from Scotland to see me. There's no way I'm putting you out on the street to look for somewhere to stay." She avoided his gaze. Her landlady was visiting her sister in Balham for the weekend. She would never know. No one would ever know. "The spare room's through there. We can move the settee through and you can sleep on it."

John still hesitated. "Meta…"

"We're not arguing about it, John." Without waiting for any further protests Meta opened the door to the spare room. John hesitated for just a moment, then he picked up his battered brown suitcase and walked with it into the other room and after that they managed to manhandle the bed settee through from Meta's living room. Then they stood for a moment getting their breath back.

"Put your hat and coat back on." Meta danced past him, running to get her own coat and then they set off. It was a fair walk to the West End, but they could have walked twice as far without noticing.

Meta showed John the Shaftsbury Memorial, which Londoners now simply referred to as 'Eros'. As they stood looking at the winged statue, John suddenly darted away from her and ran across the road.

Meta saw him go up to one of the flower girls. He came back with a rose. He smiled and handed it to her. Meta blushed. Then she kissed him on the cheek and took his hand, and they walked down to the Trafalgar Square, then past the Lyons teashop and along the Strand past the unlit Tivoli theatre, until they came to the Savoy.

"Is this where we're going for dinner?" John smiled at her as they watched an elderly gentleman in evening dress help his wife out of a cab.

She laughed. "Next time you're in London, John."

They crossed over the road and checked two or three menus of the restaurants next to the fruit market in Covent Garden. Meta realised that John might not have very much money and in the end they contented themselves with a small cheap restaurant not far from the fruit market.

The little restaurant was packed and the food turned out to be very tasty, not that they noticed. They had eyes for no one else. There were lots of uniforms in the room but the war seemed a long way away. They were the last to leave. They only realised it because they heard the staff locking the doors behind them when they left.

That night Meta fell asleep almost as soon as her head touched her pillow, but not John. He opened his suitcase. He looked at the uniform still packed as he had folded it. He lay awake on the bed settee listening to the different sounds of a strange new place, but it wasn't the strangeness of his surroundings or the new noises that kept him awake. Those weren't the thoughts going through his head.

CHAPTER 6

PARTING

The sun breaking through her curtains woke Meta early the next morning. She lay and savoured the warmth of her bed. She hadn't felt so contented for a long time. Mr. Fairfax was forgotten. Only one person filled her thoughts, John McBride.

Eventually, she got up and busied herself in her little kitchen, hoping that the noise would wake John and that he would come through and talk to her while she made breakfast. She still hadn't asked him why he was in London or what his visit meant. Dare she hope he had given up thoughts of becoming a priest? Was that what he had come to tell her? The more she thought about it the more she decided not to ask. If she avoided that minefield maybe they could at least become friends again.

"Good morning, Meta." She almost jumped out of her skin. She hadn't heard John come into the kitchen.

"Goodness, you gave me a fright."

"I'm sorry," but he smiled as he said it.

She pushed him towards the kitchen table. "Sit down, I'll make you some breakfast, then we can go and explore London."

The sun was shining as they approached Westminster Pier. They saw a steamer was about to leave. They ran towards it and the two old men getting ready to cast off the mooring ropes held on while they paid their pennies, and as soon as they were aboard the gangplank was lifted and the steamboat chugged out into the river. The breeze caught Meta's hat and she just managed to catch it before it blew away. It made them laugh.

At Greenwich, they walked through the park and then across Black-heath to the village. They found a little teashop where they had tea and some scones which Meta had not tasted since she left Scotland.

John was quiet and pensive, but Meta didn't ask him any questions she was happy just to be with him. If John didn't feel the need to talk, then neither did she, being with him was enough so they just walked hand in hand. This time when they parted she was determined they would remain friends. She wasn't going to let him just walk away again.

It was chilly on the way back on the steamer and John took off his jacket and put it round her shoulders and then put his arm round her to keep her warm. She liked feeling the warmth of his body against hers.

As she let John into her rooms she said, "Thank you for a lovely day John. I really enjoyed myself."

"I enjoyed it too…" He held onto her hand. "Meta there's something I've got to tell you."

"Hold on. Wait until I make us some tea." She smiled at him and then pulled her hand away. She tried to ignore his troubled look as she made her way through to the kitchen.

As she busied herself in the kitchen she thought about what John wanted to say. Please, please don't spoil it. Don't ruin our day. Just say you're willing for us to be friends.

She handed John his tea and sat opposite him waiting for him to speak. For some time, they sat in silence before John spoke.

He put the tea on the table beside him and said very quietly, "Meta… I'm going to France." Meta wasn't sure that she had heard him. France? Was the Church sending John to France?

"I've left Trinity College. I've enlisted in the army. I have to report to Shorncliffe barracks on Monday."

She could not believe what John was saying. John was going to France as a soldier. Men were dying there every day, thousands of them. The newspapers were full of it, but that wasn't their world. Yes, she had seen the uniforms in the streets. Terrible things were happening but not to her, not to John.

He wasn't a soldier. He must not to go to France. "But John you're going to be a priest. What about the priesthood?"

"I gave up my studies at Trinity College some time ago." Meta searched John's face trying to understand. For so long she had wished to hear John say what he just had, and now the words just sent a dreadful chill through her body.

"Does Father MacDonald know?"

"Yes, he was disappointed. I think your grandfather was too."

"What did my grandfather say to you?"

"He told me I must do whatever I thought right. He suggested I should speak to you. That's why he gave me your address."

Meta struggled to understand what John was telling her, but the enormity of it was too much. All her hopes were dashed by one short phrase. "… I'm going to France."

"I still love you Meta…"

"…then why do you have to go to France?" The words that she had longed for John to utter, now meant nothing.

He shrugged his shoulders. "It's something I have to do. I feel it's my duty."

"Duty?"

Without looking at her he told her about the death of his two friends and then he looked up at her and somehow she knew it was too late. There was nothing she could do.

He stood up. "Do you want me to leave?"

What was he saying? As he got out of his chair she stood up and flung her arms round his neck. Didn't he know how much she loved him, how she had longed to see him, to hear his voice, to feel his body against hers? She hugged him with all her might. Then quite shamelessly she searched for his mouth with hers, and as they held each other, their longing for each other melted into a long lingering kiss.

The following day was Bank Holiday Monday so she walked with John to Charing Cross station where he was to catch the train to Folkestone. John was wearing his uniform. The station was packed. Soldiers were milling about everywhere. She was amazed to see so many uniforms in one place.

They lingered at the ticket barrier, holding hands, not bearing to let go of one another, prolonging the agony as lovers do when they know they must part; hoping that time will stand still, knowing it will not. Neither of them could bring themselves to say goodbye. The guard blew his whistle and then the steam engine too let out a deafening blast on its own whistle. John hugged Meta quickly, one final time.

"Look after yourself Meta," and then he ran for the train. Willing hands pulled him through the door as the packed train slowly began to pull away. Meta watched straining to catch one last glimpse of him, only giving up when finally the last coach of the train was out of sight. Then she turned and walked away, oblivious to the hordes of people milling about around her in the station concourse. Her only thoughts were of John.

This time she knew their separation would be so much harder, for now they were lovers.

CHAPTER 7

META AND MR. FAIRFAX

The day started more or less as normal. Meta was a little early as she walked across the schoolyard. The war news was bad again and she hadn't had a letter for over three weeks. Since John had left for France, she felt even more lonely than she had before.

The sinking of the Lusitania off the south coast of Ireland had upset her; so many innocent passengers had died, but what was worse, so many of them had been children. Now the Germans had shot a nurse, someone who was only helping wounded British and French soldiers. It shocked Meta to the core. It was simple, cold-blooded murder.

It was almost immediately after assembly that Mr. Fairfax had appeared. He knocked on Meta's classroom door, but before she could say, "Come in," he was through the door. There were beads of perspiration on his florid face. Something serious must have happened. She looked at him, waiting the reason for his abrupt, unsettling entrance, but Mr. Fairfax did not enlighten her, instead in a loud voice he said, "Miss Costello please would you identify Anna Smith for me." Mr Fairfax turned away from Meta and stood facing the class with his arms folded, sternly surveying the children in anticipation of Meta's answer.

"Mr. Fairfax, perhaps if you would explain…"

"…In a moment Miss Costello, now do as I ask."

Meta hesitated. "Anna, stand up please."

Anna stood up immediately.

Mr. Fairfax glared at the child. As she returned his gaze, the words came spitting out of his mouth, "Anna Smith you are a German!"

The child looked at Mr. Fairfax in total bewilderment and then the dreadful significance of what the headmaster had said registered.

"I'm not! I'm not!"

The poor child's denial was vehement, but Mr. Fairfax ignored her. He carried on remorselessly, "Your father's name is not Smith, it is Schmidt."

The small girl stood there utterly confused and defenceless.

"I'm not German!" The child banged the desk in front of her with her small, clenched fist.

"Mr. Fairfax I don't think…"

"…Please Miss Costello do not interrupt. This is a serious matter affecting the integrity of this school of which I am the headmaster." For just a moment Meta hoped that Mr. Fairfax was just being his usual pompous self, but her hopes were stillborn for Mr. Fairfax wasn't finished.

"The Germans are barbarians. Their soldiers butcher and mutilate women and defenceless young children." Meta couldn't believe what she was hearing. In front of Mr. Fairfax was a young child, but Mr. Fairfax was addressing her as if she was a war criminal. How could he see Anna as someone responsible for the dreadful atrocities occurring in Europe?

"Your presence in this school cannot be tolerated a moment longer. You must leave. Immediately! You are not to dare set foot in this school again. Do you hear me?" As Mr. Fairfax raised his voice to threaten the child, he also raised an imperious finger and pointed to the classroom door.

"Go! Get out!" He spat out the words with a violence that made Meta shudder.

For a moment, there was absolute silence in the classroom. All the other children watched in horrified silence as slowly Anna walked down the aisle between the desks. Then the child walked across the front of her entire class in a slow death march to the classroom door. All the way she kept her eyes cast down on the floor. As she reached for the door handle to open the door, she turned and looked at Meta. The silent appeal in her dark brown eyes was heartrending.

The scenario that had unfolded in front of Meta didn't seem real and yet it was.

"Mr. Fairfax, surely…" She got no further.

"…Miss Costello I will not tolerate the presence of this German girl in my school. If you wish to discuss the matter any further you may do so in my study when school finishes for the day." Without giving Meta a chance to say anything more Mr. Fairfax strode to the door. He grabbed Anna by the arm and forcibly marched her through the doorway and out of the classroom.

For a moment there was only a stunned silence. One of the younger boys started to cry. He sniffed as his nose began to run. Meta looked at the unhappy row of faces in front of her. One of the children in the front row broke the silence. He raised his hand but he didn't wait as he normally would for Meta's permission to speak. "Please Miss, Anna ain't a German. She was born here." There was a murmur of agreement from some of the other children.

To-day's behaviour, denouncing the child before her class in this way, as if Anna was some sort of poisonous boil that had to be lanced to save the health, no, the "integrity" of the school, was unbelievable. Meta was stunned. The child had no choice as to where her parents were born. Mr. Fairfax had assessed her as some kind of fifth columnist when the only evidence that he had that Anna and her parents were anything but loyal citizens of their adopted country appeared to be that they had a German surname.

The man was a fool. He didn't know the difference between prejudice and patriotism. She wanted to storm after the headmaster, but even if she could leave her class she knew it would be pointless. Mr. Fairfax would not listen to her. She could see him standing in his room rocking on his heels and pontificating about how he was only fulfilling his patriotic duty. However Meta disliked the fact, the country was at war, questioning Mr. Fairfax's patriotism at a time like this would get her nowhere with him, it might even alienate some of the other staff.

Her attention was brought back to the classroom by one of her pupil's, Emma Freeman. "What are we going to do now Miss?"

"We will do what we were doing before. Emma, you were going to recite the six times table."

"Miss, I meant …"

"I will speak to the headmaster later. Now, commence!"

Meta didn't mean to be unkind but her pupils needed to forget what had occurred. They needed to concentrate on something else. Once Emma had finished her recitation, Meta started firing off mental arithmetic questions at her pupils, turning it into a competition so that she gained their interest.

When the hand bell rang at the end of school she still hadn't worked out how she was going to sort out the dreadful mess her headmaster had created. First, she needed to talk to Anna and tell her she would do her best to help her, tackling Mr. Fairfax would have to wait.

CHAPTER 8

META DECIDES TO FIGHT BACK

Meta passed a number of two up and two down terraced houses before she came to the tenement block about half a mile from the school where Anna's parents lived. There was a woman standing on the corner made up and dressed in such a way that Meta realised she was in a neighbour-hood where young unaccompanied women were unlikely to be identified as schoolteachers.

The entrance to the building was dark, unwelcoming and smelt un-pleasantly. She tried not let her unease affect her as she walked down the dark narrow corridor that led to the stairs.

"What do you want?" Meta gave an involuntary jump. An old man was sitting on the stone steps. She had not seen him in the gloom.

"I'm looking for Mr. and Mrs. Smith and their daughter Anna."

The old man stood up, hawked and then spat out a lump of phlegm on the stone floor just in front of where Meta was standing.

"Bloody Huns!" Then he shuffled off into the darkness. Meta started to climb the stairs. Even if she had to knock on every door in the block she was determined to find the Smiths, but the first door she knocked on was opened by her pupil. Meta smiled at the distraught face in front of her.

"Hello Anna, are your parents home?"

Anna shook her head.

"Can I come in? I'd like to wait for them." Anna stood aside to let her teacher pass, wiping her face with the back of her sleeve as Meta passed. The Smith family lived in one barely furnished room.

"My parents don't know yet, Miss. What am I going to tell them? Mr. Fairfax says I must never come back to school."

"Are they still at work?"

Anna nodded. "They don't get back until after six, Miss. My parents both work down the Whitechapel Road, my mother's a seamstress and my father works as a tailor." Meta could see Anna was proud of her parents.

Meta looked around, at the sparsely furnished room. Curtains partly hid a bed in one corner. The only other furniture were two well worn armchairs. There was a book on one of them.

"What are you reading?" Meta picked up the book. It was by Charles Dickens.

Although Anna as one of the better readers in her class it hardly seemed possible that her pupil was reading Dickens until Meta remembered that she had been exactly the same age as Anna when her grandfather had given her the very same book.

"Tell me the story. What's it about?"

Meta listened to Anna telling Dickens' story of redemption. Her young pupil had the gift of storytelling and Meta was not aware of Anna's mother opening the door until she closed it behind her.

When Meta turned round she was shocked at Mrs. Smith's appearance. There were pouches under her eyes and the skin was discoloured, almost as if it were bruised. She had lost weight since Meta had last seen her outside the school some months before and she looked as if she hadn't slept. Meta tried not to show her surprise.

"Good evening, Mrs. Smith. I'm Meta Costello, Anna's teacher. I've…"

"Yes, I remember you," but despite what Mrs. Smith said, her expression remained vacant. Then a look of concern appeared. "What has happened? Has Anna done something wrong? Is she in trouble?"

"No, of course not Mrs. Smith…It's just that Mr. Fairfax, the headmaster, believes that you're German and…he feels that Anna shouldn't come to school if that's the case."

Mrs. Smith's whole body crumpled, and she slumped into the other armchair.

"Oh God, has it come to that now? They want to punish our children." The emotion in Mrs. Smith's voice caused her slight accent to become more apparent. She looked at Meta with haunted eyes.

"Are you from Germany?" Meta didn't mean it to sound like an accusation, but Mrs. Smith flinched at her words.

For a moment Mrs. Smith said nothing. She looked at Meta uncertainly and then she turned to Anna and asked her to make a pot of tea.

"My husband is from Germany, I'm not… I'm Polish." Mrs. Smith hesitated before she decided to go on. "The Germans and the Poles have been enemies for centuries." She gave a bitter laugh. "Our peoples hate each other. We used to live the other side of the border from Hans and his family." Mrs. Smith shook her head. "We should never have even been friends. It should never have happened, but it did. Our families would not accept it."

"I'm sorry Mrs. Smith I didn't mean to…"

Meta's apology tailed off and Mrs. Smith carried on, "We managed to get on a boat to England with some of the Jewish refugees from my country. The Jews were kind to us when we arrived, that's how Hans got his tailoring job."

Meta realised what a sacrifice Emma's mother must have made. It would be heart breaking if that sacrifice was for nothing. Meta felt her anger at Mr. Fairfax's behaviour rekindling.

"That was over twenty years ago. We'd almost forgotten we had not lived here all our lives, but then the war came…" Mrs. Smith paused again. "It didn't happen straight away, but in the last few months…" Mrs. Smith shook her head as she thought of what had happened. "First of all Hans was beaten up in the street. I found him lying in the gutter. They'd broken his glasses. He's almost blind without them. He must have been lying there for three or four hours before I found him. Nobody had tried to help him."

Meta listened hopelessly as Anna's mother told her how people she thought were friends now crossed the street to avoid her. How people spat as she passed them in the street. Yet, Mrs. Smith said, they had done nothing. The accident of her husband's birth they could not change.

"What can we do, Miss Costello? We are too old to run away again, and where would we run to?" Mrs. Smith looked at Meta knowing there was no answer to her question.

As Meta listened to the anguish in Mrs. Smith's voice she despaired as well. She had secretly hoped that Mr. Fairfax had been mistaken about

Anna's parentage. Even if he was proved to be right, Meta had hoped she would be able to approach the parents of the other children, and friends and neighbours in the locality, and there would be enough local people to force Mr. Fairfax to change his mind. Now she found that the Smiths were social outcasts. Her wild notion of uniting parents and neighbours against Mr. Fairfax's decision had vanished into thin air. Many of the local people had probably goaded Mr. Fairfax into throwing Anna out of school.

Just then Anna came back from the other end of the room with the tea. Meta looked at Anna. She didn't care how unrealistic she was being, Mr. Fairfax had to change his decision.

"I'm sorry to hear of all your troubles Mrs. Smith. You mustn't worry about Anna. I'll collect her on the way to school to-morrow. Anna's done nothing wrong. I'll make sure Mr. Fairfax changes his mind." Meta spoke without thinking. Almost straight away she realised she was being stupid, but then she saw the look on Mrs. Smith's face and she couldn't bring herself to dash the woman's hopes. All she could do was smile as she stood up.

"I must go now. I'll see you in the morning, Anna. We can walk to school together."

As Meta walked along the street she realised more and more how thoughtless she had been. What an earth had made her say what she had? It was one thing to feel sorry for people. It was another to raise their hopes only to dash them the following morning. She had only made matters worse, much worse.

A moment later she stumbled and fell, cannoning into the man walking the other way. He just managed to catch her from falling flat on her face.

"I'm terribly sorry. I'm afraid I wasn't looking where I was going." The man in dark clothing smiled his forgiveness.

"I'm the Reverend Michael Kinnear," Meta looked more closely at the friendly clergyman. She knew the name from somewhere.

"You look as if you have a lot on your mind, young lady." Despite everything Meta smiled. The Reverend Michael Kinnear looked only two or three years older that she was.

Meta adjusted her hat and looked around. "I'm afraid you're right." She had no idea at all where she was. "I'm a bit lost as well."

She held out her hand. "I'm Meta Costello."

"Where are you trying to get to?"

"Mile End station," she explained.

The priest shook his head, "Not the way you're going I'm afraid. Let me show you the way. It's past the church."

As they walked along the street together Meta learnt that the Reverend Michael Kinnear was the local Church of England minister for the parish. Then it came to her, where she had come across the name, the Reverend Kinnear was on the Board of Governors of Alma School.

"Aren't you a governor of Alma Elementary School?"

"Yes. Do you know it?"

"I teach there. I think you were supposed to be on the interview panel that appointed me, but you were called away to a bereavement."

He looked at her more closely. "Well, it looks like the panel made the correct decision without my help."

Meta laughed. "I'm afraid I still don't know many of the local people or my way round the neighbourhood."

"Well, I can vouch for the fact you don't know your way around," the priest gave her a friendly smile, "but you must know a lot of local people. As I remember it the classes at Alma are much larger than they should be."

"Yes. It's difficult getting teachers now, and it's more difficult to get to know the parents. All the mothers are working now."

"Yes, that is a problem, but they are sorely needed with all the men away in France."

As they passed the church the priest pointed to the small living quarters next door and the church hall and paused for a moment. "Would you care for a cup of tea before you go? You look as though you could do with one…" He gave Meta another of his shy friendly smiles. "At least it will give you a chance to get to know the local vicar."

CHAPTER 9

THE REVEREND KINNEAR

The Reverend Kinnear shook his head as Meta described how Mr. Fairfax had treated Anna Smith, but he listened to her without any interruption.

"I have to do something Reverend, it's not just for Anna, it's for all the children. Young children don't just need discipline, they need understanding and encouragement as well. The way Anna's been treated is so unfair. She's done nothing wrong. Why should she be punished?"

When she finished the Reverend Kinnear sat silently for some time, clearly giving the matter some thought.

"I shouldn't say too much before speaking to Mr. Fairfax, Miss Costello, but if he has behaved as you have described I cannot accept his behaviour. I think his decision is ill advised and …un-Christian."

Meta looked at him hopefully. "I am more than willing to raise his behaviour with the other governors and to try and get Mr. Fairfax to reverse his decision as regards…" The Reverend Kinnear got no further before Meta interrupted.

"…That is very kind of you Reverend, but I've told Anna I will take her back to school to-morrow. It could take weeks if we need to get the governors get involved."

The Reverend Kinnear shook his head. "Frankly, I think you might have been …" he paused looking at Meta as he chose his words "…a bit hasty to tell Anna's mother what you did Miss Costello."

"I know. I know. I was desperate to give them hope …to help them. I just can't let them down after what has happened to them."

"What do you suggest, Miss Costello? I don't mean to be unsympathetic, because I know what you did was done with the best of intentions… and I accept that Mr. Fairfax's behaviour leaves a lot to be desired, but he is the headmaster … I don't see what you or I can do about his decision other than what I have proposed."

Meta sat in silence. How could she face Anna? She dreaded having to tell her mother she could do nothing for them after all, but she had to be realistic, as Reverend Kinnear was being. If only she could give Anna and her mother something that they could hold onto whilst the vicar tried to convince the other governors to let her pupil return to school.

"Well, the least I can do is try and make sure that Anna gets some schooling. I'll ask her mother if I can teach her in my own time after school."

"That's very generous of you Miss Costello. I think that's all you can do for now. I'll try and raise the issue with the other governors as soon as possible…" He paused and looked at her earnestly, "…but some of them may well be sympathetic to Mr. Fairfax's actions. I think you have to realise Miss Costello that the recent Zeppelin raids have made a lot of people very angry, and Mr. Fairfax has been headmaster for a long time."

Meta knew the airship raids had made a lot of people frightened. "You will try though?" It was all so unfair on Anna.

The Reverend Kinnear smiled at her, "I will try, I promise you."

"Don't look so worried Miss Costello. If you continue to give Anna and her mother hope and the support that you have there's a way out of this." Meta smiled gratefully. She picked up her teacup and then he did likewise and there was silence for a moment.

"The problem is that Anna's going to miss her classmates."

"I don't see how that can be avoided, Miss Costello."

"Well…I thought of something that might help."

"Yes?" The Reverend Kinnear wondered what was coming.

"I've been thinking for some time of a way to try help the parents at the school. A lot of the mothers are now working at the munition factory over at Woolwich. They often don't get home until long after their children get back from school."

"It's not just a problem at Alma Elementary School I can assure you Miss Costello."

"Well, the church hall here isn't far from the school…I was wondering whether it might be free after school finishes?"

"Yes, most days I think."

"Well…"

"Tell me what you have in mind Miss Costello."

Meta had to be at Anna's home early to ensure she arrived before her mother left for work. Even so Anna's father had already gone. Mrs. Smith asked her to sit down.

"Mrs. Smith since we met yesterday I have spoken to one of the governors of the school, the Reverend Kinnear."

Mrs. Smith nodded. "I know him, he's very young for a priest."

"He was as shocked as I am by Mr. Fairfax's behaviour, and he has agreed to ask the other governors to persuade the headmaster to let Anna back to school."

"Do you think the other governors will do that?"

"I don't know Mrs Smith, but I do believe he will try as hard as he can to help Anna." She paused. "I think that is the only way that we can get Mr. Fairfax to change his decision." Meta steeled herself to go on. "I'm afraid it's going to take longer than I thought."

"Your priest, he's so young." Mrs. Smith gave Meta a worried look. "I know it cannot be done as quickly as we would like, but will he try and raise it soon?"

"As soon as he possibly can…but it won't be possible for Anna to go back for a week or two." Possibly longer, thought Meta.

"What am I going to do if I can't go back to school?" It was Anna who spoke.

"Well Anna, what if I were to teach you on your own for a few days? I'll leave you some exercises every morning and I'll come and see how you've got on after school each day."

The change in Anna's worried expression proved Reverend Kinnear was right. All Mrs. Smith and Anna needed was hope.

By the end of two weeks Meta was exhausted. After she finished at school, she taught Anna at home and the rest of her spare time, including her weekends, she spent with the Reverend Kinnear sorting out the Church Hall.

Meta didn't tell Mr. Fairfax what she was proposing to do. It was outside school hours and it wasn't on the school premises. She explained to those parents who came to collect their children from school what she had arranged with the Reverend Kinnear and most of them were more than happy for their children to come along.

As regards the "latch key" children in the class, those who were on their own after school, she told them all that if they wanted to join in the after school arrangements they must tell their mothers or they would all get into trouble, and she gave them all notes to take home, although she had grave doubts that the notes would get there or be read if they did.

On the first day she escorted just over half her class from the school gates to the Church Hall where Anna was waiting. They were quite excited to see her again. She had been popular with her fellow pupils.

Meta knew that Anna and the rest of the class would quickly become disenchanted if they thought they were only being made to do more schoolwork so she made sure the after-school arrangement involved them in lots of different things like storytelling and playacting.

Emma Freeman's mother came along to see what was happening, and offered to help out. That made a difference. Soon nearly all Meta's class from Alma Elementary School had joined her after school club.

CHAPTER 10

META'S CONFRONTATION
WITH MR. FAIRFAX

Matters progressed without any problems for three weeks. On the third Friday as Meta walked across the playground she found Mr. Fairfax standing in her path.

"Where are you going with those children Miss Costello?"

"The children and I are leaving the school premises, headmaster."

"I can see that Miss Costello, but where are you taking them?" Mr. Fairfax didn't say she was being impertinent but his belligerence, said exactly that. She wondered if she should tell Mr. Fairfax what he was demanding to know, but she'd had enough of his arrogance and bullying.

"Well?" The headmaster stood blocking her path to the playground exit. "Does this involve that German girl?" She realised that Mr. Fairfax only wanted to know so that he could persecute Anna a bit more. There was no way she was going to allow that, but she didn't want a row in front of the children. "Please excuse me Mr. Fairfax." When the headmaster did not move, Meta stepped to one side, and started to walk round him.

Mr. Fairfax was not quick enough to block Meta's path again and so he seized her firmly by the arm.

The unexpected pull on her arm caused Meta to lose her balance and down she went. She hit the hard surface of the playground with her left arm trapped under her body. She gasped as she felt a sharp stab of pain from her arm and as she rolled over she knew from the pain and the angle of her arm that she had broken it.

Mr. Fairfax stood there frozen to the spot.

A moment later Miss Thompson pushed through Meta's pupils. "Are you alright Miss Costello?"

Meta could only shake her head. She had a searing pain in her arm. Costello needs a doctor, Mr. Fairfax."

"She just tripped. It was an accident."

"We can deal with how it happened later, headmaster, but now Miss Costello needs someone to see to her arm."

"It was an accident. You saw it was an accident, didn't you Miss Thompson?"

Miss Thompson ignored the headmaster's question and turned towards Meta's pupils, a number of whom looked quite shaken.

"Emma. Emma Freeman."

"Yes, Miss Thompson."

"Run along to Dr. Morrison's by the Church Hall and ask him if he can come over to the school to help Miss Costello. Tell him we think she's gone and broken her arm."

Emma ran off.

"Are you able to get up Miss Costello?" Asked Miss Thompson.

"If someone will help me."

Miss Thompson looked around for Mr. Fairfax to assist her, but the headmaster had started to walk away.

"Here give me your good hand." Miss Thompson helped Meta her feet. "Let's get you inside and get you a cup of tea."

"What about the children? I'm supposed to be taking them to the Church Hall until six o'clock."

"I'll send them all home for today. I'll go down to the Church Hall later and explain what's happened."

Meta wanted to argue but she was still too shocked by her fall and the pain in her arm. "Where's the headmaster?"

Miss Thompson looked round. Mr. Fairfax was disappearing into the school building.

Meta Costello received her summons to attend the Committee Meeting of the Education Authority well before her broken arm had healed. Reverend Kinnear escorted her, and she was pleased to have his presence. He had instigated Anna's appeal directly with the Education Authority. After hearing of the incident in the playground he felt there was no point in speaking to Mr. Fairfax. Meta found the proceedings intimidating, from the austere Council building to the formality of the actual meeting.

"There are two issues relating to Alma Elementary School that this Committee has been asked to consider. The expulsion of Anna Smith from Alma Elementary School and …an allegation of an assault in the school playground." Meta listened to the Chairman's formal opening statement with surprise. She had left matters to the Reverend Kinnear. She had mentioned the playground incident to him, but she had not expected it would be raised at the meeting.

"I intend the Committee should consider the alleged assault first." Meta looked at the Reverend Kinnear, sitting next to her. He seemed unsurprised.

A moment later the Chairman asked if she would come forward. He asked Meta to give her version of the playground incident. Meta gave her evidence rather haltingly. She had not expected the incident to be part of the formal hearing.

She explained the arrangement she had with the Reverend Kinnear for children to use the Church Hall after school. "I don't think the headmaster approved of what I was doing. I didn't want to have an argument with him in front of the children, so I tried to walk round him. He grabbed hold of my arm and I lost my balance".

"Thank you, Miss Costello. Mr. Fairfax, perhaps you could tell us your version of what occurred."

The headmaster appeared even more flustered than Meta, but he must have been warned that the issue would be raised at the meeting. This was a formal hearing into his behaviour.

He told the Committee that he had tried to ask Meta where she was going with her class after school. "Quite a legitimate question I think you'll agree Mr. Chairman. Miss Costello has been particularly unhelpful since I expelled the German girl from the school and she refused to answer my question. She tried to walk past me and she tripped as she did so. If she hadn't been in such a hurry it wouldn't have happened. It was just a simple accident Mr. Chairman. It was very unfortunate."

"You never touched Miss Costello?"

"No, of course not."

One of the Chairman's colleagues, a young man wearing thick pebble glasses, lent across and whispered to him.

"Is Miss Thompson present?"

"I am." Meta heard Miss Thompson's voice from the back of the room. Another surprise, Meta had not realised that Miss Thompson was present up until that moment.

"Would you come forward please."

Miss Thompson's version of the event was very different to Mr. Fairfax's and it was delivered in a much more confident and forceful manner.

"Did Mr. Fairfax touch Miss Costello at all during this incident in the playground?"

"Yes. He grabbed Miss Costello by the arm to try and stop her getting past him and he pulled her back towards him. That caused Miss Costello to lose her balance. She landed awkwardly on her arm and broke it, as you can see."

The Committee members all looked at Mr. Fairfax. The Chairman said, "Would you like to ask Miss Thompson any questions Mr. Fairfax?"

Mr. Fairfax looked flustered. "I don't think…Mr. Chairman, Miss Thompson has been a problem for me at Alma School for a long time. Both she and Miss Costello are… They both have problems keeping discipline, particularly Miss Costello. They frequently question my authority."

There was silence in the room for a moment, and then the Chairman spoke. "Are you telling us that Miss Costello and Miss Thompson have made up their version of this incident?"

"Yes…I mean no."

"Well, which is it?"

"There was an incident in the playground but I was not responsible for Miss Costello's injury."

"Are you suggesting that Miss Costello and Miss Thompson are making up the fact that you pulled Miss Costello's arm so that you can be blamed for something you did not do. That they are doing this is because you have complained about their ability to keep discipline?" Mr. Fairfax appeared not to know what to say. "Is that correct?"

There was a long silence. "Well, I might have held my arm out, but I think Miss Thompson is mistaken. I never touched Miss Costello."

"I wasn't asking that Mr. Fairfax. I was asking if you were suggesting that two of your teachers have deliberately lied to us out of spite towards yourself."

"I don't know the reason they are saying what they are, Mr. Chairman, but Miss Costello's fall was a pure accident."

Mr. Fairfax discomfiture was more than obvious now. Meta watched as the Chairman carried on remorselessly.

"Did you write to the Miss Costello or Miss Thompson about these disciplinary problems?"

"Well…no."

"Did you raise them with anybody else …any of the governors?"

"No."

"So, there is no record that there was any problem and yet you are saying that they are lying to us because you had criticised them for their disciplinary inadequacies?"

"I spoke to them about it."

After this exchange the Committee adjourned for a short time.

"Mr. Fairfax this Committee is satisfied that you assaulted Miss Costello. What is worse this occurred in front of pupils at your school. We also believe that that you have not been entirely truthful with this Committee." The Chairman paused. "It is the unanimous decision of the Committee that you should be asked to tender your resignation from your post as Headmaster of Alma Elementary School."

Mr. Fairfax stood there looking stunned. Meta was shocked too. Everyone, including the Chairman was looking at the headmaster waiting for him to say something, but the headmaster just stood there with his mouth open.

"These proceedings are now adjourned." They all stood up and the Committee left the room. Suddenly it appeared to register with Mr. Fairfax what had happened, and he rushed out the door pursuing the Committee. Meta heard was the headmaster's voice calling out as he disappeared down the corridor, "Mr. Chairman a word if you please…"

A week after the headmaster's dismissal, Miss Thompson was invited to act as temporary headmistress of Alma Elementary School, an appointment that was subsequently made permanent. One of her first decisions was to rescind Anna's expulsion.

Despite that, and Mr. Fairfax's departure, Meta decided that her time at the Alma Elementary School should come to an end.

Before she told Miss Thompson, she thanked her for her support. "I don't think I would have convinced the Committee without your help."

"I think you would Miss Costello."

Meta shook her head.

"You were honest, and you are not a bully."

"They didn't know Mr. Fairfax was a bully."

Miss Thompson looked at Meta for a moment before she spoke. "Do you remember the committee member sitting on the right of the Chairman."

Meta thought back. She remembered the bespectacled young man who had lent forward and obviously reminded the Chairman of Miss Thompson's presence. "Yes, I think so."

"He used to be a pupil here. Now he's secretary of the local Labour Party. I don't think Mr. Fairfax recognised him - though he should have. He caned that boy nearly every day. The boy had poor eyesight. Mr. Fairfax kept punishing him for his clumsiness. I tried to intervene. I'm afraid I only made matters worse."

"I'm sure that things like that are now in the past Miss Thompson."

"I hope so, but we need teachers like you, Miss Costello. I think you should seriously reconsider your decision to leave."

Meta was touched by Miss Thompson's words but her mind was made up, "I'm sorry but I've decided there's something else I must do"

"I'm sorry too. What are you intending to do?"

"I have a friend fighting in France. I want to try and do something that's more directly involved with what's going on over there."

Miss Thompson just nodded, "If you ever change your mind, do get in touch with me." Her new headmistress appeared to be about say something more, but then thought better of it, so Meta turned to leave. As she reached the door she heard Miss Thompson say quite softly, "Good luck."

Now that John McBride was fighting in the trenches Meta decided she couldn't just to sit and wait for his letters to tell her he was still alive. She had made up her mind to train as a nurse.

She wrote both to her grandfather and John and told them of her intention, but she told neither that she would try to be transferred to France once she was qualified. Her grandfather would only worry, and she didn't want to give John any false hopes.

It was clear that there was little possibility of John McBride being given leave in England. The British Army did not give ordinary soldiers home leave. They were too frightened the men would not come back to the front so this was only way she could think of getting to see John again.

CHAPTER 11

TRAINING AND JOHN'S FIRST SORTIE

John McBride's rejection of the priesthood was caused in large part by the regimentation he faced in his Seminary. If he had not been assigned to assist in the theological college's infirmary he might have quit his religious training even earlier than he did. Ironically John now found himself engulfed in an even more authoritarian regime than the one he had left behind.

Surprisingly, the physical training was less of a problem for him than many of the other recruits. Since his days swimming in the North Sea he had tried to keep fit, even during his clerical training, and he found he had an aptitude for the more practical side of his army instruction. He could soon strip and clean his rifle quicker than any of the other recruits, but each night he lay awake with one thought in his mind. Killing human beings.

He tried to convince himself he could do it, but more and more he dreaded the moment when his training would be put to the test. Then he realised that he must stop thinking about it. His training was meant to teach him to kill without thinking and that was the only way he would manage it when the time came. So, at the training camp at Etaples he stuck his bayonet into the straw sacks with a ferocity that satisfied the most dedicated of his drill sergeants, and he waited. He waited for that moment to come when he would know the answer to the question that he kept asking himself, and which would only be answered in real combat.

John McBride's commanding officer found John difficult to assess. He was different. He wasn't quite sure how a Scot like John had found himself in his unit. Nearly all his company was made up of Londoners mainly from the East End, but then he had come all the way from Ireland to join up, so the fact that McBride had found his way into a London recruiting office wasn't all that strange.

There was something apart from his Scottish heritage that made McBride stand out from the others, but he couldn't put his finger on what it was. Gradually from censoring McBride's letters he pieced together that McBride had once trained for the priesthood and that he was in love with a schoolteacher. He felt a tinge of jealousy that McBride had someone he longed to return to, someone waiting for him. He hoped McBride's obvious commitment to his training would enable him to survive but he doubted the young man was prepared for the horrors they were about to face.

The other recruit that Richard Lawson noticed early on was Andy Freeman. The two men became friends whilst they were training at Etaples. Captain Lawson didn't understand why at first. One came from lowland Scotland, the other from the East End of London; characterwise too they were total opposites. Then he discovered that John McBride's girlfriend taught in an elementary school in London near where Andy Freeman lived.

As well as being a good soldier, Andy Freeman had the ability to get the best out of others. Captain Lawson gave him his sergeant's stripes early on. He'd thought of making McBride an NCO as well, but when he proposed it, McBride refused the promotion. He had said he would prefer to be designated as one of the company's stretcher bearers. Captain Lawson wondered at first if McBride was looking for a safe option and that he didn't realise that stretcher bearers often ran even greater risks than the wounded they tried to save. When he pointed that out to McBride all the man had said was, "I'd like to be where I might be of some use, sir. I don't know how good I'll be at killing people, but I do have some medical training." So, Captain Lawson told him that when the time came he would remember his request and he let him remain a private soldier.

Despite McBride's fear that he didn't have the same propensity for fighting and killing as most of the other recruits, the other men liked him. Freeman, because he knew John McBride's history, nicknamed him

"Padre" and the nickname stuck. Maybe because of that a lot of the men confided in John McBride, they brought him their troubles for there was no chaplain with their unit.

Captain Richard Lawson struggled to hide his feelings. They had barely relieved the previous unit that had occupied their trench when he received orders to carry out a reconnaissance mission. It was bad enough that the trench they now occupied had been left in an awful state. The previous company had been desperate to get out. They'd been forgotten about by the powers that be and left in occupation of the trench for far too long. Instead of trying to improve their lot they'd let breastworks crumble, the dugouts were foul and there were holes in the protective barbed wire. Their company commander had given Richard Lawson the barest amount of information on handover. Now Captain Lawson found he was being given what he considered to be a dangerous, pointless exercise by someone on the HQ staff who had probably never been near the front line; or maybe they had and thought this was good way of avoiding the boredom that had obviously affected the previous occupants of their trench.

Lawson was ordered to make a sortie into the enemy trench opposite. He and his men were to take some prisoners so that they could be brought back and interrogated. Captain Lawson was totally unconvinced of the need for the proposed foray. Their sector of the line was quiet. There was nothing to suggest any troop movements on the part of the Germans as far as he could ascertain, and these days there were aircraft that could spot major troop movements. If this was simply a question of keeping his men occupied it was sheer stupidity. Boredom wasn't the problem. Staying alive was, that …and not freezing to death. The temperature in the last few days had dropped drastically.

He had to decide who should lead this unwelcome sortie. He had been forbidden to lead it, so his second in command, Lieutenant Harboard would have to do it. He summoned him and Sergeant Freeman.

"Any ideas as to who you want to take?

"Might I suggest Garstone and McBride, sir?" Sergeant Freeman spoke before Lieutenant Harboard had a chance to say anything. Garstone's name didn't surprise Captain Lawson but after his discussion with McBride he wasn't sure about Freeman's second choice.

"Why do you want to take McBride?" Captain Lawson wanted to make sure that Freeman didn't just want to keep his friend close by him.

"He's reliable, sir."

"What do you think Hardboard?"

"He may not look it sir, but he's the fittest man apart from Freeman we've got." Captain Lawson nodded. That made sense. Manhandling prisoners back across no man's land would be a struggle.

Richard Lawson didn't quite know how to articulate his concerns but he pressed his second in command. "He's a bit... different from the others."

"Maybe, but I think Freeman's right. He's dependable." Richard Lawson hesitated for a moment and then he decided to leave the choice up to men who were going to be taking all the risks.

"If we manage to cut the wire. Freeman and you four drop into the trench. We can only bring back two prisoners at the most." Those were Lieutenant Hardboard's orders to his men.

The German wire was thicker and denser than the British wire. It had been extremely difficult to cut. God alone knew how they had got to the wire without being spotted, probably luck and the atrocious weather. It was freezing cold.

They dropped into the trench, and still there was not a German in sight. John McBride had a bag full of Mills bombs that Andy Freeman had given him to carry. Their luck appeared to continue for as they jumped down into the German trench they landed quite close to the opening of a German dugout. All the Germans seemed to be inside. It was a quiet night and they had obviously decided there was no reason to stay out in the bitter weather. Even the British wouldn't be stupid enough to do anything in the sub-zero temperature outside.

There were proper wooden doors covering the opening to the dugout, not wooden planks as the British had, but with one ferocious double kick from Andy Freeman the doors buckled inwards.

"Chuck that bag in...as far as you can."

John lobbed the bag of Mills bombs through the door with all his might. Somebody inside shouted something in German as Andy Freeman followed up by chucking a single live bomb in after John's bag.

251

Suddenly there was lots of shouting from inside the dugout and outside a German soldier came hurtling round the bend in the trench towards them. At least one soldier had been left outside the dugout in the cold to patrol the trench.

Freeman was the first to react. He reversed his rifle and hammered the stock into the man's midriff. The man was down on his knees gasping for air. A further blow to the head and, despite his helmet, the German was out cold.

"Get down!" Yelled Freeman and as John McBride hit the floor of the trench there was the sound first of Freeman's bomb going off followed almost straight away by a second massive explosion. A blast of fire shot out from the dugout entrance. For a moment here was silence, then there were agonising screams and everything was total confusion.

"Out, out. Move!" Lieutenant Harboard was shouting at them from above the trench.

"Garstone get up that firestep. McBride grab that German bastard. Go. Go!" Freeman was shouting now.

There was no time for a second prisoner. Jimmy Garstone scrambled out of the trench. He turned around and he and the other men held out their hands to grab the unconscious prisoner from John McBride.

"Look out!" Round the bend from the opposite direction to the one the first German had come from came another soldier running a full tilt, but Andy Freeman already had his rifle raised. He fired at point blank range and one side of the German's face disintegrated as he collapsed to the ground. John barely heard the German's screams of agony.

Then they were out of the trench and running as fast as they could. McBride had the unconscious German captive slung over his shoulders in a fireman's lift. He was over halfway back to the British trench when he tripped and fell. Almost at the same instant as he fell a fusillade came from further down the German line. The Germans were fully awake now. Mortar shells started exploding in No Man's Land. The whole area was erupting.

"Freeman give me your rifle. You and McBride grab the Hun, one arm each. Garstone stay here with me. Go. Go!" Yelled Lieutenant Hardboard.

With one arm over each of their shoulders Andy Freeman and John McBride stumbled forward bending as low as they could, carrying the limp and unconscious German. It seemed an age before they found one of the gaps in the wire but when they finally reached the lip of the trench it was Captain Lawson who pulled them into the trench and then a number of willing hands caught them and their German prisoner as they tumbled into the trench.

Lieutenant Harboard waited behind to see if the Germans would send anyone out from their trench into No Man's Land. For half an hour they waited, the shooting started to die down, but Harboard knew that they had to wait for much longer than that. After another hour and a half Hardboard decided they should make their own run for the British trench. Garstone made it. Hardboard didn't. He hadn't waited quite long enough.

CHAPTER 12

KATHERINE LEARNS JOHN IS IN FRANCE

When she had read her son's letter to Meta, Katherine had not been able to control her fury, but in the weeks and months after her niece had left for London she gradually realised what a mistake she had made.

She had been so elated when she finally discovered John was studying to be a priest that she couldn't believe that her niece would jeopardise the future she had begun to envision for him. She had been unable to contain herself.

Just when she thought that God had signified his forgiveness to her by allowing her son to be ordained as a priest, Meta had threatened to ruin all her hopes. Her loathing for Michael Costello that she had managed to bury over the years had resurfaced and she had lashed out at Meta. Meta the young girl, who despite Katherine's hatred for her father, she had grown to love.

It was only when Meta had left for London that Katherine understood what she had done. She had wanted to punish Meta for her innocence, for the very same failings she, Katherine had once had. Now she realised how unfair she had been to lay the wrong done to her by Michael Costello at Meta's door.

It was her husband Seamus who made her realise she had gone too far. "You should at least have let Meta say goodbye to you." That one sentence had made her think, for Seamus never criticised her. It had not taken her long after that for her to realise he was right.

For a time after her sister's death, Katherine had deliberately tried to avoid getting too close to Meta, but as she walked along the River Leven the sense of loss she now felt brought home to her that her feelings for her niece were much stronger than she had ever admitted, but now it was too late. Instead of trying to help her orphaned niece, she had driven Meta away. It was only now that she admitted how much she loved Michael Costello's daughter.

For a long time there was little she could do. Once her son returned to his seminary, Katherine was in the dark as to what he was up to, and once Meta was in London she heard nothing from her. Yet all she could think of as she went on her long solitary walks was her fear of what might happen to the two of them. Although once more her heart ached there was nothing she could do but stand and stare out over the River Leven.

She watched the waters go swirling and rushing by, giving no heed to her thoughts of the two children she held so dear, but who for different reasons she had never been able to show her love for. Once again she had no one to talk to. She could not confess to Father MacDonald that she knew John McBride was her son. She sighed. She could never reveal her secret, never mention it to anyone. She had to live with that.

Then things changed.

Katherine continued to have lunch with her father every Sunday. After she and her husband Seamus attended church on a Sunday morning, the two of them would return to Melville House with Brian O'Malley. Relations between her father and Seamus had improved. Gradually the two had grown closer. She found her own relationship with Seamus had also changed. To her surprise she realised Seamus had not married her out of convenience, Seamus loved her.

The three of them were seated round the dining room table when her father said right out of the blue, "I had a letter from Meta this week. She said we shouldn't worry about these Zeppelin raids. None of the bombing has been near her." Katherine mind had been elsewhere but now she paid close attention.

"Did she have any other news?" It was Seamus who asked the question that Katherine was on the point of asking.

"Not much. She said that she's finding the headmaster at her school quite difficult." Then without thinking there might be any particular significance in what he said, Brian O'Malley had continued. "She did say that she had heard from John McBride, apparently he had written to her from France to say he was safe, or as safe as anyone can be out there in the trenches."

Katherine fought hard to control her reaction, which was as well because her husband had turned to look at her. She just managed to retain her composure, but only just, for her father too had looked over at her. He remembered how upset she had been when the young man's intentions to join the priesthood had been threatened by his involvement with Meta. Of course, she would be disappointed to learn that his choice of vocation had indeed come to nought, even more so that he had joined the army, but that thought was interrupted by Seamus.

"The papers seem to believe that there is likely to be another offensive soon," said Seamus and Brian O'Malley turned his attention back to his son-in-law.

"Let's hope it goes better than the previous ones," and the two men began to discuss the progress of the war in France and Katherine Thomson turned away from them hoping that her inner turmoil had not registered with either of them. She did not notice the glances Seamus gave her as she sat deep in thought.

She had thought that John and Meta had safely gone their separate ways. That was the one thing about her intervention she did not regret, but that was not the case. She made up her mind. She needed to contact Meta. Her father clearly had her latest address. She had thought of asking for it before, but she had feared her father would refuse it after her vicious row with Meta.

When there was a lull in the conversation between her husband and her father Katherine spoke, "Father, I think I should write to Meta and apologise for my behaviour towards her before she left."

What Brian O'Malley's daughter had said didn't fully register with him straight away. It certainly it took him a moment to realise that Katherine appeared to be admitting that she might have been at fault with her previous behaviour. Seamus was surprised too, but he was pleased to hear Katherine's change of heart. He'd liked his wife's niece and he always felt Katherine had behaved far too strictly towards Meta when she was younger although he had never said anything.

For a moment Brian O'Malley hesitated. He still feared Katherine was not over her hatred of Meta's father, but if his daughter had genuinely changed her mind about Meta then he ought to do what he could to heal the long-standing family rift. If Katherine was not being genuine what real harm could a letter from her do? Meta was strong enough to ignore a letter.

"By all means Katherine let me have a letter and I will enclose if with mine next time I write to her."

Until he had Meta's permission he was not going to let Katherine know of Meta's exact whereabouts.

CHAPTER 13

CAPTAIN LAWSON
REMEMBERS CAROLINE

Captain Richard Lawson's unit was well under strength. He hoped his promised re-enforcements would arrive before he went back down the line.

He lay awake on his bed worrying. How long would these new men last? They needed to be taught how to avoid needless risks and there was never enough time for that. They would face snipers and shelling from the day they arrived in the front line. Their basic training was aimed at teaching them how to kill people, not how to stay alive. Maybe they would learn from Sergeant Freeman and from Garstone, or even McBride, but it would take time. Time they didn't have.

It was going to rain. Rain wasn't just unpleasant it was depressing but there was nothing he could do about it.

To-morrow he had been told to attend a briefing at headquarters before they went back to the front. He hoped he wasn't going to be given any more bad news.

His mind drifted back to thoughts of Caroline Mansfield. He tried to put her out of his mind, but the more he tried to do that the more he thought about her. He had censored some letters the previous evening and the loving way John McBride had expressed himself to his girlfriend had made him think of Caroline.

Caroline Mansfield was the woman Richard Lawson had intended to marry until his grandfather intervened. She had sued him for breach of promise of marriage. That had been bad enough, but worse had followed. Someone had leaked the matter to the newspapers. The case had become something of a cause célèbre. It had even appeared in 'The Times' newspaper.

His grandfather had told him he had to fight the case to vindicate the family name but Richard Lawson's heart had not been in it. Whatever the legal position was, he believed he was in the wrong. Caroline Mansfield had succeeded with her claim.

He remembered only too well the humiliating cross-examination by her Counsel, Serjeant Sullivan. He was an Irish Serjeant-at-law but he had also been called to the English Bar and was entitled to appear in the English Courts. He had asked Lawson straight out the question upon which the whole case had turned.

"You promised to marry Miss Mansfield, didn't you?" He had hesitated momentarily before he replied. "I don't think so."

Sullivan had pounced. "You don't think so? You don't think so? Come now Captain Lawson either you promised to marry Caroline Mansfield or you didn't." His own Counsel had told him not to equivocate and he hadn't meant to do so but he hadn't wanted to suggest outright that Caroline was lying.

In vain he'd tried to explain that he had told Caroline he would marry her once his father had given his consent, that any promise he had made was conditional on that consent.

Sergeant Sullivan was relentless, "And did you father consent, Captain Lawson?"

"No"

"…And the reason for that was that your father died in a hunting accident."

"That is correct."

"So you promised to marry Miss Mansfield, but it was subject to a condition, and when that condition could never be fulfilled you thought that gave you the opportunity to renege on you promise?"

"It wasn't like that."

"It wasn't like that?'

"No. Obviously then I asked my grandfather."

"Why?"

"…because by that time I was his direct heir."

Serjeant Sullivan had peered at him over his round rimmed glasses. "I see, and had you informed Miss Mansfield that your promise to marry her was subject to your grandfather's consent?

"No but…"

"…And your grandfather refused his consent didn't he?"

"Yes, so…"

"Isn't the truth Captain Lawson that you promised to marry Caroline Mansfield and then you tried to find every excuse you possibly could to avoid going through with that promise."

Before he could say anything else Serjeant Sullivan had sat down and Richard Lawson had turned and looked at the jury and all he could see was a sea of hostile faces.

A few days later his grandfather had called Richard Lawson a "wimp" to his face - in front of one of his brother officers. Richard Lawson had been ostracized from that moment on. He'd resigned his commission in the regiment he had fought with in South Africa, the regiment in which his grandfather had once been colonel, and he had gone to the family estate in Ireland and hidden away there.

He'd written a final plea for forgiveness to Caroline Mansfield. He spent hours composing it, trying to apologise for his unforgiveable behaviour, for a wrong it was too late to right. At the end of it he'd tried to let her know how much he still loved her. His final words were from a poem that he felt reflected his loss. He'd written,

> "I only know the Summer sang in me
> A little while,
> That sings in me no more."

He had received the letter back torn in two.

He tried to improve his grandfather's neglected estate in Ireland in small ways. Some of the family's tenants were treated appallingly and he'd tried to intervene where he could. He was told that things had been so bad on the estate that there had been violence in the past.

He might have stayed in Ireland for the rest of his life. It was a place his grandfather never visited, but then the war had come. Sometime after the outbreak of hostilities he'd received another letter. Not a letter exactly, an envelope. The envelope had a white feather in it.

He didn't think it had come from Caroline, more likely one of his former brother officers.

Eventually he'd travelled to London and joined up, avoiding his old army contacts. Now after over a year at the front he was a Captain, the rank he given up years before.

He looked at the threatening sky. There was no point in regrets. In a few days he'd probably be dead along with most of his men.

There was a knock on his door. The ever-present army didn't give you time for your own thoughts.

"Come in." A moment later his batman was in the doorway.

"The new recruits will be here at noon, sir. Lieutenant Newman wants to know if you will be wanting to address the men or whether you want him to deal with matters."

"Tell him I want to see the replacements myself when they arrive." Captain Lawson didn't want his new second in command to be the first the new recruits heard from. He was not the man to instil confidence in them. "Let me know when they're all here."

Half an hour later there was another knock on the door. It was Lieutenant Newman. Richard Lawson tried not to show his irritation with his new second-in-command. He felt Newman was the one weak link in his command. Maybe it was because his predecessor Lieutenant Hardboard had been so reliable. Hardboard had had a baby face, but he had common sense and knew what he was doing. He had joined the territorials whilst still at Dulwich College and he'd shot for his college at Oxford. Newman was a lousy shot. He couldn't hit a barn door at a hundred yards. In fact, he probably couldn't even hit a barn at that distance. Captain Lawson knew he had to stop these facetious thoughts. The real problem with Newman was his inability to relate to the men he commanded. He had no idea how to inspire confidence in them.

"Excuse me sir."

"Yes Newman?"

"The rest of the men are here."

"Thank you. Parade the new men outside in half an hour and I'll speak to them then."

When the men were presented, Richard Lawson went down the line and spoke to each one. More importantly he learnt all their names and memorised them.

CHAPTER 14

VAD TRAINING.

The first morning after Meta moved into the hostel attached to her training hospital an explosion shook the whole building. Meta had been woken by one of the other occupants leaving her room, but it was still almost dark, and she had not yet forced herself out of her bed to face the day. Her heartbeat was racing. She was convinced for a moment that they were experiencing a Zeppelin bombing raid but when she opened the door to the hallway she discovered it was only the gas geyser from the shared bathroom next door to her room exploding into action.

Meta was attached to St. Bartholomew's Hospital in London for her training, but this was actually taking place out in Camberwell. She had given up her rooms that she rented as a teacher and moved into the hostel attached to the training hospital. There were two other trainees in her cold, cramped room. Despite the explosion and the initial and intermittent visits by a plumber, the bathroom water heater refused to yield anything like hot water.

When her turn came to use the bathroom in the morning, Meta discovered either the pilot light had gone out, or even if had not, the gas jets refused to light up straight away when the hot water tap was turned on. Meta would wait in fearful anticipation for up to half a minute before the gas water heater exploded into action shaking the whole building. She was so frightened of it that there were times when she decided she wouldn't take the risk of washing in the tepid water it produced. However, after hours working with the wounded in the hospital she just had to have a wash, so she did so using freezing cold water that left her teeth chattering.

In theory there was a straightforward tram ride from the hostel to the hospital over Denmark Hill but the early morning trams were nearly always full of the munitions workers going to work and as often as not Meta and her fellow trainees had a two mile walk to work lugging their bags with their clean uniforms which they had to change into before they were allowed to go on the wards.

The Matron, a professional nurse, resented having VAD's as trainees, they didn't have the necessary medical training and if matters had been left to her they probably never would. She gave Meta and the other VAD's all the most menial jobs and criticised everything they did. She seemed to take against her Scottish trainee in particular.

Meta might well have given up. The offer of re-employment by Miss Thompson became more and more attractive every day, but her thoughts of John McBride drove her on. She could not abandon him. Somehow, she would qualify and get to France. It was the only way she would get to see him again or at least get near him and reading his letters she was convinced that he needed her now more than ever.

So, she gritted her teeth, emptied bed pans, scrubbed floors and washed sheets and refused to answer back. She'd learnt something from her days working for Mr. Fairfax.

The next great "victory" on the Western front changed matters. They were only given a few hours warning before the first ambulance started arriving. Soon there was a string of ambulances outside the hospital that stretched for miles.

There was no time for demarcation disputes. There were too many men to deal with. The first day of dealing with the wounded from the Battle of the Somme Meta didn't get back to the lodgings until the following morning. It seemed strange to be taking the tram in the opposite direction. She was totally exhausted. She only had time for two or three hours sleep and a quick wash. This time she was almost grateful for the gas water heater shaking her awake. By two o'clock she was back at the hospital. She barely slept for the next ten days. None of the hospital staff did. She found herself doing everything from changing bandages, to assisting the doctors as they operated, to laying out dead bodies. The most difficult times though were when she had to try and comfort the men she knew were going to die, particularly those who knew themselves that they had no hope.

It would have been easier if she had heard from John McBride, but for some reason there were no letters from the front. A silence had descended.

CHAPTER 14

THE TRENCHES

John McBride could see the second and third rows of grey men running towards them, and then he heard the chatter of the machine guns and he saw the men fall, flung about like so much lifeless flotsam, falling to the ground in contorted poses.

"Fire!" He heard the command from Captain Lawson and they all started firing their rifles and John had no time for anything else but working his rifle; but still they came. The first row had reached the barbed wire. He watched one of the Germans with wire cutters feverishly trying to cut through the wire. For a moment John hesitated, the man was so close. For a moment he remembered his religious vows but then he knew that was a different time, a different life to this. Now it was kill or be killed and he pulled the trigger on his rifle.

He barely felt the recoil. The first time he had fired a rifle his shoulder had been bruised for a fortnight, but that too was a long time ago. His first shot missed the German, the second sent the man spinning round so that he fell backwards onto the barbed wire. The body lay there impaled with its arms outspread to the sky.

Now some of the enemy were through the barbed wire and running towards them. The front man was carrying a spade and not a rifle and as he jumped into the trench, he swung it about him like an axe. He saw the man next to Andy Freeman go down his head almost severed from his body by one flailing blow from the spade. As the body hit the bottom of the trench he realised it was Fred Brooke who had been felled. The

German's next strike knocked Andy Freeman's rifle flying from his hands as he tried to parry the blow and for a moment Andy Freeman stood defenceless before the German. John lunged forward with his rifle and saw the look of disbelief and surprise on the German's face as he thrust the bayonet right into the German's body under his rib cage, burying it up to the hilt, then he twisted it and pulled it out just like he had been trained to do, but this time it wasn't the straw sack. This time he saw the flesh, the blood… the entrails.

"Fall back, fall back," for a moment the command didn't register, but then they were out of the trench and running for their lives back to the support trenches behind them.

As he ran John wondered why he had not heard the word "retreat", but maybe he had. It was all happening so fast. Then another thought flashed through his mind. When it came to hand to hand fighting the man in the trenches who had nothing but his bare hands was a dead man. Those that lived fought with weapons, whatever weapons came to hand. Andy Freeman now had the spade from the German that John had killed. There was no time to be afraid now. Albert Fortune, the young recruit fresh from university had shot a German at point blank range. Maybe he still looked like a schoolboy but when it came to it he had killed just like any other animal bent on self-preservation. Just like John.

And then suddenly it was over. One moment the trench was full of enemy soldiers and the next moment they were dead or gone; and then the cry went up from Captain Lawson, "Forward!"

John and the others were out of the support trench they had re-treated to and they were running back to the trench from which they had fled. Was it hours, or minutes before? John had no idea of how long the fighting had been going on for. The rest of the battle was a blur, but none of the subsequent attacks were as bad as that first one.

Young Albert Fortune survived his first baptism of fire, but Alan Sheppey like Fred Brooke didn't. He died as they ran for the support trench. Alan Sheppey was the one Andy Freeman had asked to keep an eye out for Albert. Everyone needed someone to look out for them.

If Andy Freeman hadn't been there for him, John McBride knew he wouldn't have survived as long as he had, so once Alan Sheppey was killed John McBride told Andy Freeman he would keep an eye on Albert. When

John next thought of Meta he wondered how much experience of life young Albert had managed to have before being trapped in the terrible world that they now found themselves. He couldn't believe that there had been any woman in Albert's life.

CHAPTER 15

KATHERINE'S DECISION

It took Katherine a few weeks to work out what she must do. She had to find out where John was serving in France and which regiment he had enlisted with. Without that information there was little she could do. Until she could find that out she could only wait. Whilst John was serving in France and Meta was teaching in London they were a safe distance apart, but that could end at any time. What if John were given leave and came back to visit Meta? They were brother and sister. They had to know.

She tried to put her mind at rest. Over dinner one evening she spoke to Seamus about the fighting in France. He and her father avidly followed developments. She asked him what happened to the men in France.

"What do you mean Katherine?"

"Are their families allowed to go to France to see them when they aren't fighting? Do the men get leave to see their wives? Are they allowed home to see their children?"

"I don't think that's possible Katherine. It isn't practical. Certainly, very few enlisted men get leave to come back to this country and their wives aren't allowed out to France. They don't want anything to distract the men from the fighting and there would be nowhere for them to stay anyhow."

Katherine tried not show how relieved she was at her husband's response.

"It seems very unfair when the men are fighting in a different country."

"This war isn't fair on anybody Katherine."

Meta had responded to her aunt's first letter in a guarded manner. However more important than the content from Katherine's point of view was that Meta wrote directly to her and included details of the new address she had just moved to. Katherine felt sure a fuller reconciliation would be possible given time, but she didn't feel she could just to wait for that to happen. She needed information about John from her niece as soon as possible.

Her father was surprised and also concerned when Katherine suggested going to London to see how Meta was getting on, but when he found that Seamus was encouraging her visit, he gave her trip his blessing. He'd started to trust Seamus judgment, particularly as regards Katherine, and he dearly hoped that Katherine and Meta could get over the vicious quarrel that had driven Meta away.

Aunt Katherine arrived unannounced at the hospital in Denmark Hill. Although Meta and her aunt had parted on bitter terms her aunt's arrival was a welcome diversion from the endless horrors of dealing with so many wounded and dying men. Her aunt had gone first to Meta's lodgings and then one of the other nurses had directed her aunt to the hospital where Meta was working.

The fact that Aunt Katherine had not only found her way to the hospital but had managed an interview with Matron said a lot for the force of Katherine Thompson's personality. She even persuaded Matron to give her niece a long enough break so that Meta could see her aunt who had travelled all the way from Scotland because of her concern for her niece.

Had Katherine arrived a few days earlier Matron would not have agreed, but the day Katherine arrived at Denmark Hill was the first day that they had received no fresh intake of wounded and Matron had grudgingly admitted that Meta Costello's recent work during the crisis they had just come through had been outstanding. No nurse, qualified or not, could have done more, so Katherine and her niece were able to have afternoon tea at a small café next to the Green in Camberwell. Her aunt was interested in everything Meta had done since she came to London.

"I knew you wouldn't have difficulty teaching here in London. Both the Sisters at the convent and Father MacDonald thought you were a natural teacher."

"It was more difficult than I thought it would be Aunt Katherine but teaching the children here certainly opened my eyes. I am glad I decided to come London."

"I'm pleased that some good came out of my unpleasantness." Meta looked at her aunt. Her aunt's behaviour had been a lot more than unpleasant. It took her a moment to appreciate her aunt was probably coming as close as she ever would to apologising.

The waitress came across with the scones her Aunt had ordered, "I'm not sure that you aren't wasted here nursing these poor wounded souls."

"Teaching is a very worthwhile occupation Aunt Katherine and no doubt when this is all over I will return to it, but for the moment this is where I feel I'm needed and where I think I can do the most good." Katherine did not to push the point.

"I was surprised to hear that John McBride had gone to France." Meta searched her aunt's face. Why was her aunt still interested in John McBride?

"Have you heard from him. I think I ought to write and apologise to him as well." Katherine chose her words carefully. "I liked the young man. I thought he would make an excellent priest. I thought you might dissuade him from what I thought was his obvious vocation…but it seems that the war has done that. I think I should apologise for trying to break up…your friendship."

As they finished their tea the discussion moved onto home and Levenside. "Your Uncle Seamus has been helping your grandfather out with lot of his business affairs recently. I think that's been a great help. Your grandfather's not getting any younger, although he still goes to the Tannyard every day." Meta nodded. She didn't really know about her grandfather's business interests, but she knew his whole life had been built round his building firm.

Eventually they stood up. "Do give Uncle Seamus and my grandfather my love."

"I will, I will." For a moment Meta thought her Aunt Katherine was going to embrace her, something she'd never done even when Meta was a child, but the moment passed. Instead, she held out her hand to Meta. "I'm pleased I came to see you Meta." She paused and then added, "Don't forget to send me John McBride's address. Look after yourself, you look terribly tired. Try to get some rest."

If only that was possible, if only. Meta watched her Aunt's departing figure.

Katherine stayed one night in London before returning to Levenside but she hardly slept. She didn't know if John McBride had been to see Meta in London. Meta had only told her he had written to her. At first, Katherine had condemned her father for giving John McBride Meta's address. Why had he been so stupid, so thoughtless? But, of course, he didn't know her secret, and he must never know.

For the moment there was no problem, but what about the future? John was writing to Meta from France, Katherine was no fool. Meta's Matron had told her Meta was trying to get posted to a hospital in France. That could only be for one reason. She wanted to see John. More than that she wanted to be with him.

Thank God he was in France, a fleeting meeting in London was one thing, but it was obvious that Meta wanted much more than that. That must never happen. She waited for two weeks, two agonising weeks, before she received Meta's letter. Meta thanked her for her unexpected visit and told her how it had been such a relief to be able to talk about things other than the war and hear about Levenside. Then, there at the bottom of the letter was a postscript with John McBride's British Army postal address.

She sat up all night drafting a letter. Then she tore it up. What she had to tell John she must tell him to his face. She stood up and stared out the window. What she wanted was impossible.

The next day she sat down again at Seamus' desk and wrote a second letter, but she didn't finish it. What was the point? What she needed to say couldn't be set out in a letter. She needed to speak to her son face to face.

Over and over again she asked the same question. What should she do? She was wracked by indecision, but always she came to the same terrible conclusion. She must tell John the truth, but how could she do that if she couldn't speak to him. She couldn't believe her son was in France, fighting in the trenches. What had happened? He was going to be a priest.

Would he accept her abandoning him as a baby? Would he forgive her? The question haunted her. Maybe if she could explain to him how she had suffered, what she had been through, then just maybe he would understand she had no other choice.

There was no way to tell her son all that in a letter, but she tried. She no longer had the excuse that she had nowhere to send a letter, but the longer she wrestled with the problem the more it became obvious to her that she could not write the letter she wanted to. The fuller she tried to make her explanation the more she came to accept that her letter was one she could not send. Letters to soldiers in the trenches were read by other people.

Eventually she wrote a short letter. There was so much more that she wished to tell her son when she acknowledged for the first time that she was his mother, but in the end she decided that did not matter as long as it served its purpose and, after she re-read it, she believed it would. John had to be told the truth. She could only pray she was right.

"Dear John,

I am writing to apologise for the manner in which I acted when I learned you had first met my niece Meta and had become friends with her. My behaviour was inexcusable to anyone who was unaware of all the facts.

It may be that you will find it easier to understand it if I tell you that I had a son before I married, and if he were in France now how fearful I would be for his safety.

I decided before my son was born that he should be adopted. Father MacDonald helped to arrange the adoption for me and he found two admirable people who lived in Eyemouth to look after my child.

More importantly I must tell you that the father of my child was Michael Costello, Meta's father.

I hope that by telling you this you will understand my behaviour and more importantly why I have written to you now. I hope that after this dreadful war is over you may feel able to resume your ecclesiastical training.

I pray for your safety.
Yours sincerely,

Katherine Thomson"

She had wanted to sign it with all her love, but she decided against that. If she ever saw him again that would be when she would tell him how much she loved him. How much she had always loved him.

She locked the letter in her sideboard.

She would not send it just yet, but if she learnt that Meta had got her wish to go to France she would have no alternative, then the letter would have to be sent.

END OF PART THREE

PART 4

THE FINAL RECKONING

Chapter 1

Albert Fortune dies

Meta Costello felt quite apprehensive as she boarded the ferry. It was her first venture away from dry land, but the crossing to France was uneventful. The Channel was almost flat calm and as she watched the sun shining on the chalk of the white cliffs slowly disappearing behind them, she felt no regret at leaving her homeland, only a sense of achievement.

However, once they were in France the remaining journey was not so pleasant. Although there was a railway station near to the vast tented military camp at Etaples the troops were given priority for what rail transport was available and so once they were off the ferry they were loaded into the back of a motor lorry which had seen much better days and whose suspension if it had ever had any, was now non-existent. When they were dropped off some distance from the camp Meta and her companions barely noticed the long walk it was such a relief to get down from the vehicle.

All Meta could think of as they walked along the dusty road was that two long years of waiting were nearly over. She had crossed the English Channel, the great divide that separated her from John McBride was no longer there. She was now closer to him than she had been since their heartrending farewell at Charing Cross station two years before.

If John managed to get leave now, it would be possible for them to see each other again. She would be able to listen to his voice, to hold him, even to kiss him and feel the warmth of his body against hers.

She had to stop her mind running away with those thoughts. She and the five other nurses with her had been given an hour to settle into their tented accommodation before their first meeting with matron. Meta knew from experience at Denmark Hill that her first priority must be to ensure that her new superior had no grounds to complain about her commitment to her work.

She hadn't made up her mind whether she was going to write and let her grandfather know she was in France. There was no need to make an immediate decision about that. It was only John who she really wanted to know she was in France.

Death was never far away in the trenches but unless you ignored it, you couldn't carry on with life. John McBride had come to understand that early on in France but Albert Fortune's death he found very difficult to erase from his thoughts.

It occurred on one of those days when not very much was happening. Albert was killed by a single bullet from a German marksman just as it was getting dark. John had been standing just a few yards away, trying to forget his surroundings. He had allowed his thoughts to wander back to Scotland, to his home in Eyemouth and to Meta. He didn't notice that Albert instead of stepping down from the fire-step he was standing watch on, had lifted his head a fraction above the parapet to drink from his canteen.

At first John wasn't sure that Albert was dead. The impact of the bullet, no more than a loud thud, made him turn just as the young man's body toppled over and his canteen fell from his hand. It wasn't until he turned Albert over that John saw Albert had been killed outright. One moment a living being, the next moment… nothing.

Just the day before Albert had talked to John about dying. Maybe he had a premonition or maybe it was just the one thought that he like so many of the men couldn't get out of his head. He told John that if there was another attack like the first one he'd been involved in, he didn't think he would survive it. He listened while John tried to allay his fears, but when John finished Albert insisted that John promise to send a letter for him if he did not survive. He told John he carried it with him inside his battle dress pocket all the time.

The letter consisted of two folded pieces of paper. John was about to read it when he saw Lieutenant Newman turning the corner into their section of the trench and so he slipped the letter inside his own battle dress. He hadn't seen Newman at all during their last two look out sessions.

"What's happened to Fortune?"

John turned and looked at Albert without speaking. The Lieutenant bent down and turned Fortune's body to one side. When he saw the disfigurement that the fatal wound had made to Albert Fortune, he turned back to John. His face grey, his expression suffused with anger.

"You were supposed to be looking after him McBride..." Newman's face was right in front of John's and John could smell the alcohol on his breath. Then before John McBride could reply Newman turned away and strode back along the trench. John watched Newman disappear round the corner of the trench. He stood looking after him without moving until eventually they came and took Albert Fortune's body away.

Later when he was on his own again, away from the prying eyes of Lieutenant Newman, John read the young man's letter. Albert Fortune had written to the only woman there had been in his life.

Dear Mother

I hope that you will never read this letter but even in the short time I have been here I have come realise how temporary our existence in this world can be and I want to write a few words to help you with the grief that you will have to face once you are informed of my death.

I know that you had high expectations of what I might achieve in this life, particularly when I won my scholarship, and I know that when you receive this letter it will dash those hopes. Can I say that even in my short life I have already achieved the only thing I really wanted. You and my father are the most important people in my life and I only wanted you to be proud of me and I know you both are. No son could ask for more.

My only regret was that I did not have enough time to do more for you both to repay all your love and all the sacrifices that you made for me.

I know you found it difficult to understand why I could not finish my studies before enlisting but you both brought me up with a strong sense of duty and I felt fighting for my country was where my duty lay, I could not leave that obligation to others and not feel guilty.

I hope there will come a time when you can smile again. Remember my death will not be an end to my life if I live on in your memories and when you remember me, I hope you will still do so with pride.

I was not afraid to die, but I was always afraid of losing your love and affection. Now I have nothing to fear.

Your loving son
Albert

John enclosed Albert Fortune's letter with one of his own. It might be some added comfort to Mrs. Fortune. He knew Captain Lawson would also write to her but she might appreciate some words from the person who was with Albert at the very moment when he died. He waited to post it until they were moved back from the front line. He didn't want Lieutenant Newman to see it.

CHAPTER 2

LIEUTENANT NEWMAN'S
ALLEGATIONS

John Mc Bride lay inside of his dugout. That is, most of him did. Not all of the four men allocated to his dugout could fit into the space allocated to them underground, so John lay with his legs protruding a few inches out into the trench. They only had two hours for sleep. He was close to exhaustion. He prayed nobody would trip over his feet.

Meta was leaning over to kiss him. He felt the wetness of her kiss as her lips brushed his face. Then he felt the rain that was seeping through the dug-out roof. It was falling onto his face. He heard the rustle of a rat behind him running across the dug-out floor. He tried to blot out his surroundings. He thought of Meta's letter so full of want and longing, and he started to cry. He tried to stifle the sobs, but his body shook. He cried until the ache inside him was so intense that he could not supress the moan that he let out. He fought not scream out loud. He lay there like a wounded animal, but there was no injury to be seen. The wound was deep inside his head. Invisible to everyone except himself. All he could do was to lie there and let his tears mingle with the rain as it ran down his cheeks.

The next day they were taken out of the line for two weeks rest. They were billeted in a barn but when it came time to sleep John couldn't despite his exhaustion. Was this war the retribution he must suffer for forsaking his God? Was he was being shown purgatory while he still lived? No, that couldn't be, good men like Andy Freeman and Jimmy Garstone were being punished alongside him. What wrong had they done in God's eyes?

He couldn't adjust to the quietness.

He lay listening, waiting for the thud of shellfire, for the crack of a rifle shot. His nerves were so raw that the silence brushed across them like a hard piece of chalk across a slate blackboard. They were an open sore. The silence made him want to scream out loud. Just when he thought he couldn't bear it any more he saw a figure get up and walk outside. It was Andy Freeman. John followed him out. Andy's solitary figure was looking up at the stars. For a while the two men just stood there in silent communion.

"It's so bloody quiet, Padre." John nodded in the darkness but said nothing. You couldn't see the silence nor touch it, but it was there, cloaking the two of them like a physical presence. Then Andy Freeman rested his hand briefly on John McBride's shoulder and then he turned and made his way back inside the building leaving John alone with his thoughts.

It was a long time before John could bring himself to follow.

The next day they went to the local *estaminet* for a meal. Jimmy Garstone had been told the food was good and he was right. There was only one dish, a beef stew with lots of garlic in it. They all drank too much wine. John didn't normally drink, and he knew deep down it wouldn't help him, but he drank all the same.

As they made their way back, he was surprised to see Captain Lawson ahead of them in the distance. He must have been to the *estaminet* too, but none of them had noticed him. Lawson was quite old still to be a Captain. Most of the other officers pushed off altogether during these rest periods, but Lawson didn't. He wondered why an officer who had so obviously been passed over, bothered so much about what happened to his men?

"When was the last time you saw Lieutenant Newman, Andy?"

"Why, padre? Are you missing him?"

"No. It's just that Captain Lawson goes out of his way to look after us and Newman does just the opposite. He's either making life unpleasant or he's simply not there at all." He looked over at Andy Freeman and he stumbled as he almost missed his footing. The road they were on was badly rutted and he had drunk far too much. "Something must have hurt him rather badly."

There was a pause as Andy Freeman considered what John had said. "Well, he needs to get over it. He's trouble for you. When I came back from our bath he was in our billet and he was looking for your kit. Said he needed to check on something."

"My kit? What did you do?"

Andy Freeman smiled. "I showed him Garstone's and when he said it wasn't your kit I told him yours must have gone for de-lousing." Andy Freeman gave him a wink. "I wasn't sure if you'd been up to no good so I thought it best not to take a chance. Nosey bugger, Lieutenant Newman, if you ask me."

"… Newman blames me for Albert's death."

Andy Freeman looked away before he replied. "Yes, I know. It's funny how upset he's been about Albert's death." Andy paused and then he added, "Actually, there's nothing odd about it. You know Newman's a queer don't you?"

John stopped walking and so Andy Freeman did too. "I think Newman was in love with Albert. He was jealous of how Albert seemed able to talk to you." John wasn't shocked he just wondered how he had failed to understand the situation when apparently it had been so obvious to Andy Freeman. Probably because he'd been too close to it. Now he understood what had been going through Lieutenant Newman's mind and it all made sense to him.

Poor man.

"You realise the implication of what you are saying Newman?"

"Yes sir."

"It means a Court Martial."

"I realise that sir."

"A General Court Martial."

"I wouldn't be suggesting that charges should be brought if I wasn't satisfied both as to the serious nature of the matter and that there was clear evidence of wrongdoing, sir"

"Tell me again what you say happened?"

"I saw Private McBride taking something from Private Fortune's body after Private Fortune was dead."

"…And what was that."

"I thought it looked like a letter, sir."

"That's all?"

"No sir. He also stole a cigarette case from the boy."

"…From Private Fortune?"

"Yes, sir."

"Are you sure? How do you know that?"

"I found it when I searched Private McBride's belongings after we came back here from the trenches, sir."

"How did you know it was Private Fortune's cigarette case?"

"I gave it to Fortune, sir."

Captain Lawson gave his second-in-command a searching look. "Why?"

"Private Fortune was finding it difficult in the trenches. The men were giving him a hard time because he looked so young and the shelling was getting to him, sir. I gave him a cigarette to smoke one day and he asked me if smoking made a man look older." Newman paused and shrugged his shoulders. "So, I gave him my cigarette case. I thought something like that would make him realise that he wasn't on his own."

Captain Lawson looked at Newman. The sentiments sounded admirable, but they were out of character. He simply couldn't visualise the Lieutenant behaving in the way he was describing.

"…And the letter? You said you saw McBride take a letter from Fortune's dead body."

"I didn't find the letter, sir…"

"…but you saw him take the letter?

"Yes sir."

"Do you have the cigarette case?" Newman nodded. "You'd better let me have it."

Newman took the cigarette case from his pocket and Captain Lawson saw that the lieutenant's hand was shaking.

"That's all Newman."

It wasn't until his second-in-command had gone that he glanced at what Newman had given him. There was an inscription in very small lettering on the back. 'To my beloved nephew from General Arthur Rawlinson."

CHAPTER 3

THE GERMAN BREAKTHROUGH

When he learnt that a new offensive was likely in the next few days Captain Lawson decided to postpone any action against John McBride. Lieutenant Newman had protested but he felt that having one of his men arrested by the Provost Marshal on the day they were to go up the line would have been worst possible action that could be taken as regards morale. He declined to do it. He didn't give a damn about the consequences.

The briefing at headquarters had been short. Intelligence reports showed that thousands of German troops had been transferred from the Eastern front. There had been a big build-up of supplies and equipment by the Germans in readiness for a new offensive.

Captain Lawson was told that his unit was being allocated a secondary defensive position in case the Germans were successful in making a breakthrough.

"If you can hold that high point over here when the Germans advance you'll be in just the right position to attack their flank." Captain Lawson had peered at the map. The high point had no name. Someone on the General Staff had given it a number. Hill 105 was its only identification. He bent forward so he could see the contours on the map. It wasn't much of a hill, more an area of raised ground.

"We're not sure when the Germans are going to try their breakthrough, but you should get the usual twenty-four-hour barrage before they press forward."

As he started to leave the building, he found the Colonel was alongside him, "How's young Newman shaping up?"

Richard Lawson was about say something non-commital like it was too early to tell but the Colonel went on. "His uncle's quite close to Haig you know." The Colonel turned to look at Richard Lawson. "Newman got a bit too friendly with one of the other young officers. Rawlinson decided to post them both out to the front…different units, of course. We heard last week Newman's chum was killed. I don't know if Newman knows yet." What the Colonel had told him had made Captain Lawson stop walking.

"Tugela Heights wasn't it?"

Richard Lawson tried to adjust his thoughts. "Sir?"

"You were at Tugela Heights, weren't you?" Richard Lawson nodded. "This isn't same as South Africa, is it?"

"No sir. It's quite different." Richard Lawson couldn't think of anything else to say.

The Colonel was studying him. "Good luck, Lawson."

The German push took them all by surprise. They had been given only a rudimentary trench to occupy and although they had spent the day trying to improve it Captain Lawson was still not happy with it.

For almost the first time in the entire war the Germans decided to use the element of surprise. Although there was heavy barrage further up the line, there was no artillery barrage before they launched their attack in Captain Lawson's sector. Sergeant Freeman was on guard duty and he saw the small groups of Germans as they came running forward. He thought at first it was just a small sortie rather than a major breakthrough attempt because the enemy was not in the usual attack formation of one long line.

Two of those groups were through the lightly manned British lines in front of their position almost before Sergeant Freeman had pointed them out, but the Germans didn't move onto the position Captain Lawson was holding. The enemy simply went round them.

Richard Lawson was perhaps one of the first to realise that this offensive by the Germans was something different. He recalled the way the Boers used to fight. This wasn't the trench warfare that they had become used to on the Western front. The Germans were moving fast and in small groups, like the Boer commandos. Within a matter of hours, the advance by the German troops had effectively cut off Captain Lawson and his men from the British lines. Gradually the sound of rifle fire moved away into the distance.

For the rest of the day Captain Lawson waited. He told his men to keep their heads down, to ignore any enemy units unless they approached the hill. The higher ground they were on was important. The Colonel had been right about that.

They continued to wait and then night started to fall, and it was only then that Captain Lawson knew for sure that there was not going to be any British counter-attack. He and his men were on their own, stranded behind the new German lines. They had to try and retreat or they would be wiped out or captured whenever the Germans decided to deal with them. They'd dug in as best they could but there was no way that they could hold their position unaided.

"Sergeant Freeman, I want you and Garstone to take a look behind us. Head northwest. See if there's way back through the Germans. You've got an hour. If you're not back by then we will move out in that direction and you'll just have to find us."

"Yes sir." He watched the two men as they started to move carefully down the side of the incline. He prayed that they wouldn't run straight into the Germans. Freeman was a lucky soldier, but luck had a way of running out just at the wrong moment.

Just before the expiry of Captain Lawson's time limit Freeman was back. Was there a way to break through back to wherever the new British lines were? There were gaps he said, areas the Germans had left unoccupied but how far back the British lines were he had been unable to ascertain.

Freeman led them in single file. Captain Lawson followed immediately behind. Bringing up the rear of the column were Garstone, John McBride and Lieutenant Newman. Richard Lawson tried to visualise the terrain from the map he had gone over with the Colonel but in the dark it was virtually impossible. What he did remember was that well back, possibly four or five miles behind the British lines was a canal. It had been mentioned to him as the basis of a final fall-back position in the unlikely event that that was necessary. If the British had fallen back beyond that there, their hopes of re-joining the British line were minimal, probably non-existent. However, a breakthrough of that distance had not occurred before. He tried to remain optimistic.

Chapter 4

The Canal

It took them over three hours to work their way back to the canal. Detours to avoid German encampments slowed them down, as did the darkness. There was some moonlight, but clouds covered the moon intermittently and they had to halt from time to time when that happened.

As soon as Sergeant Freeman spotted the canal Captain Lawson halted the men. He waited until Newman brought up the rear, then he told the men to rest and took Lieutenant Newman and Sergeant Freeman to one side.

"We've got to find a way across this canal. I recall there were a couple of bridges on the map I was shown but if our men have fallen back across the canal…and that seems to be the case they'll have blown the bridges or the Germans will have them well guarded. The men need a rest. Newman do you think you can reconnoitre the canal along to the right? Freeman, can you do the same to our left?" The two men nodded their assent.

"What are we looking for, sir?" Asked Freeman.

"We need to check the bridges, but I doubt they are our way across. Look for boats…anything or any way that we might get across this canal that the Germans may not have had time to spot."

"Freeman you take Garstone with you. Newman you take one of the other men. You've got half an hour but come back earlier if you find anything we can use." He paused. "If you run into any Germans, I'm afraid you're on your own."

Captain Lawson looked as the two men faded away into the darkness. He didn't expect that they would find a crossing they could use, but he wasn't going to give up hope just yet. He made a rapid tour of the lookouts on the perimeter of their current position then he returned to the rest of the company. It was only then that he realised who Lieutenant Newman had selected to take with him.

John McBride was surprised to be picked out by Lieutenant Newman. He hadn't spoken to the Newman since the Lieutenant's formal complaint against him. He and Garstone had brought up the rear of their retreat from the hill with Lieutenant Newman but nobody had spoken. Silence had been essential as they tried to slip through the German lines.

Now they moved slowly alongside each other as they progressed along the towpath that ran beside the canal. It was deserted as far as John McBride could see. They carefully checked the undergrowth as they went forward. Once they were out of sight of the remainder of the company the Lieutenant spoke, "McBride there's something I need to say to you." John McBride slowed. "I want to apologise. I want you to know I'm going to withdraw the charges I've made against you."

John McBride didn't say anything. There wasn't anything to say. Lieutenant Newman had stopped walking so John did too.

"I'm afraid my feelings about Fortune affected my judgment. I was …very fond of him you know." John McBride said nothing.

"I loved that boy." John could just make out in the darkness that Lieutenant Newman was looking straight at him. "Do you understand?"

Newman's next words came out in a rush before John could respond. "The pain was too much for me. I had to…I wanted to take it out on someone…and I was jealous of your friendship with Fortune. I tried to tell him how I felt but he…"

"I think we should keep moving sir. We don't have much time."

"Yes, yes of course. I just wanted to tell you…What I wanted to tell you was that when this is over, I'll be withdrawing all the charges against you."

John started forward again, and they walked on in silence.

Then John spoke. "I think Albert was grateful for the support you gave him, sir."

"Did he tell you that?"

"Yes. Yes, he did." John turned and looked straight across at Lieutenant Newman. Before he had come to France John McBride had believed that lying was sinful. Now he thought differently. Many of the men in his company had come to John McBride with their fears or seeking some form of absolution from him. He had always tried to send them away with some small positive thought to cling onto. Now his instincts told him that Newman was close to breaking point. A few kind words was all the support he could offer. If he lied it was a kindness and no one but he would ever know. No one but God, and John McBride had stopped worrying long ago about what God thought about him.

Then John caught sight of a building ahead. As they moved carefully forward a boathouse loomed out of the darkness up ahead.

Sergeant Freeman was the first to return. His report to Captain Lawson was short and to the point. There was no good news. He hadn't come across any Germans until he found himself within sight of one of the bridges. The reason then became obvious, the Germans had taken the bridge and it was still intact. The enemy was on the other side of the canal. There was no way over the canal in the direction Sergeant Freeman had gone, but even if they could get across Captain Lawson now knew they would still have fight their way through to the new British lines.

"They've twice as many men as we have both sides of the bridge, sir. I'm afraid there's no chance of us getting across there, sir"

Sergeant Freeman hesitated, "Is Lieutenant Newman back yet sir?" Captain Lawson shook his head. "The longer he's away the more likely he's found something."

"Yes sir."

Lawson didn't expect any better news when his Lieutenant showed up and he didn't think Freeman was convinced by what he said but he had to appear optimistic. He was pretty sure the other bridges had been taken, blown up or captured, but he had to wait. Until he knew for certain he couldn't let any of his men see that he had given up hope of getting them back to their own lines.

Captain Lawson's concern for the other two men grew. The ten minutes before Newman came back with MacBride seemed more like an hour. "We didn't come across any Germans or any bridges." Captain Lawson tried to keep his face expressionless, even though he knew in the moonlight Newman could barely see his features. His Lieutenant continued, "I think we may have found something that will get us across the canal…or rather Private McBride may have, sir." He turned to John McBride. "Tell Captain Lawson what you found, McBride."

"Well sir, we came across some sheds by the canal. It's somewhere where the French repair their boats. It looked like the Germans have smashed up all the boats that were in use, but I saw that there was a small boat out of the water on the other side of the canal. It's very small I think that's why the Germans didn't bother with it, but Lieutenant Newman agreed we should check it out, so I swam over to it." Captain Lawson looked rather sharply at his second in command. "I managed to drag it into the water. It was more or less watertight. It can only hold 3 or 4 men. One rower and three others."

Only now did Captain Lawson notice John McBride's bedraggled features. Although his uniform was dry, he was shivering.

"Are you alright McBride?"

"Yes sir, now I've got my uniform back on." The man must have stripped naked to swim the canal and the water must have been freezing. McBride read his thoughts. "It was a bit cold, sir but I used to swim in the North Sea up at Eyemouth."

Lieutenant Newman spoke, "McBride managed to get the boat to this side of the canal and we tied it up. It's a bit waterlogged but I don't think it will sink before we get back. I think with the rest of the company we can get it out of the water. McBride found a tarpaulin which he says he can lash round it to make it more watertight."

"Tell the men we're moving out." As Lieutenant Newman made to start away he added, "Lucky you took McBride with you. He's probably the only man in the company who can swim." Newman hesitated, checked his stride for a moment, turned as if he was about to say something, and then ran on to gather up the men.

They manhandled the boat out of the canal and once it was out of the water Sergeant Freeman and John McBride confirmed it was useable. McBride and Freeman, with a bit of help from Garstone, lashed a section of tarpaulin around the hull of the boat at the only point where McBride thought it had a leak.

"Is there any more rope lying around? Get the men to check the sheds, Newman." Within five minutes Newman and a couple of the men returned with several coiled ropes.

"Right, Sergeant Freeman I want you to take three men and row the boat across the canal…You can row can't you?"

"Yes sir. I was brought up next to the Thames."

Captain Lawson looked at his men now clustered around him. "Can anyone else row?" No hands went up. He wasn't surprised he remembered making a fool of himself on the Serpentine when he had tried to impress Caroline Mansfield many years ago.

"Right, we'll tie a length of rope to the boat and pull it back across. We can get it across quicker that way and the extra man doesn't need to be a rower. Sergeant Freeman, you're in charge on the other side until I get across."

"Yes, sir."

"Lieutenant Newman you take Garstone with you and set up watch about four hundred yards further up the towpath. I think that's the mostly likely direction the Germans may come from. From what Freeman told me the Germans at the bridge are happy to sit tight where they are. If you see any Germans get back here as quick as you can."

The first boatload of men with Sergeant Freeman took an agonisingly long time to get across the canal even though Freeman was a capable rower. The boat moved slowly crabwise in an ungainly fashion, probably because of the tarpaulin lashed to it. Eventually it reached the other side and after that they were able to haul it back across using the ropes. The next journey after that took less time. However, the boat was not as watertight as they had thought the and the men had to bale with their helmets to prevent the boat becoming too waterlogged. It persuaded Captain Lawson against trying to pack the boat with more than four men.

The operation to get his company across the river was taking an agonising amount of time and he worried that he wouldn't be able to get everyone across the canal before it was daylight. He didn't start to relax until the second to last boatload was almost across. Only McBride and two other men, together with Lieutenant Newman and Private Garstone remained with him on his side of the canal.

As the boat was being pulled back for the last time Garstone came running hell for leather along the towpath.

"There are Germans coming. Lieutenant Newman says he'll hold them for as long as he can, sir."

"How far away is he?"

CHAPTER 5

THE WOUNDED ARRIVE AT ETAPLES

The first knowledge Meta and the other nurses had of the German of-fensive was when the trains coming back from the front began to be filled with wounded soldiers. What started as a trickle soon became a steady stream of injured packed into the carriages or even open trucks as the fighting began to increase. Soon Meta found herself working longer and longer shifts just as she had at Denmark Hill after the Battle of the Somme, but somehow this was different. Now she had a much more immediate connection to the fighting.

Meta had more experience than most of the other nurses so she was one of the first to be delegated to the gruesome job of assisting in the operating theatre. However, she did not mind. She could cope with open wounds and severed limbs but what she found almost unbearable was to sit and comfort the dying or lie to the living about their crippled bodies because that gave her too much time to think. What if John McBride was to be the next crippled or dying man whose final words she had to listen to?

CHAPTER 6

A FIGHTING RETREAT

"Garstone I'm going on across with the next lot of the men." Richard Lawson didn't want to leave any of his men on the wrong side of the canal, but he knew he couldn't risk staying. He had to be with the rest of the company. He still had to get as many of them as possible back to the British lines.

"After I'm across, pull the boat back and wait and see if the Lieutenant makes it back. McBride see if you can work your way up to Lieutenant Newman. If you get through to him tell him that I have ordered him to fall back. Tell him we've got all the men across and that the boat's waiting for him and you and Garstone. If you can't get through to him don't hang about double back here and we'll pull you and Garstone back across." He paused, "If the shooting stops, you'll know there is no point in going any further just get back here to Garstone as soon as you can." He looked at the two men. "Do you understand?" They both nodded. "Good luck."

He got the last of the men into the boat and signalled to Sergeant Freeman to pull them across. He could still hear some shooting further up the towpath so Lieutenant Newman was still alive but once the Germans sent more men down the towpath he knew his second-in-command's only hope was to retreat as fast as he could back to the boat. On the other side he got the remaining men out as quickly as he could and signalled to Garstone to pull the boat back.

It was Sergeant Freeman who saw them first, he had moved further up along the bank with a couple of men to see if he could spot Lieutenant

Newman on the other side and perhaps give him covering fire if there were any Germans actually on the towpath. Newman and McBride were not clearly visible but there was faint bit of daylight and after while he saw them partly hidden by a bush close to the tow path.

Shortly after that Captain Lawson moved up to join Sergeant Freeman. Freeman pointed to the towpath past where he had spotted Lieutenant Newman and McBride but as they both looked across the river they saw what looked like two Germans working their way round behind the Lieutenant.

"Lieutenant Newman is trapped sir, unless we can take out the Germans between him and the boathouse he and McBride will never make it back to Garstone." The Germans were now moving back up through the bushes towards Newman and McBride.

A moment later one of the Germans moved out of the bushes onto to the towpath to try and get a clear shot at Newman and McBride. Andy Freeman didn't hesitate he pulled his rifle into his shoulder and fired. The German dropped and Freeman quickly shifted his aim to try and fell the other encircling German but he was too far into the bushes. It was still too dark and it was impossible to see if Andy Freeman's two further shots had taken the second man out.

"They're going to have to make a run for it now. Sergeant Freeman try and give them covering fire if you can. I'll send up some more men to give you hand. I'll stay with the rest to give Newman and McBride covering fire when they get back to the boat and start crossing." Then without waiting for a response Captain Lawson was off back down the tow path.

"I think we're cut off from the boathouse, sir." John McBride was only telling Lieutenant Newman what he already knew.

"It depends how many of them have managed to get round us McBride. It looks like they're trying to give us covering fire from the other bank. We might just be able to make a run for it if we go now."

Lieutenant Newman seemed a changed man to John McBride. "I'll count to three and then we'll go. Alright?" Newman stood up ready to run hoping by doing so the men on the other side of the canal would realise what he intended, but before he could start his count of three a shot ran out and he fell to the ground. "Damn."

297

John McBride could see blood coming from the Lieutenant's leg. There was no way they could make a run for it now.

CHAPTER 7

CROSSING THE CANAL

John McBride appreciated the situation straight away and so did Lieutenant Newman.

"McBride make a run for the boat now. That's an order. I can hold the Germans in front of us for a bit. Go!"

John McBride didn't move. "Give me your belt sir."

"What?"

"We've got to stop the bleeding."

"What are you talking about McBride? Run man! Run!"

John McBride shook his head. "Listen Lieutenant the best chance for us and for Garstone is if we cross the canal here."

"What are you talking about McBride? I can't swim."

"Doesn't matter sir. I can tow you across. Once we're both in the canal put your hands on my shoulders and try let yourself float. Now let's get your boots off and give me your belt." John tied the belt tightly round Lieutenant Newman's leg above his wound.

The Germans further up the canal continued exchanging shots with Andy Freeman and his men and the other German had either been hit or moved so far back into the undergrowth that he could no longer see John McBride and Newman so the two of them managed to get into the water before any of the Germans saw what they were attempting. However, halfway across the canal things changed. The Germans spotted them, and a fusillade of shots ripped up the surface of the water around and behind John McBride.

"Rapid fire!" Andy Freeman's tried to intensify his men's response to the Germans on the far bank. A number of the enemy soldiers pulled further back into the undergrowth on their side of the canal.

"Come on padre. Come on." Nobody heard Andy Freeman's words because he didn't speak them out loud. Then he noticed that a gap had opened up between John McBride and Lieutenant Newman. The lieutenant's head, the only part of his body above water, was face down and drifting away. He was no longer holding onto John McBride's shoulders.

It took John McBride longer to realise this than it did Andy Freeman, but when McBride did Andy Freeman saw him turn round and start to swim back towards the Lieutenant. When they discussed matters afterwards everyone from Captain Lawson down believed John McBride would have made it if he carried on swimming to the bank, but he wouldn't leave Lieutenant Newman.

"God alone knows why." Jimmy Garstone said to Andy Freeman later. Only John McBride could have told them what was in his mind.

Andy Freeman could only watch helplessly as John McBride managed to lift Lieutenant Newman's head up out of the water and then seconds later another bullet struck McBride.

Sergeant Freeman and a short distance away Captain Lawson watched powerless as the two bodies floated lifelessly in the water.

Then the Germans turned their aim onto the far bank and Captain Lawson ordered Sergeant Freeman and the other men further back into the undergrowth for protection.

CHAPTER 8

THEY MAKE IT BACK

Captain Lawson couldn't let the shock of losing two of his men affect what he now had to do. It was still fairly dark. He got his men moving as quickly as he could. The Germans were on the other side of the canal, but they would have no difficulty crossing it and he had no doubt they would do so as soon as they got themselves organised.

As far as possible he would have to take his men across countryside rather than following the roads. To add to his difficulties, he had no map to follow. All he could do was to decide on a compass bearing and then they set off. Away from the canal they were in an open field. He took his men across it as fast as possible. They needed somewhere to hide up during the daytime. There was some woodland in the distance but the Germans would know that was a likely place to hide so he took his men straight through that. Then he slowed the pace down and sent Sergeant Freeman ahead to see if there was anywhere that was suitable to hide until the following night.

By mid-morning they were hidden in one of the outbuildings of a deserted farm. The inhabitants had fled the approaching Germans. They stayed there all day without any incident. The pursuing Germans from the canal seemed to have lost interest when they failed to make immediate contact.

The reaction to the loss of John McBride and Lieutenant Newman varied. In Sergeant Freeman's case it was clear. He wanted blood to avenge his loss. Captain Lawson had to restrain him if they sighted

301

passing German patrols. To get through they had to keep their heads down and stay out of sight. Among the remaining members of Captain Lawson's company their attitudes varied but in every case it was clear that they felt the loss of John McBride profoundly. Even more than the loss of Albert Fortune.

It took them two weeks to get back to the retreating British lines. Not that there was a defined British line to get back to anymore. They followed the same procedure. Hiding during the day, only moving at night and for the most part travelling cross country rather than using the roads.

Then one minute they were in an area where the only soldiers they could see were German and the next they were being challenged by a platoon of a British rear guard unit.

There was a Major in command of a motley assortment of troops in the small village they had been attempting to skirt around. He laughed when Captain Lawson asked if he knew where Lawson's regiment might be.

"God alone knows. You best stay here with us for the time being. I've been told to try and hold this village. I've got two platoons out covering each side to let me know if the Germans try to go round us. It was one of those you ran into.

It was several weeks before the German advance totally ran out of steam and Captain Lawson found himself back with what was left of his unit and before he saw the Colonel again.

"I can't say I expected to see you back again Lawson. The General was quite impressed with your report. He didn't think his nephew would make a soldier, but you seemed to have done it. By the way he's recommended you for a Military Cross"

Captain Lawson just stared at his superior. He said nothing. He shook his head. All he could think of was he was being thanked by a man for letting his nephew get killed and was even giving him a medal for it. What a bloody ridiculous war.

"I think he'd like to talk to you about it, but I've told him you deserve some leave so that can wait." Maybe the colonel understood how he felt.

CHAPTER 9

META LEARNS OF
JOHN MCBRIDE'S DEATH

There is no easy way to tell somebody of the death of a loved one. Meta learnt of John McBride's death in a letter from Captain Lawson.

John's commanding officer had struggled to write it. He had rewritten many of the words over, over again, "I deeply regret to inform you, …it is with great sadness that I have to inform you…It is my sad duty to have to tell you…" but there is no way that the finality of the news he had to convey could be softened. He could write words that later might give the recipient something to cling to in the future, but the initial devastation that the news itself would bring could not be lessened.

Meta didn't cry. She was still holding Captain Lawson's letter when she collapsed. Matron and the doctor who examined her both diagnosed extreme exhaustion, Meta's thoughts that one of the wounded might be John McBride had kept her working long after she should have stopped, but it turned out that it was more than exhaustion that caused her collapse. Meta had contracted pneumonia. For days she lay on her sick bed and her Matron feared that one of her favourite nurses would not survive. Such was the affection Matron felt for her subordinate that it was she who had decided to sit with Meta on the night when the doctors came to the conclusion that Meta's time had come.

Meta seemed to have lost the will to live. Matron could not remember what she said to Meta. Normally she was a woman of few words but that night she just talked and talked. She told Meta she was not alone, that others cared. She talked of her own home in Ireland, of the stream than ran close to it and how she and her brother loved to skim stones across it when she was a child. Throughout the night she placed cold compresses onto Meta's brow and bathed her face and arms with cold water.

That night Meta did not die, the worst of her fevers broke and in the morning she spoke for the first time in days. As she lay quietly trying to gather her strength she remembered how vividly in her sleep she had visualised the River Leven even feeling the coolness through her fingers as she dipped her hand into the river's fast flowing waters.

There was no question of Meta going back to work. For a few days she was unable to even get out of her camp bed but gradually she improved until it was decided that was fit enough to travel and could be invalided home.

Alex Field met her train when it's arrived in London. Her arrival on this occasion was much different from their original meeting. There was no need for a platform ticket to meet the troop train on which Meta had been given a travel warrant. Alex Field barely recognised the thin gaunt figure of Brian O'Malley's granddaughter, but he ensured that Meta had a good night's rest and the following morning he put her safely on the train to Glasgow. Her grandfather and Aunt Katherine met Meta from there.

On the local train back to Levenside from Glasgow she told them both of the death of John McBride and how much it had saddened her. Her grandfather was full of commiserations, but her aunt was strangely silent and said nothing further on the journey back to Levenside. She said goodbye to Meta at the door to her grandfather's house and although she said she would call and see Meta once she had settled in, it was several days before she saw her aunt again.

Then, about a week later her aunt appeared and suggested that they go out for a walk along the River Leven. Each day after that they walked either along the river, or up Kinnell Hill. Meta found herself pouring her heart out, and Aunt Katherine listened. Once or twice Meta thought her Aunt Katherine wanted to tell her something but in the end her aunt just listened. Gradually all the long daily walks together with large bowls of Scotch broth, prepared specially for Meta by her grandfather's long-serving housekeeper, meant Meta's health recovered.

Life has to go on and Meta had to decide what to do. Her first instinct was to resume her life in Levenside, but it was not long before she knew that would not work. London and France had broadened her horizons, but more than that Levenside held too many memories of John McBride. To start her new life she had to avoid too many memories. She needed to think of the future now, not the past.

It was her old headmistress that helped her decide what to do. Meta had enjoyed teaching. It was something worthwhile and her former headmistress had not forgotten her. So, when Miss Thompson's letter arrived informing her that there was a vacancy at Alma Primary School and asking if there was any possibility that she might now be interested in returning to teaching, Meta accepted the offer.

This time when she went round to see her aunt to say goodbye her Aunt Katherine welcomed her in.

"I've enjoyed having you back here Meta. So has your grandfather and Uncle Seamus. This is your home. Remember that and remember that you're more than welcome anytime you wish to come back. I'll miss our walks together."

Her grandfather also made it clear how much he would love for her to stay so that in the end Meta almost changed her mind, but she only hesitated for a short while. In her heart she knew that for time being at least leaving Levenside was what she had to do.

CHAPTER 10

MAJOR LAWSON
TRAVELS TO SCOTLAND

It was not until Richard Lawson saw the effect of John Bride's death had on the other men in his company that he realised what an exceptional person that John McBride had been. He tried to convey that fact when he wrote to John McBride's parents in Eyemouth and his fiancé, but it hadn't been possible to capture the essence of the man in the letters he wrote however hard he had tried.

After the Armistice Captain Lawson was transferred back to London but he was not demobbed straight away. There was a lot of administrative work involved in discharging so many soldiers and his colonel (the man who given him Hill 105 to hold) was occupied in some way with the peace process and he asked Richard Lawson to stay on as his assistant. He seemed to think Richard Lawson was good at administrative work. Better than he had been as a soldier Captain Lawson told himself, but the army seemed to realise he had some ability as a soldier as well because Richard Lawson now held the rank of major.

However, whilst he sat at his desk or when he was walking in St. James Park or through Green Park, Major Lawson often found himself thinking of John McBride. His wasteful death preyed on Richard Lawson's mind. He found that he wanted to know more about the family of the young man who had trained as a priest but had died fighting in a war that should never have taken place.

Although he knew that John McBride's fiancé had lived in London during the war she was originally from Scotland, a place called Levenside, somewhere near Glasgow; and that John McBride's parents were from Eyemouth a little fishing village on or near the English/Scottish border. After two or three months thought he asked if he could take a week's leave so that he could take a brief break in Scotland. His request was granted.

He had previously written to John McBride's parents and told them he would be visiting Edinburgh in the near future and had asked if he could visit them as he intended to return to London via Berwick-on-Tweed. He received a response inviting him to visit the McBrides in Eyemouth whenever he wished and telling him that as they ran a bed and breakfast establishment as well as the general store in Eyemouth he would be very welcome to stay overnight if he wished.

He went first to Levenside, travelling up via Glasgow. There was a station hotel which he booked into for the night. The following morning he went to look for Meta Costello.

He had no difficulty in finding out where she lived. Nearly everybody he spoke to knew her to be a member of the O'Malley family. She was the granddaughter of Brian O'Malley a leading member of the town's business community who lived in one of the impressive stone houses on one of the hills above Levenside.

Richard Lawson had not written to Meta as he had to the McBride family and when he knocked on the brass knocker of the O'Malley residence he discovered that had been a serious mistake. The elderly, but fit looking housekeeper, who answered the door announced with regret that Meta Costello was not at home. She had left for London the previous week and was not expected to return for some time.

There was nothing he could do but leave his card and ask if it might be forwarded on so that she knew of his visit. Kate gave the card to Katherine Thomson who arrived from a long walk along the River Leven, shortly after Richard Lawson's departure.

When Richard Lawson returned to his hotel, he discovered he had just missed the train he needed to catch if he was to get to Edinburgh that day so he decided to leave Levenside the following day. After lunch he set out to explore Levenside.

The town did not impress him much apart from the stone-built houses on of the hills overlooking the town, one of which was home to Meta and her family, but the surrounding countryside did. He walked along the River Leven and then up one of the hills the locals told him was called Kinnell Hill. The view at the top was particularly stunning. The sun had come out just as he reached the top and he had watched impressed as the shadows of the numerous small white clouds in the blue sky scudded across the fields of heather down below.

Edinburgh was a city Richard Lawson had visited once before and fallen in love with. He stayed overnight at the North British Station Hotel. He rather liked the fact that the hotel kept its clock three minutes fast so that guests wouldn't miss their trains. The following day he walked up through Advocates Close, and then down the Royal Mile to Holyrood Palace. After that he walked to the top of Arthur's Seat where he stood in the sunshine looking at the marvellous view of Edinburgh. He wondered if he would ever meet Meta Costello, and then he mulled over what he might say to ease the grief and sadness that he expected to encounter when he went on to visit Eyemouth.

What immediately struck Richard Lawson when he met John's father, Matthew McBride, was that he had an entirely white head of hair. Christine McBride told him her husband's hair had turned white almost overnight after they had received the telegram informing them of John's death. That was really the only visible mark that Richard Lawson could see that John McBride's death had made on his family.

Because he knew of John McBride's ecclesiastical training perhaps he should not have been surprised by the fact that John's parents, or at least his mother, had strong religious beliefs. When her husband was out of earshot Christine McBride confided in Richard Lawson that she thought that she had found it easier to cope with John's death than her husband because of her faith. Although John had never completed his ecclesiastical training, she told Richard Lawson that God would not be hold that against him. "Don't worry Major Lawson I have no doubt that he has now gone to a far better place. One day I will join him." Richard Lawson found himself thinking there was a lot to be said for blind faith if it could take away the pain and grief of losing somebody so obviously loved as John McBride had been by his mother. There was little he could think of to comfort her, but he had to acknowledge she had little need of any additional comfort.

John's father took Richard Lawson for a long walk over to Coldingham from Eyemouth. He showed him the Sands where John McBride loved to swim. It was there that he told Richard Lawson that John McBride was an adopted son. "We loved him just as much as if he were our natural child. My wife and I didn't have any child of our own. Our dear friend Father MacDonald knew how much we both wanted a child and he arranged for us to adopt John when he was a very young baby."

Matthew McBride looked out across the North Sea. "I think my wife feels John was a gift from God because the Church and Father Mac-Donald arranged for us to adopt him. I don't know about that, but I do know is how rewarding it was for us to have a child even for the short time that we did. He gave us a lot of happiness whilst he was alive. I'm grateful for your letter and what you've now told me, but I couldn't be prouder of John than I already am."

His visit to the McBrides had been to try and alleviate their grief if he could, but as he said his goodbyes he had to acknowledge that there had been no need. They had dealt with their loss in their own way. In-deed, as he walked up the incline to Eyemouth railway station, he realised that it was he who had benefitted talking to them. Somehow it had lifted a lot of the sadness that had lain heavily upon his shoulders for many months. He did not mention Meta Costello to them, nor did they talk of her to him.

CHAPTER 11

RICHARD LAWSON
MEETS META COSTELLO

It was some weeks before Richard Lawson received a letter from Meta. He had by then given up any thoughts of hearing from her. Her letter regretted she had missed his visit to Levenside and offered to meet with him in London if that were convenient.

He spent a week-end wondering where he should suggest they meet. He did not think inviting her to his Park Lane address was the right thing to do. It didn't seem the right venue for what he wanted to say. In the end, he thought that she might find meeting for afternoon tea in Hyde Park and a walk through the gardens afterwards might be more sensible and it seemed that it was for she wrote back fairly quickly accepting his invitation.

It put them at the mercy of the weather. He prayed for good weather and he was in luck for when he woke on the morning they had arranged to meet the sun was already shining.

He arrived early at the tea rooms. He decided not to go in but to sit beside the Serpentine to kill time. Twenty minutes later he saw a striking young woman walk past. Something told him it was John McBride's fiancé, and he followed her the short distance to the tea rooms. He saw that she sat down at the table he had reserved and so he introduced himself.

For a moment looking at Meta's striking blue eyes Richard Lawson was at a loss for words. He had thought long and hard about what he intended to say to Meta but he found he couldn't articulate the words he had decided upon. Somehow the words now escaped him. Meta Costello did not seem to notice.

"Major Lawson it is kind of you to arrange to see me. I know from what John told me in his letters how much he appreciated serving in your company."

"I can assure you I very much appreciated his serving under my command." He knew he sounded formal and stilted, even rather pompous, so he stumbled on trying not to make an idiot of himself, "I very much regret that he is not here so I can thank him for all the support he gave me and the other men he served with." That sounded even worse, but she smiled and at last he started to recover himself.

"I have seen a friend of John's recently who also served with you, Andy Freeman. I don't know if you recall him?"

'Of course, another remarkably able soldier."

"His sister has a child at the school where I am teaching." Soon she was telling him about her return to teaching. How much she enjoyed it and how worthwhile she found educating young children. "As you know my family are from Scotland and they've tried to persuade me to return there. I know my grandfather misses me a lot, but I think I've fallen in love with London and the children at the school I'm teaching at." Meta Costello carried on talking and was such easy company that Richard Lawson found he was enjoying himself. He hadn't realised how tense he had been before their meeting.

"What are you intending to do with yourself Major? I see you're still in uniform." He was impressed that she could tell his rank from his uniform but then he remembered her service as a nurse in France.

"Only briefly. I was asked to stay on for short time in an administrative capacity…to help with the demobilisation." He smiled. "I think my Colonel decided that I was a better administrator that a soldier." He saw that Meta smiled too, but she could see from his medal ribbons that he was being modest.

They talked on as if they had been friends for some time, not just two people meeting for the first time until eventually their waitress approached Richard Lawson to ask if she could bring him their bill as the tea rooms were about to close.

As he stood up, he said, "I have enjoyed meeting you Miss Costello, despite the circumstances." He smiled. "I wonder if you might be willing to see me again…." He saw the hesitation in her expression, and he paused wondering if she had found his request inappropriate. He quickly added, "…Perhaps in a month or two…"

Meta Costello did not reply straight away and so to avoid her any embarrassment he asked her how she was getting home. "I will be taking the underground railway from Victoria."

"May I walk you to the station?" He didn't want to say goodbye.

"That would be kind." They walked together but neither of them spoke and he could tell that Meta Costello's mood had changed. The smiling face in the tea rooms had been replaced by a sad expression. He kicked himself for trying to make more out of their meeting than the brief encounter it should have been. "I'm sorry." He couldn't think of anything else to say, but Meta Costello didn't seem to have heard him.

When they reached the station they stopped and she turned towards him.

"Major Lawson I have enjoyed our meeting and I might well like to meet you again in the future." She looked at him closely before she continued. "However, I have to tell you that my thoughts are still very much with John and… while that is the case, despite today I think that I would not be very good company."

"I quite understand. Please forgive me."

"There's nothing you need to seek forgiveness for. You have been very kind. I have your address and maybe if I feel in need of company in the future, I will write to you." She gave him a smile, but it was a wan smile. "Thank you again for to-day."

As he walked away back to Park Lane. He wanted to kick himself. How could he have been so crass.

Several weeks after his first meeting with Meta Costello, just when he had decided that he was unlikely to hear from her again, he received a letter from her.

Meta had mentioned her meeting with Major Lawson to her headmistress Miss Thompson, and told her how she had enjoyed his company. When she mentioned the possibility that they might meet again in the future Miss Thompson had encouraged her to do so, but despite her advice she hesitated. Two things forced Meta's hand. She bumped into Emma Freeman's mother in the street who told her how her brother still talked of Captain Lawson. Then Miss Thompson bought Meta two theatre tickets for her birthday and told her she should get Major Lawson to accompany her to the play.

"Dear Major Lawson,

I have been given the present of a couple of theatre tickets for a play which is running at the Theatre Royal in Haymarket. The play is 'General Post' by J.E. Harold Terry.

It's a comedy.

I wonder if you might be willing to accompany me. It might cheer us both up.

I assure you I will not be offended if do not wish to accept this invitation.

Yours very sincerely,
Meta Costello"

CHAPTER 12

THE DEATH OF FATHER MCDONALD

Brian O'Malley had never fully recovered his health since he'd been in-jured in the Great Fire. Mentally he didn't feel it had affected him, but physically he did not have the same strength.

He depended a lot on Seamus Thomson. Brian had to acknowledge that he wouldn't have been able to cope with all his business interests without Katherine's husband, her "man of business". The butcher who had become a successful businessman. Once Brian was sure he could trust Seamus he had taken him more and more into his confidence.

Seamus had changed. Brian O'Malley remembered how disap-pointed he had been with Seamus when he had first married Katherine. Seamus seemed to have no mind of his own, always at Katherine's beck and call. What Brian had eventually realised was not that Seamus was a weak character, but he was hopelessly in love with his wife.

It was only when Seamus was dealing with his wife that he had no mind of his own. Once her mother had died Katherine had developed a coldness about her that made it difficult for Brian to believe that some-one could be in love with her as he had been with her mother, but then one day he realised he was wrong. Seamus' behaviour which he had crit-icised in the past, was not caused by his having no mind of his own but because his overriding wish was to make his wife happy and to love him. At first, Seamus had felt that the only way he could do that was to give his wife whatever she wanted.

Then sometime after the fire in Levenside, or certainly by the time they had learnt of the death of the young priest, John McBride, who

Meta Costello had seemed so attached to, Seamus had started to make the decisions in the Thomson household. Once more Katherine became a recluse, but also Brian noticed that his daughter had started to defer to her husband for the first time.

Brian missed his daughter Grace more and more. He often took the book of poetry that Father MacDonald had given him down from his book-shelf and read the first verse of "The Dying Girl". The description of the consumptive young woman reminded him of Grace with her striking blue eyes and her long flowing hair. Meta had inherited much of those striking looks. He started to read.

> *From a Munster vale they brought her,*
> *From the pure and balmy air;*
> *An Ormond peasant's daughter,*
> *With blue eyes and golden hair.*
> *They brought her to the city*
> *And she faded slowly there —*
> *Consumption has no pity*
> *For blue eyes and golden hair.*

There was a postscript written by Father MacDonald at the back of the book. "Brian. This poem reminded me so much of your beautiful, lovely girl."

Father MacDonald had told him that the author had died relatively early at the age of forty. After going to America, he had written a number of songs that the Irish regiments sang in the Civil War before ironically he had died of consumption.

Brian felt the loss badly when he learnt Father MacDonald had passed away, but the news of the priest's death was not unexpected. What was unexpected was the letter that the priest had arranged to be delivered to Brian after his death and which now lay in front of him on his desk.

"Dear Brian,

I am sorry that I never had the courage to tell you what is contained in this letter before I died, but I have always felt bound by a promise I made to Katherine many years ago.

Katherine had a child by Michael Costello…"

Brian O'Malley re-read the words. He struggled to grasp their import. **"Katherine had a child, by Michael Costello…"** With difficulty, he stood up from his chair. Surely this letter was just the ramblings of a senile old man? He limped over to the sideboard and poured himself a whisky.

"…At her request I arranged to have the child adopted. She made me promise that, during my lifetime I would never tell you of the existence of her child. If you receive this letter you will know that I am now released from the undertaking I gave.

I hope and believe that you will forgive my behaviour, but what I hope for more is that this letter will also enable you to forgive Katherine for some of her behaviour over the years that I know you have found unacceptable.

The burden of this secret has haunted me throughout my lifetime and has grown heavier with time.

Katherine's child was John McBride…"

Dear God.

"…and it is a matter of sincere regret that I was not able to make you aware of the fact that he was your grandson before he died in France.

I write in the hope of your forgiveness both for myself and for Katherine.

Please remember me in your prayers.

Your friend in Jesus"

Brian sat back down at his desk. If what his old friend had written was true, it explained so much. He sat there for some time in disbelief, but each time he re-read the letter the more he realised that that Father MacDonald's letter spoke the truth. The words were not an old man rambling.

How could he have been so blind? God what Katherine must have gone through and he, instead of giving her love and support, had rejected everything she had tried to tell him. Why oh, why had nobody opened his eyes? Why had the truth been kept secret? It had only caused so much more heartbreak. He had failed his daughter. He hadn't been there for her when she needed him. No wonder she had remained so distant after Grace had married Michael Costello. Would she ever forgive him? Why had she not told him her secret?

Never had he felt so alone. How he wished that Father MacDonald were still there. He needed the old man's advice so badly, but dear God, it was too late for that. If only the priest had confided in him while he was still alive.

Brian poured himself another whisky.

There were decisions he had to make, but he would have to make them alone. Even Seamus could not help him to deal with this.

He had forced his eldest daughter to deny her own child. He could hardly imagine the suffering that must have caused her. No wonder she had behaved towards her sister Grace and Michael as she had done. How difficult she must have found it to look after her sister's child when she been forced to deny her own.

What could he do to make amends?

Maybe if he destroyed Father MacDonald's letter, that would be end to it. Katherine would be able to go to her grave without ever having to acknowledge the truth to anyone and her secret would have died with John McBride in France.

He walked over to the fire that was burning in the grate holding the letter in his hand. He stood there indecisively with the flames in front of him.

For all his faults he was not a coward and that was the coward's way out. Furthermore, he had to think of Meta too. What of the rift between Katherine and Meta? Yet another wound he had caused. Didn't Meta need to know the truth? Would that heal the wound between them? Would the truth be too devastating?

He walked back to his desk with the letter still in his hand and sat back down. For quite a time he sat there pondering on the questions he had asked himself, without coming up with the answers.

Then he opened his desk drawer and took out his granddaughter's last letter.

"Dear Grandfather,

*I have met the man I intend to marry, **Major Richard Lawson**. I would like to bring him to Levenside so that I can introduce him to you. He knew my father in South Africa and John McBride served under him in France. I am sure that there is so much the two of you will want to talk about when you meet."*

All his life Brian O'Malley had been obsessed with the Lawson family. He had continued to live so much in the past that he had been blind to what was going on around him. Failing to realise the future needs of his own family, unfairly blaming Katherine for driving Michael Costello to his death in South Africa when in reality it was Michael's own behaviour that had forced him to leave Levenside.

Then when after her death he had read the letter Grace had received from Michael Costello's commanding officer in South Africa, instead of accepting it as the heartfelt letter of compassion that it was meant to be, an expression of regret at the death of a courageous soldier, based on no real evidence, he had decided that Lieutenant Richard Lawson was seeking absolution for being in part responsible for his son-in-law's death. After that he had continued to take such steps as he could to ensure that he could ruin the Lawson family.

Brian O'Malley went to the little Davenport desk in the far corner of his study. From one of the side drawers he took out a bulky envelope. It contained a bundle of title deeds. He checked through the documents as he had several times before. Then he put them in the large envelope together with a letter of instructions to Alex Field in London.

"Dear Alex

My granddaughter has recently informed me of her intention to marry Major Richard Lawson, who you may recall having met as young man. I enclose with this letter the title deeds to the house in Park Lane left to him by his grandfather. I have discharged the borrowings made on the property by his grandfather. Please let him know that this is a wedding gift and return the title deeds to him.

No doubt you will receive an invitation my daughter's wedding and I look forward to meeting you at that happy event.

Yours as ever,

Brian O'Malley"

He started to write a letter to Katherine trying to put into words the heartfelt apology he wanted to make, but each time he reread what he had written he realised that a letter was not enough. He had to speak to Katherine and request her forgiveness in person, however painful that might be. Seeking forgiveness in a letter was a cowardly way of facing up to the grievous mistakes he had made but writing it down was a start to his making amends and it enabled him to marshal in his mind all the things he needed to say and hopefully right all the wrongs that he had done his eldest daughter. As Father MacDonald had once told him it is only those sinners that showed true contrition that are truly forgiven by those who they have wronged.

Once he had finished the letter, he decided he would wait to the morning to decide if he had the courage to face his daughter in person rather give the letter to her.

He sat at his desk a little longer. If only Katherine had shared her secret all those years ago.

What should he do as regards Meta? She deserved to know the truth, but wouldn't it be kinder for her not to know? How would she feel once she knew the truth about John McBride?

He drained his glass. He usually concluded each day by writing in the journal he had kept ever since Mr. Paget had taught him to write, even if it was just a short entry. This evening, perhaps the most momentous of his life, he decided to make one of the shortest entries in it.

"Today I learnt Katherine's secret." He wrote nothing more, instead he placed Father MacDonald's letter inside his latest journal and locked it away in the cabinet where he kept all his previous journals. After a moment's hesitation he took the key from the cabinet and placed it in the same envelope as the letter he had written to Katherine. Before he sealed the envelope he added a postscript to his letter. *Although I think it is a matter for you whether you reveal the secret you have kept for so long, I feel that Meta has a right to know it. My own secrets you will find in my journals which I will leave for you to read when I have gone to meet my dear friend Father MacDonald.*

Then Brian O'Malley made his way upstairs to bed. He felt so tired. The emotion he felt was raw and painful.

CHAPTER 13

META RETURNS TO LEVENSIDE

It was the middle of the night when Brian O'Malley awakened. He was sweating. His thoughts were racing and so was his heart. Meta must never know Katherine's secret. He must destroy Father MacDonald's letter. He would speak to Katherine, admit how badly he had wronged her, but Meta must never know her aunt's secret.

Seamus Thomson had taken to visiting Brian O'Malley every day to discuss business. That morning he found his father-in-law lying beside his bed. It appeared he had tried to get up during the night.

Seamus summoned Dr. Cunningham to Melville House and the doctor diagnosed a heart attack as the cause of death. He had been worried about Brian O'Malley's health for some time and he had half expected something to happen for several months.

For the doctor the death of Brian O'Malley and that of Father MacDonald was the passing of the old generation. The death of his two old friends caused even the hardened Dr. Cunningham to shed a tear in the secrecy of his home. The doctor had acknowledged long ago that Brian O'Malley had been responsible for his never leaving Levenside, despite the professional lures of Glasgow. As the death registered he decided that he would wish to die in harness, like Brian O'Malley.

Seamus entered the old man's study. He would try and ease the pain of his wife's loss by dealing with as much of Brian O'Malley's affairs as he could. His father-in-law had entrusted him with a set of keys to his safe. He opened it and found the letter and package addressed to Alex Field. He had had previous dealings with Brian's lawyer. A very efficient but rather cold man he thought. He decided he would simply post the letter and package on. Alex Field would know what to do with the contents. There were two other envelopes. One unsealed was addressed in Brian O'Malley's handwriting to Katherine. The other envelope had originally been sealed but over time the seal had deteriorated. It bore the transcription "to be given to Katherine in the event of my death". It was in a hand he did not recognise.

Seamus Thomson broke the news to his wife. When he asked her to sit down, Katherine looked at him without any emotion. Her expression did not change even after he had spoken.

"Is there anything I can do, Katherine?"

"You had best inform Meta. She will need to be here for the funeral."

"I meant for you Katherine."

"No, nothing. I think I'll go to my room."

"I'll bring you up a cup of tea."

"Thank you." He watched her walk out of the room.

When he took the tea to her room Katherine was still dry-eyed. She sat staring in the distance and did not acknowledge his presence. He put down the tray with Katherine's tea on it. "There were two letters in your father's safe addressed to you. They're on the tray." Briefly he laid a hand on his wife's shoulder, and then he walked downstairs.

Katherine looked at the two letters. She recognised the handwriting. One was from her father. The other one she realised with a shock was from her sister. She wondered why her father had kept it from her for all these years. Why had it lain unopened in his safe for all these years?

"Dear Kate,

I am entrusting Meta to your care. I know you will do what I ask because of your sense of duty to our family, but also because I believe despite how badly I have wronged you, you still love me.

However, I want you to know that I understand how onerous a task that it will be because of her father's behaviour towards you so I think you should know the truth about my marriage.

Michael married me not out of love but out of a sense of duty. I was with child at the time of our wedding but not long after our wedding I lost the baby. His grief over the loss of that child was far greater than mine and at first I did not understand the reason.

However, very shortly after the baby died Michael decided that we must leave Levenside. I did not want to go. I felt if we moved away, I could never be reconciled with you. I pleaded with him to stay.

It was then he explained to me how much he had been in love with you **and that he was still in love with you**. He said that seeing you all the time was unbearable and that the only way our marriage was ever to work was if we left Levenside and travelled as far away as possible, so I agreed to leave.

Once we were in South Africa Michael tried to make our marriage work and thanks to the birth of Meta we were not unhappy, but I knew Michael's heart remained in Levenside.

Michael had little luck as a prospector so he went back to what he knew best, building work, and he was able to make a reasonable amount of money, but nearly all the work he did was for the Boers and once war broke out that work ceased.

We moved to Durban and it was agreed that once the fighting was over we would return to Scotland. Michael said that what he could not live with was never having had the chance to explain to you just how much he had loved you.

He believed that although the two of you could never be together again that just knowing that would help you get over the wrong that he had done to you. I do not know if that is true but that is what he believed and I feel duty bound to tell you that for his sake, for your sake, but most of all for Meta's sake.

Your loving sister
Grace"

"…he was still in love with you." Katherine re-read the words. Then she let out a heart-rending moan. The moan of a wounded animal, so loud that Seamus could hear it from the downstairs kitchen. He retraced his steps and found his wife sobbing and rocking backwards and forwards in her chair. He did not hesitate. He lifted her up and held her tightly in her arms and she clung to him as she gave way to her unbearable grief.

322

For a long time after her sister Grace had died, Katherine and her father had remained estranged, but recently as Brian O'Malley's health had started to deteriorate, Seamus had noticed they had grown closer. It was a shame that her father had died when he had. Part of Katherine's unhappiness he believed was that she had missed that opportunity to become really close again to her father.

Now he put on his coat and made his way down the hill to the Post Office and sent a telegram to London. Then he made his way back to the Howes Road. He had called Dr Cunningham and he had given Katherine a sedative and Seamus had put his wife to bed to try and rest.

As soon as she saw the Post Office boy standing there with the envelope in his hand, Meta knew its contents. She decided immediately to travel up to Scotland. She sent a short note round to Major Lawson at his Park Lane address. She was surprised when he responded almost immediately informing her that he would accompany her to Levenside and so the following evening, when Meta arrived in Levenside, Richard Lawson was by her side.

Two days later as they left Melville House to commence the formal procession to Our Lady of St. Augusta's, Katherine took Meta's arm in hers and the two women led the silent funeral procession as it moved slowly down the hill past the view that had first attracted Brian O'Malley to Levenside. Seamus Thomson walked beside his wife, and the tall figure of Major Lawson could be seen on the other side next to Meta. The route down to the church was lined by inhabitants of Levenside. Nowhere were the lines of people on either side of the road less than three or four persons deep.

As the coffin approached the Church of Our Lady of St. Augusta's an elderly lawyer on the opposite side of the road removed his top hat as he stared straight ahead.

As it processed down the aisle, at the back of the packed church a frail old lady stood trying to blend into to the darkness. Maureen O'Connor had also come to say her own final goodbye.

Two weeks later Katherine Thomson took her niece for a walk-up Kinnell Hill. The hill that held so many memories for the two of them. Katherine had read her father's letter and all of his journals, but what had finally made up her mind was the letter contained in the second envelope her husband had given her. The letter that Grace had written to her just before her death.

As they looked out over the view of the River Leven that Katherine had found so striking so many years before, she told her niece her secret.

THE END

ACKNOWLEDGEMENTS

I would like to acknowledge and thank Cathy Allum and all my friends at the Arvon Foundation without whom this book would not have been written.

Printed in Great Britain
by Amazon

79206047R00189